KU-428-574

'Nora Roberts is the very best there is—
she's superb in everything she does.'
— *Romantic Times Magazine*

'John Grisham, watch your back!'
— *Entertainment Weekly*

In the still of the night
danger and mystery
lead to passion!

Together in this classic volume of
romantic suspense
Night Shift and *Night Shadow*

from NORA ROBERTS

put two sisters in peril
and send two sexy, protective,
extraordinary men to keep
them safe…

NORA ROBERTS

Number one *New York Times* best-selling author Nora Roberts is 'a word artist, painting her story and characters with vitality and verve,' according to the *Los Angeles Daily News*. She has published over one hundred novels, and her work has been optioned and made into films, excerpted in *Good Housekeeping*, translated into over twenty-five different languages and published all over the world.

In addition to her amazing success in mainstream, Nora remains committed to writing for her Silhouette® romance audience, who took her to their hearts with her very first book. With over 40 million copies of her books in print worldwide, and six titles on the *New York Times* best-seller list in one year—including *The MacGregor Brides*—Nora Roberts is truly a publishing phenomenon.

NORA
ROBERTS

NIGHT TALES

™ SILHOUETTE®

*Silhouette and Colophon are registered trademarks of
Harlequin Books S.A., used under licence.*

*First published in Great Britain 2001
Silhouette Books, Eton House, 18-24 Paradise Road,
Richmond, Surrey TW9 1SR*

NIGHT TALES © Harlequin Books S.A. 2001

The publisher acknowledges the copyright holders of the
individual works as follows:

Night Shift © Nora Roberts 1991
Night Shadow © Nora Roberts 1991

ISBN 0 373 04725 8

121-1001

*Printed and bound in Spain
by Litografia Rosés S.A., Barcelona*

Dear Reader,

The night is a time for danger, mystery—and romance. And *Night Tales* is a special collection that brings together two connected books in one volume. These books feature characters who are creatures of the night, whether for work or play—or love.

There's something intriguing about night people. The way they think, the way they live. In *Night Shift*, Cilla O'Roarke loves being the voice of the night hours during her DJ shift—until a dangerous stalker forces her to share her evenings with devastatingly handsome police dectective Boyd Fletcher.

Sometimes night is the only place for a hero who lives for the kind of justice that is often found outside the law. Gage Guthrie in *Night Shadow* is just this kind of man—and the perfect hero to rile Deborah O'Roarke, a beautiful lawyer who only plays by the rules.

I hope you enjoy these stories. Look for *Night Shield*, a brand-new *Night Tales* story, and watch what happens when Boyd's by-the-book detective daughter has to work side by side, night after night, with a dangerously sexy stranger she isn't sure she should trust. *Night Shield* is available this month from Silhouette Sensation®.

All the best,

Nora Roberts

Also available from Silhouette® Books by

NORA ROBERTS

NIGHT SHIFT

To Kay in Denver
And with appreciation to the staff of WQCM

Chapter 1

"All right, night owls, it's coming up on midnight, and you're listening to KHIP. Get ready for five hits in a row. This is Cilla O'Roarke, and darling, I'm sending this one straight out to you."

Her voice was like hot whiskey, smooth and potent. Rich, throaty, touched with the barest whisper of the South, it might have been fashioned for the airwaves. Any man in Denver who was tuned in to her frequency would believe she was speaking only to him.

Cilla eased up on the pot on the mixer, sending the first of the five promised hits out to her listeners. Music slid into the booth. She could have pulled off her headphones and given herself three minutes and twenty-two seconds of silence. She preferred the sound. Her affection for music was only one of the reasons for her success in radio.

Her voice was a natural attribute. She'd talked herself into her first job—at a low-frequency, low-budget station in rural Georgia—with no experience, no résumé and a brand-new high school diploma. And she was perfectly aware that it was her voice that had landed her that position. That and her willingness to work for next to nothing, make coffee and double as the station's receptionist. Ten years later, her voice was hardly her only qualification. But it still often turned the tide.

She'd never found the time to pursue the degree in communications she still coveted. But she could double—and had—as engineer, newscaster, interviewer and program director. She had an encyclopedic memory for songs and recording artists, and a respect for both. Radio had been her home for a decade, and she loved it.

Her easygoing, flirtatious on-air personality was often at odds with the intense, organized and ambitious woman who rarely slept more than six hours and usually ate on the run. The public Cilla O'Roarke was a sexy radio princess who mingled with celebrities and had a job loaded with glamour and excitement. The private woman spent an average of ten hours a day at the station or on station business, was fiercely determined to put her younger sister through college and hadn't had a date in two years of Saturday nights.

And didn't want one.

Setting the headphones aside, she rechecked her daily log for her next fifteen-minute block. For the space of time it took to play a top 10 hit, the booth was silent. There was only Cilla and the lights and gauges on the control board. That was how she liked it best.

When she'd accepted the position with KHIP in Denver six months before, she'd wrangled for the 10:00-p.m.-to-2-a.m. slot, one usually reserved for the novice deejay. A rising success with ten years experience behind her, she could have had one of the plum day spots when the listening audience was at its peak. She preferred the night, and for the past five years she'd carved out a name for herself in those lonely hours.

She liked being alone, and she liked sending her voice and music out to others who lived at night.

With an eye on the clock, Cilla adjusted her headphones. Between the fade-out of hit number four and the intro to hit number five, she crooned out the station's number four and the intro to hit number five, she crooned out the station's call letters and frequency. After a quick break when she popped in a cassette of recorded news, she would begin her favorite part of her show. The request line.

She enjoyed watching the phones light up, enjoyed hearing the voices. It took her out of her booth for fifty minutes every night and proved to her that there were people, real people with real lives, who were listening to her.

She lit a cigarette and leaned back in her swivel chair. This would be her last quiet moment for the next hour.

She didn't appear to be a restful woman. Nor, despite the voice, did she look like a smoldering femme fatale. There was too much energy in her face and in her long, nervous body for either. Her nails were unpainted, as was her mouth. She rarely found time in her schedule to bother with polish and paint. Her dark brandy-brown eyes were nearly closed as she allowed her body to charge up. Her lashes were long, an inheritance from her dreamy father. In contrast to the silky lashes and the pale, creamy complexion, her features were strong and angular. She had been blessed with a cloud of rich, wavy black hair that she ruthlessly pulled back, clipped back or twisted up in deference to the headphones.

With an eye on the elapsed-time clock, Cilla crushed out the cigarette and took a sip of water, then opened her mike. The On Air sign glowed green.

"That was for all the lovers out there, whether you've got someone to cuddle up with tonight or you wish you did. Stay tuned. This is Cilla O'Roarke, Denver. You're listening to KHIP. We're coming back with our request line."

As she switched on the tape for a commercial run, she glanced up. "Hey, Nick. How's it going?"

Nick Peters, the college student who served as an intern at the station, pushed up his dark-framed glasses and grinned. "I aced the Lit test."

"Way to go." She gratefully accepted the mug of steaming coffee he offered. "Is it still snowing?"

"Stopped about an hour ago."

She nodded and relaxed a little. She'd been worrying about Deborah, her younger sister. "I guess the roads are a mess."

"Not too bad. You want something to go with that coffee?"

She flicked him a smile, her mind too busy with other things to note the adoration in his eyes. "No, thanks. Help yourself to some stale doughnuts before you sign out.'' She hit a switch and spoke into the mike again.

As she read the station promos, he watched her. He knew it was hopeless, even stupid, but he was wildly in love with her. She was the most beautiful woman in the world to him, making the women at college look like awkward, gangling shadows of what a real woman should be. She was strong, successful, sexy. And she barely knew he was alive. When she noticed him at all, it was with a distractedly friendly smile or gesture.

For over three months he'd been screwing up his courage to ask her for a date. And fantasizing about what it would be like to have her attention focused on him, only him, for an entire evening.

She was completely unaware. Had she known where his mind had led him, Cilla would have been more amused than flattered. Nick was barely twenty-one, seven years her junior chronologically. And decades younger in every other way. She liked him. He was unobtrusive and efficient, and he wasn't afraid of long hours or hard work.

Over the past few months she'd come to depend on the coffee he brought her before he left the station. And to enjoy knowing she would be completely alone as she drank it.

Nick glanced at the clock. ''I'll, ah, see you tomorrow.''

''Hmm? Oh, sure. Good night, Nick.'' The moment he was through the door, she forgot about him. She punched one of the illuminated buttons on the phone. ''KHIP. You're on the air.''

''Cilla?''

''That's right. Who's this?''

"I'm Kate."

"Where are you calling from, Kate?"

"From home—over in Lakewood. My husband's a cab driver. He's working the late shift. We both listen to your show every night. Could you play 'Peaceful, Easy Feeling' for Kate and Ray?"

"You got it, Kate. Keep those home fires burning." She punched the next button. "KHIP. You're on the air."

The routine ran smoothly. Cilla would take calls, scribbling down the titles and the dedications. The small studio was lined with shelves crammed with albums, 45s, CDs, all labeled for easy access. After a handful of calls she would break to commercials and station promos to give herself time to set up for the first block of songs.

Some of the callers were repeaters, so she would chat a moment or two. Some were the lonely, calling just to hear the sound of another voice. Mixed in with them was the occasional loony that she would joke off the line or simply disconnect. In all her years of handling live phones, she couldn't remember a moment's boredom.

She enjoyed it tremendously, chatting with callers, joking. In the safety of the control booth she was able, as she had never been able face-to-face, to relax and develop an easy relationship with strangers. No one hearing her voice would suspect that she was shy or insecure.

"KHIP. You're on the air."

"Cilla."

"Yes. You'll have to speak up, partner. What's your name?"

"That doesn't matter."

"Okay, Mr. X." She rubbed suddenly damp palms on the thighs of her jeans. Instinct told her she would have trouble with this one, so she kept her finger hovering over the seven-second-delay button. "You got a request?"

"I want you to pay, slut. I'm going to make you pay. When I'm finished, you're going to thank me for killing you. You're never going to forget."

Cilla froze, cursed herself for it, then cut him off in the midst of a rage of obscenities. Through strict control she kept her voice from shaking. "Wow. Sounds like somebody's a little cranky tonight. Listen, if that was Officer Marks, I'm going to pay those parking tickets. I swear. This one goes out to Joyce and Larry."

She shot in Springsteen's latest hit single, then sat back to remove the headphones with trembling hands.

Stupid. She rose to pluck out the next selection. After all these years she should have known better than to freak over a crank call. It was rare to get through a shift without at least one. She had learned to handle the odd, the angry, the propositions and the threats as skillfully as she had learned to handle the control board.

It was all part of the job, she reminded herself. Part of being a public personality, especially on the night shift, where the weird always got weirder.

But she caught herself glancing over her shoulder, through the dark glass of the studio to the dim corridor beyond. There were only shadows, and silence. Beneath her heavy sweater, her skin was shivering in a cold sweat. She was alone. Completely.

And the station's locked, she reminded herself as she

cued up the next selection. The alarm was set. If it went off, Denver's finest would scream up to the station within minutes. She was as safe here as she would be in a bank vault.

But she stared down at the blinking lights on the phone, and she was afraid.

The snow had stopped, but its scent lingered in the chill March air. As she drove, Cilla kept the window down an inch and the radio up to the maximum. The combination of wind and music steadied her.

Cilla wasn't surprised to find that Deborah was waiting up for her. She pulled into the driveway of the house she'd bought only six months before and noted with both annoyance and relief that all the lights were blazing.

It was annoying because it meant Deborah was awake and worrying. And it was a relief, because the quiet suburban street seemed so deserted and she felt so vulnerable. She switched off the ignition, cutting the engine and the sounds of Jim Jackson's mellow all-night show. The instant of total silence had her heart leaping into her throat.

Swearing at herself, she slammed the car door and, hunched in her coat against the wind, dashed up the stairs. Deborah met her at the door.

"Hey, don't you have a nine-o'clock class tomorrow?" Stalling, Cilla peeled off her coat and hung it in the closet. She caught the scent of hot chocolate and furniture polish. It made her sigh. Deborah always resorted to housecleaning when she was tense. "What are you doing up at this hour?"

"I heard. Cilla, that man—"

"Oh, come on, baby." Turning, Cilla wrapped her arms around her sister. In her plain white terry-cloth robe, Deborah still seemed twelve years old to her. There was no one Cilla loved more. "Just one more harmless nut in a fruitcake world."

"He didn't sound harmless, Cilla." Though several inches shorter, Deborah held Cilla still. There was a resemblance between them—around the mouth. Both their mouths were full, passionate and stubborn. But Deborah's features were softer, curved rather than angular. Her eyes, thickly lashed, were a brilliant blue. They were drenched now with concern. "I think you should call the police."

"The police?" Because this option had simply not occurred to her, Cilla was able to laugh. "One obscene call and you have me dashing to the cops. What kind of nineties woman do you take me for?"

Deborah jammed her hands in her pockets. "This isn't a joke."

"Okay, it's not a joke. But Deb, we both know how little the police could do about one nasty call to a public radio station in the middle of the night."

With an impatient sigh, Deborah turned away. "He really sounded vicious. It scared me."

"Me too."

Deborah's laugh was quick, and only a little strained. "You're never scared."

I'm always scared, Cilla thought, but she smiled. "I was this time. It shook me enough that I fumbled the delay button and let it broadcast." Fleetingly she wondered how much flak she'd get for that little lapse the next day. "But he didn't call back, which proves it was a one-shot deal. Go to bed," she said, passing a hand over her sister's dark, fluffy hair. "You're never going to be the best lawyer in Colorado if you stay up pacing all night."

"I'll go if you go."

Knowing it would be hours before her mind and body settled down, Cilla draped an arm over her sister's shoulders. "It's a deal."

He kept the room dark, but for the light of a few sputtering candles. He liked the mystic, spiritual glow of them, and their dreamy religious scent. The room was small, but it was crammed with mementos—trophies from his past. Letters, snapshots, a scattering of small china animals, ribbons faded by time. A long-bladed hunting knife rested across his knees, gleaming dully in the shifting light. A well-oiled .45 automatic rested by his elbow on a starched crocheted doily.

In his hand he held a picture framed in rosewood. He stared at it, spoke to it, wept bitter tears over it. This was the only person he had ever loved, and all he had left was the picture to press to his breast.

John. Innocent, trusting John. Deceived by a woman. Used by a woman. Betrayed by a woman.

Love and hate entwined as he rocked. She would pay. She would pay the ultimate price. But first she would suffer.

The call—one single ugly call—came every night. By the end of a week, Cilla's nerves were frazzled. She wasn't able to make a joke of it, on or off the air. She was just grateful that now she had learned to recognize the voice, that harsh, wire-taut voice with that undercurrent of fury, and she would cut him off after the first few words.

Then she would sit there in terror at the knowledge that he would call back, that he was there, just on the other side of one of those blinking lights, waiting to torment her.

What had she done?

After she dropped in the canned news and commercial spots at 2:00 a.m., Cilla rested her elbows on the table and dropped her head into her hands. She rarely slept well or deeply, and in the past week she had managed only a few snatches of real sleep. It was beginning to tell, she knew, on her nerves, her concentration.

What had she done?

That question haunted her. What could she possibly have done to make someone hate her? She had recognized the hate in the voice, the deep-seated hate. She knew she could sometimes be abrupt and impatient with people. There were times when she was insensitive. But she had never deliberately hurt anyone. What was it she would have to pay for? What crime, real or imagined, had she committed that caused this person to focus in on her for revenge?

Out of the corner of her eye she saw a movement. A shadow amid the shadows in the corridor. Panic arrowed into her, and she sprang up, jarring her hip against the console. The voice she had disconnected barely ten minutes before echoed in her head. She watched, rigid with fright, as the knob on the studio door turned.

There was no escape. Dry-mouthed, she braced for a fight.

"Cilla?"

Heart thudding, she lowered slowly into her chair, cursing her own nerves. "Mark."

"Sorry, I must have scared you."

"Only to death." Making an effort, she smiled at the station manager. He was in his middle thirties, and he was drop-dead gorgeous. His dark hair was carefully styled and on the long side, adding more youth to his smooth and tanned face. As always, his attire was carefully hip. "What are you doing here at this hour?"

"It's time we did more than talk about these calls."

"We had a meeting just a couple of days ago. I told you—"

"You told me," he agreed. "You have a habit of telling me, and everybody else."

"I'm not taking a vacation." She spun around in her chair to face him. "I've got nowhere to go."

"Everybody's got somewhere to go." He held up a hand before she could speak. "I'm not going to argue about this anymore. I know it's a difficult concept for you, but I am the boss."

She tugged at the hem of her sweatshirt. "What are you going to do? Fire me?"

He didn't know that she held her breath on the challenge. Though he'd worked with her for months, he hadn't scratched deep enough beneath the surface to understand how precarious was her self-esteem. If he had threatened her then, she would have folded. But all he knew was that her show had pumped new life into the station. The ratings were soaring.

"That wouldn't do either of us any good." Even as she let out the pent-up breath, he laid a hand on her shoulder. "Look, I'm worried about you, Cilla. All of us are."

It touched her, and, as always, it surprised her. "All he does is talk." For now. Scooting her chair toward the turntables, she prepared for the next music sweep.

"I'm not going to stand by while one of my people is harassed. I've called the police."

She sprang up out of her chair. "Damn it, Mark. I told you—"

"You told me." He smiled. "Let's not go down that road again. You're an asset to the station. And I'd like to think we were friends."

She sat down again, kicking out her booted feet. "Sure. Hold on." Struggling to concentrate, she went on-air with a station plug and the intro for the upcoming song. She gestured toward the clock. "You've got three minutes and fifteen seconds to convince me."

"Very simply, Cilla, what this guy's doing is against the law. I should never have let you talk me into letting it go this long."

"If we ignore him, he'll go away."

"Your way isn't working." He dropped his hand onto her shoulder again, patiently kneading the tensed muscles there. "So we're going to try mine. You talk to the cops or you take an unscheduled vacation."

Defeated, she looked up and managed a smile. "Do you push your wife around this way?"

"All the time." He grinned, then leaned down to press a kiss on her brow. "She loves it."

"Excuse me."

Cilla jerked back in what she knew could easily be mistaken for guilt. The two people in the doorway of the booth studied her with what she recognized as professional detachment.

The woman looked like a fashion plate, with a flow of dark red hair cascading to her shoulders and small, elegant sapphires at her ears that matched her eyes. Her complexion was the delicate porcelain of a true redhead. She had a small, compact body and wore a neatly tailored suit in wild shades of blue and green.

The man beside her looked as if he'd just spent a month on the range driving cattle. His shaggy blond hair was sun-streaked and fell over the collar of a denim work shirt. His jeans were worn and low at the hips, snug over what looked to Cilla to be about three feet of leg. The hems were frayed. Lanky, he slouched in the doorway, while the woman stood at attention. His boots were scuffed, but he wore a classically cut tweed jacket over his scruffy shirt.

He didn't smile. Cilla found herself staring, studying his face longer than she should have. There were hollows beneath his cheekbones, and there was the faintest of clefts in his chin. His tanned skin was taut over his facial bones, and his mouth, still unsmiling, was wide and firm. His eyes, intent enough on her face to make her want to squirm, were a clear bottle green.

"Mr. Harrison." The woman spoke first. Cilla thought there was a flicker of amusement in her eyes as she stepped forward. "I hope we gave you enough time."

Cilla sent Mark a killing look. "You told me you'd called them. You didn't tell me they were waiting outside."

"Now you know." He kept a hand on her shoulder,

but this time it was more restraining than comforting. "This is Ms. O'Roarke."

"I'm Detective Grayson. This is my partner, Detective Fletcher."

"Thank you again for waiting." Mark gestured her, then her partner, in. The man lazily unfolded himself from the doorjamb.

"Detective Fletcher and I are both used to it. We could use a bit more information."

"As you know, Ms. O'Roarke has been getting some disturbing calls here at the station."

"Cranks." Cilla spoke up, annoyed at being talked around. "Mark shouldn't have bothered you with it."

"We're paid to be bothered." Boyd Fletcher eased a lean hip down on the table. "So, this where you work?"

There was just enough insolence in his eyes to raise her hackles. "I bet you're a hell of a detective."

"Cilla." Tired and wishing he was home with his wife, Mark scowled at her. "Let's cooperate." Ignoring her, he turned to the detectives again. "The calls started during last Tuesday's show. None of us paid much attention, but they continued. The last one came in tonight, at 12:35."

"Do you have tapes?" Althea Grayson had already pulled out her notebook.

"I started making copies of them after the third call." At Cilla's startled look, Mark merely shrugged. "A precaution. I have them in my office."

Boyd nodded to Althea. "Go ahead. I'll take Ms. O'Roarke's statement."

"Cooperate," Mark said to Cilla, and led Althea out.

In the ensuing silence, Cilla tapped a cigarette out of her dwindling pack and lit it with quick, jerky movements. Boyd drew in the scent longingly. He'd quit only six weeks, three days and twelve hours ago.

"Slow death," he commented.

Cilla studied him through the haze of smoke. "You wanted a statement."

"Yeah." Curious, he reached over to toy with a switch. Automatically she batted his fingers aside.

"Hands off."

Boyd grinned. He had the distinct feeling that she was speaking of herself, as well as her equipment.

She cued up an established hit. After opening her mike, she did a backsell on the song just fading—the title, the artist, the station's call letters and her name. In an easy rhythm, she segued into the next selection. "Let's make it quick," she told him. "I don't like company during my shift."

"You're not exactly what I expected."

"I beg your pardon?"

No, indeed, he thought. She was a hell of a lot more than he'd expected. "I've caught your show," he said easily. "A few times." More than a few. He'd lost more than a few hours' sleep listening to that voice. Liquid sex. "I got this image, you know. Five-seven." He took a casual glance from the top of her head, down her body, to the toe of her boots. "I guess I was close there. But I took you for a blonde, hair down to your waist, blue eyes, lots of…personality." He grinned again, enjoying the annoyance in her eyes. Big brown eyes, he noted. Definitely different, and more appealing than his fantasy.

"Sorry to disappoint you."

"Didn't say I was disappointed."

She took a long, careful drag, then deliberately blew the smoke in his direction. If there was one thing she knew how to do, it was how to discourage an obnoxious male.

"Do you want a statement or not, Slick?"

"That's what I'm here for." He took a pad and the stub of a pencil out of his jacket pocket. "Shoot."

In clipped, dispassionate terms, she ran through every call, the times, the phrasing. She continued to work as she spoke, pushing in recorded tapes of commercials, cuing up a CD, replacing and selecting albums.

Boyd's brow rose as he wrote. He would check the tapes, of course, but he had the feeling that she was giving him word-for-word. In his job he respected a good memory.

"You've been in town, what? Six months?"

"More or less."

"Make any enemies?"

"A salesman trying to hawk encyclopedias. I slammed the door on his foot."

Boyd spared her a glance. She was trying to make light of it, but she had crushed out her cigarette and was now gnawing on her thumbnail. "Dump any lovers?"

"No."

"Have any?"

Temper flashed in her eyes again. "You're the detective. You find out."

"I would—if it was personal." His eyes lifted again in a look that was so direct, so completely personal, that her palms began to sweat. "Right now I'm just

doing my job. Jealousy and rejection are powerful mo-
tivators. According to your statements, most of the
comments he made to you had to do with your sexual
habits.''

Bluntness might be her strong suit, but she wasn't
about to tell him that her only sexual habit was absti-
nence. ''I'm not involved with anyone at the moment,''
she said evenly.

''Good.'' Without glancing up, he made another
note. ''That was a personal observation.''

''Look, Detective—''

''Cool your jets, O'Roarke,'' he said mildly. ''It was
an observation, not a proposition.'' His dark, patient
eyes took her measure. ''I'm on duty. I need a list of
the men you've had contact with on a personal level.
We'll keep it to the past six months for now. You can
leave out the door-to-door salesman.''

''I'm not involved.'' Her hands clenched as she rose.
''I haven't been involved. I've had no desire to be
involved.''

''No one ever said desire couldn't be one-sided.''
At the moment he was damn sure his was.

She was suddenly excruciatingly tired. Dragging a
hand through her hair, she struggled for patience.
''Anyone should be able to see that this guy is hung
up on a voice over the radio. He doesn't even know
me. He's probably never seen me. An image,'' she
said, tossing his own words back at him. ''That's all I
am to him. In this business it happens all the time. I
haven't done anything.''

''I didn't say you had.''

There was no teasing note in his voice now. The
sudden gentleness in it had her spinning around, blink-

ing furiously at threatening tears. Overworked, she told herself. Overstressed. Overeverything. With her back to him, she fought for control.

Tough, he thought. She was a tough lady. The way her hands balled at her sides as she fought with her emotions was much more appealing, much sexier, than broken sighs or helpless gestures could ever be.

He would have liked to go to her, to speak some word of comfort or reassurance, to stroke a hand down her hair. She'd probably bite it off at the wrist.

"I want you to think about the past few months, see if you can come up with anything, however small and unimportant, that might have led to this." His tone had changed again. It was brisk now, brisk and dispassionate. "We can't bring every man in the greater Denver area in for questioning. It doesn't work that way."

"I know how cops work."

The bitterness in her voice had his brows drawing together. There was something else here, but this wasn't the time to dig into it.

"You'd recognize the voice if you heard it again."

"Yes."

"Anything familiar about it?"

"Nothing."

"Do you think it was disguised?"

She moved her shoulders restlessly, but when she turned back to him she had herself under control. "He keeps it muffled and low. It's, ah…like a hiss."

"Any objections to me sitting in on tomorrow night's show."

Cilla took another long look at him. "Barrels of them."

He inclined his head. "I'll just go to your boss."

Disgusted, she reached for her cigarettes. He closed his firm hard-palmed hand over hers. She stared down at the tangled fingers, shocked to realize that her pulse had doubled at the contact.

"Let me do my job, Cilla. It'll be easier all around if you let Detective Grayson and me take over."

"Nobody takes over my life." She jerked her hand away, then jammed it into her pocket.

"Just this small part of it, then." Before she could stop him, he reached out and tucked her hair behind her ear. "Go home and get some sleep. You look beat."

She stepped back, made herself smile. "Thanks, Slick. I feel a lot better now."

Though she grumbled, she couldn't prevent him waiting until she signed off and turned the studio over to the all-night man. Nor did her lack of enthusiasm discourage him from walking her out to her car, reminding her to lock her door and waiting until she'd driven away. Disturbed by the way he'd looked at her—and the way she'd reacted—she watched him in the rearview mirror until he was out of sight.

"Just what I needed," she muttered to herself. "A cowboy cop."

Moments later, Althea joined Boyd in the parking lot. She had the tapes in her bag, along with Mark's statement. "Well, Fletcher—" she dropped a friendly hand on his shoulder "—what's the verdict?"

"She's tough as nails, hardheaded, prickly as a briar patch." With his hands in his pockets, he rocked back on his heels. "I guess it must be love."

Chapter 2

She was good, Boyd thought as he downed his bitter coffee and watched Cilla work. She handled the control board with an automatic ease that spoke of long experience—switching to music, to recorded announcements, to her own mike. Her timing was perfect, her delivery smooth. And her fingernails were bitten to the quick.

She was a package full of nerves and hostility. The nerves she tried to hide. She didn't bother with the hostility. In the two hours they'd been in the booth together, she had barely spoken a word to him. A neat trick, since the room was barely ten by ten.

That was fine. As a cop, he was used to being where he wasn't wanted. And he was just contrary enough to enjoy it.

He liked his job. Things like annoyance, animosity and belligerence didn't concern him. The simple fact was that negative emotions were a whole lot easier to deal with than a .45 slug. He'd had the opportunity to be hit with both.

Though he would have been uncomfortable with the term philosopher, he had a habit of analyzing everything down to its most basic terms. A the root of this was an elemental belief in right and wrong. Or— though he would have hesitated to use the phrase— good and evil.

He was savvy enough to know that crime often did pay, and pay well. Satisfaction came from playing a part in seeing that it didn't pay for long. He was a patient man. If a perpetrator took six hours or six months to bring down, the results were exactly the same. The good guys won.

Stretching out his long legs, he continued to page through his book while Cilla's voice washed over him. Her voice made him think of porch swings, hot summer nights and the sound of a slow-moving river. In direct contrast was the tension and restless energy that vibrated from her. He was content to enjoy the first and wonder about the second.

He was driving her crazy. Just being there. Cilla switched to a commercial, checked her playlist and deliberately ignored him. Or tried to. She didn't like company in the booth. It didn't matter that when she had coolly discouraged conversation he had settled back with his book—not the Western or men's adventure she had expected, but a dog-eared copy of Steinbeck's *East of Eden*. It didn't matter that he had been patiently quiet for nearly two hours.

He was there. And that was enough.

She couldn't pretend that the calls had stopped, that

they meant nothing, that her life was back on its normal track. Not with this lanky cowboy reading the great American novel in the corner of the booth, so that she had to all but climb over him to get to the albums stored on the back wall. He brought all her nerves swimming to the surface.

She resented him for that, for his intrusion, and for the simple fact that he was a cop.

But that was personal, she reminded herself. She had a job to do.

"That was INXS taking you to midnight. It's a new day, Denver. March 28, but we're not going out like a lamb. It's eighteen degrees out there at 12:02, so tune in and heat up. You're listening to KHIP, where you get more hits per hour. We've got the news coming up, then the request line. Light up those phones and we'll rock and roll."

Boyd waited until she'd run through the news and moved to a commercial before he marked his place in his book and rose. He could feel the tension thicken as he sat in the chair next to Cilla.

"I don't want you to cut him off."

She stiffened and struggled to keep her voice carelessly sarcastic. "My listeners don't tune in for that kind of show, Slick."

"You can keep him on the line, on the studio speakers, without sending it on air, right?"

"Yes, but I don't want to—"

"Cut to a commercial or some music," Boyd said mildly, "but keep him on the line. We might get lucky and trace the call."

Her hands were balled into fists in her lap as she stared at the lights that were already blinking on the phone. He was right. She knew he was right. And she hated it.

"This is an awful lot of trouble for one loose screw."

"Don't worry." He smiled a little. "I get paid the same whether the screws are loose or tight."

She glanced down at the clock, cleared her throat, then switched on her mike. "Hello, Denver, this is Cilla O'Roarke for KHIP. You're listening to the hottest station in the Rockies. This is your chance to make it even hotter. Our request lines are open. I'll be playing what you want to hear, so give me a call at 555-KHIP. That's 555-5447."

Her finger trembled slightly as she punched the first lit button.

"This is Cilla O'Roarke. You're on the air."

"Hi, Cilla, this is Bob down in Englewood."

She closed her eyes on a shudder of relief. He was a regular. "Hey, Bob. How's it going?"

"Going great. My wife and I are celebrating our fifteenth anniversary tonight."

"And they said it wouldn't last. What can I play for you, Bob?"

"How about 'Cherish' for Nancy from Bob."

"Nice choice. Here's to fifteen more, Bob."

With her pen in one hand, she took the second call, then the third. Boyd watched her tighten up after each one. She chatted and joked. And grew paler. At the first break, she pulled a cigarette out of the pack, then fumbled with a match. Silently Boyd took the matches from her and lit one for her.

"You're doing fine."

She took a quick, jerky puff. Patient, he waited in

silence for her to respond. "Do you have to watch me?"

"No." Then he smiled. It was a long, lazy smile that had her responding in spite of herself. "A man's entitled to some fringe benefits."

"If this is the best you can do, Slick, you ought to look for another line of work."

"I like this one." He rested the ankle of his boot on his knee. "I like it fine."

It was easier, Cilla decided, to talk to him than to stare at the blinking lights on the phone and worry. "Have you been a cop long?"

"Going on ten years."

She looked at him then, struggling to relax by concentrating on his face. He had calm eyes, she thought. Dark and calm. Eyes that had seen a lot and learned to live with it. There was a quiet kind of strength there, the kind women—some women—were drawn to. He would protect and defend. He wouldn't start a fight. But he would finish one.

Annoyed with herself, she looked away again, busying herself with her notes. She didn't need to be protected or defended. She certainly didn't need anyone to fight for her. She had always taken care of herself. And she always would.

"It's a lousy job," she said. "Being a cop."

He shifted. His knee brushed her thigh. "Mostly."

Instinctively she jiggled her chair for another inch of distance. "It's hard to figure why anyone would stick with a lousy job for ten years."

He just grinned. "I guess I'm in a rut."

She shrugged, then turned to her mike. "That was for Bill and Maxine. It's 12:20, and our request lines

are still open. That's 555-5447.'' After one quick
breath, she punched a button. ''KHIP. You're on the
air.''

It went smoothly, so smoothly that she began to relax. She took call after call, falling into her old, established rhythm. Gradually she began to enjoy the music
again, the flow of it. The pulsing lights on the phone
no longer seemed threatening. By 12:45 she was sure
she was going to make it through.

Just one night, she told herself. If he didn't call tonight, it would be over. She looked at the clock,
watched the seconds tick by. Eight more minutes to go
and she would turn the airwaves over to Jackson. She
would go home, take a long, hot bath and sleep like a
baby.

''KHIP, you're on the air.''

''Cilla.''

The hissing whisper shot ice through her veins. She
reached over reflexively to disconnect, but Boyd
clamped a hand over her wrist and shook his head. For
a moment she struggled, biting back panic. His hand
remained firm on hers, his eyes calm and steady.

Boyd watched as she fought for control, until she
jammed in a cassette of commercials. The bright,
bouncy jingles transmitted as she put the call on the
studio speaker.

''Yes.'' Pride made her keep her eyes on Boyd's.
''This is Cilla. What do you want?''

''Justice. I only want justice.''

''For what?''

''I want you to think about that. I want you to think
and wonder and sweat until I come for you.''

''Why?'' Her hand flexed under Boyd's. In an instinctive gesture of reassurance, he linked his fingers with hers. "Who are you?"

"Who am I?" There was a laugh that skidded along her skin. "I'm your shadow, your conscience. Your executioner. You have to die. When you understand, only when you understand, I'll end it. But it won't be quick. It won't be easy. You're going to pay for what you've done."

"What have I done?" she shouted. "For God's sake, what have I done?"

He spit out a stream of obscenities that left her dazed and nauseated before he broke the connection. With one hand still covering hers, Boyd punched out a number on the phone.

"You get the trace?" he demanded, then bit off an oath. "Yeah. Right." Disgusted, he replaced the receiver. "Not long enough." He reached up to touch Cilla's pale cheek. "You okay?"

She could hardly hear him for the buzzing in her ears, but she nodded. Mechanically she turned to her mike, waiting until the commercial jingle faded.

"That about wraps it up for this morning. It's 1:57. Tina Turner's going to rock you through until two. My man Jackson's coming it to keep all you insomniacs company until 6:00 a.m. This is Cilla O'Roarke for KHIP. Remember, darling, when you dream of me, dream good."

Light-headed, she pushed away from the console. She only had to stand up, she told herself. Walk to her car, drive home. It was simple enough. She did it every morning of her life. But she sat where she was, afraid her legs would buckle.

Jackson pushed through the door and stood there,

hesitating. He was wearing a baseball cap to cover his healing hair transplant. "Hey, Cilla." He glanced from her to Boyd and back again. "Rough night, huh?"

Cilla braced herself, pasted on a careless smile. "I've had better." With every muscle tensed, she shoved herself to her feet. "I've got them warmed up for you, Jackson."

"Take it easy, kid."

"Sure." The buzzing in her ears was louder as she walked from the booth to snatch her coat from the rack. The corridors were dark, catching only a faint glow from the lobby, where the security lights burned. Disoriented, she blinked. She didn't even notice when Boyd took her arm and led her outside.

The cold air helped. She took big, thirsty gulps of it, releasing it again in thin plumes of white smoke. "My car's over there," she said when Boyd began to pull her toward the opposite end of the lot.

"You're in no shape to drive."

"I'm fine."

"Great. Then we'll go dancing."

"Look—"

"No, you look." He was angry, furious. He hadn't realized it himself until that moment. She was shaking, and despite the chill wind her cheeks were deadly pale. Listening to the tapes hadn't been the same as being there when the call came through, seeing the blood drain out of her face and her eyes glaze with terror. And not being able to do a damn thing to stop it. "You're a mess, O'Roarke, and I'm not letting you get behind the wheel of a car." He stopped next to his car and yanked open the door. "Get in. I'll take you home."

She tossed the hair out of her eyes. "Serve and protect, right?"

"You got it. Now get in before I arrest you for loitering."

Because her knees felt like jelly, she gave in. She wanted to be asleep, alone in some small, quiet room. She wanted to scream. Worse, she wanted to cry. Instead, she rounded on Boyd the second he settled in the driver's seat.

"You know what I hate even more than cops?"

He turned the key in the ignition. "I figure you're going to tell me."

"Men who order women around just because they're men. I don't figure that as a cultural hang-up, just stupidity. The way I look at it, that's two counts against you, Detective."

He leaned over, deliberately crowding her back in her seat. He got a moment's intense satisfaction out of seeing her eyes widen in surprise, her lips part on a strangled protest. The satisfaction would have been greater, he knew, if he had gone on impulse and covered that stubborn, sassy mouth with his own. He was certain she would taste exactly as she sounded—hot, sexy and dangerous.

Instead, he yanked her seat belt around her and fastened it.

Her breath came out in a whoosh when he took the wheel again. It had been a rough night, Cilla reminded herself. A tense, disturbing and unsettling night. Otherwise she would never have sat like a fool and allowed herself to be intimidated by some modern-day cowboy.

Her hands were shaking again. The reason didn't seem to matter, only the weakness.

"I don't think I like your style, Slick."

"You don't have to." She was getting under his skin, Boyd realized as he turned out of the lot. That was always a mistake. "Do what you're told and we'll get along fine."

"I don't do what I'm told," she snapped. "And I don't need a second-rate cop with a John Wayne complex to give me orders. Mark's the one who called you in, not me. I don't need you and I don't want you."

He braked at a light. "Tough."

"If you think I'm going to fall apart because some creep calls me names and makes threats, you're wrong."

"I don't think you're going to fall apart, O'Roarke, any more than you think I'm going to pick up the pieces if you do."

"Good. Great. I can handle him all by myself, and if you get your kicks out of listening to that kind of garbage—" She broke off, appalled with herself. Lifting her hands, she pressed them to her face and took three deep breaths.

"I'm sorry."

"For?"

"For taking it out on you." She dropped her hands into her lap and stared at them. "Could you pull over for a minute?"

Without a word, he guided the car to the curb and stopped.

"I want to calm down before I get home." In a deliberate effort to relax, she let her head fall back and her eyes close. "I don't want to upset my sister."

It was hard to hold on to rage and resentment when the woman sitting next to him had turned from barbed wire to fragile glass. But if his instincts about Cilla were on target, too much sympathy would set her off again.

"Want some coffee?"

"No thanks." The corners of her mouth turned up for the briefest instant. "I've poured in enough to fuel an SST." She let out a long, cleansing breath. The giddiness was gone, and with it that floating sense of unreality. "I am sorry, Slick. You're only doing your job."

"You got that right. Why do you call me Slick?"

She opened her eyes, made a brief but comprehensive study of his face. "Because you are." Turning away, she dug in her bag for a cigarette. "I'm scared." She hated the fact that the admission was shaky, that her hand was unsteady as she struck a match.

"You're entitled."

"No, I'm really scared." She let out smoke slowly, watching a late-model sedan breeze down the road and into the night. "He wants to kill me. I didn't really believe that until tonight." She shuddered. "Is there any heat in this thing?"

He turned the fan on full. "It's better if you're scared."

"Why?"

"You'll cooperate."

She smiled. It was a full flash of a smile that almost stopped his heart. "No, I won't. This is only a momentary respite. I'll be giving you a hard time as soon as I recover."

"I'll try not to get used to this." But it would be easy, he realized, to get used to the way her eyes warmed when she smiled. The way her voice eased over a man and made him wonder. "Feeling better?"

"Lots. Thanks." She tapped out her cigarette as he guided the car back on the road. "I take it you know where I live."

"That's why I'm a detective."

"It's a thankless job." She pushed her hair back from her forehead. They would talk, she decided. Just talk. Then she wouldn't have to think. "Why aren't you out roping cattle or branding bulls? You've got the looks for it."

He considered a moment. "I'm not sure that's a compliment, either."

"You're fast on the draw, Slick."

"Boyd," he said. "It wouldn't hurt you to use my name." When she only shrugged, he slanted her a curious look. "Cilla. That'd be from Priscilla, right?"

"No one calls me Priscilla more than once."

"Why?"

She sent him her sweetest smile. "Because I cut out their tongues."

"Right. You want to tell me why you don't like cops?"

"No." She turned away to stare out the side window. "I like the nighttime," she said, almost to herself. "You can do things, say things, at three o'clock in the morning that it's just not possible to do or say at three o'clock in the afternoon. I can't even imagine what it's like to work in the daylight anymore, when people are crowding the air."

"You don't like people much, do you?"

"Some people." She didn't want to talk about herself, her likes and dislikes, her successes, her failures.

She wanted to talk about him—to satisfy her curiosity, and to ease her jangled nerves. "So, how long have you had the night shift, Fletcher?"

"About nine months." He glanced at her. "You meet an...interesting class of people."

She laughed, surprised that she was able to. "Don't you just? Are you from Denver?"

"Born and bred."

"I like it," she said, surprising herself again. She hadn't given it a great deal of thought. It had simply been a place that offered a good college for Deborah and a good opportunity for her. Yet in six months, she realized, she had come close to sinking roots. Shallow ones, but roots nonetheless.

"Does that mean you're going to stick around?" He turned down a quiet side street. "I did some research. It seems two years in one spot's about your limit."

"I like change," she said flatly, closing down the lines of communication. She didn't care for the idea of anyone poking into her past and her private life. When he pulled up in her driveway, she was already unsnapping her seat belt. "Thanks for the ride, Slick."

Before she could dash to her door, he was beside her. "I'm going to need your keys."

They were already in her hand. She clutched them possessively. "Why?"

"So I can have your car dropped off in the morning."

She jingled them, frowning, as she stood under the front porch light. Boyd wondered what it would be like to walk her to her door after an ordinary date. He wouldn't keep his hands in his pockets, he thought ruefully. And he certainly would scratch this itch by kissing her outside the door.

Outside, hell, he admitted. He would have been through the door with her. And there would have been more to the end of the evening than a good-night kiss.

But it wasn't a date. And any fool could see that there wasn't going to be anything remotely ordinary between them. Something. That he promised himself. But nothing remotely resembling the ordinary.

"Keys?" he repeated.

After going over her options, Cilla had decided his was best. Carefully she removed a single key from the chain, which was shaped like a huge musical note. "Thanks."

"Hold it." He placed the palm of his hand on the door as she unlocked it. "You're not going to ask me in for a cup of coffee?"

She didn't turn, only twisted her head. "No."

She smelled like the night, he thought. Dark, deep, dangerous. "That's downright unfriendly."

The flash of humor came again. "I know. See you around, Slick."

His hand dropped onto hers on the knob, took a firm hold. "Do you eat?"

The humor vanished. That didn't surprise him. What did was what replaced it. Confusion. And—he could have sworn—shyness. She recovered so quickly that he was certain he'd imagined it.

"Once or twice a week."

"Tomorrow." His hand remained over hers. He couldn't be sure about what he'd thought he saw in her eyes, but he knew her pulse had quickened under his fingers.

"I may eat tomorrow."

"With me."

It amazed her that she fumbled. It had been years since she'd experienced this baffling reaction to a man. And those years had been quiet and smooth. Refusing a date was as simple as saying no. At least it always had been for her. Now she found herself wanting to smile and ask him what time she should be ready. The words were nearly out of her mouth before she caught herself.

"That's an incredibly smooth offer, Detective, but I'll have to pass."

"Why?"

"I don't date cops."

Before she could weaken, she slipped inside and closed the door in his face.

Boyd shuffled the papers on his desk and scowled. The O'Roarke case was hardly his only assignment, but he couldn't get his mind off it. Couldn't get his mind off O'Roarke, he thought, wishing briefly but intensely for a cigarette.

The veteran cop sitting two feet away from him was puffing away like a chimney as he talked to a snitch. Boyd breathed in deep, wishing he could learn to hate the smell like other nonsmokers.

Instead, he continued to torture himself by drawing in the seductive scent—that, and the other, less appealing aromas of a precinct station. Overheated coffee, overheated flesh, the cheap perfume hovering around a pair of working girls who lounged resignedly on a nearby bench.

Intrusions, he thought, that he rarely noticed in the

day-to-day scheme of things. Tonight they warred with his concentration. The smells, the sound of keyboards clicking, phones ringing, shoes scuffing along the linoleum, the way one of the overhead lights winked sporadically.

It didn't help his disposition that for the past three days Priscilla Alice O'Roarke had stuck fast to his mind like a thick, thorny spike. No amount of effort could shake her loose. It might be because both he and his partner had spent hours at a time with her in the booth during her show. It might be because he'd seen her with her defenses down. It might be because he'd felt, fleetingly, her surge of response to him.

It might be, Boyd thought in disgust. Then again, it might not.

He wasn't a man whose ego was easily bruised by the refusal of a date. He liked to think that he had enough confidence in himself to understand he didn't appeal to every woman. The fact that he'd appealed to what he considered a healthy number of them in his thirty-three years was enough to satisfy him.

The trouble was, he was hung up on one woman. And she wasn't having any of it.

He could live with it.

The simple fact was that he had a job to do now. He wasn't convinced that Cilla was in any immediate danger. But she was being harassed, systematically and thoroughly. Both he and Althea had started the ball rolling, questioning men with priors that fit the M.O., poking their fingers into Cilla's personal and professional life since she had come to Denver, quietly investigating her co-workers.

So far the score was zip.

Time to dig deeper, Boyd decided. He had Cilla's résumé in his hand. It was an interesting piece of work in itself. Just like the woman it belonged to. It showed her bouncing from a one-horse station in Georgia—which accounted for that faint and fascinating Southern drawl—to a major player in Atlanta, then on to Richmond, St. Louis, Chicago, before landing—feet first, obviously—in Denver at KHIP.

The lady likes to move, he mused. Or was it that she needed to run? That was a question of semantics, and he intended to get the answer straight from the horse's mouth.

The one thing he could be sure of from the bald facts typed out in front of him was that Cilla had pulled herself along the road to success with a high school diploma and a lot of guts. It couldn't have been easy for a woman—a girl, really, at eighteen—to break into what was still a largely male-dominated business.

"Interesting reading?" Althea settled a hip on the corner of his desk. No one in the station house would have dared whistle at her legs. But plenty of them looked.

"Cilla O'Roarke." He tossed the résumé down. "Impressions?"

"Tough lady." She grinned as she said it. She'd spent a lot of time razzing Boyd about his fascination with the sultry voice on the radio. "Likes to do things her own way. Smart and professional."

He picked up a box of candy-coated almonds and shook some into his hand. "I think I figured all that out myself."

"Well, figure this." Althea took the box and carefully selected one glossy nut. "She's scared down to the bone. And she's got an inferiority complex a mile wide.''

''Inferiority complex.'' Boyd gave a quick snort and kicked back in his chair. ''Not a chance.''

With the same careful deliberation, Althea chose another candied almond. ''She hides it behind three feet of steel, but it's there.'' Althea laid a hand on the toe of his boot. ''Woman's intuition, Fletcher. That's why you're so damn lucky to have me.''

Boyd snatched the box back, knowing Althea could, and would, methodically work her way through to the last piece. ''If that woman's insecure, I'll eat my hat.''

''You don't have a hat.''

''I'll get one and eat it.'' Dismissing his partner's instincts, he gestured toward the files. ''Since our man isn't letting up, we're going to have to go looking elsewhere for him.''

''The lady isn't very forthcoming about her past.''

''So we push.''

Althea considered a moment. Then she shifted her weight gracefully, recrossed her legs. ''Want to flip a coin? Because the odds are she'll push back.''

Boyd grinned. ''I'm counting on it.''

''It's your turn in the booth tonight.''

''Then you start with Chicago.'' He handed her the file. ''We got the station manager, the landlord.'' He scanned the sheet himself. He intended to go far beyond what was printed there, but he would start with the facts. ''Use that sweet, persuasive voice of yours. They'll spill their guts.''

''Thousands have.'' She glanced over idly as an associate shoved a swearing suspect with a bloody nose into a nearby chair. There was a brief tussle, and a spate of curses followed by mumbled threats. "God, I love this place."

"Yeah, there's no place like home." He snatched up what was left of his coffee before his partner could reach for it. "I'll work from the other end, the first station she worked for. Thea, if we don't come up with something soon, the captain's going to yank us."

She rose. "Then we'll have to come up with something."

He nodded. Before he could pick up the phone, it rang. "Fletcher."

"Slick."

He would have grimaced at the nickname if he hadn't heard the fear first. "Cilla? What is it?"

"I got a call." A quick bubble of laughter worked its way through. "Old news, I guess. I'm at home this time, though, and I— Damn, I'm jumping at shadows."

"Lock your doors and sit tight. I'm on my way. Cilla," he said when there was no response. "I'm on my way."

"Thanks. If you could break a few traffic laws getting here, I'd be obliged."

"Ten minutes." He hung up. "Thea." He caught her before she could complete the first call. "Let's move."

Chapter 3

She had herself under control by the time they got to her. Above all, she felt foolish to have run to the police—to him—because of a phone call.

Only phone calls, Cilla assured herself as she paced to the window and back. After a week of them she should have a better handle on it. If she could tone down her reaction, convince the caller that what he said and how he said it left her unaffected, they would stop.

Her father had taught her that that was the way to handle bullies. Then again, her mother's solution had been a right jab straight to the jaw. While Cilla saw value in both viewpoints, she thought the passive approach was more workable under the circumstances.

She'd done a lousy job of it with the last call, she admitted. Sometime during his tirade she'd come uncomfortably close to hysteria, shouting back, pleading, meeting threats with threats. She could only be grateful that Deborah hadn't been home to hear it.

Struggling for calm, she perched on the arm of a chair, her body ruler-straight, her mind scrambling. After the call she had turned off the radio, locked the doors, pulled the drapes. Now, in the glow of the lamplight, she sat listening for a sound, any sound, while she scanned the room. The walls she and Deborah had painted, the furniture they had picked out, argued about. Familiar things, Cilla thought. Calming things.

After only six months there was already a scattering of knickknacks, something they hadn't allowed themselves before. But this time the house wasn't rented, the furniture wasn't leased. It was theirs.

Perhaps that was why, though they'd never discussed it, they had begun to fill it with little things, useless things. The china cat who curled in a permanent nap on the cluttered bookshelf. The foolishly expensive glossy white bowl with hibiscus blossoms painted on the rim. The dapper frog in black tie and tails.

They were making a home, Cilla realized. For the first time since they had found themselves alone, they were making a home. She wouldn't let some vicious, faceless voice over the phone spoil that.

What was she going to do? Because she was alone, she allowed herself a moment of despair and dropped her head into her hands. Should she fight back? But how could she fight someone she couldn't see and didn't understand? Should she pretend indifference? But how long could she keep up that kind of pretense, especially if he continued to invade her private hours, as well as her public ones?

And what would happen when he finally wearied of talk and came to her in person?

The brisk knock on the door had her jolting, had her pressing a hand between her breasts to hold in her suddenly frantic heart.

I'm your executioner. I'm going to make you suffer. I'm going to make you pay.

"Cilla. It's Boyd. Open the door."

She needed a moment more, needed to cover her face with her hands and breathe deep. Steadier now, she crossed to the door and opened it.

"Hi. You made good time." She nodded to Althea. "Detective Grayson." Cilla gestured them inside, then leaned her back against the closed door. "I feel stupid for calling you all the way out here."

"Just part of the job," Althea told her. The woman was held together by very thin wires, she decided. A few of them had already snapped. "Would you mind if we all sat down?"

"No. I'm sorry." Cilla dragged a hand through her hair. She wasn't putting on a very good show, she thought. And she prided herself on putting on a good show. "I could, ah, make some coffee."

"Don't worry about it." He sat on an oatmeal-colored couch and leaned back against sapphire-blue pillows. "Tell us what happened."

"I wrote it down." The underlying nerves showed in her movements as she walked to the phone to pick up a pad of paper. "A radio habit," she said. "The phone rings and I start writing." She wasn't ready to admit that she didn't want to repeat the conversation out loud. "Some of it's in O'Roarke shorthand, but you should get the drift."

He took the pad from her and scanned the words. His gut muscles tightened in a combination of fury and revulsion. Outwardly calm, he handed the note to his partner.

Cilla couldn't sit. Instead, she stood in the center of the room, twisting her fingers together, dragging them apart again to tug at her baggy sweatshirt. "He's pretty explicit about what he thinks of me, and what he intends to do about it."

"Is this your first call at home?" Boyd asked her.

"Yes. I don't know how he got the number. I— We're not listed."

Althea put the pad aside and took out her own. "Who has your home number?"

"The station." Cilla relaxed fractionally. This was something she could deal with. Simple questions, simple answers. "It would be on file at the college. My lawyer—that's Carl Donnely, downtown. There are a couple of guys that Deb sees. Josh Holden and Darren McKinley. A few girlfriends." She ran through the brief list. "That's about it. What I'm really concerned about is—" She spun around as the door opened behind her. "Deb." Relief and annoyance speared through her. "I thought you had evening classes."

"I did." She turned a pair of big, smoldering blue eyes on Boyd and Althea. "Are you the police?"

"Deborah," Cilla said, "you know better than to cut classes. You had a test—"

"Stop treating me like a child." She slapped the newspaper she was carrying into Cilla's hand. "Do you really expect me to go along like nothing's wrong? Damn it, Cilla, you told me it was all under control."

So she'd made the first page of section B, Cilla thought wearily. Late-night radio princess under siege. Trying to soothe a growing tension headache, she rubbed her fingers at her temple. "It is under control. Stuff like this makes good copy, that's all."

"No, that's not all."

"I've called the police," she snapped back as she tossed the paper aside. "What else do you want?"

There was a resemblance between the two, Boyd noted objectively. The shape of the mouth and eyes. While Cilla was alluring and sexy enough to make a man's head turn a 360, her sister was hands-down gorgeous. Young, he thought. Maybe eighteen. In a few years she'd barely have to glance at a man to have him swallow his tongue.

He also noted the contrasts. Deborah's hair was short and fluffed. Cilla's was long and untamed. The younger sister wore a deep crimson sweater over tailored slacks that were tucked into glossy half boots. Cilla's mismatched sweats bagged and hit on a variety of colors. The top was purple, the bottoms green. She'd chosen thick yellow socks and orange high-tops.

Their tastes might clash, he mused, but their temperaments seemed very much in tune.

And when the O'Roarke sisters were in a temper, it was quite a show.

Shifting only slightly, Althea whispered near his ear. "Obviously they've done this before."

Boyd grinned. If he'd had popcorn and a beer, he would have been content to sit through another ten rounds. "Who's your money on?"

"Cilla," she murmured, crossing one smooth leg. "But the sister's a real up-and-comer."

Apparently weary of beating her head against a brick wall, Deborah turned. "Okay." She poked a finger at Boyd. "You tell me what's going on."

"Ah…"

"Never mind." She zeroed in on Althea. "You."

Biting back a smile, Althea nodded. "We're the investigating officers on your sister's case, Miss O'Roarke."

"So there is a case."

Ignoring Cilla's furious look, Althea nodded again. "Yes. With the station's cooperation, we have a trace on the studio line. Detective Fletcher and I have already interrogated a number of suspects who have priors for obscene or harassing phone calls. With this latest development, we'll put a tap on your private line."

"Latest development." It only took Deborah a moment. "Oh, Cilla, not here. He didn't call you here." Temper forgotten, she threw her arms around her sister. "I'm sorry."

"It's nothing for you to worry about." When Deborah stiffened, Cilla drew back. "I mean it, Deb. It's nothing for either of us to worry about. We've got the pros to do the worrying."

"That's right." Althea rose. "Detective Fletcher and I have over fifteen years on the force between us. We intend to take good care of your sister. Is there a phone I can use to make some arrangements?"

"In the kitchen," Deborah said before Cilla could comment. She wanted a private interview. "I'll show you." She paused and smiled at Boyd. "Would you like some coffee, Detective?"

"Thanks." He watched her—what man wouldn't?—as she walked from the room.

"Don't even think about it," Cilla mumbled.

"Excuse me?" But he grinned. It didn't take a detective to recognize a mother hen. "Your sister—Deborah, right?—she's something."

"You're too old for her."

"Ouch."

Cilla picked up a cigarette and forced herself to settle on the arm of a chair again. "In any case, you and Detective Grayson seem well suited to each other."

"Thea?" He had to grin again. Most of the time he forgot his partner was a woman. "Yeah, I'm one lucky guy."

Cilla ground her teeth. She hated to think she could be intimidated by another woman. Althea Grayson was personable enough, professional enough. Cilla could even handle the fact that she was stunning. It was just that she was so *together*.

Boyd rose to take the unlit cigarette from her fingers. "Jealous?"

"In your dreams, Slick."

"We'll get into my dreams later." He lifted her chin up with a fingertip. "Holding on?"

"I'm fine." She wanted to move, but she had the feeling he wouldn't give her room if she stood. And if she stood it would be much too easy to drop her head on his shoulder and just cave in. She had responsibilities, obligations. And her pride. "I don't want Deb mixed up in this. She's alone here at night while I'm at work."

"I can arrange to have a cruiser stationed outside."

She nodded, grateful. "I hate it that somewhere along the line I've made a mistake that might put her in danger. She doesn't deserve it."

Unable to resist, he spread his fingers to cup her cheek. "Neither do you."

It had been a long time since she'd been touched, allowed herself to be touched, even that casually. She managed to shrug. "I haven't figured that out yet." She gave a little sigh, wishing she could close her eyes and turn her face into that strong, capable hand. "I've got to get ready to go to the station."

"Why don't you give that a pass tonight?"

"And let him think he's got me running scared?" She stood then. "Not on a bet."

"Even Wonder Woman takes a night off."

She shook her head. She'd been right about him not giving her room. Her escape routes were blocked by the chair on one side and his body on the other. Tension quivered through her. Pride kept her eyes level. He was waiting, damn him. And unless he was blind or stupid he would see that this contact, this connection with him, left her frazzled.

"You're crowding me, Fletcher."

In another minute, just one more minute, he would have given in to impulse and pulled her against him. He would have seen just how close to reality his fantasy was. "I haven't begun to crowd you, O'Roarke."

Her eyes sharpened. "I've had enough threats for one day, thanks."

He wanted to strangle her for that. Slowly, his eyes on hers, he hooked his thumbs in his pockets. "No threat, babe. Just a fact."

Deborah decided she'd eavesdropped long enough and cleared her throat. "Coffee, Detective Fletcher." She passed him a steaming mug. "Thea said black, two sugars."

"Thanks."

"I'm going to hang around," she said, silently daring Cilla to argue with her. "They should be here in an hour or so to hook up the phone." Then, she put her hands on Cilla's shoulders and kissed both of her cheeks. "I haven't missed a class this semester, Simon."

"Simon?" Boyd commented.

"Legree." With a laugh, Deborah kissed Cilla again. "The woman's a slave driver."

"I don't know what you're talking about." Cilla moved aside to gather up her purse. "You ought to catch up on your reading for U.S. studies. Your political science could use a boost. It wouldn't hurt to bone up on Psychology 101." She pulled her coat from the closet. "While you're at it, the kitchen floor needs scrubbing. I'm sure we have an extra toothbrush you could use on it. And I'd like another cord of wood chopped."

Deborah laughed. "Go away."

Cilla grinned as she reached for the doorknob. Her hand closed over Boyd's. She jolted back before she could stop herself. "What are you doing?"

"Hitching a ride with you." He sent Deborah a quick wink as he pulled Cilla out the door.

"This is ridiculous," Cilla said as she strode into the station.

"Which?"

"I don't see why I have to have a cop in the studio with me night after night." She whipped off her coat as she walked—a bit like a bullfighter swirling a cape, Boyd thought. Still scowling, she reached for the door of a small storage room, then shrieked and stumbled back against Boyd as it swung open. "Jeez, Billy, you scared the life out of me."

"Sorry." The maintenance man had graying hair, toothpick arms and an apologetic grin. "I was out of window cleaner." He held up his spray bottle.

"It's okay. I'm a little jumpy."

"I heard about it." He hooked the trigger of the bottle in his belt, then gathered up a mop and bucket. "Don't worry, Cilla. I'm here till midnight."

"Thanks. Are you going to listen to the show tonight?"

"You bet." He walked away, favoring his right leg in a slight limp.

Cilla stepped inside the room and located a fresh bottle of stylus cleaner. Taking a five-dollar bill out of her bag, she slipped it into a pile of cleaning rags.

"What was that for?"

"He was in Vietnam," she said simply, and closed the door again.

Boyd said nothing, knowing she was annoyed he'd caught her. He chalked it up to one more contradiction.

To prep for her shift, she went into a small lounge to run over the daily log for her show, adding and deleting as it suited her. The program director had stopped screaming about this particular habit months before. Another reason she preferred the night shift was the leeway it gave her.

"This new group," she muttered.

"What?" Boyd helped himself to a sugared doughnut.

"This new group, the Studs." She tapped her pencil against the table. "One-shot deal. Hardly worth the airtime."

"Then why play them?"

"Got to give them a fair shake." Intent on her work, she took an absent bite of the doughnut Boyd held to her lips. "In six months nobody will remember their names."

"That's rock and roll."

"No. The Beatles, Buddy Holly, Chuck Berry, Springsteen, Elvis—that's rock and roll."

He leaned back, considering her. "Ever listen to anything else?"

She grinned, then licked a speck of sugar from her top lip. "You mean there *is* something else?"

"Have you always been one-track?"

"Yeah." She pulled a band of fabric out of her pocket. With a couple of flicks of the wrist she had her hair tied back. "So what kind of music do you like?"

"The Beatles, Buddy Holly, Chuck—"

"Well, there's hope for you yet," she interrupted.

"Mozart, Lena Horne, Beaujolais, Joan Jett, Ella Fitzgerald, B.B. King..."

Her brow lifted. "So, we're eclectic."

"We're open-minded."

She leaned back a moment. "You're a surprise, Fletcher. I guess I figured you for the loving-and-hurting, drinking-and-cheating type."

"In music appreciation or personality?"

"Both." She glanced at the clock. "It's show time."

Wild Bob Williams, who had the six-to-ten slot, was just finishing up his show. He was short, paunchy and middle-aged, with the voice of a twenty-year-old stud. He gave Cilla a brief salute as she began sorting through 45s and albums.

"Mmm, the long-legged filly just walked in." He

hit a switch that had an echoing heartbeat pounding. "Get ready out there in KHIP land, your midnight star's rising. I'm leaving you with this blast from the past." He potted up "Honky Tonk Woman."

He swung out of his chair and stretched his rubbery leg muscles. "Hey, honey, you okay?"

"Sure." She set her first cut on the turntable and adjusted the needle.

"I caught the paper."

"No big deal, Bob."

"Hey, we're family around here." He gave her shoulder a quick squeeze. "We're behind you."

"Thanks."

"You're the cop?" he asked Boyd.

"That's right."

"Get this guy soon. He's got us all shaking." He gave Cilla another squeeze. "Let me know if you need anything."

"I will. Thanks."

She didn't want to think about it, couldn't afford to think about it, with thirty seconds to air. Taking her seat, she adjusted the mike, took a series of long, deep breaths, ran a one-two-three voice check, then opened her mike.

"All right, Denver, this is Cilla O'Roarke coming to you on number one, KHIP. You've got me from ten till two in the a.m. We're going to start off giving away one hundred and nine dollars. We've got the mystery record coming up. If you can give me the title, the artist and the year, you've got yourself a fistful of cash. That number is 555-5447. Stand by, 'cause we're going to rock."

The music blasted out, pleasing her. She was in control again.

"Elton John," Boyd said from behind her. "'Honky Cat.' Nineteen seventy…two."

She turned in her chair to face him. He was looking damned pleased with himself, she thought. That half grin on his face, his hands in his pockets. It was a shame he was so attractive, a bloody crying shame. "Well, well, you surprise me, Slick. Remind me to put you down for a free T-shirt."

"I'd rather have a dinner."

"And I'd rather have a Porsche. But there you go— Hey," she said when he took her hand.

"You've been biting your nails." He skimmed a thumb over her knuckles and watched her eyes change. "Another bad habit."

"I've got lots more."

"Good." Instead of sitting back in the corner, he chose a chair beside her. "I didn't have time to get a book," he explained. "Why don't I watch you work?"

"Why don't you—" She swore, then punched a button on the phone. He'd nearly made her miss her cue. "KHIP. Can you name the mystery record?"

It took five calls before she had a winner. Trying to ignore Boyd, she put on another cut while she took the winner's name and address.

As if she didn't have enough on her mind, she thought. How was she supposed to concentrate on her show when he was all but sitting on top of her? Close enough, she realized, that she could smell him. No cologne, just soap—something that brought the mountains to mind one moment and quiet, intimate nights the next.

She wasn't interested in either, she reminded herself. All she wanted was to get through this crisis and get her life back on an even keel. Attractive men came and went, she knew. But success stayed—as long as you were willing to sweat for it.

She shifted, stretching out to select a new record. Their thighs brushed. His were long and as hard as rock. Determined not to jolt, she turned her head to look into his eyes. Inches apart, challenge meeting challenge. She watched as his gaze dipped down to linger on her mouth. And it lifted again, desire flickering. Music pulsed in her ears from the headphones she stubbornly wore so that she wouldn't have to speak to him. They were singing of hot nights and grinding needs.

Very carefully, she moved away. When she spoke into the mike again, her voice was even huskier.

He rose. He'd decided it was his only defense. He'd meant to annoy her, to distract her from the inevitable phone call that would come before the night was over. He'd wanted her mind off it, and on him. He wouldn't deny that he'd wanted her to think of him. But he hadn't known that when he'd succeeded she would tie him up in knots.

She smelled like midnight. Secret and sinful. She sounded like sex. Hot and inviting. Then you looked into her eyes, really looked, and saw simple innocence. The man that combination wouldn't drive mad either had never been born or was already dead.

A little distance, Boyd told himself as he moved quietly out of the studio. A lot of objectivity. It wouldn't do either one of them any good to allow his emotions to get so tangled up with a woman he was supposed to protect.

When she was alone, Cilla made a conscious effort to relax, muscle by muscle. It was just because she was already on edge. It was a comfort to believe that. Her reaction to Boyd was merely an echo of the tension she'd lived with for more than a week. And he was trying to goad her.

She blew the hair out of her eyes and gave her listeners a treat—two hits in a row. And herself another moment to calm.

She hadn't figured him out yet. He read Steinbeck and recognized Elton John. He talked slow and lazy— and thought fast. He wore scarred boots and three-hundred-dollar jackets.

What did it matter? she asked herself as she set up for the next twenty minutes of her show. She wasn't interested in men. And he was definitely a man. Strike one. She would never consider getting involved with a cop. Strike two. And anyone with eyes could see that he had a close, even intimate relationship with his knockout partner. She'd never been one to poach on someone else's property.

Three strikes and he's out.

She closed her eyes and let the music pour through her. It helped, as it always did, to calm her, or lift her up, or simply remind her how lucky she was. She wasn't sharp and studious like Deborah. She wasn't dedicated, as their parents had been. She had little more than the education required by law, and yet she was here, just where she wanted to be, doing just what she wanted to do.

Life had taught her one vital lesson. Nothing lasted

forever. Good times or bad, they passed. This nightmare, however horrid it was at this point in time, would be over eventually. She only had to get through it, one day at a time.

"That was Joan Jett waking you up as we head toward eleven-thirty. We've got a news brief coming up for you, then a double shot of Steve Winwood and Phil Collins to take us into the next half hour. This is KHIP, and the news is brought to you by Wildwood Records."

She punched in the prerecorded cassette, then scanned the printout of the ads and promos she would read. By the time Boyd came back, she was into the next block of music and standing up to stretch her muscles.

He stopped where he was, trying not to groan as she lifted her arms to the ceiling and rotated her hips. In time to the music, he was sure, as she bent from the waist, grabbed her ankles and slowly bent and straightened her knees.

He'd seen the routine before. It was something she did once or twice during her four-hour stint. But she thought she was alone now, and she put a little more rhythm into it. Watching her, he realized that the ten-minute break he'd taken hadn't been nearly long enough.

She sat again, pattered a bit to the audience. Her headphones were around her neck now, as she'd turned the music up for her own pleasure. As it pulsed, she swayed.

When he put a hand on her shoulder, she bolted out of the chair. "Easy, O'Roarke. I brought you some tea."

Her heart was like a trip-hammer in her chest. As it slowed, she lowered to the table. "What?"

"Tea," he repeated, offering her a cup. "I brought you some tea. You drink too much coffee. This is herbal. Jasmine or something."

She'd recovered enough to look at the cup in distaste. "I don't drink flowers."

"Try it. You might not hit the ceiling the next time someone touches you." He sipped a soft drink out of the bottle.

"I'd rather have that."

He took another sip, a long one, then passed the bottle to her. "You're almost halfway there."

Like Boyd, she looked at the clock. It was nearing midnight. This had once been her favorite leg of the show. Now, as she watched the second hand tick away, her palms began to sweat.

"Maybe he won't call tonight, since he got me at home."

He settled beside her again. "Maybe."

"But you don't think so."

"I think we take it a step at a time." He put a soothing hand at the back of her neck. "I want you to try to keep calm, keep him on the line longer. Ask questions. No matter what he says, just keep asking them, over and over. He may just answer one and give us something."

She nodded, then worked her way through the next ten minutes. "There's a question I want to ask you," she said at length.

"All right."

She didn't look at him, but drained the last swallow

of the cold drink to ease her dry throat. "How long will they let me have a baby-sitter?"

"You don't have to worry about it."

"Let's just say I know something about how police departments work." It was there in her voice again, that touch of bitterness and regret. "A few nasty calls don't warrant a hell of a lot of attention."

"You're life's been threatened," he said. "It helps that you're a celebrity, and that there's already been some press on it. I'll be around for a while."

"Mixed blessings," she muttered, then opened the request line.

The call came, as she had known it would, but quickly this time. On call number five, she recognized the voice, battled back the urge to scream and switched to music. Without realizing it, she groped for Boyd's hand.

"You're persistent, aren't you?"

"I want you dead. I'm almost ready now."

"Do I know you? I like to think I know everyone who wants to kill me."

She winced a little at the names he spewed at her and tried to concentrate on the steady pressure of Boyd's fingers at the base of her neck.

"Wow. I've really got you ticked off. You know, buddy, if you don't like the show, you've just got to turn it off."

"You seduced him." There was a sound of weeping now, fueled with fury. "You seduced him, tempted him, promised him. Then you murdered him."

"I…" She was more shocked by this than by any of the gutter names he had called her. "Who? I don't know what you're talking about. Please, who—"

The line went dead.

As she sat there, dazed and silent, Boyd snatched up the phone. "Any luck? Damn it." He rose, stuffed his hands in his pockets and began pacing. "Another ten seconds. We'd have had him in another ten seconds. He has to know we've got it tapped." His head snapped around when Nick Peters entered, his hands full of sloshing coffee. "What?"

"I—I—I—" His Adam's apple bobbed as he swallowed. "Mark said it was okay if I stayed through the show." He swallowed again. "I thought Cilla might want some coffee."

Boyd jerked a thumb toward the table. "We'll let you know. Can you help her get through the rest of the show?"

"I don't need help." Cilla's voice was icy-calm. "I'm fine, Nick. Don't worry about it." She put a steady hand on the mike. "That was for Chuck from Laurie, with all her love." She aimed a steady look at Boyd before she punched the phone again. "KHIP, you're on the air."

She got through it. That was all that mattered. And she wasn't going to fall apart the way she had the other night. Cilla was grateful for that. All she needed to do was think it all through.

She hadn't objected when Boyd took the wheel of her car. Relinquishing the right to drive was the least of her worries.

"I'm coming in," Boyd said after he parked the car. She just shrugged and started for the door.

Very deliberately she hung up her coat and pried off her shoes. She sat, still without speaking, and lit a cigarette. The marked cruiser outside had relieved her mind. Deborah was safe and asleep.

"Look," she began once she'd marshaled her thoughts. "There really isn't any use going into this. I think I have it figured out."

"Do you?" He didn't sit down. Her icy calm disturbed him much more than hysterics or anger would have. "Fill me in."

"It's obvious he's made a mistake. He has me mixed up with someone else. I just have to convince him."

"Just have to convince him," Boyd repeated. "And how do you intend to do that?"

"The next time he calls, I'll make him listen." She crossed an arm across her body and began to rub at the chill in her shoulder. "For God's sake, Fletcher, I haven't murdered anyone."

"So you'll tell him that and he'll be perfectly reasonable and apologize for bothering you."

Her carefully built calm was wearing thin. "I'll make him understand."

"You're trying to make yourself believe he's rational, Cilla. He's not."

"What am I supposed to do?" she demanded, snapping the cigarette in two as she crushed it out. "Whether he's rational or not, I have to make him see he's made a mistake. I've never killed anyone." Her laugh was strained as she pulled the band from her hair. "I've never seduced anyone."

"Give me a break."

Anger brought her out of the chair. "What do you see me as, some kind of black widow who goes around luring men, then knocking them off when I'm finished?

Get the picture, Fletcher. I'm a voice, a damn good one. That's where it ends.''

"You're a great deal more than voice, Cilla. We both know that." He paused, waiting for her to look at him again. "And so does he."

Something trembled inside her—part fear, part longing. She wanted neither. "Whatever I am, I'm no temptress. It's an act, a show, and it has nothing to do with reality. My ex-husband would be the first to tell you I don't even have a sex drive."

His eyes sharpened. "You never mentioned you'd been married."

And she hadn't intended to, Cilla thought as she wearily combed a hand through her hair. "It was a million years ago. What does it matter?"

"Everything applies. I want his name and address."

"I don't know his address. We didn't even last a year. I was twenty years old, for God's sake." She began to rub at her forehead.

"His name, Cilla."

"Paul. Paul Lomax. I haven't seen him for about eight years—since he divorced me." She spun to the window, then back again. "The point is, this guy's on the wrong frequency. He's got it into his head I— what?—used my wiles on some guy, and that doesn't wash."

"Apparently he thinks it does."

"Well, he thinks wrong. I couldn't even keep one man happy, so it's a joke to think I could seduce legions."

"That's a stupid remark, even for you."

"Do you think I like admitting that I'm all show, that I'm lousy in bed?" She bit off the words as she paced. "The last man I went out with told me I had ice water for blood. But I didn't kill him." She calmed a little, amused in spite of herself. "I thought about it, though."

"I think it's time you start to take this whole business seriously. And I think it's time you start taking yourself seriously."

"I take myself very seriously."

"Professionally," he agreed. "You know exactly what to do and how to do it. Personally...you're the first woman I've met who was so willing to concede she couldn't make a man dance to her tune."

"I'm a realist."

"I think you're a coward."

Her chin shot up. "Go to hell."

He wasn't about to back off. He had a point to prove, to both of them. "I think you're afraid to get close to a man, afraid to find out just what's inside. Maybe you'd find out it's something you can't control."

"I don't need this from you. You just get this man off my back." She started to storm past him but was brought up short when he grabbed her arm.

"What do you say to an experiment?"

"An experiment?"

"Why don't you give it a try, O'Roarke—with me? It should be safe, since you can barely stand the sight of me. A test." He took her other arm. "Low-risk." He could feel the anger vibrate through her as he held her. Good. For reasons he couldn't have begun to name, he was just as angry. "Five to one I don't feel a thing." He drew her inches closer. "Want to prove me wrong?"

Chapter 4

They were close. She had lifted one hand in an unconscious defensive gesture and now her fingers were splayed across his chest. She could feel his heartbeat, slow and steady, beneath her palm. She focused her resentment on that even rhythm as her own pulse jerked and scrambled.

"I don't have to prove anything to you."

He nodded. The barely banked fury in her eyes was easier for him to handle than the glaze of fear it replaced. "To yourself, then." Deliberately he smiled, baiting her. "What's the matter, O'Roarke? Do I scare you?"

He'd pushed exactly the right button. They both knew it. He didn't give a damn if it was temper that pushed her forward. As long as she moved.

She tossed her hair back and slowly, purposefully slid her hand from his chest to his shoulder. She wanted a reaction, hang him. He only lifted a brow and, with that faint smile playing around his mouth, watched her.

So he wanted to play games, she thought. Well, she was up for it. Tossing common sense aside, she pressed her lips to his.

His were firm, cool. And unresponsive. With her eyes open, she watched his remain patient, steady, and hatefully amused. As her hand balled into a fist on his shoulder, she snapped her head back.

"Satisfied?"

"Not hardly." His eyes might have been calm. That was training. But if she had bothered to monitor his heartbeat she would have found it erratic. "You're not trying, O'Roarke." He slid a hand down to her hip, shifting her balance just enough to have her sway against him. "You want me to believe that's the best you can do?"

Angry humiliation rippled through her. Cursing him, she dragged his mouth to hers and poured herself into the kiss.

His lips were still firm, but they were no longer cool. Nor were they unresponsive. For an instant the urge to retreat hammered at her. And then needs, almost forgotten needs, surged. A flood of longings, a storm of desires. Overwhelmed by them, she strained against him, letting the power and the heat whip through her, reminding her what it was like to sample passion again.

Every other thought, every other wish, winked out. She could feel the long, hard length of him pressed against her, the slow, deliberate stroke of his hands as they moved up her back and into her hair. His mouth, no longer patient, took and took from hers until the blood pounded like thunder in her head.

He'd known she would pack a punch. He'd thought he was prepared for it. In the days he'd known her he'd imagined tasting her like this dozens of times. He'd imagined what it would be like to hold her against him, to hear her sigh, to catch the fevered scent of her skin as he took his mouth over her.

But reality was much more potent than any dream had been.

Chain lightning. She was every bit as explosive, as turbulent, as potentially lethal. The current sparked and sizzled from her into him, leaving him breathless, dazed and churning. Even as he groaned against the onslaught, he felt her arch away from the power that snapped back into her.

She shuddered against him and made a sound—part protest, part confusion—as she tried to struggle away.

He'd wrapped her hair around his hand. He had only to tug gently to have her head fall back, to have her eyes dark and cloudy on his.

He took his time, letting his gaze skim over her face. He wanted to see in her eyes what he had felt. The reflection was there, that most elemental yearning. He smiled again as her lips trembled open and her breath came fast and uneven.

"I'm not finished yet," he told her, then dragged her against him again and plundered.

She needed to think, but her thoughts couldn't fight their way through the sensations. Layers of them, thin and silky, seemed to cover her, fogging the reason, drugging the will. Before panic could slice through, she was rocketing up again, clinging to him, opening for him, demanding from him.

He knew he could feast and never be full. Not when her mouth was hot and moist and ripe with flavor. He knew he could hold yet never control. Not when her body was vibrating from the explosion they had ignited together. The promise he had heard in her voice, seen in her eyes, was here for the taking.

Unable to resist, he slid his hands under her sweatshirt to find the warmed satin skin beneath. He took, possessed, exploited, until the ache spreading through his body turned to pain.

Too fast, he warned himself. Too soon. For both of them. Holding her steady, he lifted his head and waited for her to surface.

She dragged her eyes open and saw only his face. She gulped in air and tasted only his flavor. Reeling, she pressed a hand to her temple, then let it fall to her side. "I...I want to sit down."

"That makes two of us." Taking her arm, he led her to the couch and sat beside her.

She worked on steadying her breathing, focused on the dark window across the room. Maybe with enough time, enough distance, she would be able to convince herself that what had just happened had not been life-altering.

"That was stupid."

"It was a lot of things," he pointed out. "Stupid doesn't come to mind."

She took one more deep breath. "You made me angry."

"It isn't hard."

"Listen, Boyd—"

"So you *can* say it." Before she could stop him, he stroked a hand down her hair in a casually intimate gesture that made her pulse rate soar again. "Does that mean you don't use a man's name until you've kissed him?"

"It doesn't mean anything." She stood up, hoping she'd get the strength back in her legs quicker by pacing. "Obviously we've gotten off the track."

"There's more than one." He settled back, thinking it was a pleasure to watch her move. There was something just fine and dandy about watching the swing of long feminine legs. As she paced, nervous energy crackling, he tossed an arm over the back of the couch and stretched out his legs.

"There's only one for me." She threw him a look over her shoulder. "You'd better understand that."

"Okay, we'll ride on that one for a while." He could afford to wait, since he had every intention of switching lines again, and soon. "You seem to have some kind of screwy notion that the only thing that attracts men to you is your voice, your act. I think we just proved you wrong."

"What just happened proved nothing." If there was anything more infuriating than that slow, patient smile of his, she had yet to see it. "In any case, that has nothing to do with the man who's calling me."

"You're a smart woman, Cilla. Use your head. He's fixed on you, but not for himself. He wants to pay you back for something you did to another man. Someone you knew," he continued when she stopped long enough to pick up a cigarette. "Someone who was involved with you."

"I've already told you, there's no one."

"No one now."

"No one now, no one before, no one for years."

Having experienced that first wave of her passion, he found that more than difficult to believe. Still, he nodded. "So it didn't mean as much to you. Maybe that's the problem."

"For God's sake, Fletcher, I don't even date. I don't have the time or the inclination."

"We'll talk about your inclinations later."

Weary, she turned away to stare blindly through the glass. "Damn it, Boyd, get out of my life."

"It's your life we're talking about." There was an edge to his voice that had her holding back the snide comment she wanted to make. "If there's been no one in Denver, we'll start working our way back. But I want you to think, and think hard. Who's shown an interest in you? Someone who calls the station more than normal. Who asks to meet you, asks personal questions. Someone who's approached you, asked you out, made a play."

She gave a short, humorless laugh. "You have."

"Remind me to run a make on myself." His voice was deceptively mild, but she caught the underlying annoyance and frustration in it. "Who else, Cilla?"

"There's no one, no one who's pushed." Wishing for a moment's, just a moment's, peace of mind, she pressed the heels of her hands against her eyes. "I get calls. That's the idea. I get some that ask me for a date, some that even send presents. You know, candy-and-flower types. Nothing very sinister about a bunch of roses."

"There's a lot sinister about death threats."

She wanted to speak calmly, practically, but she

couldn't keep the nastiness out of her voice. "I can't remember everyone who's called and flirted with me on the air. Guys I turn down stay turned down."

He could only shake his head. It was a wonder to him that such a sharp woman could be so naive in certain situations. "All right, we'll shoot for a different angle. You work with men—almost all men—at the station."

"We're professionals," she snapped, and began biting her nails. "Mark's happily married. Bob's happily divorced. Jim's a friend—a good one."

"You forgot Nick."

"Nick Peters? What about him?"

"He's crazy about you."

"What?" She was surprised enough to turn around. "That's ridiculous. He's a kid."

After a long study, he let out a sigh. "You really haven't noticed, have you?"

"There's nothing to notice." More disturbed than she wanted to admit, she turned away again. "Look, Slick, this is getting us nowhere, and I'm..." Her words trailed off, and her hand crept slowly toward her throat.

"And you're what?"

"There's a man across the street. He's watching the house."

"Get away from the window."

"What?"

Boyd was already up and jerking her aside. "Stay away from the windows and keep the door locked. Don't open it again until I get back."

She nodded and followed him to the door. Her lips pressed together as she watched him take out his weapon. That single gesture snapped her back to reality. It had been a smooth movement, not so much practiced as instinctive. Ten years on the force, she remembered. He'd drawn and fired before.

She wouldn't tell him to be careful. Those were useless words.

"I'm going to take a look. Lock the door behind me." Gone was the laid-back man who had taunted her into an embrace. One look at his face and she could see that he was all cop. Their eyes changed, she thought. The emotion drained out of them. There was no room for emotion when you held a gun. "If I'm not back in ten minutes, call 911 for backup. Understood?"

"Yes." She gave in to the need to touch his arm. "Yes," she repeated.

After he slipped out, she shoved the bolt into place and waited.

He hadn't buttoned his coat, and the deep wind of the early hours whipped through his shirt. His weapon, warmed from sitting in its nest against his side, fitted snug in his hand. Sweeping his gaze right, then left, he found the street deserted, dark but for the pools of light from the streetlamps spaced at regular intervals. It was only a quiet suburban neighborhood, cozily asleep in the predawn hours. The night wind sounded through the naked trees in low moans.

He didn't doubt Cilla's words—wouldn't have doubted it even if he hadn't caught a glimpse through her window of a lone figure on the opposite sidewalk.

Whoever had been there was gone now, probably alerted the moment Cilla had spotted him.

As if to punctuate Boyd's thoughts, there was the

sound of an engine turning over a block or two away. He swore but didn't bother to give chase. With that much of a lead, it would be a waste of time. Instead, he walked a half block in each direction, then carefully circled the house.

Cilla had her hand on the phone when he knocked.

"It's okay. It's Boyd."

In three hurried strides, she was at the door. "Did you see him?" she demanded the moment Boyd stepped inside.

"No."

"He was there. I swear it."

"I know." He relocked the door himself. "Try to relax. He's gone now."

"Relax?" In the past ten minutes she'd had more than enough time to work herself from upset to frantic. "He knows where I work, where I live. How in God's name am I ever supposed to relax again? If you hadn't scared him off, he might have—" She dragged her hands through her hair. She didn't want to think about what might have happened. Didn't dare.

Boyd didn't speak for a moment. Instead, he watched as she slowly, painfully brought herself under control. "Why don't you take some time off, stay home for a few days? We'll arrange for a black-and-white to cruise the neighborhood."

She allowed herself the luxury of sinking into a chair. "What difference does it make if I'm here or at the station?" She shook her head before he could speak. "And if I stayed home I'd go crazy thinking about it, worrying about it. At least at work I have other things on my mind."

He hadn't expected her to agree. "We'll talk about

it later. Right now you're tired. Why don't you go to bed? I'll sleep on the couch.''

She wanted to be strong enough to tell him it wasn't necessary. She didn't need to be protected. But the wave of gratitude made her weak. ''I'll get you a blanket.''

It was almost dawn when he dragged himself home. He'd driven a long time—from one sleepy suburb to another, into an eerily quiet downtown. Covering his trail. The panic had stayed with him for the first hour, but he'd beaten it, made himself drive slowly, carefully. Being stopped by a roving patrol car could have ruined all of his plans.

Under the heavy muffler and cap he was wearing he was sweating. In the thin canvas tennis shoes his feet were like ice. But he was too accustomed to discomfort to notice.

He staggered into the bathroom, never turning on a light. With ease he avoided his early-warning devices. The thin wire stretched from the arm of the spindly chair to the arm of the faded couch. The tower of cans at the entrance to his bedroom. He had excellent night vision. It was something he'd always been proud of.

He showered in the dark, letting the water run cold over his tensed body. As he began to relax, he allowed himself to draw in the fragrance of soap—his favorite scent. He used a rough, long-handled brush to violently scrub every inch of his skin.

As he washed, the dark began to lessen with the first watery light of dawn.

Over his heart was an intricate tattoo of two knives, blades crossed in an X. With his fingers he caressed them. He remembered when it had still been new, when he had shown it to John. John had been so impressed, so fascinated.

The image came so clearly. John's dark, excited eyes. His voice—the way he spoke so quickly that the words tumbled into each other. Sometimes they had sat in the dark and talked for hours, making plans and promises. They were going to travel together, do great things together.

Then the world had interfered. Life had interfered. The woman had interfered.

Dripping, he stepped from the shower. The towel was exactly where he had placed it. No one came into this room, into any of his rooms, to disturb his carefully ordered space. Once he was dry, he pulled on faded pajamas. They reminded him of the childhood he'd been cheated out of.

As the sun came up, he made two enormous sandwiches and ate them standing in the kitchen, leaning over the sink so that the crumbs wouldn't fall to the floor.

He felt strong again. Clean and fed. He was outwitting the police, making fools of them. And that delighted him. He was frightening the woman, bringing terror into every day of her life. That excited him. When the time was right, he would do everything he'd told her he would do.

And still it wouldn't be enough.

He went into the bedroom, shut the door, pulled the shades and picked up the phone.

Deborah strolled out of her room in a white teddy, a thin blue robe that reached to midthigh, flapping open. Her toenails were shocking pink. She'd painted them the night before to amuse herself as she'd crammed for an exam.

She was muttering the questions she thought would be on the exam she had scheduled at nine. The questions came easily enough, but the answers continued to bog down at some crossroads between the conscious and the unconscious. She hoped to unblock the answers with a quick shot of coffee.

Yawning, she stumbled over a boot, pitched toward the couch, then let out a muffled scream as her hand encountered warm flesh.

Boyd sat up like a shot, his hand already reaching for his weapon. With their faces close, he stared at Deborah—the creamy skin, the big blue eyes, the tumble of dark hair—and relaxed.

"Good morning."

"I—Detective Fletcher?"

He rubbed a hand over his eyes. "I think so."

"I'm sorry. I didn't realize you were here." She cleared her throat and belatedly remembered to close her robe. Still fumbling, she glanced up the stairs and automatically lowered her voice. Her sister wasn't a sound sleeper under the best of circumstances. "Why are you here?"

He flexed a shoulder that had stiffened during his cramped night on the couch. "I told you I was going to look after Cilla."

"Yes, you did." Her eyes narrowed as she studied him. "You take your job seriously."

"That's right."

"Good." Satisfied, she smiled. In the upheaval and confusion of her nineteen years, she had learned to make character judgments quickly. "I was about to make some coffee. I have an early class. Can I get you some?"

If she was anything like her sister, he wouldn't get any more sleep until he'd answered whatever questions were rolling around in her head. "Sure. Thanks."

"I imagine you'd like a hot shower, as well. You're about six inches too long to have spent a comfortable night on that couch."

"Eight," he said, rubbing the back of his stiff neck. "I think it's more like eight."

"You're welcome to all the hot water you want. I'll start on the coffee." As she turned toward the kitchen, the phone rang. Though she knew Cilla would pick it up before the second ring, she stepped toward it automatically. Boyd shook his head. Reaching over, he lifted the receiver and listened.

With her hands clutching the lapels of her robe, Deborah watched him. His face remained impassive, but she saw a flicker of anger in his eyes. Though brief, it was intense enough to make her certain who was on the other end of the line.

Boyd disconnected mechanically, then punched in a series of numbers. "Anything?" He didn't even bother to swear at the negative reply. "Right." After hanging up, he looked at Deborah. She was standing beside the couch, her hands clenched, her face pale. "I'm going upstairs," he said. "I'll take a rain check on that coffee."

"She'll be upset. I want to talk to her."

He pushed aside the blanket and rose, wearing only his jeans. "I'd appreciate it if you'd let me handle it this time."

She wanted to argue, but something in his eyes stopped her. She nodded. "All right, but do a good job of it. She isn't as tough as she likes people to think."

"I know."

He climbed the stairs to the second floor, walked past an open door to a room where the bed was tidily made. Deborah's, he decided, noting the rose-and-white decor and the feminine bits of lace. Pausing at the next door, he knocked, then entered without waiting for an answer.

She was sitting in the middle of the bed, her knees drawn up close to her chest and her head resting on them. The sheets and blankets were tangled, a testimony to the few hours of restless sleep she'd had.

There were no bits of feminine lace here, no soft, creamy colors. She preferred clean lines rather than curves, simplicity rather than flounces. In contrast, the color scheme was electric, and anything but restful. In the midst of the vibrant blues and greens, she seemed all the more vulnerable.

She didn't look up until he sat on the edge of the bed and touched her hair. Slowly she lifted her head. He saw that there were no tears. Rather than the fear he'd expected, there was an unbearable weariness that was even more disturbing.

"He called," she said.

"I know. I was on the extension."

"Then you heard." She looked away, toward the window, where she could see the sun struggling to burn away a low bank of clouds. "It was him outside last night. He said he'd seen me, seen us. He made it sound revolting."

"Cilla—"

"He was watching!" She spit out the words. "Nothing I say, nothing I do, is going to make him stop. And if he gets to me, he's going to do everything he said he'd do."

"He's not going to get to you."

"How long?" she demanded. Her fingers clenched and unclenched on the sheets as her eyes burned into his. "How long can you watch me? He'll just wait. He'll wait and keep calling, keep watching." Something snapped inside her, and she picked up the bedside phone and heaved it across the room. It bounced against the wall, jangling as it thudded to the floor. "You're not going to stop him. You heard him. He said nothing would stop him."

"This is just what he wants." Boyd took her by the arms and gave her one quick shake. "He wants you to fall apart. He wants to know he's made you fall apart. If you do, you're only helping him."

"I don't know what to do," she managed. "I just don't know what to do."

"You've got to trust me. Look at me, Cilla." Her breath was hitching, but she met his eyes. "I want you to trust me," he said quietly, "and believe me when I say I won't let anything happen to you."

"You can't always be there."

His lips curved a little. He gentled his hold to rub his hands up and down her arms. "Sure I can."

"I want—" She squeezed her eyes shut. How she hated to ask. Hated to need.

"What?"

Her lips trembled as she fought for one last handhold on control. "I need to hold on to something." She let out an unsteady breath. "Please."

He said nothing, but he gathered her close to cradle her head on his shoulder. Her hands, balled into fists, pressed against his back. She was trembling, fighting off a wild bout of tears.

"Take five, O'Roarke," he murmured. "Let loose."

"I can't." She kept her eyes closed and held on. He was solid, warm, strong. Dependable. "I'm afraid once I do I won't be able to stop."

"Okay, let's try this." He tilted her head up and touched his lips gently to hers. "Think about me. Right here." His mouth brushed hers again. "Right now." Easy, patient, he stroked her rigid back. "Just me."

Here was compassion. She hadn't known a kiss from a man could hold it. More than gentle, more than tender, it soothed frayed nerves, calmed icy fears, cooled hot despair. Her clenched hands relaxed, muscle by muscle. There was no demand here as his lips roamed over her face. Just understanding.

It became so simple to do as he'd asked. She thought only of him.

Hesitant, she brought a hand to his face, letting her fingers skim along his beard-roughened cheek. Her stomach unknotted. The throbbing in her head quieted. She said his name on a sigh and melted against him.

He had to be careful. Very careful. Her complete and total surrender had his own needs drumming. He ignored them. For now she needed comfort, not passion. It couldn't matter that his senses were reeling from her, the soft give of her body, the rich taste of her mouth. It couldn't matter that the air had thickened so that each breath he took was crowded with the scent of her.

He knew he had only to lay her back on the bed

among the tangled sheets. And cover her. She wouldn't resist. Perhaps she would even welcome the heat and the distraction. The temporary respite. He intended to be much more to her.

Battling his own demons, he pressed his lips to her forehead, then rested his cheek on her hair.

"Better?"

On one ragged breath, she nodded. She wasn't sure she could speak. How could she tell him that she wanted only to stay like this, her arms around him, his heart beating against hers? He'd think she was a fool.

"I, uh...didn't know you could be such a nice guy, Fletcher."

He wanted to sigh, but he found himself grinning. "I have my moments."

"Yeah. Well, that was certainly above and beyond."

Maybe, just maybe, she wasn't really trying to needle him. He pulled back, put a hand under her chin and held it steady. "I'm not on duty. When I kiss you, it's got nothing to do with my job. Got it?"

She'd meant to thank him, not annoy him. There was a warning in his eyes that had her frowning. "Sure."

"Sure," he repeated, then rose to jam his hands in his pockets in disgust.

For the first time she noted that he wore only his jeans, unsnapped and riding low. The sudden clutching in her stomach had nothing to do with fear and left her momentarily speechless.

She wanted him. Not just to hold, not just for a few heated kisses. And certainly not just for comfort. She wanted him in bed, the way she couldn't remember ever wanting a man before. She could look at him—the long, lean, golden line of torso, the narrow hips, the dance of muscle in his arms as he balled his hands—and she could imagine what it would be like to touch and be touched, to roll over the bed in one tangled heap of passion. To ride and be ridden.

"What the hell's wrong with you now?"

"What?"

Eyes narrowed, he rocked back on his heels as she blinked at him. "Taking a side trip, O'Roarke?"

"I, ah…" Her mouth was dry, and there was a hard knot of pressure in her gut. What would he say if she told him where her mind had just taken her, taken them? She let her eyes close. "Oh, boy," she whispered. "I think I need some coffee." And a quick dip in a cold lake.

"Your sister was fixing some." He frowned as he studied her. He thought of Deborah for a moment, of how she had nearly fallen on top of him wearing hardly more than a swatch of white lace. He'd appreciated the long, lissome limbs. What man wouldn't? But looking at her hadn't rocked his system.

And here was Cilla—sitting there with her eyes shadowed, wearing a Broncos football jersey that was two sizes too big. The bright orange cotton was hardly seductive lingerie. If he stood there one more moment, he would be on his knees begging for mercy.

"How about breakfast?" His voice was abrupt, not even marginally friendly. It helped to bring her thoughts to order.

"I never eat it."

"Today you do. Ten minutes."

"Look, Slick—"

"Do something with your hair," he said as he walked out of the room. "You look like hell."

He found Deborah downstairs in the kitchen, fully dressed, sipping a cup of coffee. That she was waiting for him was obvious. The moment he stepped into the room she was out of her chair.

"She's fine," he said briefly. "I'm going to fix her some breakfast."

Though her brow lifted at this information, she nodded. "Look, why don't you sit down? I'll fix some for both of you."

"I thought you had an early class."

"I'll skip it."

He headed for the coffee. "Then she'll be mad at both of us."

She had to smile as he poured a cup, then rooted through a drawer for a spoon for the sugar. "You already know her very well."

"Not well enough." He drank half the cup and felt nearly human again. He had to think of Cilla. It would be safe enough, he hoped, if he kept those thoughts professional. "How much time do you have?"

"About five minutes," she said as she glanced at her watch.

"Tell me about the ex-husband."

"Paul?" There was surprise in her eyes, in her voice. "Why?" She was shaking her head before he could answer. "You don't think he has anything to do with what's going on here?"

"I'm checking all the angles. The divorce…was it amicable?"

"Are they ever?"

She was young, Boyd thought, nodding, but she was sharp. "You tell me."

"Well, in this case, I'd say it was as amicable—or

as bland as they get.'' She hesitated, torn. If it was a question of being loyal to Cilla or protecting her, she had to choose protection. ''I was only about twelve, and Cilla was never very open about it, but my impression was, always has been, that he wanted it.''

Boyd leaned back against the counter. ''Why?''

Uncomfortable, Deborah moved her shoulders. ''He'd fallen in love with someone else.'' She let out a hiss of breath and prayed Cilla wouldn't see what she was doing as a betrayal. ''It was pretty clear that they were having problems before I came to live with them. It was right after our parents had died. Cilla had only been married a few months, but...well, let's say the honeymoon was over. She was making a name for herself in Atlanta, and Paul—he was very conservative, a real straight arrow. He'd decided to run for assemblyman, I think it was, and Cilla's image didn't suit.''

''Sounds like it was the other way around to me.''

She smiled then, beautifully, and moved over to top off his coffee. ''I remember how hard she was working, to hold her job together, to hold everything together. It was a pretty awful time for us. It didn't help matters when the responsibility for a twelve-year-old was suddenly dumped on them. The added strain— well, I guess you could say it hastened the inevitable. A couple of months after I moved in, he moved out and filed for divorce. She didn't fight it.''

He tried to imagine how it would have been. At twenty, she'd lost her parents, accepted the care and responsibility of a young girl and watched her marriage crumble. ''Sounds to me like she was well rid of him.''

''I guess it doesn't hurt to say I never liked him very much. He was inoffensive. And dull.''

"Why did she marry him?"

"I think it would be more appropriate to ask me," Cilla said from the doorway.

Chapter 5

The something she had done with her hair was to pull it back in a ponytail. It left her face unframed, so the anger in her eyes was that much easier to read. Along with the jersey she'd slept in, she'd pulled on a pair of yellow sweatpants. It was a deceptively sunny combination. Her hands were thrust into their deep pockets as she stood, directing all her resentment at Boyd.

"Cilla." Knowing there was a time to argue and a time to soothe, Deborah stepped forward. "We were just—"

"Yes, I heard what you were just." She shifted her gaze to Deborah. The edge of her temper softened. "Don't worry about it. It's not your fault."

"It's not a matter of fault," Deborah murmured. "We care what happens to you."

"Nothing's going to happen. You'd better get going, Deb, or you'll be late. And it appears that Detective Fletcher and I have things to discuss."

Deborah lifted her hands and let them fall. She shot one sympathetic glance toward Boyd, then kissed her sister's cheek. "All right. You'd never listen to reason at this hour anyway."

"Get an A," was all Cilla said.

"I intend to. I'm going to catch a burger and a movie with Josh, but I'll be back before you get home."

"Have a good time." Cilla waited, not moving an inch until she heard the front door close. "You've got a hell of a nerve, Fletcher."

He merely turned and slipped another mug off the hook behind the stove. "Want some coffee?"

"I don't appreciate you grilling my sister."

He filled the mug, then set it aside. "I left my rubber hose in my other suit."

"Let's get something straight." She walked toward him, deliberately keeping her hands in her pockets. She was dead sure she'd hit him if she took them out. "If you have any questions about me, you come to me. Deborah is not involved in any of this."

"She's a lot more forthcoming than her sister. Got any eggs?" he asked as he opened the refrigerator.

She managed to restrain the urge to kick the door into his head. "You know, for a minute upstairs you had me fooled. I actually thought you had some heart, some compassion."

He found a half-dozen eggs, some cheese and a few miserly strips of bacon. "Why don't you sit down, O'Roarke, and drink your coffee?"

She swore at him, viciously. Something shot into his eyes, something dangerous, but he picked up a skillet and calmly began to fry the bacon. "You'll have to do better than that,'' he said after a moment. "After ten years on the force there's not much you could call me and get a rise."

"You had no right." Her voice had quieted, but the emotion in it had doubled. "No right to dredge all that up with her. She was a child, devastated, scared to death. That entire year was nothing but hell for her, and she doesn't need you to make her remember it."

"She handled herself just fine." He broke an egg into a bowl, then crushed the shell in his hand. "It seems to me you're the one with the problem."

"Just back off."

He had her arm in a tight grip so quickly that she had no chance to evade. His voice was soft, deadly, with temper licking around the edges. "Not a chance."

"What happened back then has nothing to do with what's happening now, and what's happening now is the only thing that concerns you."

"It's my job to determine what applies." With an effort, he reeled himself in. He couldn't remember when anyone had pushed him so close to the edge so often. "If you want me to put it to rest, then spell it out for me. Ex-spouses are favored suspects."

"It was eight years ago." She jerked away and, needing something to do with her hands, snatched up her coffee. It splattered over the rim and onto the counter.

"I find out from you or I find out from someone else. The end result's the same."

"You want me to spell it out? You want me to strip bare? Fine. It hardly matters at this point. I was twenty, I was stupid. He was beautiful and charming and smart—all the things stupid twenty-year-old girls think they want.''

She took a long sip of hot coffee, then automatically reached for a washcloth to mop up the spill. ''We only knew each other a couple of months. He was very persuasive, very romantic. I married him because I wanted something stable and real in my life. And I thought he loved me.''

She was calmer now. She hadn't realized that the anger had drained away. Sighing, she turned, mechanically reaching for plates and flatware. ''It didn't work—almost from day one. He was disappointed in me physically and disillusioned when he saw that I believed my work was as important as his. He'd hoped to convince me to change jobs. Not that he wanted me to quit altogether. He wasn't against my having a career, even in radio—as long as it didn't interfere with his plans.''

''Which were?'' Boyd asked as he set the bacon aside to drain.

''Politics. Actually, we met at a charity event the station put on. He was trying to charm up votes. I was promoting. That was the basic problem,'' she murmured. ''We met each other's public personalities.''

''What happened?''

''We got married—too fast. And things went wrong—too fast. I was even considering his idea that I go into marketing or sales. I figured I should at least give it a shot. Then my parents... I lost my parents, and brought Deborah home.''

She stopped speaking for a moment. She couldn't talk of that time, couldn't even think of the fears and the griefs, the pain and the resentments.

"It must have been rough."

She shrugged the words away. "The bottom line was, I couldn't handle another upheaval. I needed to work. The strain ate away at what shaky foundation we had. He found someone who made him happier, and he left me." She filled her mug with coffee she no longer wanted. "End of story."

What was he supposed to say? Boyd wondered. Tough break, kid? We all make mistakes? You were better off without the jerk? No personal comments, he warned himself. They were both edgy enough.

"Did he ever threaten you?"

"No."

"Abuse you?"

She gave a tired laugh. "No. No. You're trying to make him into the bad guy, Boyd, and it won't play. We were simply two people who made a mistake because we got married before we knew what we wanted."

Thoughtful, Boyd scooped eggs onto her plate. "Sometimes people hold resentments without even being aware of it. Then one day they bust loose."

"He didn't resent me." Sitting, she picked up a piece of bacon. She studied it as she broke it in two. "He never cared enough for that. That's the sad, sad truth." She smiled, but there wasn't a trace of humor in her eyes. "You see, he thought I was like the woman he heard on the radio—seductive, sophisticated, sexy. He wanted that kind of woman in bed. And outside the bedroom he wanted a well-groomed, well-mannered, attentive woman to make his home. I was neither." She shrugged and dropped the bacon on her plate again. "Since he wasn't the attentive, reliable and understanding man I thought he was, we both lost out. We had a very quiet, very civilized divorce, shook hands and went our separate ways.''

"If there was nothing more to it, why are you still raw?''

She looked up then, eyes somber. "You've never been married, have you?''

"No.''

"Then I couldn't begin to explain. If you want to run a check on Paul, you go ahead, but it's a waste of time. I can guarantee he hasn't given me a thought since I left Atlanta.''

He doubted that any man who had ever been close to her would be able to push her completely out of his mind, but he would let that ride for the moment. "You're letting your eggs get cold.''

"I told you I don't eat breakfast.''

"Humor me.'' He reached over, scooped up a forkful of eggs from her plate and held them to her lips.

"You're a pest,'' she said after she swallowed them. "Don't you have to check in or something?''

"I already did—last night, after you went up to bed.''

She toyed with the food on her plate, eating a bite or two to keep him from nagging her. He had stayed, she reminded herself, long after his duty shift was over. She owed him for that. And she always paid her debts.

"Look, I appreciate you hanging around, and I know it's your job to ask all kinds of personal and embarrassing questions. But I really want you to leave Deb out of it.''

"As much as I can.''

"Spring break's coming up. I'm going to try to convince her to head for the beach."

"Good luck." He sipped, watching her over the rim of his mug. "You might pull it off if you went with her."

"I'm not running from this." After pushing her half-eaten breakfast aside, she rested her elbows on the table. "After the call this morning, I was pretty close to doing just that. I thought about it—and after I did I realized it's not going to stop until I figure it out. I want my life back, and that's not going to happen until we know who he is and why he's after me."

"It's my job to find him."

"I know. That's why I've decided to cooperate."

He set his mug aside. "Have you?"

"That's right. From now on, my life's an open book. You ask, I'll answer."

"And you'll do exactly what you're told?"

"No." She smiled. "But I'll do exactly what I'm told if it seems reasonable." She surprised them both by reaching over to touch his hand. "You look tired, Slick. Rough night?"

"I've had better." He linked his fingers with hers before she could withdraw them. "You look damn good in the morning, Cilla."

There it was again—that fluttering that started in her chest and drifted down to her stomach. "A little while ago you said I looked like hell."

"I changed my mind. Before I clock in I'd like to talk to you about last night. About you and me."

"That's not a good idea."

"No, it's not." But he didn't release her hand. "I'm a cop, and you're my assignment. There's no getting around that.'' She nearly managed a relieved breath before he continued. ''Any more than there's any getting around the fact that I want you so much it hurts.''

She went very still, so still she could hear the sound of her own heartbeat drumming in her head. Very slowly she moved her eyes, only her eyes, until they met his. They were not so calm now, she thought. There was a fire there, barely banked. It was exciting, terrifyingly exciting.

''Lousy timing,'' he continued when she didn't speak. ''But I figure you can't always pick the right time and the right place. I'm going to do my job, but I think you should know I'm having trouble being objective. If you want someone else assigned to you, you'd better say so now.''

''No.'' She answered too quickly, and she forced herself to backtrack. ''I don't think I'm up to breaking in a new cop.'' Keep it light, she warned herself. ''I'm not crazy about having one at all, but I'm almost used to you.'' She caught herself gnawing on her thumbnail and hastily dropped her hand into her lap. ''As for the rest, we're not children. We can…handle it.''

He knew he shouldn't expect her to admit the wanting wasn't all one-sided. So he would wait a little while longer.

When he rose, she sprang up so quickly that he laughed. ''I'm going to do the dishes, O'Roarke, not jump on you.''

''I'll do them.'' She could have kicked herself. ''One cooks, one cleans. O'Roarke rules.''

''Fine. You've got a remote at noon, right?''

''How did you know?''

"I checked your schedule. Leave enough time for us to drop by my place so I can shower and change."

"I'm going to be in a mall with dozens of people," she began. "I don't think—"

"I do." With that, he left her alone.

Boyd was lounging on the couch with the paper and a last cup of coffee when Cilla came downstairs. He glanced over, and the casual comment he'd been about to make about her being quick to change died before it reached his tongue. He was glad he was sitting down.

She wore red. Vivid, traffic-stopping red. The short leather skirt was snug at the hips and stopped at midthigh. The jeans she usually wore hadn't given him a true measure of how long her legs were, or how shapely. The matching jacket crossed over her body to side snaps at the waist. It made him wonder what she was wearing beneath it.

She'd done something to her hair. It was still tumbled, but more artfully, and certainly more alluringly. And her face, he noted as he finally stood. She'd fiddled with that, as well—enough to highlight her cheekbones, accent her eyes, slicken her lips.

"Stupid," she muttered as she struggled with an earring. "I can never figure out why hanging things from your ears is supposed to be attractive." On a sigh, she stared down at the dangling columns and the little gold back in her palm. "Either these are defective or I am. Are you any good at this?"

She'd walked to him, her hand held out. Her scent was wheeling in his head. "At what?"

"Putting these in. I don't wear them for weeks at a

time, so I've never really gotten the hang of it. Give me a hand, will you?''

He was concentrating on breathing, nice, slow, even breaths. ''You want me to put that on for you?''

She rolled her eyes impatiently. ''You catch on fast, Slick.'' She thrust the earring into his hand, then tucked the hair behind her right ear. ''You just slide the post through, then fasten the little doodad on the back. That's the part I have trouble with.''

He muttered something, then bent to the task. There was a pressure in his chest, and it was building. He knew he would never get that scent out of his system. Swearing softly, he struggled to pinch the tiny fastening with his fingertips.

''This is a stupid system.''

''Yeah.'' She could barely speak. She'd known the minute he touched her that she'd made an enormous mistake. Bursts of sensations, flashes of images, were rushing into her. All she could do was stand still and pray he'd hurry up and finish.

The back of his thumb brushed up and down over her jaw. His fingertips grazed the sensitive area behind her ear. His breath fluttered warm against her skin until she had to bite back a moan.

She lifted an unsteady hand. ''Listen, why don't we just forget it?''

''I've got it.'' Letting out a long breath, he stepped back an inch. He was a wreck. But some of the tension eased when he looked at her and saw that she was far from unaffected. He managed to smile then and flicked a finger over the swaying gold columns. ''We'll have to try that again…when we've got more time.''

Since no response she could think of seemed safe,

she gave none. Instead, she retrieved his coat and her own from the closet. She set his aside and waited while he slipped into his shoulder holster. Watching him give his weapon a quick, routine check brought back memories she wanted to avoid, so she looked away. Pulling open the door, she stepped into the sunlight and left him to follow when he was ready.

He made no comment when he joined her.

"Do you mind if I tune the station in?" she asked as they settled into his car.

"It's on memory. Number three."

Pleased, she turned it on. The morning team was chattering away, punctuating their jokes with sound effects. They plugged an upcoming concert, promised to give another pair of tickets away during the next hour, then invited the listening audience to the mall to see Cilla O'Roarke live and in person.

"She'll be giving away albums, T-shirts and concert tickets," Frantic Fred announced.

"Come on, Fred," his partner broke in. "You know those guys out there don't care about a couple of T-shirts. They want to—" he made loud, panting noises—"see Cilla." There was a chorus of wolf whistles, growls and groans.

"Cute," Boyd muttered, but Cilla only chuckled.

"They're supposed to be obnoxious," she pointed out. "People like absurdity in the morning when they're dragging themselves out of bed or fighting traffic. Last quarter's Arbitron ratings showed them taking over twenty-four percent of the target audience."

"I guess you get a kick out of hearing some guy pant over you."

"Hey, I live for it." Too amused to be offended,

she settled back. He certainly had a nice car for a cop. Some sporty foreign job that still smelled new. She was never any good with makes and models. "Come on, Slick, it's part of the act."

He caught himself before he could speak again. He was making a fool of himself. His own investigation had verified that both morning men were married, with tidy homes in the suburbs. Frantic Fred and his wife were expecting their first child. Both men had been with KHIP for nearly three years, and he'd found no cross-reference between their pasts and Cilla's.

Relaxing as the music began, Cilla gazed out the window. The day promised to be warm and sunny. Perhaps this would be the first hint of spring. And her first spring in Colorado. She had a weakness for the season, for watching the leaves bud and grow, the flowers bloom.

Yet in spring she would always think of Georgia. The magnolias, the camellias, the wisterias. All those heady scents.

She remembered a spring when she'd been five or six. Planting peonies with her father on a warm Saturday morning while the radio counted down the Top 40 hits of the week. Hearing the birds without really listening, feeling the damp earth under her hands. He'd told her they would bloom spring after spring and that she would be able to see them from her window.

She wondered if they were still there—if whoever lived in that house cared for them.

"Cilla?"

She snapped back. "What?"

"Are you all right?"

"Sure, I'm fine." She focused on her surroundings.

There were big trees that would shade in the summer, trimmed hedges for privacy. A long, gently sloping hill led to a graceful three-story house fashioned from stone and wood. Dozens of tall, slender windows winked in the sunlight. "Where are we?"

"My house. I've got to change, remember?"

"Your house?" she repeated.

"Right. Everyone has to live somewhere."

True enough, she thought as she pushed the door open. But none of the cops she had ever known had lived so well. A long look around showed her that the neighborhood was old, established and wealthy. A country-club neighborhood.

Disconcerted, she followed Boyd up a stone path to an arched door outlined in etched glass.

Inside, the foyer was wide, the floors a gleaming cherry, the ceilings vaulted. On the walls were paintings by prominent twentieth-century artists. A sweep of stairway curved up to the second floor.

"Well," she said. "And I thought you were an honest cop."

"I am." He slipped the coat from her shoulders to toss it over the railing.

She had no doubts as to his honesty, but the house and all it represented made her nervous. "And I suppose you inherited all this from a rich uncle."

"Grandmother." Taking her arm, he led her through a towering arch. The living room was dominated by a stone fireplace topped with a heavy carved mantel. But the theme of the room was light, with a trio of windows set in each outside wall.

There was a scattering of antiques offset by modern

sculpture. She could see what she thought was a dining room through another arch.

"That must have been some grandmother."

"She was something. She ran Fletcher Industries until she hit seventy."

"And what is Fletcher Industries?"

He shrugged. "Family business. Real estate, cattle, mining."

"Mining." She blew out a breath. "Like gold?"

"Among other things."

She linked her fingers together to keep from biting her nails. "So why aren't you counting your gold instead of being a cop?"

"I like being a cop." He took her restless hand in his. "Something wrong?"

"No. You'd better change. I have to be there early to prep."

"I won't be long."

She waited until he had gone before she sank onto one of the twin sofas. Fletcher Industries, she thought. It sounded important. Even prominent. After digging in her bag for a cigarette, she studied the room again.

Elegant, tasteful, easily rich. And way out of her league.

It had been difficult enough when she'd believed they were on fairly equal terms. She didn't like to admit it, but the thought had been there, in the back of her mind, that maybe, just maybe, there could be a relationship between them. No, a friendship. She could never be seriously involved with someone in law enforcement.

But he wasn't just a cop now. He was a rich cop. His name was probably listed on some social register.

People who lived in houses like this usually had roman numerals after their names.

Boyd Fletcher III.

She was just Priscilla Alice O'Roarke, formerly from a backwater town in Georgia that wasn't even a smudge on the map. True, she had made something of herself, by herself. But you never really pulled out your roots.

Rising, she walked over to toss her cigarette in the fireplace.

She wished he would hurry. She wanted to get out of this house, get back to work. She wanted to forget about the mess her life was suddenly in.

She had to think about herself. Where she was going. How she was going to get through the long days and longer nights until her life was settled again. She didn't have the time, she couldn't afford the luxury of exploring her feelings for Boyd. Whatever she had felt, or thought she was feeling, was best ignored.

If ever there were two people more mismatched, she couldn't imagine them. Perhaps he had stirred something in her, touched something she'd thought could never be touched again. It meant nothing. It only proved that she was alive, still functioning as a human being. As a woman.

It would begin and end there.

The minute whoever was threatening her was caught, they would go their separate ways, back to their separate lives. Whatever closeness they had now was born of necessity. When the necessity passed, they would move apart and forget. Nothing, she reminded herself, lasted forever.

She was standing by the windows when he came

back. The light was in her hair, on her face. He had never imagined her there, but somehow, when he looked, when he saw her, he knew he'd wanted her there.

It left him shaken, it left him aching to see how perfectly she fitted into his home. Into his life. Into his dreams.

She would argue about that, he thought. She would struggle and fight and run like hell if he gave her the chance. He smiled as he crossed to her. He just wouldn't give her the chance.

"Cilla."

Startled, she whirled around. "Oh. I didn't hear you. I was—"

The words were swallowed by a gasp as he yanked her against him and imprisoned her mouth.

Earthquakes, floods, wild winds. How could she have known that a kiss could be grouped with such devastating natural disasters?

She didn't want this. She wanted it more than she wanted to breathe. She had to push him away. She pulled him closer. It was wrong, it was madness. It was right, it was beautifully mad.

As she pressed against him, as her mouth answered each frenzied demand, she knew that everything she had tried to convince herself of only moments before was a lie. What need was there to explore her feelings when they were all swimming to the surface?

She needed him. However much that might terrify her, for now the knowledge and the acceptance flowed through her like wine. It seemed she had waited a lifetime to need like this. To feel like this. Trembling and strong, dazed and clear-eyed, pliant and taut as a wire.

His hands whispered over the leather as he molded her against him. Couldn't she see how perfectly they fitted? He wanted to hear her say it, to hear her moan it, that she wanted him as desperately as he wanted her.

She did moan as he drew her head back to let his lips race down her throat. The thudding of her pulse heated the fragrance she'd dabbed there. Groaning as it tangled in his senses, he dragged at the snaps of her jacket. Beneath he found nothing but Cilla.

She arched back, her breath catching in her throat as he captured her breasts. At his touch it seemed they filled with some hot, heavy liquid. When her knees buckled, she gripped his shoulders for balance, shuddering as his thumbs teased her nipples into hard, aching peaks.

Mindlessly she reached for him, diving into a deep, intimate kiss that had each of them swaying. She tugged at his jacket, desperate to touch him as he touched her. Her hand slid over the leather of his holster and found his weapon.

It was like a slap, like a splash of ice water. As if burned, she snatched her hand away and jerked back. Unsteady, she pressed the palm of her hand against a table and shook her head.

"This is a mistake." She paced her words slowly, as if she were drunk. "I don't want to get involved."

"Too late." He felt as if he'd slammed full tilt into a wall.

"No." With deliberate care, she snapped her jacket again. "It's not too late. I have a lot on my mind. So do you."

He struggled for the patience that had always been

part of his nature. For the first time in days he actively craved a cigarette. "And?"

"And nothing. I think we should go."

He didn't move toward her or away, but simply held up a hand. "Before we do, are you going to tell me you don't feel anything?"

She made herself look at him. "It would be stupid to pretend I'm not attracted to you. You already know you affect me."

"I want to bring you back here tonight."

She shook her head. She couldn't afford, even for an instant, to imagine what it would be like to be with him. "I can't. There are reasons."

"You've already told me there isn't anyone else." He stepped toward her now, but he didn't touch her. "If there was, I wouldn't give a damn."

"This has nothing to do with other men. It has to do with me."

"Exactly. Why don't you tell me what you're afraid of?"

"I'm afraid of picking up the phone." It was true, but it wasn't the reason. "I'm afraid of going to sleep, and I'm afraid of waking up."

He touched her then, just a fingertip to her cheek. "I know what you're going through, and believe me, I'd do anything to make it go away. But we both know that's not the reason you're backing away from me."

"I have others."

"Give me one."

Annoyed, she walked over to grab her purse. "You're a cop."

"And?"

She tossed her head up. "So was my mother." Before he could speak, she was striding back into the foyer to get her coat.

"Cilla—"

"Just back off, Boyd. I mean it." She shoved her arms into her coat. "I can't afford to get churned up like this before a show. For God's sake, my life's screwed up enough right now without this. If you can't let it alone, I'll call your captain and tell him I want someone else assigned. Now you can take me to the mall or I can call a cab."

One more push and she'd be over the edge, he thought. This wasn't the time for her to take that tumble. "I'll take you," he said. "And I'll back off. For now."

Chapter 6

He was a man of his word, Cilla decided. For the rest of that day, and all of the next, they discussed nothing that didn't relate directly to the case.

He wasn't distant. Far from it. He stuck with her throughout her remote at the mall, subtly screening all the fans who approached her for a word or an autograph, all the winners who accepted their T-shirts or their albums.

It even seemed to Cilla that he enjoyed himself. He browsed through the record racks, buying from the classical, pop and jazz sections, chatted with the engineer about baseball and kept her supplied with a steady supply of cold soft drinks in paper cups.

He talked, but she noted that he didn't talk *to* her, not the way she'd become accustomed to. They certainly had conversations, polite and impersonal conversations. And not once, not even in the most casual of ways, did he touch her.

In short, he treated her exactly the way she'd thought she wanted to be treated. As an assignment, and nothing more.

While he seemed to take the afternoon in stride, even offering to buy her a burger between the end of the remote and the time she was expected back in the studio, she was certain she'd never spent a more miserable afternoon in her life.

It was Althea who sat with her in the booth over her next two shifts, and it was Althea who monitored the calls. Why Boyd's silence, and his absence, made it that much more difficult for her to concentrate, Cilla couldn't have said.

It was probably some new strategy, she decided as she worked. He was ignoring her so that she would break down and make the first move. Well, she wouldn't. She hit her audience with Bob Seger's latest gritty rock single and stewed.

She'd wanted their relationship to be strictly professional, and he was accommodating her. But he didn't have to make it seem so damned easy.

Undoubtedly what had happened between them—or what had almost happened between them—hadn't really meant that much to him. That was all for the best. She would get over it. Whatever it was. The last thing she needed in her life was a cop with a lazy smile who came from a moneyed background.

She wished to God she could go five minutes without thinking about him.

While Cilla juggled turntables, Althea worked a crossword puzzle. She had always been able to sit for hours at a time in contented silence as long as she could exercise her mind. Cilla O'Roarke, she mused, was a different matter. The woman hadn't mastered the fine art of relaxation. Althea filled the squares with her neat, precise printing and thought that Boyd was just the man to teach her how it was done.

Right now, Cilla was bursting to talk. Not to ask questions, Althea thought. She hadn't missed the quick disappointment on Cilla's face when Boyd hadn't been the one to drive her to the station for her night shift.

She's dying to ask me where he is and what he's doing, Althea thought as she filled in the next word. But she doesn't want me to think it matters.

It wasn't possible for her not to smile to herself. Boyd had been pretty closemouthed himself lately. Althea knew he had run a more detailed check on Cilla's background and that he had found answers that disturbed him. Personally, she thought. Whatever he had discovered had nothing to do with the case or he would have shared it with his partner.

But, no matter how close they were, their privacy was deeply respected. She didn't question him. If and when he wanted to talk it through, she would be there for him. As he would be there for her.

It was too bad, she decided, that when sexual tension reared its head, men and women lost that easy camaraderie.

Abruptly Cilla pushed away from the console. "I'm going to get some coffee. Do you want some?"

"Doesn't Nick usually bring some in?"

"He's got the night off."

"Why don't I get it?"

"No." Restlessness seemed to vibrate from her. "I've got nearly seven minutes before the tape ends. I want to stretch my legs."

"All right."

Cilla walked to the lounge. Billy had already been there, she noted. The floor gleamed, and the coffee mugs were washed and stacked. There was the lingering scent of the pine cleaner he always used so lavishly.

She poured two cups and as an afterthought stuck one leftover and rapidly hardening pastry in her pocket.

With a cup in each hand, she turned. In the doorway she saw the shadow of a man. And the silver gleam of a knife. With a scream, she sent the mugs flying. Crockery smashed and shattered.

"Miss O'Roarke?" Billy took a hesitant step into the light.

"Oh, God." She pressed the heel of one hand to her chest as if to force out the air trapped there. "Billy. I thought you were gone."

"I—" He stumbled back against the door when Althea came flying down the hallway, her weapon drawn. In an automatic response, he threw his hands up. "Don't shoot. Don't. I didn't do nothing."

"It's my fault," Cilla said quickly. She stepped over to put a reassuring hand on Billy's arm. "I didn't know anyone was here, and I turned around—" She covered her face with her hands. "I'm sorry," she managed, dropping them again. "I overreacted. I didn't know Billy was still in the station."

"Mr. Harrison had a lunch meeting in his office." He spoke quickly, his eyes darting from Althea to Cilla. "I was just getting to it." He swallowed audibly. "Lots of—lots of knives and forks left over."

Cilla stared at the handful of flatware he held and

felt like a fool. "I'm sorry, Billy. I must have scared you to death. And I've made a mess of your floor."

"That's okay." He grinned at her, relaxing slowly as Althea holstered her weapon. "I'll clean it right up. Good show tonight, Miss O'Roarke." He tapped the headphones that he'd slid around his neck. "You going to play any fifties stuff? You know I like that the best."

"Sure." Fighting nausea, she made herself smile. "I'll pick something out just for you."

He beamed at her. "You'll say my name on the air?"

"You bet. I've got to get back."

She hurried back to the booth, grateful that Althea was giving her a few moments alone. Things were getting pretty bad when she started jumping at middle-aged maintenance men holding dinner knives.

The best way to get through the nerves was to work, she told herself. Keeping her moves precise, she began to set up for what she called the "power hour" between eleven and midnight.

When Althea came back, bearing coffee, Cilla was inviting her audience to stay tuned for more music. "We've got ten hits in a row coming up. This first one's for my pal Billy. We're going back, way back, all the way back to 1958. It ain't Dennis Quaid. It's the real, the original, the awesome Jerry Lee Lewis with 'Great Balls of Fire.'"

After pulling off her headphones, she gave Althea a wan smile. "I really am sorry."

"In your place I probably would have gone through the roof." Althea offered her a fresh mug. "Been a lousy couple of weeks, huh?"

"The lousiest."

"We're going to get him, Cilla."

"I'm hanging on to that." She chose another record, took her time cuing it up. "What made you become a cop?"

"I guess I wanted to be good at something. This was it."

"Do you have a husband?"

"No." Althea wasn't sure where the questions were leading. "A lot of men are put off when a woman carries a gun." She hesitated, then decided to take the plunge. "You might have gotten the impression that there's something between Boyd and me."

"It's hard not to." Cilla lifted a hand for silence, then opened the mike to link the next song. "You two seem well suited."

As if considering it, Althea sat and sipped at her coffee. "You know, I wouldn't have figured you for the type to fall into the clichéd, sexist mind-set that says that if a man and woman work together they must be playing together."

"I didn't." Outraged, Cilla all but came out of her chair. At Althea's bland smile, she subsided. "I did," she admitted. Then her lips curved. "Kind of. I guess you've had to handle that tired line quite a bit."

"No more than you, I imagine." She gestured, both hands palms out, at the confines of the studio. "An attractive woman in what some conceive of as a man's job."

Even that small patch of common ground helped her to relax. "There was a jock in Richmond who figured I was dying to, ah…spin on his turntable."

Understanding and amusement brightened Althea's eyes. "How'd you handle it?"

"During my show I announced that he was hard up for dates and anyone interested should call the station during his shift.'' She grinned, remembering. "It cooled him off.'' She turned to her mike to plug the upcoming request line. After an update on the weather, a time check and an intro for the next record, she slipped her headphones off again. "I guess Boyd wouldn't be as easily discouraged.''

"Not on your life. He's stubborn. He likes to call it patience, but it's plain mule-headed stubbornness. He can be like a damn bulldog.''

"I've noticed.''

"He's a nice man, Cilla, one of the best. If you're really not interested, you should make it clear up front. Boyd's stubborn, but he's not obnoxious.''

"I don't want to be interested,'' Cilla murmured. "There's a difference.''

"Like night and day. Listen, if the question's too personal, tell me to shut up.''

A smile tugged at Cilla's mouth. "You don't have to tell me that twice.''

"Okay. Why don't you want to be interested?''

Cilla chose a compact disc, then backed it up with two 45s. "He's a cop.''

"So if he was an insurance salesman you'd want to be interested?''

"Yes. No.'' She let out a huff of breath. Sometimes it was best to be honest. "It would be easier. Then there's the fact that I made a mess of the one serious relationship I've had.''

"All by yourself?''

"Mostly.'' She sent out the cut from the CD. "I'm

more comfortable concentrating on my life, and Deborah's. My work and her future."

"You're not the type that would be happy for long with comfortable."

"Maybe not." She stared down at the phone. "But I'd settle for it right now."

So she was running scared, Althea thought as she watched Cilla work. Who wouldn't be? It had to be terrifying to be hounded and threatened by some faceless, nameless man. Yet she was handling it, Althea thought, better than she was handling Boyd and her feelings about him.

She had them, buckets of them. Apparently she just didn't know what to do with them.

Althea kept her silence as the calls began to come in. Cilla was afraid of the phone, afraid of what might be on the other end. But she answered, call after call, moving through them with what sounded like effortless style. If Althea hadn't been in the studio, watching the strain tighten Cilla's face, she would have been totally fooled.

She gave them their music and a few moments of her time. If her hand was unsteady, her finger still pushed the illuminated button.

Boyd had entered her life to protect it, not threaten it. Yet she was afraid of him. With a sigh, Althea wondered why it was that women's lives could be so completely turned upside down by the presence of a man.

If she ever fell in love herself—which so far she'd had the good sense to avoid—she would simply find a way to call the shots.

The tone of Cilla's voice had her snapping back.

Recognizing the fear, sympathizing with it, Althea rose to massage her rigid shoulders.

"Keep him talking," she whispered. "Keep him on as long as you can."

Cilla blocked out what he said. She'd found it helped her keep sane if she ignored the vicious threats, the blood-chilling promises. Instead she kept her eye on the elapsed-time clock, grimly pleased when she saw that the one-minute mark had passed and he was still on the line.

She questioned him, forcing herself to keep her voice calm and even. He liked it best when she lost control, she knew. He would keep threatening until she began to beg. Then he would cut her off, satisfied that he had broken her again.

Tonight she struggled not to hear, just to watch the seconds tick away.

"I haven't hurt you," she said. "You know I haven't done anything to you."

"To him." He hissed the words. "He's dead, and it's because of you."

"Who did I hurt? If you'd tell me his name, I—"

"I want you to remember. I want you to say his name before I kill you."

She shut her eyes and tried to fill her head with sound as he described exactly how he intended to kill her.

"He must have been very important to you. You must have loved him."

"He was everything to me. All I had. He was so young. He had his whole life. But you hurt him. You betrayed him. An eye for an eye. Your life for his. Soon. Very soon."

When he cut her off, she turned quickly to send out the next record. She would backsell it, Cilla told herself. Her voice would be strong again afterward. Ignoring the other blinking lights, she pulled out a cigarette.

"They got a trace." Althea replaced the receiver, then moved over to put a hand on Cilla's shoulder. "They got a trace. You did a hell of a job tonight, Cilla."

"Yeah." She closed her eyes. Now all she had to do was get through the next hour and ten minutes. "Will they catch him?"

"We'll know soon. This is the first real break we've had. Just hang on to that."

She wanted to be relieved. Cilla leaned back as Althea drove her home and wondered why she couldn't accept this step as a step forward. They had traced the call. Didn't that mean they would know where he lived? They would have a name, and they would put a face, a person, together with that name.

She would go and see him. She would make herself do that. She would look at that face, into those eyes, and try to find a link between him and whatever she had done in the past to incite that kind of hate.

Then she would try to live with it.

She spotted Boyd's car at the curb in front of her house. He stood on the walk, his coat unbuttoned. Though the calendar claimed it was spring, the night was cold enough for her to see his breath. But not his eyes.

Cilla took a firm grip on the doorhandle, pushed it open. He waited as she moved up the walk toward him.

"Let's go inside."

"I want to know." She saw his eyes now and understood. "You didn't get him."

"No." He glanced toward his partner. Althea saw the frustration held under grim control.

"What happened?"

"It was a phone booth a couple miles from the station. No prints. He'd wiped it clean."

Struggling to hold on for a few more minutes, Cilla nodded. "So we're no closer."

"Yes, we are." He took her hand to warm it in his. "He made his first mistake. He'll make another."

Weary, she looked over her shoulder. Was it just her overworked nerves, or was he out there somewhere, in the shadows, close enough to see? Near enough to hear?

"Come on, let me take you inside. You're cold."

"I'm all right." She couldn't let him come with her. She needed to let go, and for that she needed privacy. "I don't want to talk about any of this tonight. I just want to go to bed. Althea, thanks for the ride, and everything else." She walked quickly to the front door and let herself inside.

"She just needs to work this out," Althea said, placing a hand on his arm.

He wanted to swear, to smash something with his hands. Instead, he stared at the closed door. "She doesn't want to let me help her."

"No, she doesn't." She watched the light switch on upstairs. "Want me to call for a uniform to stake out the house?"

"No, I'll hang around."

"You're off duty, Fletcher."

"Right. We can consider this personal."

"Want some company?"

He shook his head. "No. You need some sleep."

Althea hesitated, then let out a quiet sigh. "You take the first shift. I sleep better in a car than a bed, anyway."

There was a light frost that glittered like glass on the lawn. Cilla sighed as she studied it through her bedroom window. In Georgia the azaleas would be blooming. It had been years, more years than she could remember, since she had yearned for home. In that chill Colorado morning she wondered if she had made a mistake traveling more than halfway across the country and leaving all those places, all those memories of her childhood, behind.

Letting the curtain fall again, she stepped back. She had more to think about than an April frost. She had also seen Boyd's car, still parked at the curb.

Thinking of him, she took more time and more care dressing than was her habit. Not for a moment had she changed her mind about it being unwise to become involved with him. But it seemed it was a mistake she'd already made. The wisdom to face up to her mistakes was something she'd learned very early.

She smoothed her plum-colored cashmere sweater over her hips. It had been a Christmas present from Deborah, and it was certainly more stylish, with its high neck and its generous sleeves, than most of the clothes Cilla chose for herself. She wore it over snug black leggings and on impulse struggled with a pair of star-shaped earrings in glossy silver.

He was spread comfortably over her couch, the

newspaper open, a mug of coffee steaming in his hand. His shirt was carelessly unbuttoned to the middle of his chest and wrinkled from being worn all night. His jacket was tossed over the back of the couch, but he still wore his shoulder holster.

She had never known anyone who could melt into his surroundings so easily. At the moment he looked as though he spent every morning of his life in that spot, in her spot, lazily perusing the sports page and drinking a second cup of coffee.

He looked up at her. Though he didn't smile, his utter relaxation was soothing. "Good morning."

"Good morning." Feeling awkward, she crossed to him. She wasn't certain whether she should begin with an apology or an explanation.

"Deborah let me in."

She nodded, then immediately wished she'd worn trousers with pockets. There was nothing to do with her hands but link them together. "You've been here all night."

"Just part of the service."

"You slept in your car."

He tilted his head. Her tone was very close to an accusation. "It wasn't the first time."

"I'm sorry." On a long, shaky breath, she sat on the coffee table across from him. Their knees bumped. He found it a friendly gesture. One of the friendliest she'd made with him. "I should have let you inside. I should have known you would stay. I guess I was—"

"Upset." He passed her his coffee. "You were entitled, Cilla."

"Yeah." She sipped, wincing a bit at the added sugar. "I guess I'd talked myself into believing that you were going to catch him last night. It even—it's weird, but it even unnerved me a bit thinking about finally seeing him, finally knowing the whole story. Then, when we got here and you told me…I couldn't talk about it. I just couldn't.''

''It's okay.''

Her laugh was only a little strained. ''Do you have to be so nice to me?''

''Probably not.'' Reaching out, he touched her cheek. ''Would you feel better if I yelled at you?''

''Maybe.'' Unable to resist, she lifted a hand to his. ''I have an easier time fighting than I do being reasonable.''

''I've noticed. Have you ever considered taking a day, just to relax?''

''Not really.''

''How about today?''

''I was going to catch up with my paperwork. And I have to call a plumber. We've got a leak under the sink.'' She let her hand fall to her knees, where it moved restlessly. ''It's my turn to do the laundry. Tonight I'm spinning records at this class reunion downtown. Bill and Jim are splitting my shift.''

''I heard.''

''These reunion things…they can get pretty wild.'' She was groping, feeling more foolish by the minute. He'd taken the empty cup and set it aside, and was now holding both of her hands lightly in his. ''They can be a lot of fun, though. Maybe you'd like to come and…hang around.''

''Are you asking me to come and…hang around, like on a date?''

"I'll be working," she began, then subsided. She was getting in deep. "Yes. Sort of."

"Okay. Can I sort of pick you up?"

"By seven," she said. "I have to be there early enough to set up."

"Let's make it six, then. We can have some dinner first."

"I…" Deeper and deeper. "All right. Boyd, I have to tell you something."

"I'm listening."

"I still don't want to get involved. Not seriously."

"Mm-hmm."

"You're completely wrong for me."

"That's just one more thing we disagree on." He held her still when she started to rise. "Don't pace, Cilla. Just take a couple deep breaths."

"I think it's important we understand up front how far this can go, and what limitations there are."

"Are we going to have a romance, Cilla, or a business arrangement?"

He smiled. She frowned.

"I don't think we should call it a romance."

"Why not?"

"Because it's…because a romance has implications."

He struggled against another smile. She wouldn't appreciate the fact that she amused him. "What kind of implications?" Slowly, watching her, he brought her hand to his lips.

"Just…" His mouth brushed over her knuckles, and then, when her fingers went limp, he turned her palm up to press a kiss to its center.

"Just?" he prompted.

"Implications. Boyd—" She shivered when his teeth grazed over her wrist.

"Is that all you wanted to tell me?"

"No. Can you stop that?"

"If I really put my mind to it."

She found that her own lips had curved. "Well, put your mind to it. I can't think."

"Dangerous words." But he stopped nibbling.

"I'm trying to be serious."

"So am I." Once again he stopped her from rising. "Try that deep breath."

"Right." She did, then plunged on. "Last night, when I lay down in the dark, I was afraid. I kept hearing him, hearing that voice, everything he'd said to me. Over and over. I knew I couldn't think of it. If I did, I'd go crazy. So I thought of you." She paused, waiting for the courage to go on. "And when I thought of you it blocked out everything else. And I wasn't afraid."

His fingers tightened on hers. Her eyes were steady, but he saw that her lips trembled once before she pressed them together. She was waiting, he knew. To see what he would do, what he would say. She couldn't have known, couldn't have had any idea, that at that moment, at that one instant of time, he teetered off the edge he'd been walking and tumbled into love with her.

And if he told her that, he thought as he felt the shock of the emotions vibrate through him, she would never believe it. Some women had to be shown, convinced, not merely told. Cilla was one of them.

Slowly he rose, drawing her up with him. He gathered her close, cradling her head on his shoulder, wrapping his arms around her. He could feel her shiver of relief as he kept the embrace quiet and undemanding.

It was just what she needed. How was it he seemed always to know? To be held, only held, without words, without promises. To feel the solid warmth of his body against her, the firm grip of his hands, the steady beat of his heart.

"Boyd?"

"Yeah." He turned his head just enough to kiss her hair.

"Maybe I don't mind you being nice to me after all."

"We'll give it a trial run."

She thought she might as well go all the way with it. "And maybe I've missed having you around."

It was his turn to take a deep breath and steady himself. "Listen." He slid his hands up to her shoulders. "I've got some calls to make. After, why don't I take a look at that leak?"

She smiled. "I can look at it, Slick. What I want is to have it fixed."

He leaned forward and bit her lower lip. "Just get me a wrench."

Two hours later, Cilla had her monthly finances spread out over the secondhand oak desk in the den that doubled as her office. There were two dollars and fifty-three cents lost somewhere in her checkbook, an amount she was determined to find before she paid the neat stack of bills to her right.

Her sense of order was something she'd taught herself, something she'd clung to during the lean years, the unhappy years, the stormy years. If amid any crisis she could maintain this small island of normalcy, however bland, she believed she would survive.

''Ah!'' She found the error, pounced on it. Making the correction, she scrupulously ran her figures again. Satisfied, she filed away her bank statement, then began writing checks, starting with the mortgage.

Even that gave her an enormous sense of accomplishment. It wasn't rent, it was equity. It was hers. The house was the first thing she had ever owned other than the clothes on her back and the occasional secondhand car.

She'd never been poor, but she had learned, growing up in a family where the income was a combination of a cop's salary and the lean monthly earnings of a public defender, to count pennies carefully. She'd grown up in a rented house, and she'd never known the luxury of riding in a new car. College wouldn't have been impossible, but because of the strain it would have added to her parents' income at a time when their marriage was rocky Cilla had decided to bypass her education in favor of a job.

She didn't regret it often. She resented it only a little, at odd times. But her ability to subsidize Deborah's partial scholarship made her look back to the time when she had made the decision. It had been the right one.

Now they were slowly creeping their way up. The house wasn't simply an acquisition, it was a statement. Family, home, roots. Every month, when she paid the mortgage, she was grateful she'd been given the chance.

''Cilla?''

''What? Oh.'' She spotted Boyd in the doorway. She

started to speak again, then focused. He still had the wrench she'd given him. His hair was mussed and damp. Both his shirt and his slacks were streaked with wet. He'd rolled his sleeves up to the elbows. Water glistened on his forearms. "Oh," she said again, and choked on a laugh.

"I fixed it." His eyes narrowed as he watched her struggle to maintain her dignity. "Problem?"

"No. No, not a thing." She cleared her throat. "So, you fixed it."

"That's what I said."

She had to bite down on her lip. She recognized a frazzled male ego when she heard it. "That's what you said, all right. And since you've just saved me a bundle the least I can do is fix you lunch. What do you think about peanut butter and jelly?"

"That it belongs in a plastic lunch box with Spider-man on the outside."

"Well, I've got to tell you, Slick, it's the best thing I cook." Forgetting the bills, she rose. "It's either that or a can of tuna fish." She ran a fingertip down his shirt experimentally. "Did you know you're all wet?"

He held up one grimy hand, thought about it, then went with the impulse and rubbed it all over her face. "Yeah."

She laughed, surprising him. Seducing him. He'd heard that laugh before, over the radio, but not once since he'd met her. It was low and rich and arousing as black silk.

"Come on, Fletcher, we'll throw that shirt in the wash while you eat your sandwich."

"In a minute." He kept his hand cupped on her chin, pulling her to him with that subtle pressure alone.

When his mouth met hers, her lips were still curved. This time, she didn't stiffen, she didn't protest. With a sigh of acceptance, she opened for him, allowing herself to absorb the taste of his mouth, the alluring dance of his tongue over hers.

There was a warmth here that she had forgotten to hope for. The warmth of being with someone who understood her. And cared, she realized as his fingers skimmed over her cheek. Cared, despite her flaws.

"I guess you were right," she murmured.

"Damn right. About what?"

She took a chance, an enormous one for her, and brushed at the hair on his forehead. "It is too late."

"Cilla." He brought his hands to her shoulders again, battling back a clawing need, a ragged desire. "Come upstairs with me. I want to be with you."

His words sent the passion leaping. He could see the fire of it glow in her eyes before she closed them and shook her head. "Give me some time. I'm not playing games here, Boyd, but the ground's pretty shaky and I need to think it through." On a steadying breath, she opened her eyes, and nearly smiled. "You're absolutely everything I swore I'd never fall for."

He brought his hands down to hers and gripped. "Talk to me."

"Not now." But she laced her fingers with his. It was a sign of union that was rare for her. "I'm not ready to dig it all up right now. I'd just like to spend a few hours here like real people. If the phone rings, I'm not going to answer it. If someone comes to the door, I'm going to wait until they go away again. All

I want to do is fix you a sandwich and wash your shirt. Okay?''

"Sure." He pressed a kiss to her brow. "It's the best offer I've had in years."

Chapter 7

There was a wall of noise—the backbeat, the bass, the wail of a guitar riff. There were spinning lights, undulating bodies, the clamor of feet. Cilla set the tone with her midnight voice and stood back to enjoy the results. The ballroom was alive with sound—laughter, music, voices raised in spurts of conversation. Cilla had her finger on the controls. She didn't know any of the faces, but it was her party.

Boyd sipped a club soda and politely avoided a none-too-subtle invitation from a six-foot blonde in a skimpy blue dress. He didn't consider this a trial. He'd spent a large portion of his career watching people, and he'd never gotten bored with it.

It was a hell of a party, and he wouldn't have minded a turn on the dance floor. But he preferred keeping his eye on Cilla. There were worse ways to spend the evening.

She presided over a long table at the front of the ballroom, her records stacked, her amps turned up high. She glittered. Her silver-sequined jacket and black stovepipe pants were a whole new look in tuxedos. Her hair was full and loose, and when she turned her head the silver stars at her ears glistened.

She'd already lured dozens of couples onto the dance floor, and they were bopping and swaying elbow to elbow. Others crowded around the edges in groups or loitered at the banquet tables, lingering over drinks and conversation.

The music was loud, hot and fast. He'd already learned that was how she liked it best. As far as he could tell, the class of 75 was having the time of their lives. From all appearances, Cilla was, too.

She was joking with a few members of the graduating class, most of them male. More than a few of them had imbibed freely at the cash bar. But she was handling herself, Boyd noted. Smooth as silk.

He didn't particularly like it when a man with a lineman's chest put a beefy arm around her and squeezed. But Cilla shook her head. Whatever brush-off she used, she sent the guy off with a smile on his face.

"There's more where that came from, boys and girls. Let's take you back, all the way back to prom night, 1975." She cued up the Eagles' "One Of These Nights," then skimmed the crowd for Boyd.

When she spotted him, she smiled. Fully, so that even with the room between them he could see her eyes glow. He wondered if he could manage to get her to look at him like that when they didn't have five hundred people between them. He had to grin when she put a hand to her throat and mimed desperate thirst.

Lord, he looked wonderful, Cilla thought as she watched him turn toward the bar. Strange, she would have thought a smoke-gray jacket would look too conservative on a man for her tastes. On him, it worked. So well, she mused with a wry smile, that half the female portion of the class of 75 had their eye on him.

Tough luck, ladies, she thought. He's mine. At least for tonight.

A little surprised by where her thoughts had landed, she shook herself back and chose a slip from the pile of requests next to the turntable. A nostalgic crowd, she decided and plucked another fifteen-year-old hit from her stack.

She liked working parties, watching people dance and flirt and gossip. The reunion committee had done a top-notch job on this one. Red and white streamers dripped from the ceiling, competing with a hundred matching balloons. The dance floor glittered from the light of a revolving mirror ball. When the music or the mood called for it, she could flick a switch on a strobe light and give them a touch of seventies psychedelia.

Mixed with the scents of perfume and cologne was the fragrance of the fresh flowers that adorned each table.

"This is for Rick and Sue, those high school sweeties who've been married for twelve years. And they said it was only puppy love. We're 'Rockin' All Over The World.'"

"Nice touch," Boyd commented.

She twisted her head and smiled. "Thanks."

He handed her a soft drink heaped with ice. "I've got a reunion coming up next year. You booked?"

"I'll check my schedule. Wow." She watched as a couple cut loose a few feet away. Other couples spread out as they put the dirty in dirty dancing. "Pretty impressive."

"Mmm. Do you dance?"

"Not like that." She let out a little breath. "I wish I did."

He took her hand before she could reach for another request slip. "Why don't you play one for me?"

"Sure. Name it."

When he poked through her discs, she was too amused to be annoyed. She could reorganize later. After choosing one, he handed it to her.

"Excellent taste." She shifted her mike. "We've got ourself a wild group tonight. Y'all having fun?" The roar of agreement rolled across the dance floor. "We're going to be here until midnight, pumping out the music for you. We've got a request here for Springsteen. 'Hungry Heart.'"

Fresh dancers streamed onto the floor. Couples twined around each other to sway. Cilla turned to speak to Boyd and found herself molded against him.

"Want to dance?" he murmured.

They already were. Body fitted to body, he took her on a long, erotically slow circle. "I'm working."

"Take five." He lowered his head to catch her chin between his teeth. "Until I make love with you, this is the next best thing."

She was going to object. She was sure of it. But she was moving with him, her body fine-tuned to his. In silent capitulation, she slid her arms around his neck.

With their faces close, he smiled. Slowly, firmly, he ran his hands over her hips, up, lazily up to the sides of her breasts, then down again.

She felt as though she'd been struck by lightning.

"You've, ah, got some nice moves, Slick."

"Thanks." When their lips were a whisper apart, he shifted, leaving hers hungry as he nuzzled into her neck. "You smell like sin, Cilla. It's just one of the things about you that's been driving me crazy for days."

She wanted him to kiss her. Craved it. She moaned when his hands roamed into her hair, drawing her head back. Her eyes closed in anticipation, but he only brushed those tempting lips over her cheekbone.

Breathless, she clung to him, trying to fight through the fog of pleasure. There were hundreds of people around them, all moving to the erotic beat of the music. She was working, she reminded herself. She was—had always been—a sensible woman, and tonight she had a job to do.

"If you keep this up, I won't be able to work the turntable."

He felt her heart hammering against his. It wasn't enough to satisfy him. But it was enough to give him hope. "Then I guess we'll have to finish the dance later."

When he released her, Cilla turned quickly and chose a record at random. A cheer went up as the beat pounded out. She lifted the hair from the back of her neck to cool it. The press of bodies—or the press of one body—had driven the temperature up. She'd never realized what a dangerous pastime dancing could be.

"Want another drink?" Boyd asked when she drained her glass.

"No. I'm okay." Steadying herself, she reached for the request sheet on top of her pile. "This is a nice group," she said as she glanced across the room. "I like reunions."

"I think I figured that out."

"Well, I do. I like the continuity of them. I like seeing all these people who shared the same experience, the same little block of time. 1975," she mused, the paper dangling from her fingers. "Not the greatest era for music, with the dreaded disco onslaught, but there were a few bright lights. The Doobie Brothers were still together. So were the Eagles."

"Do you always measure time in rock and roll?"

She had to laugh. "Occupational hazard. Anyway, it's a good barometer." Tossing her hair back, she grinned at him. "The first record I spun, as a professional, was the Stones' 'Emotional Rescue.' That was the year Reagan was elected the first time, the year John Lennon was shot—and the year the Empire struck back."

"Not bad, O'Roarke."

"It's better than not bad." She considered him. "I bet you remember what was playing on the radio the first time you talked a girl into the back seat of your car."

"'Dueling Banjos.'"

"You're kidding."

"You asked."

She was chuckling as she opened the request sheet. Her laughter died. She thought for a moment her heart had stopped. Carefully she squeezed her eyes shut. But when she opened them again the boldly printed words remained.

I want you to scream when I kill you.

"Cilla?"

With a brisk shake of her head, she passed the note to Boyd.

He was here, she thought, panic clawing as she searched the room. Somewhere in this crowd of laughing, chattering couples, he was watching. And waiting.

He'd come close. Close enough to lay that innocent-looking slip of paper on her table. Close enough to look into her eyes, maybe to smile. He might have spoken to her. And she hadn't known. She hadn't recognized him. She hadn't understood.

"Cilla."

She jolted when Boyd put a hand to her shoulder, and she would have stumbled backward if he hadn't balanced her. "Oh, God. I thought that tonight, just this one night, he'd leave me alone."

"Take a break."

"I can't." Dazed, she clamped her hands together and stared around the room. "I have to—"

"I need to make a call," he told her. "I want you where I can see you."

He could still be here, she thought. Close enough to touch her. Did he have the knife? The long-bladed knife he'd so lovingly described to her? Was he waiting for the moment when the music was loud, when the laughter was at a peak, so that he could plunge it into her?

"Come on."

"Wait. Wait a minute." With her nails biting into her palms, she leaned into the mike. "We're going to take a short break, but don't cool down. I'll be back in ten to start things rocking again." Mechanically she shut off her equipment. "Stay close, will you?" she whispered.

With an arm snug around her waist, he began to lead her through the crowd. Every time they were bumped she shuddered. When a man pushed through the throng and grabbed both of her hands, she nearly screamed.

"Cilla O'Roarke." He had a pleasant, affable face dampened with sweat from a turn on the dance floor. He was beaming as Cilla stood as still as a statue and Boyd tensed beside her. "Tom Collins. Not the drink," he said, still beaming. "That's my name. I'm chairman of the reunion committee. Remember?"

"Oh." She forced her lips to curve. "Yes. Sure."

"Just wanted to tell you how thrilled we are to have you. Got a lot of fans here." He released one of her hands to sweep his arm out. "I'm about the biggest. There's hardly a night goes by I don't catch at least a part of your show. Lost my wife last year."

"I…" She cleared her throat. "I'm sorry."

"No, I mean I lost her. Came home one night and she and the furniture were gone. Never did find her— or the sectional sofa." He laughed heartily while Cilla searched for something to say. "Fact is, your show got me through some pretty lonely nights. Just wanted to thank you and tell you you're doing a hell of a job here tonight." He pressed a business card into her hand. "I'm in appliances. You just call me whenever you need a new refrigerator." He winked. "Give you a good deal."

"Thanks." It should be funny, she thought. Later it would be funny. "Nice seeing you, Tom."

"Pleasure's mine." He watched her walk away and beamed again.

Boyd steered her out of the ballroom and toward the nearest pay phone. "Hang on. Okay?"

She nodded, even managed to smile at a group of women herding toward the ladies' lounge. "I'm better now. I'm going to sit down right over there." She pointed to an arrangement of chairs and a potted plant.

Leaving Boyd digging for change, she walked over, then let her legs collapse under her.

It was a nightmare. She wished it was as simple as a nightmare so that she could wake up with the sun shining in her face. She had nearly gotten through an entire day without thinking of him.

Shaky, she pulled out a cigarette.

Perhaps it had been foolish to let herself believe he would give her a day of peace. But to have come here. The odds of him actually being one of the alumni were slim. Yet he'd gotten inside.

With her back pressed into the chair, she watched people file in and out of the ballroom. It could be any one of them, she thought, straining for some spark of recognition. Would she know him if she saw him, or would he be a complete stranger?

He could be someone standing behind her at the market, someone sitting across from her at a gas pump. He might be the man in front of her at the bank, or the clerk at the dry cleaners.

Anyone, she thought as she closed her eyes. He could be any one of the nameless, faceless people she passed in the course of a day.

Yet he knew her name. He knew her face. He had

taken away her peace of mind, her freedom. He wouldn't be satisfied until he'd taken her life.

She watched Boyd hang up the phone and waited until he crossed to her. "Well?"

"Thea's coming by to pick up the paper. We'll send it to the lab." His hand found the tensed muscle at the curve of her neck and soothed. "I don't think we'll get prints."

"No." She appreciated the fact that he didn't give her any false hope. "Do you think he's still here?"

"I don't know." That was its own frustration. "It's a big hotel, Cilla. There's no security to speak of for this event. It wouldn't be very effective to try to close it off and interrogate everyone in it. If you want to take off early, I can tell them you're sick."

"No, I don't want to do that." She took a long last drag on her cigarette. "The only satisfaction I can get is from finishing out. Proving I'm not ready to fold. Especially if he *is* still around, somewhere."

"Okay. Remember, for the next hour, I'm never going to be more than a foot away."

She put a hand in his as she rose. "Boyd, he changed his approach, writing a note. What do you think it means?"

"It could mean a lot of things."

"Such as?"

"Such as it was the most convenient way to contact you tonight. Or he's starting to get sloppy."

"Or impatient," she added, turning to him at the doorway. "Be honest with me."

"Or impatient." He cupped her face in his hands. "He has to get through me first, Cilla. I can promise that won't be an easy job."

She made herself smile. "Cops like to think they're tough."

"No." He kissed her lightly. "Cops have to be tough. Come on. Maybe you've got 'Dueling Banjos' in there. You can play it for me for old times' sake."

"Not on a bet."

She got through it. He'd never doubted that she would, and yet the way she held on despite her fears amazed and impressed him. Not once did she bog down, break down or falter. But he saw the way she studied the crowd, searched the faces as the music raged around her.

Her hands moved constantly, tapping out the beat on the table, shifting through records, fiddling with the sequined studs on her pleated shirt.

She would never be serene, he thought. She would never be soothing. She would pace her way through life driven by nerves and ambition. She would make a demanding and unsettling companion.

Not what he'd had in mind on the rare occasions he'd considered marriage and family. Not even close, he realized with a faint smile. But she was exactly what he wanted and intended to have.

He would protect her with his life. That was duty. He would cherish her for a lifetime. That was love. If the plans he'd made ran smoothly, she would understand the difference very soon.

He, too, was searching the crowd, studying the faces, watching for any sign, any movement, that would bring that quick tensing of the gut called instinct. But the music raged on. The partygoers laughed.

He saw Althea enter. And so, he thought with a

shake of his head, did most of the men in the room. He had to chuckle when he saw one woman jab her husband in the ribs as he gawked at the redhead skirting the dance floor.

"You always make an entrance, Thea."

She only shrugged. She was wearing a simple off-the-shoulder cocktail dress in basic black. "I should thank you for getting me out of what turned into an annoying evening. My date had a toothbrush in his pocket and a night of wild sex on his mind."

"Animal."

"Aren't they all?" She glanced past him to Cilla. Amusement faded, to be replaced by concern. "How's she holding up?"

"She's incredible."

She lifted one arched brow. "Partner, my sharp investigative skills lead me to believe that you are seriously infatuated with our assignment."

"I passed infatuation. I'm in love with her."

Thea's lips formed a thoughtful pout. "Is that with a lowercase or uppercase *L*?"

"That's in all caps." He looked away from Cilla to his partner. There were few others with whom he would share his private thoughts. "I'm thinking marriage, Thea. Want to be my best man?"

"You can count on me." Still, she laid a hand on his arm. "I don't want to be a drag, Boyd, but you've got to keep some perspective on this. The lady's in trouble."

He struggled against annoyance. "I can function as a cop and as a man." Because it wasn't something he wanted to discuss at length, he reached in his pocket. "Here's the note, for what it's worth."

She skimmed the message, then slipped it into her bag. "We'll see what the lab boys can do."

He only nodded. "The ex-husband looks clean." An enormous disappointment. "I finished running him through tonight. State Senator Lomax has been married for seven years, and has one point six children. He hasn't been out of Atlanta for three months."

"I finally got ahold of the station manager in Chicago. He had nothing but good things to say about Cilla. I checked out his story about being in Rochester the past week visiting his daughter. It pans. She had a girl. Seven pounds, six ounces. He faxed me the personnel files on the jocks and staff who were at the station when Cilla worked there. So far nothing."

"When I come in Monday, we'll take a closer look."

"I figured I'd go over the file this weekend. Stick close to our girl."

"I owe you one, Thea."

"You owe me more than one, but who's counting?" She started out, pausing once, then twice, to refuse the offer of a dance. Then, again, to decline a more intimate offer.

Because a party was appreciated more when it ended on a fever pitch, Cilla chose the last three songs for their beat rather than their sentiment. Jackets were off, ties were undone and careful hairstyles were limp. When the last song ended, the dance floor was jammed.

"Thank you, class of 75, you've been great. I want to see all of you back here for your twentieth."

"Good job," Boyd told her.

She was already stacking records as the crowd split off into groups. Phone numbers and addresses would be exchanged. A few of the goodbyes would be tearful. "It's not over yet."

It helped to work. She had to break down the equipment, and with the help of the hotel staff she would load it into Boyd's car. Then there would be a trip back to the station and the unloading. After that, maybe she would allow herself to think again.

"It *was* a good job."

She looked up, surprised. "Mark? What are you doing here?"

"I could say I was checking up on one of my jocks." He picked up one of the 45s and laughed. "God, don't tell me you actually played this."

"It was pretty hot in 75." Suspicious, she took it back from him. "Now, why don't you tell me what you're really doing here?"

Feeling nostalgic himself, he glanced around. He and his wife had met in high school. "I'm here to get my equipment."

"Since when does the station manager load equipment?"

"I'm the boss," he reminded her. "I can do whatever I want. And as of now…" He glanced casually at his watch. "You're on sick leave."

It was suddenly very clear. She shot an accusing look at Boyd. "I'm not sick."

"You are if I say you are," Mark countered. "If I see you at the station before your shift Monday night, you're fired."

"Damn it, Mark."

"Take it or leave it." Softening the blow, he put his hands on her shoulders. "It's business, Cilla. I've had jocks burn out from a lot less pressure than you're under. I want you for the long haul. And it's personal. You've got a lot of people worried about you."

"I'm handling it."

"Then you should be able to handle a couple of free days. Now get out of here."

"But who's going to—"

Boyd took her arm. "You heard the man."

"I hate being bullied," she muttered as he dragged her along.

"Too bad. I guess you figure KHIP is going to fall apart without you there for a weekend."

Without turning her head, she shifted her eyes and aimed a killing look at him. "That's not the point."

"No, the point is you need a rest, and you're going to get it."

She grabbed her coat before he could help her on with it. "Just what the hell am I supposed to do with myself?"

"We'll think of something."

Seething with resentment, she stalked out to the parking lot. A few stragglers from the reunion loitered around their cars. She plopped into the passenger's seat and scowled.

"Since when did *we* come into it?"

"Since, by an odd coincidence, I've also got the weekend off."

Eyes narrowed, she studied him as he conscientiously buckled her seat belt. "It smells like a conspiracy."

"You haven't seen anything yet."

He deliberately chose a cassette of classical music and popped it into the tape player before driving out of the lot.

"Mozart?" she said with a sneer.

"Bach. It's called cleansing the palate."

On a heavy sigh, she reached for a cigarette. She didn't want people worried about her, didn't want to admit she was tired. Wasn't ready to admit she was relieved. "This stuff always puts me to sleep."

"You could use the rest."

She had her teeth clenched as she punched in the lighter. "I don't appreciate you running to Mark this way."

"I didn't run to Mark. I simply called him and suggested you could use some time."

"I can take care of myself, Slick."

"Your taxes are being used to see that I take care of you."

"Have I mentioned lately how much I dislike cops?"

"Not in the past twenty-four hours."

Apparently he wasn't going to rise to any of the bait she dangled and allow her to purge her annoyance with a fight. Maybe it was for the best after all, she decided. She could use the time to catch up on her reading. The last two issues of *Radio and Records* were waiting for her attention. She also wanted to look through one of the garden magazines that had come in the mail. It would be nice to plant some summer flowers around the house, maybe some bushes. She hadn't a clue what sort of thing suited Denver's climate.

The idea made her smile. She would buy a window box, and maybe one of those hanging baskets. Perhaps that was why she didn't notice they were heading in the wrong direction until Boyd had been driving for twenty minutes.

"Where are we?" She sat up quickly, blinking.

"On 70, heading west."

"Highway 70? What the devil are we doing on 70?"

"Driving to the mountains."

"The mountains." Groggy, she pushed back her tumbled hair. "What mountains?"

"I think they're called the Rockies," he said dryly. "You might have heard of them."

"Don't get smart with me. You're supposed to be driving me home."

"I am—in a manner of speaking. I'm driving you to my home."

"I've seen your home." She jerked her thumb. "It's back that way."

"That's where I live in Denver. This is the place I have in the mountains. It's a very comfortable little cabin. Nice view. We're going for the weekend."

"*We* are not going anywhere for the weekend." She shifted in her seat to glare at him. "I'm spending the weekend at home."

"We'll do that next weekend," he said, perfectly reasonable.

"Look, Fletcher, as a cop you should know when you take somebody somewhere against their will it's considered a crime."

"You can file charges when we get back."

"Okay, this has gone far enough." It wouldn't do any good to lose her temper, she reminded herself. He was immune. "You might think you're doing this for my own good, but there are other people involved. There's no way I'm going to leave Deborah in that house alone while this maniac is running loose looking for me."

''Good point.'' He glided off at an exit and nearly had her relaxing. ''That's why she's spending a couple of days with Althea.''

''I—''

''She told me to tell you to have a good time. Oh,'' he continued while Cilla made incoherent noises, ''she packed a bag for you. It's in the trunk.''

''Just when did you plan all this?'' That fabulous voice of hers was quiet. Too quiet, Boyd decided, bracing for the storm.

''I had some free time today. You'll like the cabin. It's peaceful, not too remote, and like I said, it has a nice view.''

''As long as there's a nice high cliff I can throw you off of.''

He slowed to navigate the winding road. ''There's that, too.''

''I knew you had nerve, Fletcher, but this goes beyond. What the hell made you think you could just put me in a car, arrange my sister's life and drive me off to some cabin?''

''Must've had a brainstorm.''

''Brain damage is more like it. Get this straight. I don't like the country, I don't like rustic. I am not a happy camper, and I won't go.''

''You're already going.''

How could he stay so irritatingly calm? ''If you don't take me back, right now, I'm going to—''

''What?''

She ground her teeth. ''You have to sleep sometime.'' Her own words made her take a quantum leap. ''You creep,'' she began on a fresh wave of fury. ''If this is your way of getting me into bed, you miscalculated. I'll sit in the car and freeze first.''

"There's more than one bedroom in the cabin," he said mildly. "You're welcome to share mine, or take any of the others. It's your choice."

She slumped back in her seat, finally speechless.

Chapter 8

She didn't intend to romanticize it. Being swept away was fine in books about titled ladies and swaggering buccaneers. But it didn't play well in twentieth-century Denver.

She didn't intend to change her attitude. If the only revenge available to her was keeping a frosty distance, she would keep it very well. He wouldn't get one smile or one kind word until the entire ridiculous weekend was over.

That was why it was a shame that her first glimpse of the house was in the moonlight.

He called this a cabin? Cilla was grateful the music masked her surprised gasp. Her idea of a cabin was a squat little log structure in the middle of nowhere lacking all possible conveniences. The kind of place men went when they wanted to grow beards, drink beer and complain about women.

It was built of wood—a soft, aged wood that glowed warm in the dappled moonlight. But it was far from little. Multileveled, with interesting juts of timber and windows, it rested majestically amid the snow-dusted pine. Decks, some covered, some open, promised a breathtaking view from any direction. The metal roof glinted, making her wonder how it would be to sit inside and listen to rain falling.

But she stubbornly bit back all the words of praise and pushed out of the car. The snow came up to mid-calf and clogged in her shoes.

"Great," she muttered. Leaving him to deal with whatever luggage they had, she trudged up to the porch.

So it was beautiful, she thought. It didn't make any difference. She still didn't want to be there. But since she was, and hailing a cab wasn't a possibility, she would keep her mouth shut, choose the bedroom farthest away from his and crawl into bed. Maybe she'd stay there for forty-eight hours.

Cilla kept the first part of the vow when he joined her on the porch. The only sounds were the planks creaking under his weight and the calling of something wild in the woods. After setting their bags aside, he unlocked the door and gestured her inside.

It was dark. And freezing. Somehow that made her feel better. The more uncomfortable it was, the more justified her foul temper. Then he switched on the lights. She could only gape.

The main room at the cabin's center was huge, an open gabled structure with rough-hewn beams and a charming granite fireplace. Thick, cushy furniture was arranged around it. Its freestanding chimney rose up through the high, lofted ceiling. Above, a balcony swept the width of the room, keeping with the theme of open space and wood. In contrast, the walls were a simple white, accented with glossy built-in shelves and many-paned doors and windows.

This was nothing like the arches and curves of his house in Denver. The cabin was all straight lines and simplicity. The wide planked floors were bare. A set of gleaming steps marched straight to the next level. Beside the fireplace was an open woodbox stacked with split logs. A touch of whimsy was added by grinning brass dragons that served as andirons.

"It warms up pretty quick," Boyd said, figuring she would start talking to him again when she was ready. He flipped on the heat before he shucked off his coat and hung it on a mirrored rack just inside the door. Leaving her where she was, he crossed to the fireplace and proceeded to arrange kindling and logs.

"The kitchen's through there." He gestured as he touched a match to some crumpled newspaper. "The pantry's stocked, if you're hungry."

She was, but she'd be damned if she'd admit it. She'd been getting a perverse pleasure in watching her breath puff out in front of her. Sulking, she watched the flames rise up to lick at the logs. He even did that well, she thought in disgust. He'd probably been an Eagle Scout.

When she didn't respond, he stood up, brushing off his hands. As stubborn as she was, he figured he could outlast her. "If you'd rather just go to bed, there are four bedrooms upstairs. Not counting the sleeping porch. But it's a little cold yet to try that."

She knew when she was being laughed at. Setting

her chin, she snatched up her bag and stalked up the stairs.

It was hard to tell which room was his. They were all beautifully decorated and inviting. Cilla chose the smallest. Though she hated to admit it, it was charming, with its angled ceiling, its tiny paneled bath and its atrium doors. Dropping her bag on the narrow bed, she dug in to see just what her sister—a partner in this crime—had packed.

The big, bulky sweater and thick cords met with approval, as did the sturdy boots and rag socks. The bag of toiletries and cosmetics was a plus, though she doubted she'd waste her time with mascara or perfume. Instead of her Broncos jersey and frayed chenille robe, there was a swatch of black silk with a matching—and very sheer—peignoir. Pinned to the bodice was a note.

Happy birthday a few weeks early. See you Monday.

Love, Deborah

Cilla blew out a long breath. Her own sister, she thought. Her own baby sister. Gingerly she held up the transparent silk. Just what had Deborah had in mind when she'd packed an outfit like this? she wondered. Maybe that question was best left unanswered. So she'd sleep in the sweater, Cilla decided, but she couldn't resist running her fingertips over the silk.

It felt…well, glorious, she admitted. Rarely did she indulge herself with anything so impractical. A small section of her closet was devoted to outfits like the one she'd worn to the reunion. She thought of them more as costumes than as clothes. The rest were practical, comfortable.

Deborah shouldn't have been so extravagant, she thought. But it was so like her. With a sigh, Cilla let the silk slide through her hands.

It probably wouldn't hurt just to try it on. After all, it was a gift. And no one was going to see it.

Heat was beginning to pour through the vents. Grateful, she slipped out of her coat and kicked off her shoes. She'd indulge herself with a hot bath in that cute claw-footed tub, and then she'd crawl under that very comfortable looking quilt and go to sleep.

She meant to. Really. But the hot water lulled her. The package of bubble bath Deborah had tucked in the case had been irresistible. Now the night-spice fragrance enveloped her. She nearly dozed off, dreaming, with the frothy, perfumed water lapping over her skin.

Then there was the skylight over the tub, that small square of glass that let the stardust sprinkle through. Indulgent, Cilla thought with a sigh as she sank deeper in the tub. Romantic. Almost sinfully soothing.

It had probably been silly to light the pair of candles that sat in the deep windowsill instead of using the overhead lamp. But it had been too tempting. And as she soaked and dreamed, their scent wafted around her.

She was just making the best of a bad situation, she assured herself as she rose lazily from the tub. Unpinning her hair, she let it swing around her shoulders as she slipped into the teddy Deborah had given her.

It had hardly any back at all, she noted, just a silly little flounce that barely covered the essentials. It laced up the front, thin, glossy ribbons that crisscrossed and ended in a small bow in the center, just below her breasts. Though it barely covered them, as well, some clever structural secret lifted them up, made them look fuller.

Despite her best intentions, she traced a fingertip down the ribbons, wondering what it would be like to have Boyd unlace them. Imagining what it might be like to have his fingers brush over her just-pampered skin. Would he go slowly, one careful hook at a time, or would he simply tear at them until—

Oh Lord.

Cursing herself, she yanked open the door and dashed out of the steamy bath.

It was ridiculous to daydream that way, she reminded herself. She had never been a daydreamer. Always, always, she had known where she was going and how to get there. Not since childhood had she wasted time with fantasies that had no connection with ambition or success.

She certainly had no business fantasizing about a man, no matter how attracted she was to him, when she knew there was no possible way they could become a comfortable reality.

She would go to bed. She would shut off her mind. And she would pray that she could shut off these needs that were eating away at her. Before she could shove her bag on the floor, she saw the glass beside the bed.

It was a long-stemmed crystal glass, filled with some pale golden liquid. As she sampled it, she shut her eyes. Wine, she realized. Wonderfully smooth. Probably French. Turning, she saw herself reflected in the cheval glass in the corner.

Her eyes were dark, and her skin was flushed. She looked too soft, too yielding, too pliant. What was he doing to her? she asked herself. And why was it working?

Before she could change her mind, she slipped the thin silk over her shoulders and went to find him.

He'd been reading the same page for nearly an hour. Thinking about her. Cursing her. Wanting her. It had taken every ounce of self-possession he had to set that wine beside her bed and leave the room when he could hear her splashing lazily in the tub just one narrow door away.

It wasn't as if it were all one-sided, he thought in disgust. He knew when a woman was interested. It wasn't as if it were all physical. He was in love with her, damn it. And if she was too stupid to see that, then he'd just have to beat her over the head with it.

Laying the book on his lap, he listened to the bluesy eloquence of Billie Holiday and stared into the fire. The cheerful flames had cut the chill in the bedroom. That was the practical reason he had built a fire in here, as well as one on the main floor. But there was another, a romantic one. He was annoyed that he had daydreamed of Cilla as he set the logs and lit the kindling.

She had come to him, wearing something thin, flowing, seductive. She had smiled, held out her hands. Melted against him. When he had lifted her into his arms, carried her to the bed, they had...

Keep dreaming, he told himself. The day Cilla O'Roarke came to him of her own free will, with a smile and an open hand, would be the day they built snowmen in hell.

She had feelings for him, damn it. Plenty of them. And if she weren't so bullheaded, so determined to lock up all that incredible passion, she wouldn't spend so much time biting her nails and lighting cigarettes.

Resentful, restrictive and repressed, that was Priscilla Alice O'Roarke, he thought grimly. He picked up his wine for a mock toast. It nearly slid out of his hand when he saw her standing in the doorway.

"I want to talk to you." She'd lost most of her nerve on the short trip down the hall, but she managed to step into the room. She wasn't going to let the fact that he was sitting in front of a sizzling fire wearing nothing but baggy sweats intimidate her.

He needed a drink. After a gulp of wine, he managed a nod. He was almost ready to believe he was dreaming again—but she wasn't smiling. "Yeah?"

She was going to speak, she reminded herself. Say what was on her mind and clear the air. But she needed a sip of her own wine first. "I realize your motives in bringing me here tonight were basically well-intentioned, given the circumstances of the last couple of weeks. But your methods were unbelievably arrogant." She wondered if she sounded like as much of a fool to him as she did to herself. She waited for a response, but he just continued to stare blankly at her. "Boyd?"

He shook his head. "What?"

"Don't you have anything to say?"

"About what?"

A low sound of frustration rumbled in her throat as she stepped closer. She slammed the glass down on a table, and the remaining wine lapped close to the rim. "The least you can do after dragging me all the way up here is to listen when I complain about it."

He was barely capable of breathing, much less listening. In self-defense he took another long sip of wine. "If you had any legs—brains," he corrected, gnashing his teeth, "you'd know that a couple days away from everything would be good for you."

Anger flared in her eyes, making her all the more arousing. Behind her the flames shot high, and the light rippled through the thin silk she wore. "So you just took it on yourself to make the decision for me."

"That's right." In one jerky movement, he set the glass aside to keep it from shattering in his fingers. "If I had asked you to come here for a couple of days, you would have made a dozen excuses why you couldn't."

"We'll never know what I would have done," she countered. "Because you didn't give me the option of making my own choice."

"I'm doing my damnedest to give you the option now," he muttered.

"About what?"

On an oath, he stood up and turned away. Hands braced on the wall, he began, none too gently, to pound his forehead against it. As she watched him, confusion warred with anger.

"What are you doing?"

"I'm beating my head against the wall. What does it look like I'm doing?" He stopped, letting his forehead rest against the wood.

Apparently she wasn't the only one under too much strain, Cilla mused. She cleared her throat. "Boyd, why are you beating your head against the wall?"

He laughed and, rubbing his hands over his face, turned. "I have no idea. It's just something I've felt obliged to do since I met you." She was standing, a little uncertain now, running nervous fingertips up and down her silk lapel. It wasn't easy, but after a deep breath he found a slippery hold on control. "Why don't you go on to bed, Cilla? In the morning you can tear apart what's left of me."

"I don't understand you." She snapped out the words, then began to pace. Boyd opened his mouth but couldn't even manage a groan as he stared at the long length of her back, bare but for the sheerest of black silk, at the agitated swing of her hips, accented by the sassy little flounce. She was talking again, rapid-fire and irritated, but it was all just a buzzing in his head.

"For God's sake, don't pace." He rubbed the heel of his hand against his heart. In another minute, he was sure, it would explode out of his chest. "Are you trying to kill me?"

"I always pace when I'm mad," she tossed back. "How do you expect me to go quietly to bed after you've got me worked up this way?"

"Got you worked up?" he repeated. Something snapped—he would have sworn he heard it boomerang in his head as he reached out and snatched her arms. "I've got you worked up? That's rich, O'Roarke. Tell me, did you wear this thing in here tonight to make me suffer?"

"I…" She looked down at herself, then shifted uncomfortably. "Deborah packed it. It's all I've got."

"Whoever packed it, it's you who's packed into it. And you're driving me crazy."

"I just thought we should clear all this up." She was going to start stuttering in a minute. "Talk it through, like grown-ups."

"I'm thinking very much like a grown-up at the moment. If you want to talk, there's a chestful of big, thick wool blankets. You can wrap yourself up in one."

She didn't need a blanket. She was already much too warm. If he continued to rub his hands up and down the silk on her arms, the friction was going to cause her skin to burst into flame.

"Maybe I wanted to make you suffer a little."

"It worked." His fingers toyed with the excuse of a robe as it slid from her right shoulder. "Cilla, I'm not going to make this easy on you and drag you to that bed. I'm not saying the idea doesn't appeal to me a great deal. But if we make love, you're going to have to wake up in the morning knowing the choice was yours."

Wasn't that why she had come to him? Hoping he'd take matters out of her hands? That made her a coward—and, in a miserable way, a cheat.

"It's not easy for me."

"It should be." He slid his hands down to hers. "If you're ready."

She lifted her head. He was waiting—every bit as edgy as she, but waiting. "I guess I've been ready since I met you."

A tremor worked through him, and he struggled against his self-imposed leash. "Just say yes."

Saying it wasn't enough, she thought. When something was important, it took more than one simple word.

"Let go of my hands, please."

He held them another long moment, searching her face. Slowly his fingers relaxed and dropped away from hers. Before he could back up, she moved into him, wrapping her arms around his neck. "I want you, Boyd. I want to be with you tonight."

She brought her lips to his. There had already been enough words. Warm and willing, she sank into him.

For a moment, he couldn't breathe. The onslaught on his senses was too overwhelming. Her taste, her scent, the texture of silk against silk. There was her sigh as she rubbed her lips over his.

He remembered taking a kick in the solar plexus from one of his father's prized stallions. This left him just as debilitated. He wanted to savor, to drown, to lose himself, inch by glorious inch. But even as he slipped the robe from her shoulders she was pulling him to the bed.

She was like a whirlwind, hands racing, pressing, tugging, followed by the mad, erotic journey of her mouth. The pressure was building too fast, but when he reached for her she shimmied out of the silk and rushed on.

She didn't want him to regret wanting her. She couldn't have borne it. If she was to throw every shred of caution to the winds for this one night, she needed to know that it would matter. That he would remember.

His skin was hot and damp. She wished she could have lingered over the taste of it, the feel of it under her fingers. But she thought men preferred speed and power.

She heard him groan. It delighted her. When she tugged off his sweats, his hands were in her hair. He was murmuring something—her name, and more—but she couldn't tell. She thought she understood his urgency, the way he pulled her up against him. When he rolled over her, she whispered her agreement and took him inside her.

He stiffened. On an oath, he tried to level himself and draw back. But her hips arched and thrust against him, leaving his body no choice.

Her lips were curved when he lay over her, his face buried in her hair, his breath still shuddering. He wouldn't regret this, she thought, rubbing a soothing hand over his shoulder. And neither would she. It was more than she had ever had before. More than she had ever expected. There had been a warmth when he filled her, and a quiet contentment when she felt him spill into her. She thought how nice it would be to close her eyes and drift off to sleep with his body still warm on hers.

He was cursing himself, steadily. He was enraged by his lack of control, and baffled by the way she had rushed them both from kiss to completion. He'd barely touched her—in more ways than one. Though it was she who had set the pace at a sprint, he knew she hadn't come close to fulfillment.

Struggling for calm, he rolled away from her to stare at the ceiling. She'd set off bombs inside him, and though they had exploded, neither of them had shared the joy.

"Why did you do that?" he asked her.

Her hand paused on its way to stroke his hair. "I don't understand. I thought you wanted to make love."

"I did." He sat up, dragging the hair back from his face. "I thought you did, too."

"But I thought men liked…" She let her eyes close

as the warmth drained out of her. "I told you I wasn't very good at it."

He swore, ripely enough to have her jolting. Moving quickly, she scrambled out of bed to struggle back into the peignoir.

"Where the hell are you going?"

"To bed." Because her voice was thick with tears, she lowered it. "We can just chalk this up to one more miscalculation." She reached down for her robe and heard the door slam. Bolting up, she saw Boyd turning a key in the lock, then tossing it across the room. "I don't want to stay here with you."

"Too bad. You already made your choice."

She balled up the robe, hugging it to her chest. So he was angry, she thought. And it was the real thing this time. It wouldn't be the first fight she had had about her inadequacies in bed. Old wounds, old doubts, trickled through her until she stood rigid with embarrassment.

"Look, I did the best I could. If it wasn't good enough, fine. Just let me go."

"Wasn't good enough," he repeated. As he stepped forward, she backed up, ramming into the carved footboard. "Somebody ought to bounce you on your head and knock some sense into it. There are two people in a bed, Cilla, and what happens in it is supposed to be mutual. I wasn't looking for a damn technician."

The angry flush died away from her face until it was marble white. Her eyes filled. Pressing his fingers against his own eyes, he swore. He hadn't meant to hurt her, only to show her that he'd wanted a partner.

"You didn't feel anything."

"I did." She rubbed tears from her cheek, infuriated. No one made her cry. No one.

"Then that's a miracle. Cilla, you barely let me touch you. I'm not blaming you." He took another step, but she evaded him. Searching for patience he stood where he was. "I didn't exactly fight you off. I thought—Let's just say by the time I understood it was too late to do anything about it. I'd like to make it up to you."

"There's nothing to make up." She had herself under control again, eyes dry, voice steady. She wanted to die. "We'll just forget it. I want you to unlock the door."

He let out a huff of breath, then shrugged. When he turned to the door, she started to follow. But he only turned off the lights.

"What are you doing?"

"We tried it your way." In the moonlight, he moved across the room to light a candle, then another and another. He turned over the record that sat silent on the turntable, engaged the needle. The trembling cry of a tenor sax filled the room. "Now we try it mine."

She was starting to tremble now, from embarrassment and from fear. "I said I wanted to go to bed."

"Good." He swept her up into his arms. "So do I."

"I've had enough humiliation for one night," she said between her teeth.

She saw something in his eyes, something dark, but his voice was quiet when he spoke. "I'm sorry. I never meant to hurt you."

Though she held herself rigid, he lowered her gently to the bed. With his eyes on hers, he spread out her hair, letting his fingers linger. "I've imagined you here, in the candlelight, with your hair on my pillow.'' He lowered his lips to brush them across hers. ''Moonlight and firelight on your skin. With nothing and no one else but you for miles.''

Moved, she turned her head away. She wouldn't be seduced by words and make a fool of herself again. He only smiled and pressed his lips to her throat.

''I love a challenge. I'm going to make love with you, Cilla.'' He slipped the strap of the peignoir from her shoulder to cruise the slope with his mouth. ''I'm going to take you places you've never even dreamed of.'' He took her hand, pleased that her pulse had quickened. ''You shouldn't be afraid to enjoy yourself.''

''I'm not.''

''You're afraid to relax, to let go, to let someone get close enough to find out what's inside you.''

She tried to shift away, but his arms wrapped around her. ''We already had sex.''

''Yes, we did.'' He kissed one corner of her mouth, then the other. ''Now we're going to make love.''

She started to turn her head again, but he cupped her face with his hands. When his mouth came to hers again, her heart leaped into her throat. It was so soft, so tempting. As his fingertips glided across her face, she gave a strangled sigh. He dipped into her parted lips to tease her tongue with his.

''I don't want—'' She moaned as his teeth nipped into her bottom lip.

''Tell me what you do want.''

''I don't know.'' Her mind was already hazy. She lifted a hand to push him away, but it only lay limp on his shoulder.

"Then we'll make it multiple-choice." To please himself, and her, he ran a trail of kisses down her throat. "When I'm finished, you can tell me what you like best."

He murmured to her, soft, dreamy words that floated in·her head. Then he drugged her with a kiss, long, lazy, luxurious. Though her body had begun to tremble, he barely touched her—just those fingertips stroking along her shoulders, over her face, into her hair.

His tongue slid over the tops of her breasts, just above the fringe of black lace. Her skin was like honey there, he thought, laving the valley between. Her heart jackhammered against him, but when she reached out he took her hands in his.

Taking his time, his devastating time, he inched the lace down with his teeth. She arched up, offering herself, her fingers tensing like wires against his. He only murmured and, leaving a moist trail, eased the other curve of lace down.

His own breathing was short and shallow, but he fought back the urge to take greedily. With teasing openmouthed kisses he circled her, flicking his hot tongue over her rigid nipple until she shuddered and sobbed out his name. On a groan of pleasure, he suckled.

She felt the pressure deep inside, clenching, unclenching, to the rhythm of his clever mouth. Building, layering, growing, until she thought she would die from it.

Her breath was heaving as she writhed beneath him. Her nails dug hard into the backs of his hand as her body bowed, driven up by a knot of sensation. She heard her own cry, her gasp of relief and torment as something shattered inside her. Hot knives that turned to silky butterfly wings. A pain that brought unreasonable pleasure.

As every muscle in her body went lax, he covered her mouth with his. "Good Lord. You're incredible."

"I can't." She brought a hand up to press a palm to her temple. "I can't think."

"Don't. Just feel."

He straddled her. She was prepared for him to take her. He had already given her more than she had ever had. Shown her more than she had ever imagined. He began to unlace the peignoir with infinite care, infinite patience. His eyes were on her face. He loved being able to see everything she felt as it flickered there. Every new sensation, every new emotion. He heard the whisper of silk against her skin as he drew it down. He felt passion vibrate from her as he pressed his mouth to the quivering flesh of her stomach.

Floating, she stroked his hair, let her mind follow where her body so desperately wanted to go. This was heaven, more demanding, more exciting, more erotic, than any paradise she could have dreamed. She could feel the sheets, hot from her own body, tangled beneath her. And the shimmer of silk as it slipped slowly, slowly away. His skin, dampened from pleasure, slid over hers. When her lips parted on a sigh, she could still taste him there, rich and male. Candlelight played against her closed lids.

There was so much to absorb, so much to experience. If it went on forever, it would still end too soon.

She was his now, he knew. Much more his than she had been when he had been plunged inside her. Her body was like a wish, long and slim and pale in the moonlight. Her breath was quick and quiet. And it was his name, only his name, she spoke when he touched her. Her hands flexed on his shoulder, urging him on.

He slid down her legs, taking the silk with him, nibbling everywhere as he went. The scent of her skin was a tormenting delight he could have lingered over endlessly. But her body was restless, poised. He knew she must be aching, even as he was.

He stroked a fingertip up her thigh, along that sensitive flesh, close, so close, to where the heat centered. When he slipped inside her, she was wet and waiting.

The breathless moan came first, and then the magic of his hands had her catapulting up, over a new and higher crest. Stunned by the power of it, she arched against him, shuddering again and again as she climbed. Though her hands clutched at him, he continued to drive her with his mouth, with his clever and relentless fingers, until she shot beyond pleasure to delirium.

Then her arms were around him and they were spinning off together, rolling over on the bed like lightning and thunder. The time for patience was over. The time for greed had begun.

He fought for breath as her hands raced over him. As she had the first time, she ripped away his control. But now she was with him, beat for beat and need for need. He saw her eyes glow, dark with passion, depthless with desire. Her slick skin shimmered with it in the shadowy light.

One last time he brought his mouth down on hers, swallowing her stunned cry, as he thrust himself into her. On a half sob she wrapped her arms and legs around him, locking tight so that they could race toward madness together.

He was exhausted. Weak as a baby. And he was heavy. Using what strength he could find, Boyd rolled, taking Cilla with him so that their positions were reversed. Satisfied, he cradled her head and decided he very much liked the sensation of her body sprawled over his.

She shuddered. He soothed.

"Cold?"

She just shook her head.

Lazy as a cat, he stroked a hand down her naked back. "I might, in an hour or so, find the strength to look for the blankets."

"I'm fine."

But her voice wasn't steady. Frowning, Boyd cupped a hand under her chin and lifted it. He could see a tear glittering on her lashes. "What's this?"

"I'm not crying," she said, almost fiercely.

"Okay. What are you?"

She tried to duck her head again, but he held it firm. "You'll think I'm stupid."

"Probably the only time I couldn't think you were stupid is right after you've turned me inside out." He gave her a quick kiss. "Spill it, O'Roarke."

"It's just that I..." She let out an impatient breath. "I didn't think it was supposed to be that way. Not really."

"What way?" His lips curved. Funny, but it seemed he was getting his strength back. Maybe it was the way she was looking at him. Dazed. Embarrassed. Beautiful. "You mean, like good?" He slid his hands down to caress her bottom casually. "Or very good? Maybe you mean terrific. Or astounding."

"You're making fun of me."

"Uh-uh. I was hoping for a compliment. But you don't want to give me one. I figure you're just too stubborn to admit that my way was better than your way. But that's okay. I also figure I can keep you locked in here until you do."

"Damn it, Boyd, it's not easy for me to explain myself."

"You don't have to." There was no teasing note in his voice now. The look in his eyes made her weak all over again.

"I wanted to tell you that I never...no one's ever made me..." She gave up. "It was terrific."

"Yeah." He cupped a hand on the back of her head and brought her mouth to his. "Now we're going to shoot for astounding."

Chapter 9

Cilla wrapped her arms across her body to ward off the chill and stared out over the pine and rock. Boyd had been right again. The view was incredible.

From this angle she could see the jagged, snow-capped peaks of the circling mountains. Closer, yet still distant, she caught the faint mist of smoke from a chimney. Evergreens stood, sturdy winter veterans, their needles whistling in the rising wind. There was the harsh whisper of an icy stream. She could catch glimpses of the water, just the glint of it in the fading sun.

The shadows were long, with late afternoon casting a cool blue light over the snow. Earlier she had seen a deer nuzzling her nose into it in search of the grass beneath. Now she was alone.

She'd forgotten what it was to feel so at peace. In truth, she wondered if she had ever known. Certainly not since earliest childhood, when she had still believed in fairy tales and happy endings. It had to be too late, when a woman was nearly thirty, to start believing again.

And yet she doubted things would ever be quite the same again.

He had kept his promise. He had taken her places she had never dreamed of. In one exquisitely long night, he had shown her that love meant you could accept as well as offer, take as well as give. She had learned more than the power of lovemaking in Boyd's bed. She had learned the power of intimacy. The comfort and the glory of it. For the first time in years, she had slept deeply and dreamlessly.

She hadn't felt awkward or uncomfortable on waking with him that morning. She had felt calm. Wonderfully calm. It was almost impossible to believe that there was another world apart from this spot. A world of pain and danger and fear.

Yet there was. And it was a world she would have to face again all too soon. She couldn't hide here—not from a man who wanted her dead, nor from her own miserable memories. But wasn't she entitled to a little more time to pretend that nothing else mattered?

It wasn't right. On a sigh, she lifted her face to the dying sun. No matter how she felt—or perhaps because she had come to feel so deeply—she had to be honest with herself, and with Boyd. She wouldn't let what had started between them go any further. Couldn't, she thought, squeezing her eyes tight. It had to be better to let her heart break a little now than to have it smashed later.

He was a good man, she thought. An honest one, a

caring one. He was patient, intelligent and dedicated. And he was a cop.

She shivered and held herself more tightly.

There was a scar just under his right shoulder. Front and back, she remembered. From a bullet—that occupational hazard of law enforcement. She hadn't asked, and wouldn't, how he had come by it, when it had happened, or how near death it had taken him.

But neither could she hide from the fact that the scars she bore were as real as his.

She simply could not delude either of them into believing there was a future for them. She should never have allowed it to progress as far as it had. But that was done. They were lovers. And though she knew that was a mistake, she would always be grateful for the time she had had with him.

The logical thing to do would be to discuss the limitations of their relationship. No strings, no obligations. In all likelihood he would appreciate that kind of practicality. If her feelings had grown too far too fast, she would just have to get a grip on them.

She would simply have to talk herself out of being in love.

He found her there, leaning out on the railing as if she were straining to fly out above the pines, above the snowcapped peaks. The nerves were coming back, he noted with some frustration. He wondered if she knew how relaxed she had been that morning when she had stretched against him, waking gradually, turning to him so that they could make slow, lazy love.

Now, when he touched her hair, she jolted before she leaned back against his hand.

"I like your place, Slick."

"I'm glad." He intended to come back here with her, year after year.

Her fingers danced over the railing, then groped in her pockets. "I never asked you if you bought it or had it built."

"Had it built. Even hammered a few nails myself."

"A man of many talents. It's almost a shame to have a place like this only for weekends."

"I've been known to break away for more than that from time to time. And my parents use it now and again."

"Oh. Do they live in Denver?"

"Colorado Springs." He began to massage the tensing muscles in her shoulders. "But they travel a lot. Itchy feet."

"I guess your father was disappointed when you didn't go into the family business."

"No. My sister's carrying on the family tradition."

"Sister?" She glanced over her shoulder. "I didn't know you had a sister."

"There's a lot you don't know." He kissed her lips when they formed into a pout. "She's a real go getter. Tough, high-powered businesswoman. And a hell of a lot better at it than I would have been."

"But aren't they uneasy about you being a cop?"

"I don't think it's a day-to-day worry. You're getting chilled," he said. "Come on inside by the fire."

She went with him, moving inside and down the rear steps into the kitchen. "Mmm... What's that smell?"

"I threw some chili together." He walked over to the center island, where copper pots hung from the ceiling. Lifting the lid on a pan simmering on the range, he sniffed. "Be ready in about an hour."

"I would have helped you."

"That's okay." He selected a Bordeaux from the wine rack. "You can cook next time."

She made a feeble attempt at a smile. "So you did like my peanut-butter-and-jelly special."

"Just like Mom used to make."

She doubted that his mother had ever made a sandwich in her life. People who had that kind of money also had a houseful of servants. As she stood feeling foolish, he set the wine on the counter to breathe.

"Aren't you going to take off your coat?"

"Oh. Sure." She shrugged out of it and hung it on a hook by the door. "Is there anything you want me to do?"

"Yes. Relax."

"I am."

"You were." Selecting two glasses from above the rack, he examined them. "I'm not sure what has you tied up again, Cilla, but we're going to talk it through this time. Why don't you go sit by the fire? I'll bring out the wine."

If he read her this easily after a matter of weeks, Cilla thought as she went into the living room, how much would he see in a year? She settled on a low cushion near the fire. She wasn't going to think of a year. Or even a month.

When he came in, she offered him a much brighter smile and reached for her wine. "Thanks. It's a good thing I didn't come here before I went house-hunting. I never would have settled on a house without a fireplace."

In silence, he settled beside her. "Look at me," he

said at length. "Are you worried about going back to work?"

"No." Then she sighed. "A little. I trust you and Thea, and I know you're doing what you can, but I am scared."

"Do you trust me?"

"I said I did." But she didn't meet his eyes.

He touched a fingertip to her cheek until she faced him again. "Not just as a cop."

She winced, looked away again. "No, not just as a cop."

"And that's the trigger," he mused. "The fact that I am a cop."

"It's none of my business."

"We both know better."

"I don't like it," she said evenly. "I don't expect you to understand."

"I think I do understand." He leaned back against a chair, watching her as he sipped his wine. "I've done some checking, Cilla—necessary to the investigation. But I won't pretend that's the only reason I looked."

"What do you mean?"

"I looked into your background because I need to protect you. And I need to understand you. You told me your mother was a cop. It wasn't hard to track down what happened."

She clutched her glass in both hands and stared straight ahead, into the flames. After all these years, the pain was just as deadly. "So you punched some buttons on your computer and found out my mother was killed. Line of duty. That's what they call it. Line of duty," she repeated, her voice dull. "As if it were part of a job description."

"It is," he said quietly.

There was a flicker of fear in her eyes when she looked at him, then quickly away again. "Yeah. Right. It was just part of her job to be shot that day. Too bad about my father, though. He just happened to be in the wrong place at the wrong time. The old innocent by-stander."

"Cilla, nothing's as black-and-white as that. And nothing's that simple."

"Simple?" She laughed and dragged her hair back from her face. "No, the word's *ironic*. The cop and the public defender, who just happen to be married, are going head-to-head over a case. They never agreed. Never once can I remember them looking at any one thing from the same angle. When this happened, they were talking about a separation—again. Just a trial one, they said." With a thoughtful frown, she studied her glass. "Looks like I'm out of wine."

Saying nothing, Boyd poured her more.

"So I guess you read the official report." She swirled the wine, then drank. "They brought this little creep in for interrogation. Three-time loser—armed robbery, assault, drugs. He wanted his lawyer present while the investigating officer questioned him. Talked about making a deal. He knew there wouldn't be any deal. They had him cold, and he was going to do hard time. He had two people to blame for it—in his head, anyway. His lawyer, and the cop who had collared him."

It was painful, still so painful, to remember, to try to picture an event she hadn't seen, one that had so drastically altered her life.

"They caught the guy who smuggled him the gun,"

she said softly. "He's still doing time." Taking a moment, she soothed her throat with wine. "There they were, sitting across from each other at the table—just as they might have been in our own kitchen—arguing about the law. The sonofabitch took out that smuggled snub-nosed .22 and shot them both."

She looked down at her glass again. "A lot of people lost their jobs over that incident. My parents lost their lives."

"I'm not going to tell you that cops don't die by mistake, unnecessarily, even uselessly."

When she looked at him, her eyes were eloquent. "Good. And I don't want the crap about how proud we're supposed to be of our valiant boys in blue. Damn it, she was my mother."

He hadn't just read the reports, he'd pored over them. The papers had called it a disgrace and a tragedy. The investigation had lasted more than six months, and when it was over eight officials had resigned or been replaced.

But over and above the facts, he remembered a file picture. Cilla, her face blank with grief, standing by the two graves, clutching Deborah's hand in hers.

"It was a horrible way to lose them," he said.

She just shook her head. "Yes. But in most ways I'd already lost my mother the day she joined the force."

"She had an impressive record," Boyd said carefully. "It wasn't easy for a woman back then. And it's always tough on a cop's family."

"How do you know?" she demanded. "You're not the one who sits at home and sweats. From the day I was old enough to understand, I waited for her captain to come to the door and tell us she was dead.''

"Cilla, you can't live your life waiting for the worst.''

"I lived my life waiting for a mother. The job always came first—it came before Dad, before me, before Deb. She was never there when I needed her.'' She snatched her hand aside before he could grasp it. "I didn't care if she baked cookies or folded my socks. I just wanted her to be there when I needed her. But her family was never as important as the masses she'd sworn to serve and protect.''

"Maybe she was too focused on her career," he began.

"Don't you compare me with her.''

His brow rose. "I wasn't going to.'' Now he took her hand despite her resistance. "It sounds like you are.''

"I've had to be focused. She had people who loved her, who needed her, but she never took time to notice. Cops don't have regular hours, she'd say. Cops don't have regular lives.''

"I didn't know your mother, and I can't comment on the choices she made, but don't you think it's time to cut it loose and get on with your life?''

"I have. I've done what I had to do. I've done what I've wanted to do.''

"And you're scared to death of what you're feeling for me because of my job.''

"It's not just a job," she said desperately. "We both know it's not just a job.''

"Okay." He nodded. "It's what I do, and what I

am. We're going to have to find a way to deal with it.''

"It's your life," she said carefully. "I'm not asking you to change anything. I didn't intend to get this involved with you, but I don't regret it.''

"Thanks," he muttered, and drained his own glass.

"What I'm trying to say is that if we're reasonable I think we can keep it uncomplicated.''

He set his glass aside. "No.''

"No what?''

"No, I don't want to be reasonable, and it's already complicated.'' He gave her a long look that was very close to grim. "I'm in love with you.''

He saw the shock. It flashed into her eyes an instant before she jerked back. The color drained away from her face.

"I see that thrills the hell out of you," he muttered. Rising, he heaved a log on the fire and cursed as he watched the sparks fly.

Cilla thought it best to stay exactly where she was. "Love's a real big word, Boyd. We've only known each other a couple of weeks, and not under the most ideal circumstances. I think—''

"I'm damn tired of you thinking.'' He turned back to face her. "Just tell me what you feel.''

"I don't know.'' That was a lie, one she knew she would hate herself for. She was terrified. And she was thrilled. She was filled with regrets, and hammered by longings. "Boyd, everything that's happened has happened fast. It's as if I haven't had any control, and that makes me uneasy. I didn't want to be involved with you, but I am. I didn't want to care about you, but I do.''

"Well, I finally managed to pry that out of you."

"I don't sleep with a man just because he makes me tingle."

"Better and better." He smiled as he lifted her hand to kiss her fingers. "I make you tingle, and you care about me. Marry me."

She tried to jerk her hand free. "This isn't the time for jokes."

"I'm not joking." Suddenly his eyes were very intense. "I'm asking you to marry me."

She heard a log shift in the grate. Saw the flicker of a new flame as it cast light and shadow over his face. His hand was warm and firm on hers, holding, waiting. Her breath seemed to be blocked somewhere beneath her heart. The effort of dragging in air made her dizzy.

"Boyd—"

"I'm in love with you, Cilla." Slowly, his eyes steady on hers, he pulled her closer. "With every part of you." Soft, persuasive, his lips cruised over hers. "I only want fifty or sixty years to show you." His mouth skimmed down her throat as he lowered her to the hearth rug. "Is that too much to ask?"

"No… Yes." Struggling to clear her mind, she pressed a hand against his chest. "Boyd, I'm not going to marry anyone."

"Sure you are." He nibbled lightly at her lips as his hands began to stroke—soothing and exciting at the same time. "You just have to get used to the fact that it's going to be me." He deepened the kiss, lingering over it until her hand lost its resistance and slid to his back. "I'm willing to give you time." His lips curved as her murmured protest hummed against them. "A day or two. Maybe a week."

She shook her head. "I've already made one mistake. I'm not ever going to repeat it."

He caught her chin in his hand in a movement so quick that her eyes flew open. In his eyes was a ripe, raging fury that was rare for him, and all the more dangerous.

"Don't ever compare me with him."

She started to speak, but his fingers tightened once, briefly, and silenced her.

"Don't ever compare what I feel for you with what anyone else has felt."

"I wasn't comparing you." Her heart was hammering against his chest. "It's me. It was my mistake, mine alone. And I'm never going to make another one like it."

"It takes two people, damn it." Enraged, he braced himself over her, then took both her hands in his. "If you want to play it that way, fine. Ask yourself one question, Cilla. Has anyone else made you feel like this?"

His mouth swooped down to take hers in a hot, rough, frantic kiss that had her arching against him. In protest? In pleasure? Even she couldn't tell. Sensations swarmed through her like thousands of swirling stars, all heat and light. Before she could draw and release a breath, she was tossed into the storm.

No. Her mind all but screamed it. No one. Never. Only he had ever caused a hunger so sharp and a need so desperate. Even as her body strained against his, she struggled to remember that it wasn't enough to want. It wasn't always enough to have.

Whipped by fury and frustration, he crushed his mouth to hers, again, and then again. If only for this moment, he would prove to her that what they had together was unique to them. She would think of no one, remember nothing. Only him.

Her response tore through him, so complete, so right. The small, helpless sound that purred up from her throat shuddered into him. Like the flames that rose beside them, what they created burned and consumed. The gentle loving that had initiated them both during the night was replaced by a wild and urgent hunger that left no room for tender words and soft caresses.

She didn't want them. This was a new, a frenetic storm of needs that demanded speed and pushed for power. *Hurry.* She tore her hands from his to drag at his shirt. *Touch me.* Twin groans tangled as flesh met flesh. *More.* With a new aggression, she rolled onto him to take her mouth on a frantic race over his body. And still it wasn't enough.

His breath ragged, he stripped the layers of clothing from her, not caring about what he tore. One driving need was prominent. To possess. Hands gripped. Fingers pressed. Mouths devoured.

Agile and electric, she moved over him. Her face glowed, fragile porcelain in the firelight. Her body arched, magnificent in its new power, sheened with passion, shuddering from it, strengthened by it.

For one glorious moment she rose, witchlike, over him, her hands lifting up into her hair, her head thrown back as she lost herself in the wonder. Her body shuddered once, twice, as separate explosions burst within her. Even as she gasped, he gripped her hips and sheathed himself inside her.

He filled her. Not just physically. Even through the wracking pleasure she understood that. He, and only he, had found the key that opened every part of her. He, and only he, had found the way inside her heart, her mind. And somehow, without trying, she had found the way into his.

She didn't want to love him. She reached for his hands and gripped them tight. She didn't want to need him. Opening her eyes, she looked down at him. His eyes were dark and direct on hers. She knew, though she didn't speak, that he understood every thought in her head. On a sigh that was as much from despair as from delight, she bent down to press her mouth to his.

He could taste both the needs and the fears. He was determined to exploit the first and drive away the second. Staying deep inside her, he pushed up so that he could wrap his arms around her. He watched her eyes widen, stunned with pleasure, glazed with passion. Her fingers dug into his back. Her cry of release was muffled against his mouth seconds before he let himself go.

Bundled in a large, frayed robe, her feet covered with thick rag socks, Cilla sampled the chili. She liked sitting in the warm golden light in the kitchen, seeing the blanket of snow outside the windows, hearing the quiet moan of the wind through the pines. What surprised her, and what she wasn't ready to consider too carefully, was this feeling of regret that the weekend was almost over.

"Well?"

At Boyd's question, she looked back from the window. He sat across from her, his hair still mussed from her hands. Like her, he wore only a robe and socks.

Though it made no sense, Cilla found the meal every bit as intimate as their loving in front of the fire.

Uneasy, she broke a piece of the hot, crusty bread on her plate. She was afraid he was going to bring up marriage again.

"Well what?"

"How's the chili?"

"The— Oh." She spooned up another bite, not sure if she was relieved or disappointed. "It's great. And surprising." Nervous again, she reached for her wine. "I'd have thought someone in your position would have a cook and wouldn't know how to boil an egg."

"My position?"

"I mean, if I could afford to hire a cook I wouldn't hassle with making sandwiches."

It amused him that his money made her uncomfortable. "After we're married we can hire one if you want."

Very carefully she set down her spoon. "I'm not going to marry you."

He grinned. "Wanna bet?"

"This isn't a game."

"Sure it is. The biggest in town."

She made a low sound of frustration. Picking up her spoon again, she began to tap it against the wood. "That's such a typically male attitude. It's all a game. You Tarzan, me stupid." His laughter only enraged her further. "Why is it men think women can't resist them—for sex, for companionship, for handling the details of life? Oh, Cilla, you need me. Oh, Cilla, I just want to take care of you. I want to show you what life's all about."

He considered a moment. "I don't remember saying

any of those things. I think what I said is I love you and I want to marry you.''

"It's the same thing.''

"Not even close.'' He continued to eat, undisturbed.

"Well, I don't want to marry you, but I'm sure that won't make a difference. It never does.''

He shot her one brief and dangerous look. "I warned you not to compare me to him. I meant it.''

"I'm not just talking about Paul. I wasn't even thinking about Paul.'' After pushing her bowl aside, she sprang up to find a cigarette. "I hadn't given him a thought in years before all of this.'' She blew out an agitated stream of smoke. "And if I want to compare you to other men, I will.''

He topped off his wine, then hers. "How many others have asked you to marry them?''

"Dozens.'' It was an exaggeration, but she didn't give a damn. "But somehow I've found the strength to resist.''

"You weren't in love with them,'' he pointed out calmly.

"I'm not in love with you.'' Her voice had a desperate edge to it, and she had the sinking feeling that they both knew she was lying.

He knew, but it still hurt. The hurt settled into a dull, grinding ache in his belly. Ignoring it, he finished off his chili. "You're crazy about me, O'Roarke. You're just too pigheaded to admit it.''

"I'm pigheaded?'' Stifling a scream, she crushed out the cigarette. "I'm amazed that even you have the nerve to toss that one out. You haven't listened to a simple no since the day I met you.''

"You're right." His gaze skimmed down her. "And look where it's got me."

"Don't be so damn smug. I'm not going to marry you, because I don't want to get married, because you're a cop and because you're rich."

"You are going to marry me," he said, "because we both know you'd be miserable without me."

"Your arrogance is insufferable. It's just as irritating—and just as pathetic—as moon-eyed pleading."

"I'd rather be smug," he decided.

"You know, you're not the first jerk I've had to shake off." She snatched up her wine before she began to pace. "In my business, you get good at it." She whirled back, stabbing a finger at him. "You're almost as bad as this kid I had to deal with in Chicago. Up to now, he's taken the prize for arrogance. But even he didn't sit there with a stupid grin on his face. With him it was flowers and poetry. He was just as much of a mule, though. I was in love with him, too. But I wouldn't admit it. I needed him to take care of me, to protect me, to make my life complete." She spun in a quick circle. "What nerve! Before you, I thought he couldn't be topped. Hounding me at the station," she muttered. "Hounding me at the apartment. Sending me an engagement ring."

"He bought you a ring?"

She paused long enough for a warning look. "Don't get any ideas, Slick."

Boyd kept his voice very cool, very even. "You said he bought you a ring. A diamond?"

"I don't know." She dragged a hand through her hair. "I didn't have it appraised. I sent it back."

"What was his name?"

She waved a hand dismissively. "I don't know how I got off on this. The point I'm trying to make is—"

"I said, what was his name?"

He rose as he asked. Cilla took a confused step back. He wasn't just Boyd now. He was every inch a cop. "I— It was John something. McGill… No, McGillis, I think. Look, he was just a pest. I only brought it up because—"

"You didn't work with a John McGillis in Chicago."

"No." Annoyed with herself, she sat down again. "We're getting off the subject, Boyd."

"I told you to tell me about anyone you were involved with."

"I wasn't involved with him. He was just a kid. Star-struck or something. He listened to the show and got hung up. I made the mistake of being nice to him, and he misunderstood. Eventually I set him straight, and that was that."

"How long?" Boyd asked quietly. "Just how long did he bother you?"

She was feeling more foolish by the minute. She could barely remember the boy's face. "Three or four months, maybe."

"Three or four months," he repeated. Taking her by the arms, he lifted her to her feet. "He kept this up for three or four months and you didn't mention it to me?"

"I never thought of it."

He resisted the temptation to give her a good shake, barely. "I want you to tell me everything you remember about him. Everything he said, everything he did."

"I can't remember."

"You'd better." Releasing her, he stepped back. "Sit down."

She obeyed. He had shaken her more than he realized. She tried to comfort herself with the fact that they were no longer arguing about marriage. But he had reminded her of something she'd allowed herself to forget for hours.

"All right. He was a night stocker at a market, and he listened to the show. He'd call in on his break, and we'd talk a little. I'd play his requests. One day I did a remote—I can't remember where—and he showed up. He seemed like a nice kid. Twenty-three or four, I guess. Pretty," she remembered. "He had a pretty, sort of harmless face. I gave him an autograph. After that he started to write me at the station. Send poems. Just sweet, romantic stuff. Nothing suggestive."

"Go on."

"Boyd, really—"

"Go on."

The best she could do was a muttered oath. "When I realized he was getting in too deep, I pulled back. He asked me out, and I told him no." Embarrassed, she blew out a breath. "A couple of times he was waiting out in the parking lot when I got off my shift. He never touched me. I wasn't afraid of him. He was so pathetic that I felt sorry for him, and that was another mistake. He misunderstood. I guess he followed me home from work, because he started to show up at the apartment. He'd leave flowers and slip notes under the door. Kid stuff," she insisted.

"Did he ever try to get in?"

"He never tried to force his way in. I told you he was harmless."

"Tell me more."

She rubbed her hands over her face. "He'd just beg. He said he loved me, that he would always love me and we were meant to be together. And that he knew I loved him, too. It got worse. He would start crying when he called. He talked about killing himself if I didn't marry him. I got the package with the ring, and I sent it back with a letter. I was cruel. I felt I had to be. I'd already accepted the job here in Denver. It was only a few weeks after the business with the ring that we moved."

"Has he contacted you since you've been in Denver?"

"No. And it's not him who's calling. I know I'd recognize his voice. Besides, he never threatened me. Never. He was obsessed, but he wasn't violent."

"I'm going to check it out." He rose, then held out a hand. "You'd better get some sleep. We're going to head back early."

She didn't sleep. Neither did he. And they lay in the dark, in silence; there was another who kept vigil through the night.

He lit the candles. New ones he'd just bought that afternoon. Their wicks were as white as the moon. They darkened and flared as he set the match against them. He lay back on the bed with the picture pressed against his naked breast—against the twin blades of the tattooed knives.

Though the hour grew late, he remained alert. Anger fueled him. Anger and hate. Beside him the radio hummed, but it wasn't Cilla's voice he heard.

She had gone away. He knew she was with that man,

and she would have given herself to that man. She'd had no right to go. She belonged to John. To John, and to him.

She was beautiful, just as John had described her. She had deceptively kind eyes. But he knew better. She was cruel. Evil. And she deserved to die. Almost lovingly, he reached down a hand to the knife that lay beside him.

He could kill her the way he'd been taught. Quick and clean. But there was little satisfaction in that, he knew. He wanted her to suffer first. He wanted her to beg. As John had begged.

When she was dead, she would be with John. His brother would rest at last. And so would he.

Chapter 10

The heat was working overtime in the precinct, and so was Boyd. While Maintenance hammered away at the faulty furnace, he pored over his files. He'd long since forsaken his jacket. His shoulder holster was strapped over a Denver P.D. T-shirt that had seen too many washings. He'd propped open a window in the conference room so that the stiff breeze from outside fought with the heat still pouring through the vents.

Two of his ongoing cases were nearly wrapped, and he'd just gotten a break in an extortion scam he and Althea had been working on for weeks. There was a court appearance at the end of the week he had to prepare for. He had reports to file and calls to make, but his attention was focused on O'Roarke, Priscilla A.

Ignoring the sweat that dribbled down his back, he read over the file on Jim Jackson, KHIP's all-night man. It interested and annoyed him.

Cilla hadn't bothered to mention that she had worked with Jackson before, in Richmond. Or that Jackson had been fired for drinking on the job. Not only had he broadcast rambling streams of consciousness, but he had taken to nodding off at the mike and leaving his audience with that taboo of radio. Dead air.

He'd lost his wife, his home and his prime spot as the morning jock and program director on Richmond's number-two Top 40 station.

When he'd gotten the ax, Cilla had taken over his duties as program director. Within six months, the number-two station had been number one. And Jackson had been picked up for drunk and disorderly.

As Althea stepped into the conference room carrying two dripping cans of soda, Boyd tossed the Jackson file across the table. Saying nothing, she passed one can to Boyd, popped the top on the second, then glanced at the file.

"He's clean except for a couple of D and D's," Althea commented.

"Revenge is high on the list for this kind of harassment. Could be he's carrying a grudge because she replaced him in Richmond and outdid him." Boyd took a swig of the warming soda. "He's only had the night spot in Denver for three months. The station manager in Richmond claims Jackson got pretty bent when they let him go. Tossed around some threats, blamed Cilla for undermining his position. Plus, you add a serious drinking problem to the grudge."

"You want to bring him in?"

"Yeah. I want to bring him in."

"Okay. Why don't we make it a doubleheader?" She picked up the file on Nick Peters. "This guy looks harmless—but then I've dated harmless-looking guys before and barely escaped with my skin. He doesn't date at all." She shrugged out of her turquoise linen jacket and draped it carefully over her chair back. "It turns out that Deborah has a couple of classes with him. Over the weekend she mentioned that he pumps her for information on Cilla all the time. Personal stuff. What kind of flowers does she like? What's her favorite color? Is she seeing anyone?"

She reached in her skirt pocket and drew out a bag of jelly beans. Carefully, and after much thought, she selected a yellow one. "Apparently he got upset when Deborah mentioned that Cilla had been married before. Deborah didn't think much of it at the time—put it down to his being weird. But she was worried enough to mention it over the weekend. She's a nice kid," Althea put in. "Real sharp. She's totally devoted to Cilla." Althea hesitated. "Over the course of the weekend, she told me about their parents."

"We've already covered that ground."

"I know we did." Althea picked up a pencil, ran it through her fingers, then set it aside again. "Deborah seems to think you're good for her sister." She waited until Boyd looked up. "I just wonder if her sister's good for you."

"I can take care of myself, partner."

"You're too involved, Boyd." She lowered her voice, though it couldn't have carried over the noise outside of the closed door. "If the captain knew you were hung up, personally, with an assignment, he'd yank you. He'd be right."

Boyd kicked back in his chair. He studied Althea's face, a face he knew as well as his own. Resentment simmered in him, but he controlled it. "I can still do my job, Thea. If I had any doubts about that, I'd yank myself."

"Would you?"

His eyes narrowed. "Yeah, I would. My first priority is my assignment's safety. If you want to go to the captain, that's your right. But I'm going to take care of Cilla, one way or the other."

"You're the one who's going to get hurt," she murmured. "One way or the other."

"My life. My problem."

The anger she'd hoped to control bubbled to the surface. "Damn it, Boyd, I care about you. It was one thing when you were infatuated by her voice. I didn't even see it as a problem when you met her and had a few sparks flying. But now you're talking serious stuff like marriage, and I know you mean it. She's got trouble, Boyd. She *is* trouble."

"You and I are assigned to take care of the trouble she's got. As for the rest, it's my business, Thea, so save the advice."

"Fine." Irked, she flipped open another file. "Bob Williams—Wild Bob—is so clean he squeaks. I haven't turned up a single connection with Cilla other than the station. He has a good marriage, goes to church, belongs to the Jaycees and for the last two weeks has been accompanying his wife to Lamaze classes."

"Nothing's turned up on the morning guys." Boyd took another swallow of the soda and wished it was an ice-cold beer.

"KHIP's just one big happy family."

"So it seems," Boyd mumbled. "Harrison looks

solid, but I'm still checking. He's the one who hired her, and he actively pursued her, offering her a hefty raise and some tidy benefits to persuade her to move to Denver and KHIP.''

Althea meticulously chose a red jelly bean. ''What about the McGillis guy?''

''I'm expecting a call from Chicago.'' He opened another file. ''There's the maintenance man. Billy Lomus. War veteran—Purple Heart and a Silver Star in Nam. Did two tours of duty before the leg mustered him out. He seems to be a loner. Never stays in one place more than a year or so. He did drop down in Chicago for a while a couple years back. No family. No close friends. Settled in Denver about four months ago. Foster homes as a kid.''

Althea didn't look up. ''Rough.''

''Yeah.'' Boyd studied her bent head. There weren't many who knew that Althea Grayson had been shuffled from foster home to foster home as a child. ''It doesn't look like we're going to have much luck inside the station.''

''No. Maybe we'll do better with McGillis.'' She looked up, face calm, voice even. Only one who knew her well would have seen that she was still angry. ''You want to start with Jackson or Peters?''

''Jackson.''

''Okay. We'll try it the easy way first. I'll call and ask him to come in.''

''Thanks. Thea,'' he added before she could rise, ''you have to be hit before you can understand. I can't turn off my feelings, and I can't turn back from what I've been trained to do.''

She only sighed. ''Just watch your step, partner.''

He intended to. And while he was watching his step, he was going to watch Cilla's. She wouldn't care for that, Boyd thought as he continued to study the files. From the moment he had told her that he loved her she'd been trying to pull back.

But she wasn't afraid of him, he mused. She was afraid of herself. The deeper her feelings for him went, the more afraid she became to acknowledge them. Odd, but he hadn't known he would need the words. Yet he did. More than anything he could remember, he needed to have her look at him and tell him that she loved him.

A smile, a touch, a moan in the night—it wasn't enough. Not with Cilla. He needed the bond, and the promise, that verbal connection. Three words, he thought. A simple phrase that came easily, often too easily—and could change the structure of people's lives.

They wouldn't come easily to Cilla. If she ever pushed them through the self-doubts, the barrier of defense, the fear of being hurt, she would mean them with all of her heart. It was all he needed, Boyd decided. And he would never let her take them back.

For now he had to put aside his own wants and needs and be a cop. To keep her safe, he had to be what she feared most. For her sake, he couldn't afford to think too deeply about where their lives would go once he closed the files.

"Boyd?" Althea poked her head back in the door. "Jackson's on his way in."

"Good. We should be able to catch Peters before he checks in at the station. I want to—" He broke off when the phone rang beside him. "Fletcher." He held

up a hand to wave Althea inside. "Yeah. I appreciate
you checking into it for me." He muffled the phone
for a moment. "Chicago P.D. That's right," he continued into the receiver. "John McGillis." Taking up
a pencil, he began making notes on a legal pad. In
midstroke he stopped, fingers tightening. "When?"
His oath was strong and quiet. "Any family? He leave
a note? Can you fax it? Right." On the legal pad he
wrote in bold letters: Suicide.

In silence, Althea lowered a hip to the table.

"Anything you can get me. You're sure he didn't
have a brother? No. I appreciate it, Sergeant." He hung
up and tapped the pencil against the pad. "Son of a
bitch."

"We're sure it's the same McGillis?" Althea asked.

"Yeah. Cilla gave me the information she had on
him, plus a physical description. It's the same guy. He
cashed himself in almost five months ago." He let out
a long breath. "Slit his wrists with a hunting knife."

"It fits, Boyd." Althea leaned over to check his
notes. "You said McGillis was obsessing on Cilla, that
he'd threatened to kill himself if she didn't respond.
The guy over the phone is blaming her for the death
of his brother."

"McGillis didn't have a brother. Only child, sur-
vived by his mother."

"Brother could be an emotional term. A best
friend."

"Maybe." He knew it fitted. What worried him was
how Cilla would react. "The Chicago police are co-
operating. They're sending us what information
they've got. But I think it might be worth a trip east.
We might get a lead from the mother."

Althea nodded. "Are you going to tell Cilla?"

"Yeah, I'm going to tell her. We'll talk to Jackson and Peters first, see if we can make a connection to McGillis."

Across town, Cilla dashed from the shower to the phone. She wanted it to be Boyd. She wanted him to tell her that he'd found John McGillis happily stocking shelves in Chicago. With her hair dripping down her back, she snatched up the phone.

"Hello."

"Did you sleep with him? Did you let him touch you?"

Her damp hands shook as she gripped the receiver. "What do you want?"

"Did you make promises to him the way you made promises to my brother? Doe he know you're a whore and a murderer?"

"No. I'm not. I don't know why—"

"He'll have to die, too."

Her blood froze. The fear she thought she'd come to understand clawed viciously at her throat. "No! Boyd has nothing to do with this. It's—it's between you and me, just as you've said all along."

"He's involved now. He made his choice, like you made yours when you killed my brother. When I'm finished with him, I'm coming for you. Do you remember what I'm going to do to you? Do you remember?"

"You don't have to hurt Boyd. Please. Please, I'll do anything you want."

"Yes, you will." There was laughter, too, long, eerily lilting. "You'll do anything."

"Please. Don't hurt him." She continued to shout into the phone long after the connection went dead. With a sob tearing at her throat, she slammed the receiver down and raced to the bedroom to dress.

She had to talk to Boyd. To see him, face-to-face. To make certain he was unharmed. And to warn him, she thought frantically. She wouldn't, couldn't, lose someone else she loved.

With her hair still streaming wet, she dashed down the stairs and yanked open the door. She nearly ran over Nick Peters.

"Oh, God." Her hands clutched at her chest. "Nick."

"I'm sorry." With fumbling hands, he pushed up his glasses. "I didn't mean to scare you."

"I have to go." She was already digging in her purse for her keys. "He called. I have to get to Boyd. I have to warn him."

"Hold on." Nick picked up the keys, which she'd dropped on the stoop. "You're in no shape to drive."

"I've got to get to Boyd," she said desperately, gripping Nick by his coat. "He said he would kill him."

"You're all worked up about the cop." Nick's mouth thinned. "He looks like he can handle himself."

"You don't understand," she began.

"Yeah, I understand. I understand just fine. You went away with him." The note of accusation surprised her, and unnerved her enough that she glanced toward the black-and-white sitting at her curb. Then she shook herself. It was foolish, absolutely foolish, to be afraid of Nick.

"Nick, I'm sorry, but I don't have time to talk right now. Can we get into this later, at the station?"

"I quit." He bit off the words. "I quit this morning."

"Oh, but why? You're doing so well. You have a future at KHIP."

"You don't even know," he said bitterly. "And you don't care."

"But I do." When she reached out to touch his arm, he jerked back.

"You let me make a fool of myself over you."

Oh, God, not again. She shook her head. "Nick, no."

"You wouldn't even let me get close, and then he comes along and it's all over before you let it begin. Now they want me to come down to the police station. They want to question me." His lips trembled. "They think I'm the one who's been calling you."

"There has to be a mistake—"

"How could you?" he shouted. "How could you believe I'd want to hurt you?" He dropped the keys back into her hand. "I just came by to let you know I'd quit, so you don't have to worry about me bothering you again."

"Nick, please. Wait." But he was already striding off to his car. He didn't look back.

Because her knees were weak, Cilla lowered herself to the stoop. She needed a moment, she realized. A moment to steady herself before she got behind the wheel of a car.

How could she have been so stupid, so blind, that she couldn't see that Nick's pride and ego were on the line. Now she had hurt him, simply by being unaware.

Somehow she had to straighten out this mess her life had become. Then she had to start making amends.

Steadier, she rose, carefully locked the door, then walked to her car.

She hated police stations—had from the first. Fingering her plastic visitor's badge, she walked down the corridor. It had been scrubbed recently, and she caught the scent of pine cleaner over the ever-present aroma of coffee.

Phones rang. An incessant, strident, whirl of sound punctuated by voices raised to a shout or lowered to a grumble. Cilla turned into a doorway, to the heart of the noise, and scanned the room.

It was different from the cramped quarters where her mother had worked. And died. There was more space, less grime, and there was the addition of several computer work stations. The clickety-clack of keyboards was an underlying rhythm.

There were men and women, jackets off, shirts limp with sweat, though it was a windy fifty-five outside.

On a nearby bench, a woman rocked a fretful baby while a cop tried to distract it by jiggling a pair of handcuffs. Across the room, a young girl, surely just a teenager, related information to a trim woman cop in jeans and a sweatshirt. Silent tears coursed down the girl's face.

And Cilla remembered.

She remembered sitting in a corner of a squad room, smaller, hotter, dingier, than the one she stood in now. She had been five or six, and the baby-sitter had canceled because she'd been suffering from stomach flu. Cilla's mother had taken her to work—something about a report that couldn't wait to be written. So Cilla had sat in a corner with a doll and a Dr. Seuss book, listening to the phones and the voices. And waiting for her mother to take her home.

There had been a water cooler, she remembered. And a ceiling fan. She had watched the bubbles glug in the water and the blades whirl sluggishly. For hours. Her mother had forgotten her. Until, suffering from the same bug as her sitter, Cilla had lost her breakfast all over the squad room floor.

Shaky, Cilla wiped a hand over her damp brow. It was an old memory, she reminded herself. And not all of it. After she had been sick, her mother had cleaned her up, held her, taken her home and pampered her for the rest of the day. It wasn't fair to anyone to remember only the unhappy side.

But as she stood there she could feel all too clearly the dragging nausea, the cold sweat, and the misery of being alone and forgotten.

Then she saw him, stepping from another room. His T-shirt was damp down the front. Jackson was behind him, his hat in place, his face sheened with sweat and nerves. Flanking him was Althea.

Jackson saw her first. He took a hesitant step toward her, then stopped and shrugged. Cilla didn't hesitate. She walked to him to take his hand in both of hers.

"You okay?"

"Sure." Jackson shrugged again, but his fingers held tight on hers. "We just had to clear some things up. No big deal."

"I'm sorry. Look, if you need to talk, you can wait for me."

"No, I'm okay. Really." He lifted a hand to adjust

his cap. "I guess if you screw up once you've got to keep paying for it."

"Oh, Jim."

"Hey, I'm handling it." He gave her a quick smile. "I'll catch you tonight."

"Sure."

"We appreciate your cooperation, Mr. Jackson," Althea put in.

"I told you, anything I can do to help Cilla, I'll do. I owe you," he said to Cilla, cutting her off before she could shake her head. "I owe you," he repeated, then crossed the room into the corridor.

"I could have told you that you were wasting your time with him," Cilla stated.

Boyd only nodded. "You could have told us a lot of things."

"Maybe." She turned back to him. "I need to talk to you, both of you."

"All right." Boyd gestured toward the conference room. "It's a little quieter in here."

"You want something cold?" Althea began before they settled. "I think they've finally fixed the furnace, but it's still like an oven in here."

"No, thanks. This won't take long." She sat, Althea across from her, Boyd at the table's head. She wanted to choose her words carefully. "Can I ask why you brought Jackson in?"

"You worked together in Richmond." Boyd shoved a file aside. "He had a drinking problem that got him fired, and you took over his job. He wasn't too happy about it at the time."

"No, he wasn't."

"Why didn't you tell us about it, Cilla?"

"I didn't think of it." She lifted a hand. "I honestly didn't think of it. It was a long time ago, and Jackson's come a long way. I'm sure he told you he's been in AA for over three years. He made a point of coming to see me when I was doing my run in Chicago. He wanted me to know he didn't blame me for what had happened. He's been putting his life back together."

"You got him the job at KHIP," Boyd added.

"I put in a good word for him," she said. "I don't do the hiring. He was a friend, he needed a break. When he's sober, Jackson's one of the best. And he wouldn't hurt a fly."

"And when he's drunk he breaks up bars, threatens women and drives his car into telephone poles."

"That was a long time ago," Cilla said, struggling for calm. "And the point is, he is sober. There are some things you have to forgive and forget."

"Yes." He watched her carefully. "There are."

She thought of her mother again, and of that painful memory of the squad room. "Actually, I didn't come here to talk to you about Jackson. I got another call at home."

"We know." Althea's voice was brisk and professional. "They relayed the information to us here."

"Then you know what he said." Finding Althea's cool gaze unsympathetic, Cilla turned to Boyd. "He wants to hurt you now. He knows you're involved with me, and he's dragged you into whatever sick plans he has."

"They traced the call to another phone booth, just a couple of blocks from your house," Boyd began.

"Didn't you hear me?" Cilla slapped a fist on the

table. Pencils jumped. "He's going to try to kill you, too."

He didn't reach for her hand to soothe her. At the moment, he thought, she needed him more professionally than personally. "Since I'm protecting you, he would have had to try all along. Nothing's changed."

"Everything's changed," she burst out. "It doesn't matter to him if you're with the police or not, it only matters that you're with me. I want you off the case. I want you reassigned. I don't want you anywhere near me until this is over."

Boyd crushed a disposable cup in his hand and tossed it in a wastebasket. "Don't be ridiculous."

"I'm not being ridiculous. I'm being practical." She turned to Althea, her eyes full of pleas. "Talk to him. He'll listen to you."

"I'm sorry," she said after a moment. "I agree with him. We both have a job to do, and at the moment you're it."

Desperate, Cilla whipped back to Boyd. "I'll go to your captain myself."

"He already knows about the call."

She sprang up. "I'll tell him I'm sleeping with you."

"Sit down, Cilla."

"I'll insist he take you off the case."

"Sit down," Boyd repeated. His voice was still mild, but this time she relented and dropped back in her chair. "You can go to the captain and request another officer. You can demand one. It won't make any difference. If he takes me off the case, I'll just turn in my badge."

Her head snapped up at that. "I don't believe you."

"Try me."

He was too calm, Cilla realized. And too determined. Like a brick wall, she thought in despair. Going
head-to-head with him when he was like this was futile. "Boyd, don't you realize I couldn't handle it if
anything happened to you?"

"Yes," he said slowly. "I think I do. Then you
should realize I'm just as vulnerable where you're concerned."

"That's the whole point." She broke down enough
to take his hands. "You are vulnerable. Listen to me."
Desperate, she pulled his hand to her cheek. "For eight
years I've wondered if it had been anyone else in the
room with my mother that day, anyone else but my
father, would she have been sharper, would she have
been quicker. Would her concentration have been more
focused. Don't make me have to ask that same question about you for the rest of my life."

"Your mother wasn't prepared. I am."

"Nothing I say is going to change your mind."

"No. I love you, Cilla. One day soon you're going
to have to learn to accept that. In the meantime, you're
going to have to trust me."

She took her hand away to drop it into her lap.
"Then there's nothing more to say."

"There's this." He pulled a file closer. She was already upset, he mused. Already on edge. But they
couldn't afford to wait. "John McGillis."

Her head aching, Cilla pressed the heels of her hands
to her eyes. "What about him?"

"He's dead."

Slowly she lowered her hands. "Dead?" she repeated dully. "But he was just a kid. Are you sure? Are you sure it's the same one?"

"Yes." The man wished he could spare her this. The cop knew he couldn't. "He committed suicide about five months ago."

For a moment she only stared. The blood drained out of her face, inch by inch, until it was bone white. "Oh, God. Oh, dear God. He— He threatened, but I didn't believe—"

"He was unstable, Cilla. He'd been in and out of therapy since he was fourteen. Trouble with his mother, in school, with his contemporaries. He'd already attempted suicide twice before."

"But he was so quiet. He tried so hard to make me—" She stopped, squeezing her eyes shut. "He killed himself after I left Chicago to come here. Just as he said he would."

"He was disturbed," Althea said gently. "Deeply disturbed. A year before he contacted you he was involved with a girl. When she broke things off, he swallowed a fistful of barbiturates. He was in a clinic for a while. He'd only been out for a few weeks when he made the connection with you."

"I was cruel to him." Cilla turned her purse over and over on her lap. "Really cruel. At the time I thought it was the best way to handle it. I thought he would be hurt, maybe hate me for a little while, then find some nice girl and… But he won't."

"I'm not going to tell you it wasn't your fault, because you're smart enough to know that yourself." Boyd's voice was deliberately devoid of sympathy. "What McGillis did he did to himself. You were just an excuse."

She gave a quick, involuntary shudder. "It's not as easy for me. I don't live with death the way you do."

"It's never easy, not for anyone." He opened the file. "But there are priorities here, and mine is to make the connection between McGillis and the man we're after."

"You really think John's the reason I'm being threatened?"

"It's the only thing that fits. Now I want you to tell us everything you remember about him."

She released her death grip on the bag, then carefully folded her hands on the table. As clearly as possible, she repeated everything she'd already told him.

"Did you ever see him with anyone?" Boyd asked. "Did he ever talk about his friends, his family?"

"He was always alone. Like I told you, he used to call the station. I didn't meet him face-to-face for weeks. After I did, all he really talked about was the way he felt about me. The way he wanted us to be together." Her fingers twisted together. "He used to send me notes, and flowers. Little presents. It isn't that unusual for a fan to develop a kind of fantasy relationship with a jock. But then I began to see that it wasn't—" she cleared her throat "—it wasn't the normal kind of weird, if you know what I mean."

Boyd nodded and continued to write on the pad. "Go on."

"The notes became more personal. Not sexual so much as emotional. The only time he got out of hand was when he showed me his tattoo. He had these knives tattooed on his chest. It seemed so out of character for him, and I told him I thought it was foolish for him to mark up his body that way. We were out in the parking lot. I was tired and annoyed, and here was this kid pulling open his shirt to show me this stupid tattoo. He was upset that I didn't like it. Angry, really. It was the only time I saw him angry. He said that if it was good enough for his brother it was good enough for him.''

"His brother?'' Boyd repeated.

"That's right.''

"He didn't have a brother.''

She stopped twisting her fingers. "Yes, he did. He mentioned him a couple of times.''

"By name?''

"No.'' She hesitated, tried to think. "No,'' she repeated, more certain now. "He just mentioned that his brother was living out in California. He hadn't seen him for a couple of months. He wanted me to meet him. Stuff like that.''

"He didn't have a brother.'' Althea turned the file around to skim the top sheet again. "He was an only child.''

Cilla shook her head. "So he made it up.''

"No.'' Boyd sat back, studying his partner and Cilla in turn. "I don't think the man we're after is a figment of John McGillis's imagination.''

Chapter 11

Her head was pounding in a dull, steady rhythm that made her ears ring. It was too much to absorb all at once. The phone call, Nick's visit, the reminders at the station house. John McGillis's suicide.

For the first time in her life, Cilla was tempted to shut herself in her room, lock the door and escape into a drugged sleep. She wanted peace, a few hours of peace, without guilt, without dreams, without fears.

No, she realized. More than that, much more than that, she wanted control over her life again. She'd taken that control for granted once, but she would never do so again.

She could think of nothing to say to Boyd as he followed her into the house. She was much too tired to argue, particularly since she knew the argument would be futile on her side. He wouldn't take himself off the case. He wouldn't believe her when she told

him they could have no future. He refused to understand that in both instances she was looking out for his
best interests.

Going to the kitchen, she went directly to the cupboard above the sink. From a bottle she shook out three
extra-strength aspirin.

Boyd watched her fill a glass from the tap and swallow the pills. Her movements were automatic and just
a little jerky. As she rinsed the glass, she stared out
the window at the backyard.

There were daffodils, their yellow blooms still se-
creted in the protective green. Along the low fence they
sprang up like slender spears, promising spring. She
hadn't known they were there when she'd bought the
house.

She wished they were blooming now so that she
could see those cheerful yellow trumpets waving in the
breeze. How bad could life be if you could look
through your own window and see flowers blooming?

"Have you eaten?" he asked her.

"I don't remember." She folded her arms and
looked out at the trees. There was the faintest hint of
green along the branches. You had to look hard to see
it. She wondered how long it would take for the leaves
to unfurl and make shade. "But I'm not hungry.
There's probably something around if you are."

"How about a nap?" He brought his hands to her
shoulders and massaged them gently.

"I couldn't sleep yet." On a quiet sigh, she lifted a
hand up to lay it over his. "In a few weeks I'll have
to cut the grass. I think I'll like that. I've never had a
lawn to mow before."

"Can I come over and watch?"

She smiled, as he'd wanted her to. "I love it here," she murmured. "Not just the house, though it means a lot to stand here, just here, and look out at something that belongs to me. It's this place. I haven't really felt at home anywhere since I left Georgia. It wasn't even something I realized until I came here and felt at home again."

"Sometimes you find what you want without looking."

He was talking of love, she knew. But she was afraid to speak of it.

"Some days the sky is so blue that it hurts your eyes. If you're downtown on one of those days when the wind has swept through and cleared everything, the buildings look painted against the sky. And you can see the mountains. You can stand on the corner in the middle of rush hour and see the mountains. I want to belong here."

He turned her to him. "You do."

"I never really believed that things could last. But I was beginning to, before this. I'm not sure I can belong here, or anywhere, until I can stop being afraid. Boyd." She lifted her hands to his face. Intense, she studied him, as if to memorize every plane, every angle. "I'm not just talking about belonging to a place, but to a person. I care for you more than I've cared for anyone in my life but Deborah. And I know that's not enough."

"You're wrong." He touched his lips to hers. "It's exactly enough."

She gave him a quick, frustrated shake of her head. "You just won't listen."

"Wrong again. I listen, Cilla. I just don't always agree with what you say."

"You don't have to agree, you just have to accept."

"Tell you what—when this is over, you and I will have a nice, long talk about what we both have to accept."

"When this is over, you might be dead." On impulse, she gripped him harder. "Do you really want to marry me?"

"You know I do."

"If I said I'd marry you, would you take yourself off the case? Would you let someone else take over and go up to your cabin until it's done?"

He struggled against a bitter anger. "You should know better than to try to bribe a public servant."

"I'm not joking."

"No." His eyes hardened. "I wish you were."

"I'll marry you, and I'll do my best to make you happy if you do this one thing for me."

He set her aside and stepped back. "No deal, O'Roarke."

"Damn it, Boyd."

He jammed his hands into his pockets before he exploded. "Do you think this is some kind of trade-off? What you want for what I want? Damn you, we're talking about marriage. It's an emotional commitment and a legal contract, not a bartering tool. What's next?" he demanded. "I give up my job and you agree to have my child?"

Shock and shame robbed her of speech. She held up both hands, palms out. "I'm sorry. I'm sorry," she managed. "I didn't mean for it to sound like that. I just keep thinking of what he said today. How he said it. And I can imagine what it would be like if you weren't here." She shut her eyes. "It would be worse than dying."

"I am here." He reached for her again. "And I'm going to stay here. Nothing's going to happen to either of us."

She pulled him close, pressed her face to his throat. "Don't be angry. I just haven't got a good fight in me right now."

He relented and lifted a hand to her hair. "We'll save it for later, then."

She didn't want to think about later. Only now. "Come upstairs," she whispered. "Make love with me."

Hand in hand they walked through the empty house, up the stairs. In the bedroom she closed the door, then locked it. The gesture was a symbol of her need to lock out everything but him for this one moment in time.

The sun came strong through the windows, but she felt no need for dim lights or shadows. There would be no secrets between them here. With her eyes on his, she began to unbutton her shirt.

Only days before, she thought, she would have been afraid of this. Afraid she would make the wrong move, say the wrong word, offer too much, or not enough. He had already shown her that she had only to hold out a hand and be willing to share.

They undressed in silence, not yet touching. Did he sense her mood? she wondered. Or did she sense his? All she knew was that she wanted to look, to absorb the sight of him.

There was the way the light streamed through the

window and over his hair—the way his eyes darkened as they skimmed over her. She wanted to savor the line of his body, the ridges of muscle, the smooth, taut skin.

Could she have any idea how exciting she was? he wondered. Standing in the center of the room, her clothes pooled at her feet, her skin already flushed with anticipation, her eyes clouded and aware?

He waited. Though he wanted to touch her so badly his fingers felt singed, he waited.

She came to him, her arms lifted, her lips parted. Slim, soft, seductive, she pressed against him. Still, he waited. His name was a quiet sigh as she brought her mouth to his.

Home. The thought stirred inside her, a trembling wish. He was home to her. The strength of his arms, the tenderness of his hands, the unstinting generosity of his heart. Tears burned the backs of her lids as she lost herself in the kiss.

He felt the change, the slow and subtle yielding. It aroused unbearably. Strong, she was like a flame, smoldering and snapping with life and passion. In surrender, she was like a drug that seeped silently into his blood.

Lured by, lost in, her total submission, he lowered her to the bed. Her body was his. And so for the first time, he felt, was her mind, and her heart. He was careful to treat each gently.

So sweet, she thought dreamily. So lovely. The patient stroke of his fingers, the featherbrush of his lips, turned the bright afternoon into the rich secrets of midnight. Now that she knew where he could take her, she craved the journey all the more.

No dark thoughts. No nagging fears. Like flowers on the verge of blooming, she wanted to celebrate life, the simplicity of being alive and capable of love.

He aroused her thoroughly, thoughtfully, torturously. Her answering touch and her answering kiss were just as generous. What she murmured to him were not demands, but promises she desperately wanted to keep.

They knelt together in the center of the bed, lips curved as they touched, bodies almost painfully in tune. Her hair flowed through his fingers. His skin quivered at her light caress.

Soft, quiet sighs.

Heart-to-heart, they lowered again. Mouth teased mouth. Their eyes were open when he slid into her. Joined, they held close, absorbing a fresh riot of sensation. When they moved, they moved together, with equal wonder.

The booth seemed like another world. Cilla sat at the console, studying the controls she knew so well. Both her mind and body were sluggish. The clearsighted control she had felt for a short time with Boyd that afternoon had vanished. She wanted only for the night to be over.

He had mentioned going to Chicago the next day. She intended to encourage him. If she couldn't convince him to be reassigned, at least she would have the satisfaction of knowing he would be miles away for a day or two. Away from her, and safe, she thought.

He, whoever he was, was closing in. She could feel it. When he struck, she wanted Boyd far away.

If this man was determined to punish her for what

had happened to John McGillis, she would deal with it. Boyd had been right, to a point. She didn't blame herself for John's suicide. But she did share in the responsibility. And she couldn't keep herself from grieving for a young, wasted life.

The police would protect her, she thought as she cued up the next song. And she would protect herself. The new fear, the grinding fear, came from the fact that she didn't know how to protect Boyd.

"You're asleep at the switch," Boyd commented.

She shook herself. "No, just resting between bouts." She glanced at the clock. It was nearly midnight. Nearly time for the request line.

Once again the station was locked. There was only the two of them.

"You're nearly halfway home," he pointed out. "Look, why don't you come back to my place tonight? We can listen to my Muddy Waters records."

She decided to play dumb, because she knew it amused him. "Who?"

"Come on, O'Roarke."

It helped, a great deal, to see him grin at her. It made everything seem almost normal. "Okay, I'll listen to Muddy Whatsis—"

"Waters."

"Right—if you can answer these three music trivia questions."

"Shoot."

"Hold on." She set the next record, did a quick intro. She ruffled through her papers. "Okay, you've got three-ten to come up with them. Number one, what was the first British rock group to tour the States?"

"Ah, a trick question. The Dave Clark Five. The Beatles were the second."

"Not bad for an amateur. Number two. Who was the last performer at Woodstock."

"Jimi Hendrix. You'll have to do better, O'Roarke."

"I'm just lulling you into complacency. Number three, and this is the big one, Fletcher. What year was Buddy Holly and the Crickets' hit 'That'll Be the Day' released?"

"Going back a ways, aren't you?"

"Just answer the question, Slick."

"Fifty-six."

"Is that 1956?"

"Yeah, that's 1956."

"Too bad. It was 57. You lose."

"I want to look it up."

"Go ahead. Now you'll have to come back to my place and listen to a Rolling Stones retrospective." She yawned hugely.

"If you stay awake that long." It pleased him that she had taken a moment out to play. "Want some coffee?"

She shot him a grateful look. "Only as much as I want to breathe."

"I'll get it."

The station was empty, he thought. Since Nick Peters had gotten his ego bruised and quit, there had been no one around to brew that last pot of the evening. He, too, glanced at the clock. He wanted to have it done and be back beside her before the phones started to ring.

He'd grab her a doughnut while he was at it, Boyd

decided as he checked the corridor automatically. A little sugar would help her get through the night.

Before going to the lounge, he moved to the front of the building to check the doors. The locks were in place, and the alarm was engaged. His car was alone on the lot. Satisfied, he walked through the building and gave the same careful check to the rear delivery doors before he turned into the lounge.

It wasn't going to go on much longer. With the McGillis lead, Boyd had every confidence they would tie someone to the threats in a matter of days. It would be good to see Cilla without those traces of fear in her eyes, that tension in the set of her shoulders.

The restlessness would remain, he thought. And the energy. They were as much a part of her as the color of her hair.

He added an extra scoop of coffee to the pot and listened to her voice over the speaker as she segued from one record to the next.

That magic voice, he thought. He'd had no idea when he first heard it, when he was first affected by it, that he would fall in love with the woman behind it.

It was Joan Jett now, blasting out "I Love Rock and Roll." Though the lounge speaker was turned down to little more than a murmur, the feeling gritted out. It should be Cilla's theme song, he mused. Though he'd learned in their two days in his cabin that she was just as easily fascinated by the likes of Patsy Cline or Ella Fitzgerald.

What they needed was a good solid week in the mountains, he decided. Without any outside tensions to interfere.

He took an appreciative sniff of the coffee as it began to brew and hoped that he could get to Chicago, find the answers he needed and make the trip back quickly.

He whirled, disturbed by some slight sound in the corridor. A rustle. A creak of a board. His hand was already on the butt of his weapon. Drawing it, turning his back to the side wall, he took three careful strides to the doorway, scanning.

Getting jumpy, he told himself when he saw nothing but the empty halls and the glare of security lights. But instinct had him keeping the gun in his hand. He'd taken the next step when the lights went out.

Cursing under his breath, he moved fast. Though he held his weapon up for safety, he was prepared to use it. Above, from the speakers, the passionate music continued to throb. Up ahead he could see the faint glow of lights from the booth. She was there, he told himself. Safe in those lights. Keeping his back to the wall, skimming his gaze up and down the darkened hallway, he moved toward her.

As he rounded the last turn in the hallway before the booth, he heard something behind him. He saw the storeroom door swing open as he whirled. But he never saw the knife.

"That was Joan Jett and the Blackhearts coming at you. It's 11:50, Denver and a balmy forty-two degrees." Cilla frowned at the clock and wondered why Boyd was taking so long. "A little reminder that you can catch KHIP's own Wild Bob tomorrow at the Brown Palace Hotel downtown on 17th. And hey, if you've never been there, it's a very classy place. Tickets are still available for the banquet benefiting abused children. So open your wallets. It's twenty dollars stag, forty if you take your sweetie. The festivities start at seven o'clock, and Wild Bob will be spinning those discs for you.'' She potted up the next song. ''Now get ready for a doubleheader to take you to midnight. This is Cilla O'Roarke. We've got the news, then the request line, coming up.''

She switched off her mike. Shrugging her shoulders to loosen them, she slipped off the headphones. She was humming to herself as she checked the program director's hot clock. A canned ad was next, then she'd *seg* into the news at the top of the hour. She pushed away from the console to set up for the next segment.

It was then that she saw that the corridor beyond the glass door was dark. At first she only stared, baffled. Then the blood rushed to her head. If the security lights were out, the alarm might be out, as well.

He was here. Sweat pearled cold on her brow as she gripped the back of her chair. There would be no call tonight, because he was here. He was coming for her.

A scream rose in her throat to drown in a flood of panic.

Boyd. He had also come for Boyd.

Propelled by a new terror, she hit the door at a run. ''Boyd!'' She shouted for him, stumbling in the dark. Her forward motion stopped when she saw the shadow move toward her. Though it was only a shape, formless in the darkened corridor, she knew. Groping behind her, she stepped back. ''Where's Boyd? What have you done with him?'' She stepped back again. The lights from the booth slanted through the glass and split the dark in two.

She started to speak again, to beg, then nearly fainted with relief. "Oh, God, it's you. I didn't know you were here. I thought everyone had left."

"Everyone's gone," he answered. He moved fully into the light. And smiled. Cilla's relief iced over. He held a knife, a long-bladed hunting knife already stained with blood.

"Boyd," she said again.

"He can't help you now. No one can. We're all alone. I've waited a long time for us to be alone."

"Why?" She was beyond fear now. It was Boyd's blood on the blade, and grief left no room for fear. "Why, Billy?"

"You killed my brother."

"No. No, I didn't." She stepped back, into the booth. Hot hysteria bubbled in her throat. A cold chill sheened her skin. "I didn't kill John. I hardly knew him."

"He loved you." He limped forward, the knife in front of him, his eyes on hers. His feet were bare. He wore only camouflage pants and dark stocking cap pulled low over his graying hair and brows. Though he had smeared his face and chest and arms with black, she could see the tattoo over his heart. The twin to the one she had seen over John McGillis's.

"You were going to marry him. He told me."

"He misunderstood." She let out a quick gasp as he jabbed with the knife. Her chair toppled with a crash as she fell back against the console.

"Don't lie to me, you bitch. He told me everything, how you told him you loved him and wanted him." His voice lowered, wavered, whispered, like the voice over the phone, and had her numbed heart racing.

"How you seduced him. He was so young. He didn't understand about women like you. But I do. I would have protected him. I always protected him. He was good." Billy wiped his eyes with the hand holding the knife, then drew a gun out of his pocket. "Too good for you." He fired, ramming a bullet into the board above the controls. Cilla pressed both hands to her mouth to hold back a scream. "He told me how you lied, how you cheated, how you flaunted yourself."

"I never wanted to hurt John." She had to stay calm. Boyd wasn't dead. She wouldn't believe he was dead. But he was hurt. Somehow she had to get help. Bracing herself on the console, she reached slowly behind her and opened her mike, all the while keeping her eyes on his face. "I swear, Billy, I never wanted to hurt your brother."

"Liar," he shouted, lifting the knife to her throat. She arched back, struggling to control her shuddering. "You don't care about him. You never cared. You just used him. Women like you love to use."

"I liked him." She sucked in her breath as the knife nicked her throat. Blood trickled warm along her skin. "He was a nice boy. He—he loved you."

"I loved him." The knife trembled in his hand, but he pulled it back an inch. Cilla let out a long, quiet breath. "He was the only person I ever loved, who ever loved me. I took care of him."

"I know." She moistened her dry lips. Surely someone would come. Someone was listening. She didn't dare take her eyes from his to glance around to the phone, where the lights were blinking madly.

"He was only five when they sent me to that house. I would have hated it there, like I'd hated all the other places they'd sent me. But John lived there. He looked up to me. He cared. He needed me. So I stayed until I was eighteen. It was only a year and a half, but we were brothers.''

''Yes.''

''I joined the Army. When I'd have leave he'd sneak out to see me. His pig of a mother didn't want him to have anything to do with me, 'cause I'd gotten in some trouble.'' He fired again, randomly, and shattered the glass in the top of the door. ''But I liked the army. I liked it fine, and John liked my uniform.''

His eyes glazed over a moment, as he remembered. ''They sent us to Nam. Messed up my leg. Messed up my life. When we came back, people wanted to hate us. But not John. He was proud of me. No one else had ever been proud of me.''

''I know.''

''They tried to put him away. Twice.'' Again he squeezed the trigger. A bullet plowed into the reel-to-reel six inches from Cilla's head. Sweaty fear dried to ice on her skin. ''They didn't understand him. I went to California. I was going to find us a nice place there. I just needed to find work. John was going to write poetry. Then he met you.'' The glaze melted away from his eyes, burned away by hate. ''He didn't want to come to California anymore. He didn't want to leave you. He wrote me letters about you, long letters. Once he called. He shouldn't have spent his money, but he called all the way to California to tell me he was getting married. You wanted to get married at Christmas, so he was going to wait. I was coming back for it, because he wanted me there.''

She could only shake her head. ''I never agreed to

marry him. Killing me isn't going to change that," she said when he leveled the gun at her. "You're right, he didn't understand me. And I guess I didn't understand him. He was young. He imagined I was something I wasn't, Billy. I'm sorry, terribly sorry, but I didn't cause his death."

"You killed him." He ran the flat of the blade down her cheek. "And you're going to pay."

"I can't stop you. I won't even try. But please, tell me what you've done with Boyd."

"I killed him." He smiled a sweet, vacant smile that made the weapons he carried incongruous.

"I don't believe you."

"He's dead." Still smiling, he held the knife up to the light. "It was easy. Easier than I remembered. I was quick," he assured her. "I wanted him dead, but I didn't care if he suffered. Not like you. You're going to suffer. I told you, remember? I told you what I was going to do."

"If you've killed Boyd," she whispered, "you've already killed me."

"I want you to beg." He laid the knife against her throat again. "I want you to beg the way John begged."

"I don't care what you do to me." She couldn't feel the knife against her flesh. She couldn't feel anything. From a long way off came the wail of sirens. She heard them without emotion, without hope. They were coming, but they were coming too late. She looked into Billy's eyes. She understood that kind of pain, she realized. It came when the person who meant the most was taken from you.

"I'm sorry," she said, prepared to die. "I didn't love him."

On a howl of rage, he struck her a stunning blow against the temple with the knife handle. He had planned and waited for weeks. He wouldn't kill her quickly, mercifully. He wouldn't. He wanted her on her knees, crying and screaming for her life.

She landed in a heap, driven down by the explosive pain. She would have wept then, with her hands covering her face and her body limp. Not for herself, but for what she had lost.

They both turned as Boyd staggered to the doorway.

Seconds. It took only seconds. Her vision cleared, her heart almost burst. Alive. He was alive.

Her sob of relief turned to a scream of terror as she saw Billy raise the gun. Then she was on her feet, struggling with him. Records crashed to the floor and were crushed underfoot as they rammed into a shelf. His eyes burned into hers. She did beg. She pleaded even as she fought him.

Boyd dropped to his knees. The gun nearly slipped out of his slickened fingers. Through a pale red mist he could see them. He tried to shout at her, but he couldn't drag his voice through his throat. He could only pray as he struggled to maintain a grip on consciousness and the gun. He saw the knife come up, start its vicious downward sweep. He fired.

She didn't hear the crashing glass or the clamor of feet. She didn't even hear the report as the bullet struck home. But she felt the jerk of his body as the knife flew out of his hand. She lost her grip on him as he slammed back into the console.

Wild-eyed, she whirled. She saw Boyd swaying on

his knees, the gun held in both hands. Behind him was
Althea, her weapon still trained on the figure sprawled
on the floor. On a strangled cry, Cilla rushed over as
Boyd fell.

"No." She was weeping as she brushed the hair
from his eyes, as she ran a hand down his side and felt
the blood. "Please, no." She covered his body with
hers.

"You've got to move back." Althea bit down on
panic as she urged Cilla aside.

"He's bleeding."

"I know." And badly, she thought. Very badly.
"There's an ambulance coming."

Cilla stripped off her shirt to make a pressure bandage. Kneeling in her chemise, she bent over Boyd.
"I'm not going to let him die."

Althea's eyes met hers. "That makes two of us."

Chapter 12

There had been a sea of faces. They seemed to swim inside Cilla's head as she paced the hospital waiting room. It was so quiet there, quiet enough to hear the swish of crepe-soled shoes on tile or the whoosh of the elevator doors opening, closing. Yet in her head she could still hear the chaos of sirens, voices, the crackle of static on the police cruisers that had nosed together in the station's parking lot.

The paramedics had come. Hands had pulled her away from Boyd, pulled her out of the booth and into the cool, fresh night.

Mark, she remembered. It was Mark who had held her back as she'd run the gamut from hysteria to shock. Jackson had been there, steady as a rock, pushing a cup of some hot liquid into her hand. And Nick, white-faced, mumbling assurances and apologies.

There had been strangers, dozens of them, who had

heard the confrontation over their radios. They had crowded in until the uniformed police set up a barricade.

Then Deborah had been there, racing across the lot in tears, shoving aside cops, reporters, gawkers, to get to her sister. It was Deborah who had discovered that some of the blood on Cilla was her own.

Now, dully, Cilla looked down at her bandaged hand. She hadn't felt the knife slice into it during the few frantic seconds she had fought with Billy. The scratch along her throat where the blade had nicked her was more painful. Shallow wounds, she thought. They were only shallow wounds, nothing compared to the deep gash in her heart.

She could still see how Boyd had looked when they had wheeled him out to the ambulance. For one horrible moment, she'd been afraid he was dead. So white, so still.

But he was alive. Althea had told her. He'd lost a lot of blood, but he was alive.

Now he was in surgery, fighting to stay that way. And she could only wait.

Althea watched her pace. For herself, she preferred to sit, to gather her resources and hold steady. She had her own visions to contend with. The jolt when Cilla's voice had broken into the music. The race from the precinct to the radio station. The sight of her partner kneeling on the floor, struggling to hold his weapon. He had fired only an instant before her.

She'd been too late. She would have to live with that.

Now her partner, her friend, her family, was lying on an operating table. And she was helpless.

Rising, Deborah walked across the room to put an arm around her sister. Cilla stopped pacing long enough to stare out the window.

"Why don't you lie down?" Deborah suggested.

"No, I can't."

"You don't have to sleep. You could just stretch out on the couch over there."

Cilla shook her head. "So many things are going through my mind, you know? The way he'd just sit there and grin after he'd gotten me mad. How he'd settle down in the corner of the booth with a book. The calm way he'd boss me around. I spent most of my time trying to push him away, but I didn't push hard enough. And now he's—"

"You can't blame yourself for this."

"I don't know who to blame." She looked up at the clock. How could the minutes go by so slowly? "I can't really think about that now. The cause isn't nearly as important as the effect."

"He wouldn't want you to take this on, Cilla."

She nearly smiled. "I haven't made a habit of doing what he wanted. He saved my life, Deb. How can I stand it if the price of that is his?"

There seemed to be no comfort she could offer. "If you won't lie down, how about some coffee?"

"Sure. Thanks."

She crossed to a pot of stale coffee resting on a hot plate. When Althea joined her, Deborah poured a second cup.

"How's she holding up?" Althea asked.

"By a thread." Deborah rubbed her gritty eyes before she turned to Althea. "She's blaming herself."

Studying Althea, she offered the coffee. "Do you blame her, too?"

She hesitated, bringing the coffee to her lips first. She'd long since stopped tasting it. She looked over to the woman still standing by the window. Cilla wore baggy jeans and Mark Harrison's tailored jacket. She wanted to blame Cilla, she realized. She wanted to blame her for involving Boyd past the point of wisdom. She wanted to blame her for being the catalyst that had set an already disturbed mind on the bloody path of revenge.

But she couldn't. Neither as a cop nor as a woman.

"No," she said with a sigh. "I don't blame her. She's only one of the victims here."

"Maybe you could tell her that." Deborah passed the second cup to Althea. "Maybe that's what she needs to hear."

It wasn't easy to approach Cilla. They hadn't spoken since they had come to the waiting room. In some strange way, Althea realized, they were rivals. They both loved the same man. In different ways, perhaps, and certainly on different levels, but the emotions were deep on both sides. It occurred to her that if there had been no emotion on Cilla's part there would have been no resentment on hers. If she had remained an assignment, and only an assignment, Althea would never have felt the need to cast blame.

It seemed Boyd had not been the only one to lose his objectivity.

She stopped beside Cilla, stared at the same view of the dark studded with city lights. "Coffee?"

"Thanks." Cilla accepted the cup but didn't drink. "They're taking a long time."

"It shouldn't be much longer."

Cilla drew in a breath and her courage. "You saw the wound. Do you think he'll make it?"

I don't know. She almost said it. They both knew she'd thought it. "I'm counting on it."

"You told me once he was a good man. You were right. For a long time I was afraid to see that, but you were right." She turned to face Althea directly. "I don't expect you to believe me, but I would have done anything to keep him from being hurt."

"I do believe you. And you did what you could." Before Cilla could turn away again, Althea put a hand on her arm. "Opening your mike may have saved his life. I want you to think about that. With a wound as serious as Boyd's, every second counted. With the broadcast, you gave us a fix on the situation, so there was an ambulance on the scene almost as quickly as we were. If Boyd makes it, it's partially due to your presence of mind. I want you to think about that."

"Billy only went after him because of me. I have to think about that, as well."

"You're trying to logic out an irrational situation. It won't work." The sympathy vanished from her voice. "If you want to start passing out blame, how about John McGillis? It was his fantasy that lit the fuse. How about the system that allowed someone like Billy Lomus to bounce from foster home to foster home so that he never knew what it was like to feel loved or wanted by anyone but a young, troubled boy? You could blame Mark for not checking Billy's references closely enough. Or Boyd and me for not making the connection quicker. There's plenty of blame to pass around,

Cilla. We're all just going to have to live with our share.''

"It doesn't really matter, does it? No matter who's at fault, it's still Boyd's life on the line.''

"Detective Grayson?''

Althea snapped to attention. The doctor who entered was still in surgical greens damped down the front with sweat. She tried to judge his eyes first. They were a clear and quiet gray and told her nothing.

"I'm Grayson.''

His brow lifted slightly. It wasn't often you met a police detective who looked as though she belonged on the cover of *Vogue*. "Dr. Winthrop, chief of surgery.''

"You operated on Boyd, Boyd Fletcher?''

"That's right. He's your partner?''

"Yes.'' Without conscious thought on either side, Althea and Cilla clasped hands. "Can you tell us how he is?''

"I can tell you he's a lucky man,'' Winthrop said. "If the knife had gone a few inches either way, he wouldn't have had a chance. As it is, he's still critical, but the prognosis is good.''

"He's alive.'' Cilla finally managed to force the words out.

"Yes.'' Winthrop turned to her. "I'm sorry, are you a relative?''

"No, I… No.''

"Miss O'Roarke is the first person Boyd will want to see when he wakes up.'' Althea gave Cilla's hand a quick squeeze. "His family's been notified, but they were in Europe and won't be here for several hours yet.''

"I see. He'll be done in Recovery shortly. Then we'll transfer him to ICU. O'Roarke," he said suddenly. "Of course. My son's a big fan." He lifted her bandaged hand gently. "I've already heard the story. If you were my patient, you'd be sedated and in bed."

"I'm fine."

Frowning, he studied her pupils. "To put it in unprofessional terms, not by a long shot." His gaze skimmed down the long scratch on her throat. "You've had a bad shock, Miss O'Roarke. Is there someone who can drive you home?"

"I'm not going home until I see Boyd."

"Five minutes, once he's settled in ICU. Only five. I can guarantee he won't be awake for at least eight hours."

"Thank you." If he thought she would settle for five minutes, he was very much mistaken.

"Someone will come by to let you know when you can go down." He walked out rubbing the small of his back and thinking about a hot meal.

"I need to call the captain." It infuriated Althea that she was close to tears. "I'd appreciate it if you'd come back for me after you've seen him. I'd like a moment with him myself."

"Yes, of course. Thea." Letting her emotions rule, Cilla wrapped her arms around Althea. The tears didn't seem to matter. Nor did pride. They clung together and held on to hope. They didn't speak. They didn't have to. When they separated, Althea walked away to call her captain. Cilla turned blindly to the window.

"He's going to be okay," Deborah murmured beside her.

"I know." She closed her eyes. She did know. The

dull edge of fear was gone. "I just need to see him, Deb. I need to see him for myself."

"Have you told him you love him?"

She shook her head.

"Now might be a good time."

"I was afraid I wouldn't get the chance, and now…I don't know."

"Only a fool would turn her back on something so special."

"Or a coward." Cilla pressed her fingers to her lips. "Tonight, all night, I've been half out of my mind thinking he might die. Line of duty." She turned to face her sister. "In the line of duty, Deborah. If I let myself go, if I don't turn my back, how many other times might I stand here wondering if he'll live or die?"

"Cilla—"

"Or open the door one day and have his captain standing there, waiting to tell me that he was already gone, the way Mom's captain came to the door that day."

"You can't live your life waiting for the worst, Cilla. You have to live it hoping for the best."

"I'm not sure I can." Weary, she dragged her hands through her hair. "I'm not sure of anything right now except that he's alive."

"Miss O'Roarke?" Both Cilla and Deborah turned toward the nurse. "Dr. Winthrop said to bring you to ICU."

"Thank you."

Her heart hammered in her ears as she followed the nurse toward the corridor. Her mouth was dry, and her palms were damp. She tried to ignore the machines and monitors as they passed through the double doors into Intensive Care. She wanted to concentrate on Boyd.

He was still so white. His face was as colorless as the sheet that covered him. The machines blipped and hummed. A good sound, she tried to tell herself. It meant he was alive. Only resting.

Tentatively she reached out to brush at his hair. It was so warm and soft. As was his skin when she traced the back of her knuckles over his cheek.

"It's all over now," she said quietly. "All you have to do is rest and get better." Desperate for the contact, she took his limp hand in hers, then pressed it to her lips. "I'm going to stay as close as they'll let me. I promise." It wasn't enough, not nearly enough. She brushed her lips over his hair, his cheek, his mouth. "I'll be here when you wake up."

She kept her word. Despite Deborah's arguments, she spent the rest of the night on the couch in the waiting room. Every hour they allowed her five minutes with him. Every hour she woke and took what she was given.

He didn't stir.

Dawn broke, shedding pale, rosy light through the window. The shifts changed. Cilla sipped coffee and watched the night staff leave for home. New sounds began. The clatter of the rolling tray as breakfast was served. Bright morning voices replaced the hushed tones of night. Checking her watch, she set the coffee aside and walked out to sit on a bench near the doors of ICU. It was almost time for her hourly visit.

While she waited to be cleared, a group of three hurried down the hall. The man was tall, with a shock of gray hair and a lean, almost cadaverous face. Beside him was a trim woman, her blond hair ruffled, her suit wrinkled. They were clutching hands. Walking with them was another woman. The daughter, Cilla thought with dazed weariness. She had her father's build and her mother's face.

There was panic in her eyes. Even through the fatigue Cilla saw it and recognized it. Beautiful eyes. Dark green, just like…Boyd's.

"Boyd Fletcher," the younger woman said to the nurse. "We're his family. They told us we could see him."

The nurse checked her list. "I'll take you. Only two at a time, please."

"You go." Boyd's sister turned to her parents. "I'll wait right here."

Cilla wanted to speak, but as the woman sat on the opposite end of the bench she could only sit, clutching her hands together.

What could she say to them? To any of them? Even as she searched for words, Boyd's sister leaned back against the wall and shut her eyes.

Ten minutes later, the Fletchers came out again. There were lines of strain around the woman's eyes, but they were dry. Her hand was still gripping her husband's.

"Natalie." She touched her daughter's shoulder. "He's awake. Groggy, but awake. He recognized us." She beamed a smile at her husband. "He wanted to know what the hell we were doing here when we were supposed to be in Paris." Her eyes filled then, and, she groped impatiently for a handkerchief. "The doctor's looking at him now, but you can see him in a few minutes."

Natalie slipped an arm around her mother's waist, then her father's. "So what were we worried about?"

"I still want to know exactly what happened." Boyd's father shot a grim look at the double doors. "Boyd's captain has some explaining to do."

"We'll get the whole story," his wife said soothingly. "Let's just take a few minutes to be grateful it wasn't worse." She dropped the handkerchief back in her purse. "When he was coming around, he asked for someone named Cilla. That's not his partner's name. I don't believe we know a Cilla."

Though her legs had turned to jelly, Cilla rose. "I'm Cilla." Three pairs of eyes fixed on her. "I'm sorry," she managed. "Boyd was...he was hurt because...he was protecting me. I'm sorry," she said again.

"Excuse me." The nurse stood by the double doors again. "Detective Fletcher insists on seeing you, Miss O'Roarke. He's becoming agitated."

"I'll go with you." Taking charge, Natalie steered Cilla through the doors.

Boyd's eyes were closed again, but he wasn't asleep. He was concentrating on reviving the strength he'd lost in arguing with the doctor. But he knew the moment she entered the room, even before she laid a tentative hand on his. He opened his eyes and looked at her.

"Hi, Slick." She made herself smile. "How's it going?"

"You're okay." He hadn't been sure. The last clear memory was of Billy holding the knife and Cilla struggling.

"I'm fine." Deliberately she put her bandaged hand behind her back. Natalie noted the gesture with a frown. "You're the one hooked up to machines."

Though her voice was brisk, the hand that brushed over his cheek was infinitely tender. "I've seen you looking better, Fletcher."

He linked his fingers with hers. "I've felt better."

"You saved my life." She struggled to keep it light, keep it easy. "I guess I owe you."

"Damn right." He wanted to touch her, but his arms felt like lead. "When are you going to pay up?"

"We'll talk about it. Your sister's here." She glanced across the bed at Natalie.

Natalie leaned down and pressed a kiss to his brow. "You jerk."

"It's nice to see you, too."

"You just couldn't be a pushy, uncomplicated business shark, could you?"

"No." He smiled and nearly floated off again. "But you make a great one. Try to keep them from worrying."

She sighed a little as she thought of their parents. "You don't ask for much."

"I'm doing okay. Just keep telling them that. You met Cilla."

Natalie's gaze skimmed up, measuring. "Yes, we met. Just now."

"Make her get the hell out of here." Natalie saw the shocked hurt in Cilla's eyes, saw her fingers tighten convulsively on the bedguard.

"She doesn't have to make me go." With her last scrap of pride, she lifted her chin. "If you don't want me around, I'll—"

"Don't be stupid," Boyd said in that mild, slightly irritated voice that made her want to weep. He looked back at his sister. "She's dead on her feet. Last night was rough. She's too stubborn to admit it, but she needs to go home and get some sleep.''

''Ungrateful slob,'' Cilla managed. ''Do you think you can order me around even when you're flat on your back?''

''Yeah. Give me a kiss.''

''If I didn't feel sorry for you, I'd make you beg.'' She leaned close to touch her lips to his. At the moment of contact she realized with a new panic that she was going to break down. ''Since you want me to clear out, I will. I've got a show to prep for.''

''Hey, O'Roarke.''

She got enough of a grip on control to look over her shoulder. ''Yes?''

''Come back soon.''

''Well, well…'' Natalie murmured as Cilla hurried away.

''Well, well…'' her brother echoed. He simply could not keep his eyes open another moment. ''She's terrific, isn't she?''

''I suppose she must be.''

''As soon as I can stay awake for more than an hour at a time, I'm going to marry her.''

''I see. Maybe you should wait until you can actually stand up for an hour at a time.''

''I'll think about it. Nat.'' He found her hand again. ''It is good to see you.''

''You bet,'' she said as he fell asleep.

Cilla was almost running when she hit the double doors. She didn't pause, not even when Boyd's parents both rose from the bench. As her breath hitched and her eyes filled, she hurried down the hall and stumbled into the ladies' room.

Natalie found her there ten minutes later, curled up in a corner, sobbing wretchedly. Saying nothing, Natalie pulled out a handful of paper towels. She dampened a few, then walked over to crouch in front of Cilla.

"Here you go."

"I hate to do this," Cilla said between sobbing breaths.

"Me too." Natalie wiped her own eyes, and then, without a thought to her seven-hundred-dollar suit, sat on the floor. "The doctor said they'd probably move him to a regular room by tomorrow. They're hoping to downgrade his condition from critical to serious by this afternoon."

"That's good." Cilla covered her face with the cool, wet towel. "Don't tell him I cried."

"All right."

There was silence between them as each worked on control.

"I guess you'd like to know everything that happened," Cilla said at length.

"Yes, but it can wait. I think Boyd had a point when he told you to go home and get some sleep."

With very little effort she could have stretched out on the cool tile floor and winked out like a light. "Maybe."

"I'll give you a lift."

"No, thanks. I'll call a cab."

"I'll give you a lift," Natalie repeated, and rose.

Lowering the towel, Cilla studied her. "You're a lot like him, aren't you?"

"So they say." Natalie offered a hand to help Cilla to her feet. "Boyd told me you're getting married."

"So he says."

For the first time in hours, Natalie laughed. "We really will have to talk."

She all but lived in the hospital for the next week. Boyd was rarely alone. Though it might have frustrated him from time to time that he barely had a moment for a private word with her, Cilla was grateful.

His room was always filled with friends, with family, with associates. As the days passed and his condition improved, she cut her visits shorter and kept them farther apart.

They both needed the distance. That was how she rationalized it. They both needed time for clear thinking. If she was to put the past—both the distant past and the near past—behind her, she needed to do it on her own.

It was Thea who filled her in on Billy Lomus. In his troubled childhood, the only bright spot had been John McGillis. As fate would have it, they had fed on each other's weaknesses. John's first suicide attempt had occurred two months after Billy left for Viet Nam. He'd been barely ten years old.

When Billy had returned, bitter and wounded, John had run away to join him. Though the authorities had separated them, they had always managed to find each other again. John's death had driven Billy over the fine line of reason he had walked.

"Delayed stress syndrome," Althea said as they stood together in the hospital parking lot. "Paranoid psychosis. Obsessive love. It doesn't really matter what label you put on it."

"Over these past couple of weeks, I've asked myself

dozens of times if there was anything I could have done differently with John McGillis.'' She took in a deep breath of the early spring air. ''And there wasn't. I can't tell you what a relief it is to finally be sure of that.''

''Then you can put it behind you.''

''Yes. It's not something I can forget, but I can put it behind me. Before I do, I'd like to thank you for everything you did, and tried to do.''

''It was my job,'' Althea said simply. ''We weren't friends then. I think maybe we nearly are now.''

Cilla laughed. ''Nearly.''

''So, as someone who's nearly your friend, there's something I'd like to say.''

''Okay.''

''I've been watching you and Boyd since the beginning. Observation's also part of the job.'' Her eyes, clear and blue and direct, met Cilla's. ''I still haven't decided if I think you're good for Boyd. It's not really my call, but I like to form an opinion.''

Cilla looked out beyond the parking lot to a patch of green. The daffodils were blooming there, beautifully. ''Thea, you're not telling me anything I don't already know.''

''My point is, Boyd thinks you're good for him. That's enough for me. I guess the only thing you've got to decide now is if he's good for you.''

''He thinks he is,'' she murmured.

''I've noticed.'' In an abrupt change of mood, Althea looked toward the hospital. ''I heard he was getting out in a couple of days.''

''That's the rumor.''

''You've already been up, I take it.''

"For a few minutes. His sister's there, and a couple of cops. They brought in a flower arrangement shaped like a horseshoe. The card read Tough break, Lucky. They tried to tell him they'd confiscated it from some gangster's funeral."

"Wouldn't surprise me. Funny thing about cops. They usually have a sense of humor, just like real people." She gave Cilla an easy smile. "I'm going to go up. Should I tell him I ran into you and you're coming back later?"

"No. Not this time. Just—just tell him to listen to the radio. I'll see if I can dig up 'Dueling Banjos.'"

"'Dueling Banjos'?"

"Yeah. I'll see you later, Thea."

"Sure." Althea watched Cilla walk to her car and was grateful, not for the first time, not to be in love.

Though the first couple of nights in the booth after the shooting had been difficult, Cilla had picked up her old routine. She no longer got a flash of Boyd bleeding as he knelt by the door, or of Billy, his eyes wild, holding a knife to her throat.

She'd come to enjoy the request line again. The blinking lights no longer grated on her nerves. Every hour she was grateful that Boyd was recovering, and so she threw herself into her work with an enthusiasm she had lost for too long.

"Cilla."

She didn't jolt at the sound of her name, but swiveled easily in her chair and smiled at Nick. "Hey."

"I, ah, decided to come back."

She kept smiling as she accepted the cup of coffee he offered. "I heard."

"Mark was real good about it."

"You're an asset to the station, Nick. I'm glad you changed your mind."

"Yeah, well…" He let his words trail off as he studied the scar on the palm of her hand. The stitches had come out only days earlier. "I'm glad you're okay."

"Me too. You want to get me the Rocco's Pizza commercial?"

He nearly jumped for it, sliding it out of place and handing it to her. Cilla popped the tape in, then potted it up.

"I wanted to apologize," he blurted out.

"You don't have to."

"I feel like a jerk, especially after I heard…well, the whole story about Billy and that guy from Chicago."

"You're nothing like John, Nick. And I'm flattered that you were attracted to me—especially since you have a class with my incredibly beautiful sister."

"Deborah's nice. But she's too smart."

Cilla had her first big laugh of the month. "Thanks a lot, kid. Just what does that make me?"

"I didn't mean—" He broke off, mortally embarrassed. "I only meant—"

"Don't bury yourself." Giving him a quick grin, she turned on her mike. "Hey, Denver, we're going to keep it rocking for you for the next quarter hour. It's 10:45 on this Thursday night, and I'm just getting started." She hit them with a blast of "Guns 'n' Roses". "Now that's rock and roll," she said to herself. "Hey, Nick, why don't you…" Her words trailed off when she saw Boyd's mother in the doorway.

"Mrs. Fletcher." She sprang up, nearly strangling herself with her headphones.

"I hope I'm not disturbing you." She smiled at Cilla, nodded to Nick.

"No, no, of course not." Cilla brushed uselessly at her grimy jeans. "Um…Nick, why don't you get Mrs. Fletcher a cup of coffee?"

"No, thank you, dear. I can only stay a moment."

Nick made his excuses and left them alone.

"So," Mrs. Fletcher said after a quick study. She blinked at the posters on the wall and examined the equipment. "This is where you work?"

"Yes. I'd, ah…give you a tour, but I've got—"

"That's perfectly all right." The lines of strain were no longer around her eyes. She was a trim, attractive and perfectly groomed woman. And she intimidated the hell out of Cilla. "Don't let me interrupt you."

"No, I…I'm used to working with people around."

"I missed you at the hospital the past few days, so I thought I'd come by here and say goodbye."

"You're leaving?"

"Since Boyd is on the mend, we're going back to Paris. It's business, as well as pleasure."

Cilla made a noncommittal noise and cued up the next record. "I know you must be relieved that Boyd…well, that he's all right. I'm sure it was dreadful for you."

"For all of us. Boyd explained it all to us. You've had a horrible ordeal."

"It's over now."

"Yes." She lifted Cilla's hand and glanced at the healing wound. "Experiences leave scars. Some deeper than others." She released Cilla's hand to wander around the tiny booth. "Boyd tells me you're to be married."

"I…" She shook off the shock, cleared her throat. "Excuse me a minute." Turning to the console she segued into the next record, then pushed another switch. "It's time for our mystery record," she explained. "The roll of thunder plays over the song, then people call in. The first caller who can give me the name of the song, the artist and the year of the recording wins a pair of concert tickets. We've got Madonna coming in at the end of the month."

"Fascinating," Mrs. Fletcher smiled, a smile precisely like Boyd's. "As I was saying, Boyd tells me you're to be married. I wondered if you'd like any help with the arrangements."

"No. That is, I haven't said… Excuse me." She pounced on a blinking light. "KHIP. No, I'm sorry, wrong answer. Try again." She struggled to keep her mind clear as the calls came through. The fourth caller's voice was very familiar.

"Hey, O'Roarke."

"Boyd." She sent his mother a helpless look. "I'm working."

"I'm calling. You got a winner yet?"

"No, but—"

"You've got one now. 'Electric Avenue,' Eddy Grant, 1983."

She had to smile. "You're pretty sharp, Slick. Looks like you've got yourself a couple of concert tickets. Hold on." She switched on her mike. "We've got a winner."

Patient, Mrs. Fletcher watched her work, smiling as she heard her son's voice over the speakers.

"Congratulations," Cilla said after she'd potted up a new record.

"So, are you going to the concert with me?"

"If you're lucky. Gotta go."

"Hey!" He shouted before she could cut him off. "I haven't heard 'Dueling Banjos' yet."

"Keep listening." After a long breath, she turned back to his mother. "I'm very sorry."

"No problem, no problem at all." In fact, she'd found the interlude delightful. "About the wedding?"

"I don't know that there's going to be a wedding. I mean, there isn't a wedding." She dragged a hand through her hair. "I don't think."

"Ah, well..." That same faint, knowing smile hovered around her mouth. "I'm sure you or Boyd will let us know. He's very much in love with you. You know that?"

"Yes. At least I think I do."

"He told me about your parents. I hope you don't mind."

"No." She sat again. "Mrs. Fletcher—"

"Liz is fine."

"Liz. I hope you don't think I'm playing some sort of game with Boyd. I wouldn't ask him to change. I could never ask him to change, and I just don't know if I can live with what he does."

"Because you're afraid of his being a policeman? Afraid he might die and leave you, as your parents did?"

Cilla looked down at her hands, spread her fingers. "I guess when you trim away all the fat, that's it."

"I understand. I worry about him," she said quietly. "I also understand he's doing what he has to do."

"Yes, it is what he has to do. I've given that a lot of thought since he was hurt." Cilla looked up again, her eyes intense. "How do you live with it?"

Liz took Cilla's restless hand in hers. "I love him."

"And that's enough?"

"It has to be. It's always difficult to lose someone you love. The way you lost your parents was tragic—and, according to Boyd, unnecessary. My mother died when I was only six. I loved her very much, though I had little time with her."

"I'm sorry."

"She cut herself in the garden one day. Just a little nick on the thumb she paid no attention to. A few weeks later she was dead of blood poisoning. All from a little cut on the thumb with a pair of rusty garden shears. Tragic, and unnecessary. It's hard to say how and when a loved one will be taken from us. How sad it would be not to allow ourselves to love because we were afraid to lose." She touched a hand to Cilla's cheek. "I hope to see you again soon."

"Mrs. Fletcher—Liz," Cilla said as she stopped at the door. "Thank you for coming."

"It was my pleasure." She glanced at a poster of a bare-chested rock star with shoulder-length hair and a smoldering sneer. "Though I do prefer Cole Porter."

Cilla found herself smiling as she slipped in another tape. After the ad, she gave her listeners fifteen uninterrupted minutes of music and herself time to think.

When the request line rolled around, she was as nervous as a cat, but her mind was made up.

"This is Cilla O'Roarke for KHIP. It's five minutes past midnight and our request lines are open. Before I take a call, I've got a request of my own. This one goes to Boyd. No, it's not 'Dueling Banjos,' Slick. You're just going to have to try a new memory on for size. It's an old one by the Platters. 'Only You.' I hope you're listening, because I want you to know—'' For the first time in her career, she choked on the air. "Oh, boy, it's a lot to get out. I guess I want to say I finally figured out it's only you for me. I love you, and if the offer's still open, you've got a deal."

She sent the record out and, with her eyes closed, let the song flow through her head.

Struggling for composure, she took call after call. There were jokes and questions about Boyd, but none of the callers *was* Boyd. She'd been so certain he would phone.

Maybe he hadn't even been listening. The thought of that had her dropping her head in her hands. She had finally dragged out the courage to tell him how she felt, and he hadn't been listening.

She got through the next two hours step-by-step. It had been a stupid move, she told herself. It was unbelievably foolish to announce that you loved someone over the radio. She'd only succeeded in embarrassing herself.

The more she thought about it, the angrier she became. She'd told him to listen, damn it. Couldn't he do anything she asked him to do? She'd told him to go away, he'd stayed. She'd told him she wasn't going to marry him, he'd told everyone she was. She'd told him to listen to the radio, he'd shut it off. She'd bared her soul over the public airwaves for nothing.

"That was a hell of a request," Jackson commented when he strolled into the booth just before two.

"Shut up."

"Right." He hummed to himself as he checked the programmer's clock for his shift. "Ratings should shoot right through the roof."

"If I wanted someone to be cheerful in here, I'd have brought along Mickey Mouse."

"Sorry." Undaunted, he continued to hum.

With her teeth on edge, Cilla opened her mike. "That's all for tonight, Denver. It's 1:58. I'm turning you over to my man Jackson. He'll be with you until six in the a.m. Have a good one. And remember, when you dream of me, dream good." She kicked her chair out of the way. "And if you're smart," she said to Jackson, "you won't say a word."

"Lips are sealed."

She stalked out, snatching up her jacket and digging for her keys as she headed for the door. She was going to go home and soak her head. And if Deborah had been listening and was waiting up, it would just give her someone to chew out.

Head down, hands in her pockets, she stomped to her car. She had her hand on the doorhandle before she saw that Boyd was sitting on the hood.

"Nice night," he said.

"What—what the hell are you doing here?" Anger forgotten, she rushed around the car. "You're supposed to be in the hospital. They haven't released you yet."

"I went over the wall. Come here."

"You jerk. Sitting out here in the night air. You were nearly dead two weeks ago, and—"

"I've never felt better in my life." He grabbed her by the front of her jacket and hauled her against him for a kiss. "And neither have you."

"What?"

"You've never felt better in my life, either."

She shook her head to clear it and stepped back. "Get in the car. I'm taking you back to the hospital."

"Like hell." Laughing, he pulled her against him again and devoured her mouth.

She went weak and hot and dizzy. On a little sigh, she clung to him, letting her hands rush over his face, into his hair. Just to touch him, to touch him and know he was whole and safe and hers.

"Lord, do you know how long it's been since you've kissed me like that?" He held her close, waiting for his heart rate to level. His side was throbbing in time with it. "Those chaste little pecks in the hospital weren't enough."

"We were never alone."

"You never stayed around long enough." He pressed his lips to the top of her head. "I liked the song."

"What song? Oh." She stepped back again. "You were listening."

"I liked the song a lot." He took her hand and pressed his mouth to the scar. "But I liked what you said before it even better. How about saying it again, face-to-face?"

"I..." She let out a huff of breath.

Patient, he cupped her face in his hands. "Come on, O'Roarke." He smiled. "Spit it out."

"I love you." She said it so quickly, and with such obvious relief, that he laughed again. "Damn it, it's not funny. I really love you, and it's your fault for making it impossible for me to do anything else."

"Remind me to pat myself on the back later. You've

got a hell of a voice, Cilla.'' He wrapped his arms around her, comfortably. ''And you've never sounded better than tonight.''

''I was scared.''

''I know.''

''I guess I'm not anymore.'' She rested her head against his shoulder. ''It feels right.''

''Yeah. Just right. The offer still holds, Cilla. Marry me.''

She took her time, not because she was afraid, but because she wanted to savor it. She wanted to remember every second. The moon was full, the stars were out. She could just catch the faintest drift of those fragile spring flowers.

''There's one question I have to ask you first.''

''Okay.''

''Can we really hire a cook?''

He laughed and lowered his mouth to hers. ''Absolutely.''

''Then it's a deal.''

*   *   *   *   *

NIGHT SHADOW

With thanks to Isabel and Dan

Dear Reader,

We need heroes. One of the reasons writing romances appeals to me is it gives me the opportunity to create heroes—male and female. You know, those people who are able to triumph over adversity, emotional pain and yes, bad guys.

In *Night Shadow* I wanted to create a different kind of hero, someone a little beyond the realm of the usual. You'll find he's not the kind of guy you might meet at a party or on a train or at the checkout counter at the supermarket. In fact, the heroine meets him... Well, you only have to turn a few pages to find out, so I won't spoil it.

The point is, heroes come in all sizes and shapes. In *Night Shadow* he's just a little more, and less, than average. But he's still vulnerable to the love of a good woman. He's still forced to face the problems and joy of forging an emotional bond with that one special person. He falls in love, he makes mistakes, and he learns to compromise. *And* he chases bad guys. That's my kind of hero.

I hope he's yours.

Love,
Nora

Chapter 1

He walked the night. Alone. Restless. Ready. Clad in black, masked, he was a shadow among shadows, a whisper among the murmurs and mumbles of the dark.

He was watchful, always, for those who preyed on the helpless and vulnerable. Unknown, unseen, unwanted, he stalked the hunters in the steaming jungle that was the city. He moved unchallenged in the dark spaces, the blind alleys and violent streets. Like smoke, he drifted along towering rooftops and down into dank cellars.

When he was needed, he moved like thunder, all sound and fury. Then there was only the flash, the optical echo that lightning leaves after it streaks the sky.

They called him Nemesis, and he was everywhere.

He walked the night, skirting the sound of laughter, the cheerful din of celebrations. Instead he was drawn to the whimpers and tears of the lonely and the hopeless pleas of the victimized. Night after night, he clothed himself in black, masked his face and stalked the wild, dark streets. Not for the law. The law was too easily manipulated by those who scorned it. It was too often bent and twisted by those who claimed to uphold it. He knew, oh, yes, he knew. And he could not forget.

When he walked, he walked for justice—she of the blind eyes.

With justice, there could be retribution and the balancing of scales.

Like a shadow, he watched the city below.

Deborah O'Roarke moved quickly. She was always in a hurry to catch up with her own ambitions. Now her neat, sensible shoes clicked rapidly on the broken sidewalks of Urbana's East End. It wasn't fear that had her hurrying back toward her car, though the East End was a dangerous place—especially at night—for a lone, attractive woman. It was the flush of success. In her capacity as assistant district attorney, she had just completed an interview with a witness to one of the drive-by shootings that were becoming a plague in Urbana.

Her mind was completely occupied with the need to get back to her office and write her report so that the wheels of justice could begin to turn. She believed in justice, the patient, tenacious and systematic stages of it. Young Rico Mendez's murderers would answer for their crime. And with luck, she would be the one to prosecute.

Outside the crumbling building where she had just spent an hour doggedly pressuring two frightened young boys for information, the street was dark. All but two of the streetlights that lined the cracked sidewalk had been broken. The moon added only a fitful glow. She knew that the shadows in the narrow doorways were drunks or pushers or hookers. More than once she had reminded herself that she could have ended up in one of those sad and scarred buildings—if it hadn't been for her older sister's fierce determination to see that she had a good home, a good education, a good life.

Every time Deborah brought a case to trial, she felt she was repaying a part of that debt.

One of the doorway shadows shouted something at her, impersonally obscene. A harsh feminine cackle followed it. Deborah had only been in Urbana for eighteen months, but she knew better than to pause or to register that she had heard at all.

Her strides long and purposeful, she stepped off the curb to get into her car. Someone grabbed her from behind.

"Ooh, baby, ain't you sweet."

The man, six inches taller than she and wiry as a spring, stank. But not from liquor. In the split second it took her to read his glassy eyes, she understood that he wasn't pumped high on whiskey but on chemicals that would make him quick instead of sluggish. Using both hands, she shoved her leather briefcase into his gut. He grunted and his grip loosened. Deborah wrenched away and ran, digging frantically for her keys.

Even as her hand closed over the jingling metal in her pocket, he grabbed her, his fingers digging in at the collar of her jacket. She heard the linen rip and turned to fight. Then she saw the switchblade, its business end gleaming once before he pressed it against the soft skin under her chin.

"Gotcha," he said, and giggled.

She went dead still, hardly daring to breathe. In his eyes she saw a malicious kind of glee that would never listen to pleading or logic. Still she kept her voice low and calm.

"I've only got twenty-five dollars."

Jabbing the point of the blade against her skin, he leaned intimately close. "Uh-uh, baby, you got a lot more than twenty-five dollars." He twisted her hair around his hand, jerking once, hard. When she cried out, he began to pull her toward the deeper dark of the alley.

"Go on and scream." He giggled in her ear. "I like it when they scream. Go on." He nicked her throat with the blade. "Scream."

She did, and the sound rolled down the shadowed street, echoing in the canyons of the buildings. In doorways people shouted encouragement—to the attacker. Behind darkened windows people kept their lights off and pretended they heard nothing.

When he pushed her against the damp wall of the alleyway, she was icy with terror. Her mind, always so sharp and open, shut down. "Please," she said, though she knew better, "don't do this."

He grinned. "You're going to like it." With the tip of the blade, he sliced off the top button of her blouse. "You're going to like it just fine."

Like any strong emotion, fear sharpened her senses. She could feel her own tears, hot and wet on her cheeks, smell his stale breath and the overripe garbage that crowded the alley. In his eyes she could see herself pale and helpless.

She would be another statistic, she thought dully. Just one more number among the ever increasing victims.

Slowly, then with increasing power, anger began to burn through the icy shield of fear. She would not cringe and whimper. She would not submit without a fight. It was then she felt the sharp pressure of her keys. They were still in her hand, closed tight in her rigid fist. Concentrating, she used her thumb to push the points between her stiff fingers. She sucked in her breath, trying to channel all of her strength into her arm.

Just as she raised it, her attacker seemed to rise into the air, then fly, arms pinwheeling, into a stand of metal garbage cans.

Deborah ordered her legs to run. The way her heart was pumping, she was certain she could be in her car, doors locked, engine gunning, in the blink of an eye. But then she saw him.

He was all in black, a long, lean shadow among the shadows. He stood over the knife-wielding junkie, his legs spread, his body tensed.

"Stay back," he ordered when she took an automatic step forward. His voice was part whisper, part growl.

"I think—"

"Don't think," he snapped without bothering to look at her.

Even as she bristled at his tone, the junkie leaped up, howling, bringing his blade down in a deadly arc. Before Deborah's dazed and fascinated eyes, there was a flash of movement, a scream of pain and the clatter of the knife as it skidded along the concrete.

In less than the time it takes to draw and release a single breath, the man in black stood just as he had before. The junkie was on his knees, moaning and clutching his stomach.

"That was..." Deborah searched her whirling brain for a word, "impressive. I—I was going to suggest that we call the police."

He continued to ignore her as he took some circular plastic from his pocket and bound the still-moaning junkie's hands and ankles. He picked up the knife, pressed a button. The blade disappeared with a whisper. Only then did he turn to her.

The tears were already drying on her cheeks, he noted. And though there was a hitch in her breath, she didn't appear to be ready to faint or shoot off into hysterics. In fact, he was forced to admire her calm.

She was extraordinarily beautiful, he observed dispassionately. Her skin was pale as ivory against a disheveled cloud of ink-black hair. Her features were soft, delicate, almost fragile. Unless you looked at her eyes. There was a toughness in them, a determination that belied the fact that her slender body was shaking in reaction.

Her jacket was torn, and her blouse had been cut open to reveal the icy-blue lace and silk of a camisole. An interesting contrast to the prim, almost mannish business suit.

He summed her up, not as man to woman, but as he had countless other victims, countless other hunters. The unexpected and very basic jolt of reaction he felt disturbed him. Such things were more dangerous than any switchblade.

"Are you hurt?" His voice was low and unemotional, and he remained in shadow.

"No. No, not really." There would be plenty of bruises, both on her skin and her emotions, but she would worry about them later. "Just shaken up. I want to thank you for—" She had stepped toward him as she spoke. In the faint backsplash from the streetlight, she saw that his face was masked. As her eyes widened, he saw they were blue, a brilliant electric blue. "Nemesis," she murmured. "I thought you were the product of someone's overworked imagination."

"I'm as real as he is." He jerked his head toward the figure groaning among the garbage. He saw that there was a thin trickle of blood on her throat. For reasons he didn't try to understand, it enraged him. "What kind of a fool are you?"

"I beg your pardon?"

"This is the sewer of the city. You don't belong here. No one with brains comes here unless they have no choice."

Her temper inched upward, but she controlled it. He had, after all, helped her. "I had business here."

"No," he corrected. "You have no business here, unless you choose to be raped and murdered in an alley."

"I didn't choose anything of the sort." As her emotions darkened, the faint hint of Georgia became more prominent in her voice. "I can take care of myself."

His gaze skimmed down, lingered on the shredded blouse then returned to her face. "Obviously."

She couldn't make out the color of his eyes. They were dark, very dark. In the murky light, they seemed black. But she could read the dismissal in them, and the arrogance.

"I've already thanked you for helping me, even though I didn't need any help. I was just about to deal with that slime myself."

"Really?"

"That's right. I was going to gouge his eyes out." She held up her keys, lethal points thrusting out. "With these."

He studied her again, then gave a slow nod. "Yes, I believe you could do it."

"Damn right I could."

"Then it appears I've wasted my time." He pulled a square of black cloth from his pocket. After wrapping the knife in it, he offered it to her. "You'll want this for evidence."

The moment she held it, she remembered that feeling

of terror and helplessness. With a muffled oath, she bit back her temper. Whoever, whatever he was, he had risked his life to help her. "I am grateful."

"I don't look for gratitude."

Her chin came up as he threw her words back in her face. "For what then?"

He stared at her, into her. Something came and went in his eyes that made her skin chill again as she heard his words, "For justice."

"This isn't the way," she began.

"It's my way. Weren't you going to call the police?"

"Yes." She pressed the heel of her hand to her temple. She was a little dizzy, she realized. And more than a little sick to her stomach. This wasn't the time or the place to argue morality and law enforcement with a belligerent masked man. "I have a phone in my car."

"Then I suggest you use it."

"All right." She was too tired to argue. Shivering a bit, she started down the alley. At the mouth of it, she saw her briefcase. She picked it up with a sense of relief and put the switchblade in it.

Five minutes later, after calling 911 and giving her location and the situation, she walked back into the alley. "They're sending a cruiser." Weary, she pushed the hair back from her face. She saw the junkie, curled up tight on the concrete. His eyes were wide and wild. Nemesis had left him with the promise of what would happen to him if he was ever caught again attempting to rape.

Even through the haze of drugs, the words had rung true.

"Hello?" With a puzzled frown, she looked up and down the alley.

He was gone.

"Damn it, where did he go?" On a hiss of breath, she

leaned back against the clammy wall. She hadn't finished with him yet, not by a long shot.

He was almost close enough to touch her. But she couldn't see him. That was the blessing, and the curse, the repayment for the lost days.

He didn't reach out and was curious why he wanted to. He only watched her, imprinting on his memory the shape of her face, the texture of her skin, the color and sheen of her hair as it curved gently beneath her chin.

If he had been a romantic man, he might have thought in terms of poetry or music. But he told himself he only waited and watched to make certain she was safe.

When the sirens cut the night, he could see her rebuild a mask of composure, layer by layer. She took deep, steadying breaths as she buttoned the ruined jacket over her slashed blouse. With a final breath, she tightened her grip on her briefcase, set her chin and walked with confident strides toward the mouth of the alley.

As he stood alone in his own half world between reality and illusion, he could smell the subtle sexiness of her perfume.

For the first time in four years, he felt the sweet and quiet ache of longing.

Deborah didn't feel like a party. In her fantasy, she wasn't all glossed up in a strapless red dress with plastic stays digging into her sides. She wasn't wearing pinching three-inch heels. She wasn't smiling until she thought her face would split in two.

In her fantasy, she was devouring a mystery novel and chocolate chip cookies while she soaked in a hot bubble bath to ease the bruises that still ached a bit three days after her nasty adventure in the East End alley.

Unfortunately, her imagination wasn't quite good enough to keep her feet from hurting.

As parties went, it was a pretty good one. Maybe the music was a bit loud, but that didn't bother her. After a lifetime with her sister, a first-class rock and roll fanatic, she was well indoctrinated into the world of loud music. The smoked salmon and spinach canapés weren't chocolate chip cookies, but they were tasty. The wine that she carefully nursed was top-notch.

There was plenty of glitz and glamour, lots of cheek bussing and glad-handing. It was, after all, a party thrown by Arlo Stuart, hotel magnate, as a campaign party for Tucker Fields, Urbana's mayor. It was Stuart's, and the present administration's hope, that the campaign would end in November with the mayor's reelection.

Deborah was as yet undecided whether she would pull the lever for the incumbent, or the young upstart challenger, Bill Tarrington. The champagne and pâté wouldn't influence her. Her choice would be based on issues, not party affiliations—either social or political. Tonight she was attending the party for two reasons. The first was that she was friends with the mayor's assistant, Jerry Bower. The second was that her boss had used the right combination of pressure and diplomacy to push her through the gilded swinging doors of the Stuart Palace.

"God, you look great." Jerry Bower, trim and handsome in his tux, his blond hair waving around his tanned, friendly face, stopped beside Deborah to press a quick kiss to her cheek. "Sorry I haven't had time to talk. There was a lot of meeting and greeting to do."

"Things are always busy for the big boss's right arm." She smiled, toasting him. "Quite a bash."

"Stuart pulled out all the stops." With a politician's eye, he scanned the crowd. The mix of the rich, famous and influential pleased him. There were, of course, other aspects to the campaign. Visibility, contact with shop owners, factory workers—the blue, the gray and the white collars, press conferences, speeches, statements. But Jerry figured if he could spend a small slice of one eighteen-hour day rubbing silk elbows and noshing on canapés, he'd make the best of it.

"I'm properly dazzled," Deborah assured him.

"Ah, but it's your vote we want."

"You might get it."

"How are you feeling?" Taking the opportunity in hand, he began to fill a plate with hors d'oeuvres.

"Fine." She glanced idly down at the fading bruise on her forearm. There were other, more colorful marks, hidden under the red silk.

"Really?"

She smiled again. "Really. It's an experience I don't want to repeat, but it did bring it home, straight home to me that we've got a lot more work to do before Urbana's streets are safe."

"You shouldn't have been out there," he mumbled.

He might as well have nudged a soapbox under her feet. Her eyes lit up, her cheeks flushed, her chin angled. "Why? Why should there be any place, any place at all in the city where a person isn't safe to walk? Are we supposed to just accept the fact that there are portions of Urbana that are off-limits to nice people? If we're—"

"Hold it, hold it." He held up a surrendering hand. "The only person someone in politics can't comfortably outtalk is a lawyer. I agree with you, okay?" He snagged a glass of wine from a passing waiter and reminded himself it could be his only one of the long evening. "I was stating a fact. It doesn't make it right, it just makes it true."

"It shouldn't be true." Her eyes had darkened in both annoyance and frustration.

"The mayor's running on a tough anticrime campaign," Jerry reminded her, and gave smiling nods to constituents who wandered by. "Nobody in this city knows the statistics better than I do. They're nasty, no doubt, and we're going to push them back. It just takes time."

"Yeah." Sighing, she pulled herself away from the brink of the argument she'd had with Jerry more times than she could count. "But it's taking too much time."

He bit into a carrot slice. "Don't tell me you're going to step over to the side of this Nemesis character? 'If the law won't deal with it quickly enough, I will'?"

"No." On that she was firm. The law would mete out justice in a proper fashion. She believed in the law, even now, when it was so totally overburdened. "I don't believe in crusades. They come too close to vigilantism. Though I have to admit, I'm grateful he was tilting at windmills in that alley the other night."

"So am I." He touched her lightly on the shoulder. "When I think of what might have happened—"

"It didn't." That helpless fear was still much too close to the surface to allow her to dwell on it. "And in spite of all the romantic press he's been getting, up close and in person, he's rude and abrupt." She took another sip of wine. "I owe him, but I don't have to like him."

"Nobody understands that sentiment more than a politician."

She relaxed and laughed up at him. "All right, enough shoptalk. Tell me who's here that I should know and don't."

Jerry entertained her. He always did. For the next few minutes he gulped down canapés and put names and tax

brackets to the faces crowding the Royal Stuart ballroom. His clever and pithy comments made her chuckle.
When they began to stroll through the crowd, she
hooked her arm easily through his. It was a matter of
chance that she turned her head and, in that sea of people, focused on one single face.

He was standing in a group of five or six, with two
beautiful women all but hanging on his arms. Attractive,
yes, she thought. But the room was filled with attractive
men. His thick, dark hair framed a long, lean, somewhat
scholarly face. Prominent bones, deep-set eyes—brown
eyes, she realized, dark and rich like bittersweet chocolate. They seemed faintly bored at the moment. His
mouth was full, rather poetic looking, and curved now
in the barest hint of a smile.

He wore his tux as if he'd been born in one. Easily,
casually. With one long finger he brushed a fiery curl
off the redhead's cheek as she leaned closer to him. His
smile widened at something she said.

Then, without turning his head, he merely shifted his
gaze and locked on Deborah.

"….and she bought the little monsters a wide-screen
TV."

"What?" She blinked, and though she realized it was
absurd, she felt as though she had broken out of a spell.
"What?"

"I was telling you about Mrs. Forth-Wright's
poodles."

"Jerry, who is that? Over there. With the redhead on
one side and the blonde on the other."

Glancing over, Jerry grimaced, then shrugged. "I'm
surprised he doesn't have a brunette sitting on his shoulders. Women tend to stick to him as though he was
wearing flypaper instead of a tux."

She didn't need to be told what she could see with her own eyes. "Who is he?"

"Guthrie, Gage Guthrie."

Her eyes narrowed a bit, her mouth pursed. "Why does that sound familiar?"

"It's splashed liberally through the society section of the *World* almost every day."

"I don't read the society section." Well aware it was rude, Deborah stared stubbornly at the man across the room. "I know him," she murmured. "I just can't place how."

"You've probably heard his story. He was a cop."

"A cop." Deborah's brows lifted in surprise. He looked much too comfortable, much too much a part of the rich and privileged surroundings to be a cop.

"A good one, apparently, right here in Urbana. A few years ago, he and his partner ran into trouble. Big trouble. The partner was killed, and Guthrie was left for dead."

Her memory jogged then homed in. "I remember now. I followed his story. My God, he was in a coma for…"

"Nine or ten months," Jerry supplied. "He was on life-support, and they'd just about given him up, when he opened his eyes and came back. He couldn't hack the streets anymore, and turned down a desk job with UPD. He'd come into a plump inheritance while he was in the *Twilight Zone,* so I guess you could say he took the money and ran."

It couldn't have been enough, she thought. No amount of money could have been enough. "It must have been horrible. He lost nearly a year of his life."

Jerry picked through the dwindling supply on his plate, looking for something interesting. "He's made up for lost time. Apparently women find him irresistible. Of course that might be because he turned a three-million-dollar inheritance into thirty—and counting.'' Nipping a spiced shrimp, Jerry watched as Gage smoothly disentangled himself from the group and started in their direction. ''Well, well,'' he said softly. ''Looks like the interest is mutual.''

Gage had been aware of her since the moment she'd stepped into the ballroom. He'd watched, patient, as she'd mingled then separated herself. He'd kept up a social patter though he'd been wholly and uncomfortably aware of every move she'd made. He'd seen her smile at Jerry, observed the other man kiss her and brush a casually intimate hand over her shoulder.

He'd find out just what the relationship was there.

Though it wouldn't matter. Couldn't matter, he corrected. Gage had no time for sultry brunettes with intelligent eyes. But he moved steadily toward her.

''Jerry,'' Gage smiled. ''It's good to see you again.''

''Always a pleasure, Mr. Guthrie. You're enjoying yourself?''

''Of course.'' His gaze flicked from Jerry to Deborah. ''Hello.''

For some ridiculous reason, her throat snapped shut.

''Deborah, I'd like to introduce you to Gage Guthrie. Mr. Guthrie, Assistant District Attorney Deborah O'Roarke.''

''An A.D.A.'' Gage's smile spread charmingly. ''It's comforting to know that justice is in such lovely hands.''

''Competent,'' she said. ''I much prefer competent.''

''Of course.'' Though she hadn't offered it, he took her hand and held it for a brief few seconds.

Watch out! The warning flashed into Deborah's mind the instant her palm met his.

"Will you excuse me a minute?" Jerry laid a hand on Deborah's shoulder again. "The mayor's signaling."

"Sure." She summoned up a smile for him, though she was ashamed to admit she'd forgotten he was beside her.

"You haven't been in Urbana long," Gage commented.

Despite her uneasiness, Deborah met his eyes straight on. "About a year and a half. Why?"

"Because I'd have known."

"Really? Do you keep tabs on all the A.D.A's?"

"No." He brushed a finger over the pearl drop at her ear. "Just the beautiful ones." The instant suspicion in her eyes delighted him. "Would you like to dance?"

"No." She let out a long, quiet breath. "No, thanks. I really can't stay any longer. I've got work to do."

He glanced at his watch. "It's already past ten."

"The law doesn't have a time clock, Mr. Guthrie."

"Gage. I'll give you a lift."

"No." A quick and unreasonable panic surged to her throat. "No, that's not necessary."

"If it's not necessary, then it must be a pleasure."

He was smooth, she thought, entirely too smooth for a man who had just shrugged off a blonde and a redhead. She didn't care for the idea of being the brunette to round out the trio.

"I wouldn't want to take you away from the party."

"I never stay late at parties."

"Gage." The redhead, her mouth pouty and moist, swayed up to drag on his arm. "Honey, you haven't danced with me. Not once."

Deborah took the opportunity to make a beeline for the exit.

It was stupid, she admitted, but her system had gone

haywire at the thought of being alone in a car with him. Pure instinct, she supposed, for on the surface Gage Guthrie was a smooth, charming and appealing man. But she sensed something. Undercurrents. Dark, dangerous undercurrents. Deborah figured she had enough to deal with; she didn't need to add Gage Guthrie to the list.

She stepped out into the steamy summer night.

"Hail you a cab, miss?" the doorman asked her.

"No." Gage cupped a firm hand under her elbow. "Thank you."

"Mr. Guthrie," she began.

"Gage. My car is just here, Miss O'Roarke." He gestured to a long sleek limo in gleaming black.

"It's lovely," she said between her teeth, "but a cab will suit my needs perfectly."

"But not mine." He nodded at the tall, bulky man who slipped out of the driver's seat to open the rear door. "The streets are dangerous at night. I'd simply like to know you've gotten where you want to go, safely."

She stepped back and took a long careful study, as she might of a mug shot of a suspect. He didn't seem as dangerous now, with that half smile hovering at his mouth. In fact, she thought, he looked just a little sad. Just a little lonely.

She turned toward the limo. Not wanting to soften too much, she shot a look over her shoulder. "Has anyone ever told you you're pushy, Mr. Guthrie?"

"Often, Miss O'Roarke."

He settled beside her and offered a single long-stemmed red rose.

"You come prepared," she murmured. Had the blossom been waiting for the blonde, she wondered, or the redhead?

"I try. Where would you like to go?"

"The Justice Building. It's on Sixth and—"

"I know where it is." Gage pressed a button, and the glass that separated them from the driver slid open noiselessly. "The Justice Building, Frank."

"Yes, sir." The glass closed again, cocooning them.

"We used to work on the same side," Deborah commented.

"Which side is that?"

"Law."

He turned to her, his eyes dark, almost hypnotic. It made her wonder what he had seen when he had drifted all those months in that strange world of half life. Or half death.

"You're a defender of the law?"

"I like to think so."

"Yet you wouldn't be adverse to making deals and kicking back charges."

"The system's overburdened," she said defensively.

"Oh, yes, the system." With a faint movement of his shoulders, he seemed to dismiss it all. "Where are you from?"

"Denver."

"No, you didn't get cypress trees and magnolia blossoms in your voice from Denver."

"I was born in Georgia, but my sister and I moved around quite a bit. Denver was where I lived before I came east to Urbana."

Her sister, he noted. Not her parents, not her family, just her sister. He didn't press. Not yet. "Why did you come here?"

"Because it was a challenge. I wanted to put all those years I studied to good use. I like to think I can make a difference." She thought of the Mendez case and the four gang members who had been arrested and were even now awaiting trial. "I have made a difference."

"You're an idealist."

"Maybe. What's wrong with that?"

"Idealists are often tragically disappointed." He was silent a moment, studying her. The streetlamps and head-lights of oncoming traffic sliced into the car, then faded. Sliced, then faded. She was beautiful in both light and shadow. More than beauty, there was a kind of power in her eyes. The kind that came from the merging of intelligence and determination.

"I'd like to see you in court," he said.

She smiled and added yet one more element to the power and the beauty. Ambition. It was a formidable combination.

"I'm a killer."

"I bet you are."

He wanted to touch her, just the skim of a fingertip on those lovely white shoulders. He wondered if it would be enough, just a touch. Because he was afraid it wouldn't, he resisted. It was with both relief and frus-tration that he felt the limo glide to the curb and stop.

Deborah turned to look blankly out of the window at the old, towering Justice Building. "That was quick," she murmured, baffled by her own disappointment. "Thanks for the lift." When the driver opened her door, she swung her legs out.

"I'll see you again."

For the second time, she looked at him over her shoul-der. "Maybe. Good night."

He sat for a moment against the yielding seat, haunted by the scent she had left behind.

"Home?" the driver asked.

"No." Gage took a long, steadying breath. "Stay here, take her home when she's finished. I need to walk."

Chapter 2

Like a boxer dazed from too many blows, Gage fought his way out of the nightmare. He surfaced, breathless and dripping sweat. As the grinding nausea faded, he lay back and stared at the high ornate ceiling of his bedroom.

There were 523 rosettes carved into the plaster. He had counted them day after day during his slow and tedious recuperation. Almost like an incantation, he began to count them again, waiting for his pulse rate to level.

The Irish linen sheets were tangled and damp around him, but he remained perfectly still, counting. Twenty-five, twenty-six, twenty-seven. There was a light, spicy scent of carnations in the room. One of the maids had placed them on the rolltop desk beneath the window. As he continued to count, he tried to guess what vase had been used. Waterford, Dresden, Wedgwood. He concen-

trated on that and the monotonous counting until he felt
his system begin to level.

He never knew when the dream would reoccur. He
supposed he should have been grateful that it no longer
came nightly, but there was something more horrible
about its capricious visits.

Calmer, he pressed the button beside the bed. The
drapes on the wide arching window slid open and let in
the light. Carefully he flexed his muscles one by one,
assuring himself he still had control.

Like a man pursuing his own demons, he reviewed
the dream. As always, it sprang crystal clear in his mind,
involving all his senses.

They worked undercover. Gage and his partner, Jack
McDowell. After five years, they were more than partners. They were brothers. Each had risked his life to save
the other's. And each would do so again without hesitation. They worked together, drank together, went to
ball games, argued politics.

For more than a year, they had been going by the
names of Demerez and Gates, posing as two high-rolling
dealers of cocaine and its even more lethal offspring,
crack. With patience and guile, they had infiltrated one
of the biggest drug cartels on the East Coast. Urbana
was its center.

They could have made a dozen arrests, but they, and
the department, agreed that the goal was the top man.

His name and face remained a frustrating mystery.

But tonight they would meet him. A deal had been set
painstakingly. Demerez and Gates carried five million in
cash in their steel-reinforced briefcase. They would
exchange it for top-grade coke. And they would only
deal with the man in charge.

They drove toward the harbor in the customized

Maserati Jack was so proud of. With two dozen men for backup, and their own cover solid, their spirits were high.

Jack was a quick-thinking, tough-talking veteran cop, devoted to his family. He had a pretty, quiet wife and a young pistol of a toddler. With his brown hair slicked back, his hands studded with rings and the silk suit fitting creaselessly over his shoulders, he looked the part of the rich, conscienceless dealer.

There were plenty of contrasts between the two partners. Jack came from a long line of cops and had been raised in a third-floor walk-up in the East End by his divorced mother. There had been occasional visits from his father, a man who had reached for the bottle as often as his weapon. Jack had gone straight into the force after high school.

Gage had come from a business family filled with successful men who vacationed in Palm Beach and golfed at the country club. His parents had been closer to working class by the family standard, preferring to invest their money, their time, and their dreams in a small, elegant French restaurant on the upper East side. That dream had ultimately killed them.

After closing the restaurant late one brisk autumn night, they had been robbed and brutally murdered not ten feet from the doorway.

Orphaned before his second birthday, Gage had been raised in style and comfort by a doting aunt and uncle. He'd played tennis instead of streetball, and had been encouraged to step into the shoes of his late father's brother, as president of the Guthrie empire.

But he had never forgotten the cruelty, and the injustice of his parents' murder. Instead, he had joined the police force straight out of college.

Despite the contrasts in their backgrounds, the men had one vital thing in common—they both believed in the law.

"We'll hang his ass tonight," Jack said, drawing deeply on his cigarette.

"It's been a long time coming," Gage murmured.

"Six months prep work, eighteen months deep cover. Two years isn't much to give to nail this bastard." He turned to Gage with a wink. "Course, we could always take the five mil and run like hell. What do you say, kid?"

Though Jack was only five years older than Gage, he had always called him "kid." "I've always wanted to go to Rio."

"Yeah, me, too." Jack flicked the smoldering cigarette out of the car window where it bounced on asphalt and sputtered. "We could buy ourselves a villa and live the high life. Lots of women, lots of rum, lots of sun. How 'bout it?"

"Jenny might get annoyed."

Jack chuckled at the mention of his wife. "Yeah, that would probably tick her off. She'd make me sleep in the den for a month. Guess we'd just better kick this guy's butt." He picked up a tiny transmitter. "This is Snow White, you copy?"

"Affirmative, Snow White. This is Dopey."

"Don't I know it," Jack muttered. "We're pulling in, Pier Seventeen. Keep a bead on us. That goes for Happy and Sneezy and the rest of you dwarfs out there."

Gage pulled up in the shadows of the dock and cut the engine. He could smell the water and the overripe odor of fish and garbage. Following the instructions they'd been given, he blinked his headlights twice, paused, then blinked them twice again.

"Just like James Bond," Jack said, then grinned at him. "You ready, kid?"

"Damn right."

He lit another cigarette, blew smoke between his teeth. "Then let's do it."

They moved cautiously, Jack holding the briefcase with its marked bills and microtransmitter. Both men wore shoulder holsters with police issue .38s. Gage had a backup .25 strapped to his calf.

The lap of water on wood, the skitter of rodents on concrete. The dim half-light of a cloudy moon. The sting of tobacco on the air from Jack's cigarette. The small, slow-moving bead of sweat between his own shoulder blades.

"Doesn't feel right," Gage said softly.

"Don't go spooky on me, kid. We're going to hit the bell tonight."

With a nod, Gage fought off the ripple of unease. But he reached for his weapon when a small man stepped out of the shadows. With a grin, the man held up his hands, palms out.

"I'm alone," he said. "Just as agreed. I am Montega, your escort."

He had dark shaggy hair, a flowing moustache. When he smiled, Gage caught the glint of gold teeth. Like them, he was wearing an expensive suit, the kind that could be tailored to disguise the bulk of an automatic weapon. Montega lowered one hand carefully and took out a long, slim cigar. "It's a nice night for a little boat ride, *sí?*"

"*Sí.*" Jack nodded. "You don't mind if we pat you down? We'd feel better holding all the hardware until we get where we're going."

"Understandable." Montega lit the cigar with a slen-

der gold lighter. Still grinning, he clamped the cigar between his teeth. Gage saw his hand slip the lighter casually back into his pocket. Then there was an explosion,
the sound, the all too familiar sound of a bullet ripping
out of a gun. There was a burning hole in the pocket of
the fifteen-hundred-dollar suit. Jack fell backward.

Even now, four years later, Gage saw all the rest in
hideous slow motion. The dazed, already dead look in
Jack's eyes as he was thrown backward by the force of
the bullet. The long, slow roll of the briefcase as it
wheeled end over end. The shouts of the backup teams
as they started to rush in. His own impossibly slow motion as he reached for his weapon.

The grin, the widening grin, flashing with gold as
Montega had turned to him.

"Stinking cops," he said, and fired.

Even now, Gage could feel the hot tearing punch that
exploded in his chest. The heat, unbearable, unspeakable. He could see himself flying backward. Flying endlessly. Endlessly into the dark.

And he'd been dead.

He'd known he was dead. He could see himself. He'd
looked down and had seen his body sprawled on the
bloody dock. Cops were working on him, packing his
wound, swearing and scrambling around like ants. He
had watched it all passionlessly, painlessly.

Then the paramedics had come, somehow pulling him
back into the pain. He had lacked the strength to fight
them and go where he wanted to go.

The operating room. Pale blue walls, harsh lights, the
glint of steel instruments. The beep, beep, beep of monitors. The labored hiss and release of the respirator.
Twice he had slipped easily out of his body—like breath,
quiet and invisible—to watch the surgical team fight for

his life. He'd wanted to tell them to stop, that he didn't want to come back where he could hurt again. Feel again.

But they had been skillful and determined and had dragged him back into that poor damaged body. And for a while, he'd returned to the blackness.

That had changed. He remembered floating in some gray liquid world that had brought back primordial memories of the womb. Safe there. Quiet there. Occasionally he could hear someone speak. Someone would say his name loudly, insistently. But he chose to ignore them. A woman weeping—his aunt. The shaken, pleading sound of his uncle's voice.

There would be light, an intrusion really, and though he couldn't feel, he sensed that someone was lifting his eyelids and shining a bead into his pupils.

It was a fascinating world. He could hear his own heartbeat. A gentle, insistent thud and swish. He could smell flowers. Only once in a while, then they would be overpowered by the slick, antiseptic smell of hospital. And he would hear music, soft, quiet music. Beethoven, Mozart, Chopin.

Later he learned that one of the nurses had been moved enough to bring a small tape player into his room. She often brought in discarded flower arrangements and sat and talked with him in a quiet, motherly voice.

Sometimes he mistook her for his own mother and felt unbearably sad.

When the mists in that gray world began to part, he struggled against it. He wanted to stay. But no matter how deep he dived, he kept floating closer to the surface.

Until at last, he opened his eyes to the light.

That was the worst part of the nightmare, Gage

thought now. When he'd opened his eyes and realized he was alive.

Wearily Gage climbed out of bed. He had gotten past the death wish that had haunted him those first few weeks. But on the mornings he suffered from the nightmare, he was tempted to curse the skill and dedication of the medical team that had brought him back.

They hadn't brought Jack back. They hadn't saved his parents who had died before he'd even known them. They hadn't had enough skill to save his aunt and uncle, who had raised him with unstinting love and who had died only weeks before he had come out of the coma.

Yet they had saved him. Gage understood why.

It was because of the gift, the curse of a gift he'd been given during those nine months his soul had gestated in that gray, liquid world. And because they had saved him, he had no choice but to do what he was meant to do.

With a dull kind of acceptance, he placed his right hand against the pale green wall of his bedroom. He concentrated. He heard the hum inside his brain, the hum no one else could hear. Then, quickly and completely, his hand vanished.

Oh, it still existed. He could feel it. But even he couldn't see it. There was no outline, no silhouette of knuckles. From the wrist up, the hand was gone. He had only to focus his mind, and his whole body would do the same.

He could still remember the first time it had happened. How it had terrified him. And fascinated him. He made his hand reappear and studied it. It was the same. Wide palmed, long fingered, a bit rough with callus. The ordinary hand of a man who was no longer ordinary.

A clever trick, he thought, for someone who walks the streets at night, searching for answers.

He closed the hand into a fist, then moved off into the adjoining bathroom to shower.

At 11:45 a.m., Deborah was cooling her heels at the twenty-fifth precinct. She wasn't particularly surprised to have been summoned there. The four gang members who had gunned down Rico Mendez were being held in separate cells. That way they would sweat out the charges of murder one, accessory to murder, illegal possession of firearms, possession of controlled substances, and all the other charges on the arrest sheet. And they could sweat them out individually, with no opportunity to corroborate each other's stories.

She'd gotten the call from Sly Parino's public defense attorney at nine sharp. This would make the third meeting between them. At each previous encounter, she had held firm against a deal. Parino's public defendant was asking for the world, and Parino himself was crude, nasty and arrogant. But she had noted that each time they sat in the conference room together, Parino sweated more freely.

Instinct told her he did indeed have something to trade but was afraid.

Using her own strategy, Deborah had agreed to the meeting, but had put it off for a couple of hours. It sounded like Parino was ready to deal, and since she had him cold, with possession of the murder weapon and two eye witnesses, he'd better have gold chips to ante up.

She used her time waiting for Parino to be brought in from lockup by reviewing her notes on the case. Because she could have recited them by rote, her mind wandered back to the previous evening.

Just what kind of man was Gage Guthrie? she wondered. The type who bundled a reluctant woman into his

limo after a five-minute acquaintance. Then left that limo
at her disposal for two and a half hours. She remembered
her baffled amusement when she had come out of the
Justice Building at one o'clock in the morning only to
find the long black limo with its taciturn hulk of a driver
patiently waiting to take her home.

Mr. Guthrie's orders.

Though Mr. Guthrie had been nowhere to be seen, she
had felt his presence all during the drive from midtown
to her apartment in the lower West End.

A powerful man, she mused now. In looks, in personality, and in basic masculine appeal. She looked around
the station house, trying to imagine the elegant, just
slightly rough-around-the-edges man in the tuxedo
working here.

The twenty-fifth was one of the toughest precincts in
the city. And where, Deborah had discovered when she'd
been driven to satisfy her curiosity, Detective Gage
Guthrie had worked during most of his six years with
UPD.

It was difficult to connect the two, she mused. The
smooth, obstinately charming man, with the grimy linoleum, harsh fluorescent lights, and odors of sweat and
stale coffee underlaid with the gummy aroma of pine
cleaner.

He liked classical music, for it had been Mozart drifting through the limo's speakers. Yet he had worked for
years amid the shouts, curses and shrilling phones of the
twenty-fifth.

From the information she'd read once she'd accessed
his file, she knew he'd been a good cop—sometimes a
reckless one, but one who had never crossed the line. At
least not on record. Instead, his record had been fat with
commendations.

He and his partner had broken up a prostitution ring which had preyed on young runaways, were given credit for the arrest of three prominent businessmen who had run an underground gambling operation that had chastised its unlucky clients with unspeakable torture, had tracked down drug dealers, small and large, and had ferreted out a crooked cop who had used his badge to extort protection money from small shop owners in Urbana's Little Asia.

Then they had gone undercover to break the back of one of the largest drug cartels on the eastern seaboard. And had ended up broken themselves.

Was that what was so fascinating about him? Deborah wondered. That it seemed the sophisticated, wealthy businessman was only an illusion thinly covering the tough cop he had been? Or had he simply returned to his privileged background, his years as a policeman the aberration? Who was the real Gage Guthrie?

She shook her head and sighed. She'd been thinking a lot about illusions lately. Since the night in the alley when she'd been faced with the terrifying reality of her own mortality. And had been saved—though she firmly believed she would have saved herself—by what many people thought was no more than a phantom.

Nemesis was real enough, she mused. She had seen him, heard him, even been annoyed by him. And yet, when he came into her mind, he was like smoke. If she had reached out to touch him, would her hand have passed right through?

What nonsense. She was going to have to get more sleep if overwork caused her mind to take fantasy flights in the middle of the day.

But somehow, she was going to find that phantom again and pin him down.

"Miss O'Roarke."

"Yes." She rose and offered her hand to the young, harried-looking public defendant. "Hello again, Mr. Simmons."

"Yes, well…" He pushed tortoiseshell glasses up on his hooked nose. "I appreciate you agreeing to this meeting."

"Cut the bull." Behind Simmons, Parino was flanked by two uniformed cops. He had a sneer on his face and his hands in cuffs. "We're here to deal, so let's cut to the chase."

With a nod, Deborah led the way into the small conference room. She settled her briefcase on the table and sat behind it. She folded her hands. In her trim navy suit and white blouse she looked every inch the Southern belle. She'd been taught her manners well. But her eyes, as dark as the linen of her suit, burned as they swept over Parino. She had studied the police photos of Mendez and had seen what hate and an automatic weapon could do to a sixteen-year-old body.

"Mr. Simmons, you're aware that of the four suspects facing indictment for the murder of Rico Mendez, your client holds the prize for the most serious charges?"

"Can we lose these things?" Parino held out his cuffed hands. Deborah glanced at him.

"No."

"Come on, babe." He gave her what she imagined he thought was a sexy leer. "You're not afraid of me, are you?"

"Of you, Mr. Parino?" Her lips curved, but her tone was frigidly sarcastic. "Why, no. I squash nasty little bugs every day. You, however, should be afraid of me. I'm the one who's going to put you away." She flicked her gaze back to Simmons. "Let's not waste time, again.

All three of us know the score. Mr. Parino is nineteen and will be tried as an adult. It is still to be determined whether the others will be tried as adults or juveniles.'' She took out her notes, though she didn't need them as more than a prop. ''The murder weapon was found in Mr. Parino's apartment, with Mr. Parino's fingerprints all over it.''

''It was planted,'' Parino insisted. ''I never saw it before in my life.''

''Save it for the judge,'' Deborah suggested. ''Two witnesses place him in the car that drove by the corner of Third and Market at 11:45, June 2. Those same witnesses have identified Mr. Parino, in a lineup, as the man who leaned out of that car and fired ten shots into Rico Mendez.''

Parino began to swear and shout about squealers, about what he would do to them when he got out. About what he would do to her. Not bothering to raise her voice, Deborah continued, her eyes on Simmons.

''We have your client, cold, murder one. And the state will ask for the death penalty.'' She folded her hands on her notes and nodded at Simmons. ''Now, what do you want to talk about?''

Simmons tugged at his tie. The smoke from the cigarette Parino was puffing was drifting in his direction and burning his eyes. ''My client has information that he would be willing to turn over to the D.A.'s office.'' He cleared his throat. ''In return for immunity, and a reduction of the current charges against him. From murder one, to illegal possession of a firearm.''

Deborah lifted a brow, let the silence take a beat. ''I'm waiting for the punch line.''

''This is no joke, sister.'' Parino leaned over the table. ''I got something to deal, and you'd better play.''

With deliberate motions, Deborah put her notes back into her briefcase, snapped the lock then rose. "You're slime, Parino. Nothing, nothing you've got to deal is going to put you back on the street again. If you think you can walk over me, or the D.A.'s office, then think again."

Simmons bobbed up as she headed for the door. "Miss O'Roarke, please, if we could simply discuss this."

She whirled back to him. "Sure, we'll discuss it. As soon as you make me a realistic offer."

Parino said something short and obscene that caused Simmons to lose his color and Deborah to turn a cold, dispassionate eye on him.

"The state is going for murder one and the death penalty," she said calmly. "And believe me when I say I'm going to see to it that your client is ripped out of society just like a leech."

"I'll get off," Parino shouted at her. His eyes were wild as he lunged to his feet. "And when I do, I'm coming looking for you, bitch."

"You won't get off." She faced him across the table. Her eyes were cold as ice and never wavered. "I'm very good at what I do, Parino, which is putting rabid little animals like you away in cages. In your case, I'm going to pull out all the stops. You won't get off," she repeated. "And when you're sweating in death row, I want you to think of me."

"Murder two," Simmons said quickly, and was echoed by a savage howl from his client.

"You're going to sell me out, you sonofabitch."

Deborah ignored Parino and studied Simmons's nervous eyes. There was something here, she could smell it. "Murder one," she repeated, "with a recommendation for life imprisonment rather than the death penalty—if you've got something that holds my interest.''

"Let me talk to my client, please. If you could give us a minute.''

"Of course.'' She left the sweaty public defendant with his screaming client.

Twenty minutes later, she faced Parino again across the scarred table. He was paler, calmer, as he smoked a cigarette down to the filter.

"Deal your cards, Parino,'' she suggested.

"I want immunity.''

"From whatever charges might be brought from the information you give me. Agreed.'' She already had him where she wanted him.

"And protection.'' He'd begun to sweat.

"If it's warranted.''

He hesitated, fiddling with the cigarette, the scorched plastic ashtray. But he was cornered, and knew it. Twenty years. The public defendant had said he'd probably cop a parole in twenty years.

Twenty years in the hole was better than the chair. Anything was. And a smart guy could do pretty well for himself in the joint. He figured he was a pretty smart guy.

"I've been doing some deliveries for some guys. Heavy hitters. Trucking stuff from the docks to this fancy antique shop downtown. They paid good, too good, so I knew something was in those crates besides old vases.'' Awkward in the cuffs, he lit one cigarette from the smoldering filter of another. "So I figured I'd take a look myself. I opened one of the crates. It was packed with coke. Man, I've never seen so much snow. A hundred, maybe a hundred and fifty pounds. And it was pure.''

"How do you know?"

He licked his lips, then grinned. "I took one of the packs, put it under my shirt. I'm telling you, there was enough there to fill up every nose in the state for the next twenty years."

"What's the name of the shop?"

He licked his lips again. "I want to know if we got a deal?"

"If the information can be verified, yes. If you're pulling my chain, no."

"Timeless. That's the name. It's over on Seventh. We delivered once, maybe twice a week. I don't know how often we were taking in coke or just fancy tables."

"Give me some names."

"The guy I worked with at the docks was Mouse. Just Mouse, that's all I know."

"Who hired you?"

"Just some guy. He came into Loredo's, the bar in the West End where the Demons hang out. He said he had some work if I had a strong back and knew how to keep my mouth shut. So me and Ray, we took him up on it."

"Ray?"

"Ray Santiago. He's one of us, the Demons."

"What did he look like, the man who hired you?"

"Little guy, kinda spooky. Big mustache, couple of gold teeth. Walked into Loredo's in a fancy suit, but nobody thought to mess with him."

She took notes, nodded, prompted until she was certain Parino was wrung dry. "All right, I'll check it out. If you've been straight with me, you'll find I'll be straight with you." She rose, glancing at Simmons. "I'll be in touch."

When she left the conference room, her head was

pounding. There was a tight, sick feeling in her gut that always plagued her when she dealt with Parino's type.

He was nineteen, for God's sake, she thought as she tossed her visitor's badge to the desk sergeant. Not even old enough to vote—a privilege she would see he never attained—yet he'd viciously gunned down another human being. She knew he felt no remorse. The Demons considered drive-bys a kind of tribal ritual. And she, as a representative of the law, had bargained with him.

That was the way the system worked, she reminded herself as she stepped out of the stuffy station house into the steamy afternoon. She would trade Parino like a poker chip and hope to finesse bigger game. In the end, Parino would pay by spending the rest of his youth and most of his adult life in a cage.

She hoped Rico Mendez's family would feel justice had been served.

"Bad day?"

Still frowning, she turned, shaded her eyes and focused on Gage Guthrie. "Oh. Hello. What are you doing here?"

"Waiting for you."

She lifted a brow, cautiously debating the proper response. Today he wore a gray suit, very trim and quietly expensive. Though the humidity was intense, his white shirt appeared crisp. His gray silk tie was neatly knotted.

He looked precisely like what he was. A successful, wealthy businessman. Until you looked at his eyes, Deborah thought. When you did, you could see that women were drawn to him for a much more basic reason than money and position.

She responded with the only question that seemed apt. "Why?"

He smiled at that. He had seen her caution and her

evaluation clearly and was as amused as he was impressed by it. "To invite you to lunch."

"Oh. Well, that's very nice, but—"

"You do eat, don't you?"

He was laughing at her. There was no mistaking it. "Yes, almost every day. But at the moment, I'm working."

"You're a dedicated public servant, aren't you, Deborah?"

"I like to think so." There was just enough sarcasm in his tone to put her back up. She stepped to the curb and lifted an arm to hail a cab. A bus chugged by, streaming exhaust. "It was kind of you to leave your limo for me last night." She turned and looked at him. "But it wasn't necessary."

"I often do what others consider unnecessary." He took her hand and, with only the slightest pressure, brought her arm down to her side. "If not lunch, dinner."

"That sounds more like a command than a request." She would have tugged her hand away, but it seemed foolish to engage in a childish test of wills on a public street. "Either way, I have to refuse. I'm working late tonight."

"Tomorrow then." He smiled charmingly. "A request, Counselor."

It was difficult not to smile back when he was looking at her with humor and—was it loneliness?—in his eyes. "Mr. Guthrie. Gage." She corrected herself before he could. "Persistent men usually annoy me. And you're no exception. But for some reason, I think I'd like to have dinner with you."

"I'll pick you up at seven. I keep early hours."

"Fine. I'll give you my address."

"I know it."

"Of course." His driver had dropped her off at her doorstep the night before. "If you'll give me back my hand, I'd like to hail a cab."

He didn't oblige her immediately, but looked down at her hand. It was small and delicate in appearance, like the rest of her. But there was strength in the fingers. She kept her nails short, neatly rounded with a coating of clear polish. She wore no rings, no bracelets, only a slim, practical watch that he noted was accurate to the minute.

He looked up from her hand, into her eyes. He saw curiosity, a touch of impatience and again, the wariness. Gage made himself smile as he wondered how a simple meeting of palms could have jolted his system so outrageously.

"I'll see you tomorrow." He released her and stepped away.

She only nodded, not trusting her voice. When she slipped into a cab, she turned back. But he was already gone.

It was after ten when Deborah walked up to the antique store. It was closed, of course, and she hadn't expected to find anything. She had written her report and passed the details of her interview with Parino on to her superior. But she hadn't been able to resist a look for herself.

In this upscale part of town, people were lingering over dinner or enjoying a play. A few couples wandered by on their way to a club or a restaurant. Streetlights shot out pools of security.

It was foolish, she supposed, to have been drawn here. She could hardly have expected the doors to have been opened so she could walk in and discover a cache of drugs in an eighteenth-century armoire.

The window was not only dark, it was barred and shaded. Just as the shop itself was under a triple cloak of secrecy. She had spent hours that day searching for the name of the owner. He had shielded himself well under a tangle of corporations. The paper trail took frustrating twists and turns. So far, every lead Deborah had pursued had come up hard at a dead end.

But the stop was real. By tomorrow, the day after at the latest, she would have a court order. The police would search every nook and cranny of Timeless. The books would be confiscated. She would have everything she needed to indict.

She walked closer to the dark window. Something made her turn quickly to peer out at the light and shadow of the street behind her.

Traffic rolled noisily by. Arm in arm, a laughing couple strolled along the opposite sidewalk. The sound of music through open car windows was loud and confused, punctuated by the honking of horns and the occasional squeak of brakes.

Normal, Deborah reminded herself. There was nothing here to cause that itch between her shoulder blades. Yet even as she scanned the street, the adjoining buildings, to assure herself no one was paying any attention to her, the feeling of being watched persisted.

She was giving herself the creeps, Deborah decided. These little licks of fear were left over from her night in the alley, and she didn't care for it. It wasn't possible to live your life too spooked to go out at night, so paranoid you looked around every corner before you took that last step around it. At least it wasn't possible for her.

Most of her life she had been cared for, looked after,

even pampered by her older sister. Though she would always be grateful to Cilla, she had made a commitment when she had left Denver for Urbana. To leave her mark. That couldn't be done if she ran from shadows.

Determined to fight her own uneasiness, she skirted around the building, walking quickly through the short, narrow alley between the antique store and the boutique beside it.

The rear of the building was as secure and unforthcoming as the front. There was one window, enforced with steel bars, and a pair of wide doors, triple bolted. Here, there were no streetlamps to relieve the dark.

"You don't look stupid."

At the voice, she jumped back and would have tumbled into a line of garbage cans if a hand hadn't snagged her wrist. She opened her mouth to scream, brought her fist up to fight, when she recognized her companion.

"You!" He was in black, hardly visible in the dark. But she knew.

"I would have thought you'd had your fill of back alleys." He didn't release her, though he knew he should. His fingers braceleted her wrist and felt the fast, hot beat of her blood.

"You've been watching me."

"There are some women it's difficult to look away from." He pulled her closer, just a tug on her wrist, and stunned both of them. His voice was low and rough. She could see anger in the gleam of his eyes. She found the combination oddly compelling. "What are you doing here?"

Her mouth was so dry it ached. He had pulled her so close that their thighs met. She could feel the warm flutter of his breath on her lips. To insure some distance and some control, she put a hand to his chest.

Her hand didn't pass through, but met a warm, solid wall, felt the quick, steady beat of a heart.

"That's my business."

"Your business is to prepare cases and try them in court, not to play detective."

"I'm not playing—" She broke off, eyes narrowing. "How do you know I'm a lawyer?"

"I know a great deal about you, Miss O'Roarke." His smile was thin and humorless. "That's my business. I don't think your sister worked to put you through law school, and saw you graduate at the top of your class to have you sneaking around back entrances of locked buildings. Especially when that building is a front for some particularly ugly commerce."

"You know about this place?"

"As I said, I know a great deal."

She would handle his intrusion into her life later. Now, she had a job to do. "If you have any information, any proof about this suspected drug operation, it's your duty to give that information to the D.A.'s office."

"I'm very aware of my duty. It doesn't include making deals with scum."

Heat rushed to her cheeks. She didn't even question how he knew about her interview with Parino. It was enough, more than enough, that he was holding her integrity up to inspection. "I worked within the law," she snapped at him. "Which is more than you can say. You put on a mask and play Captain America, making up your own rules. That makes you part of the problem, not part of the solution."

In the slits of his mask, his eyes narrowed. "You seemed grateful enough for my solution a few nights ago."

Her chin came up. She wished she could face him on

her own ground, in the light. "I've already thanked you for your help, unnecessary though it was."

"Are you always so cocky, Miss O'Roarke?"

"Confident," she corrected.

"And do you always win in court?"

"I have an excellent record."

"Do you always win?" he repeated.

"No, but that's not the point."

"That's exactly the point. There's a war in this city, Miss O'Roarke."

"And you've appointed yourself general of the good guys."

He didn't smile. "No, I fight alone."

"Don't you—"

But he cut her off swiftly, putting a gloved hand over her mouth. He listened, but not with his ears. It wasn't something he heard, but something he felt, as some men felt hunger or thirst, love or hate. Or, from centuries ago when their senses were not dulled by civilization, danger.

Before she had even begun to struggle against him, he pulled her aside and shoved her down beneath him behind the wall of the next building.

"What the hell do you think you're doing?"

The explosion that came on the tail of her words made her ears ring. The flash of light made her pupils contract. Before she could close her eyes against the glare, she saw the jagged shards of flying glass, the missiles of charred brick. Beneath her, the ground trembled as the antique store exploded.

She saw, with horror and fascination, a lethal chunk of concrete crash only three feet from her face.

"Are you all right?" When she didn't answer, only

trembled, he took her face in his hand and turned it to his. "Deborah, are you all right?"

He repeated her name twice before the glassy look left her eyes. "Yes," she managed. "Are you?"

"Don't you read the papers?" There was the faintest of smiles around his mouth. "I'm invulnerable."

"Right." With a little sigh, she tried to sit up. For a moment he didn't move, but left his body where it was, where it wanted to be. Fitted against hers. His face was only inches away. He wondered what would happen— to both of them—if he closed that distance and let his mouth meet hers.

He was going to kiss her, Deborah realized and went perfectly still. Emotion swarmed through her. Not anger, as she'd expected. But excitement, raw and wild. It pumped through her so quickly, so hugely, it blocked out everything else. With a little murmur of agreement, she lifted her hand to his cheek.

Her fingers brushed his mask. He pulled back from her touch as if he'd been slapped. Shifting, he rose then helped her to her feet. Fighting a potent combination of humiliation and fury, she stepped around the wall toward the rear of the antique shop.

There was little left of it. Brick, glass and concrete were scattered. Inside the crippled building, fire raged. The roof collapsed with a long, loud groan.

"They've beaten you this time," he murmured. "There won't be anything left for you to find, no papers, no drugs, no records."

"They've destroyed a building," she said between her teeth. She hadn't wanted to be kissed, she told herself. She'd been shaken up, dazed, a victim of temporary insanity. "But someone owns it, and I'll find out who that is."

''This was meant as a warning, Miss O'Roarke. One you might want to consider.''

''I won't be frightened off. Not by exploding buildings or by you.'' She turned to face him, but wasn't surprised that he was gone.

Chapter 3

It was after one in the morning when Deborah dragged herself down the hallway toward her apartment. She'd spent the best part of two hours answering questions, giving her statement to the police and avoiding reporters. Even through the fatigue was a nagging annoyance for the man called Nemesis.

Technically he'd saved her life again. If she'd been standing within ten feet of the antique shop when the bomb had gone off, she would certainly have met a nasty death. But then he'd left her holding the bag, a very large, complicated bag she'd been forced to sort through, assistant D.A. or not, for the police.

Added to that was the fact he had shown in the short, pithy conversation they'd had, that he held no respect for her profession or her judgment. She had studied and worked toward the goal of prosecutor since she'd been eighteen. Now with a shrug, he was dismissing those years of her life as wasted.

No, she thought as she dug in her purse for her keys, he preferred to skulk around the streets, meting out his own personal sense of justice. Well, it didn't wash. And before it was over, she was going to prove to him that the system worked.

And she would prove to herself that she hadn't been the least bit attracted to him.

"You look like you had a rough night."

Keys in hand, Deborah turned. Her across-the-hall neighbor, Mrs. Greenbaum, was standing in her open doorway, peering out through a pair of cherry-red framed glasses.

"Mrs. Greenbaum, what are you doing up?"

"Just finished watching David Letterman. That boy cracks me up." At seventy, with a comfortable pension to buffer her against life's storms, Lil Greenbaum kept her own hours and did as she pleased. At the moment she was wearing a tatty terry-cloth robe, Charles and Di bedroom slippers and a bright pink bow in the middle of her hennaed hair. "You look like you could use a drink. How about a nice hot toddy?"

Deborah was about to refuse, when she realized a hot toddy was exactly what she wanted. She smiled, dropped the keys into her jacket pocket and crossed the hall. "Make it a double."

"Already got the hot water on. You just sit down and kick off your shoes." Mrs. Greenbaum patted her hand then scurried off to the kitchen.

Grateful, Deborah sank into the deep cushions of the couch. The television was still on, with an old black-and-white movie flickering on the screen. Deborah recognized a young Cary Grant, but not the film. Mrs. Greenbaum would know, she mused. Lil Greenbaum knew everything.

The two-bedroom apartment—Mrs. Greenbaum kept a second bedroom ready for any of her numerous grandchildren—was both cluttered and tidy. Tables were packed with photographs and trinkets. There was a lava lamp atop the television, with a huge brass peace symbol attached to its base. Lil was proud of the fact that she'd marched against the establishment in the sixties. Just as she had protested nuclear reactors, Star Wars, the burning of rain forests and the increased cost of Medicare.

She liked to protest, she'd often told Deborah. When you could argue against the system, it meant you were still alive and kicking.

"Here we are." She brought out two slightly warped ceramic mugs—the product of one of her younger children's creativity. She flicked a glance at the television. "*Penny Serenade,* 1941, and oh, wasn't that Cary Grant something?" After setting down the mugs, she picked up her remote and shut the TV off. "Now, what trouble have you been getting yourself into?"

"It shows?"

Mrs. Greenbaum took a comfortable sip of whiskey-laced tea. "Your suit's a mess." She leaned closer and took a sniff. "Smells like smoke. Got a smudge on your cheek, a run in your stocking and fire in your eyes. From the look in them, there's got to be a man involved."

"The UPD could use you, Mrs. Greenbaum." Deborah sipped at the tea and absorbed the hot jolt. "I was doing a little legwork. The building I was checking out blew up."

The lively interest in Mrs. Greenbaum's eyes turned instantly to concern. "You're not hurt?"

"No. Few bruises." They would match the ones she'd gotten the week before. "I guess my ego suffered a little. I ran into Nemesis." Deborah hadn't mentioned her first encounter, because she was painfully aware of her neighbor's passionate admiration for the man in black.

Behind the thick frames, Mrs. Greenbaum's eyes bulged. "You actually saw him?"

"I saw him, spoke to him and ended up being tossed to the concrete by him just before the building blew up."

"God." Lil pressed a hand to her heart. "That's even more romantic than when I met Mr. Greenbaum at the Pentagon rally."

"It had nothing to do with romance. The man is impossible, very likely a maniac and certainly dangerous."

"He's a hero." Mrs. Greenbaum shook a scarlet-tipped finger at Deborah. "You haven't learned to recognize heroes yet. That's because we don't have enough of them today." She crossed her feet so that Princess Di grinned up at Deborah. "So, what does he look like? The reports have all been mixed. One day he's an eight-foot black man, another he's a pale-faced vampire complete with fangs. Just the other day I read he was a small green woman with red eyes."

"He's not a woman," Deborah muttered. She could remember, a bit too clearly, the feel of his body over hers. "And I can't really say what he looks like. It was dark and most of his face was masked."

"Like Zorro?" Mrs. Greenbaum said hopefully.

"No. Well, I don't know. Maybe." She gave a little sigh and decided to indulge her neighbor. "He's six-one or six-two, I suppose, lean but well built."

"What color is his hair?"

"It was covered. I could see his jawline." Strong, tensed. "And his mouth." It had hovered for one long, exciting moment over hers. "Nothing special," she said quickly, and gulped more tea.

"Hmm." Mrs. Greenbaum had her own ideas. She'd

been married and widowed twice, and in between had enjoyed what she considered her fair share of affairs and romantic entanglements. She recognized the signs. "His eyes? You can always tell the make of a man by his eyes. Though I'd rather look at his tush."

Deborah chuckled. "Dark."

"Dark what?"

"Just dark. He keeps to the shadows."

"Slipping through the shadows to root out evil and protect the innocent. What's more romantic than that?"

"He's bucking the system."

"My point exactly. It doesn't get bucked enough."

"I'm not saying he hasn't helped a few people, but we have trained law enforcement officers to do that." She frowned into her mug. There hadn't been any cops around either time she had needed help. They couldn't be everywhere. And she probably could have handled both situations herself. Probably. She used her last and ultimate argument. "He doesn't have any respect for the law."

"I think you're wrong. I think he has great respect for it. He just interprets it differently than you do." Again she patted Deborah's hand. "You're a good girl, Deborah, a smart girl, but you've trained yourself to walk down a very narrow path. You should remember that this country was founded on rebellion. We often forget, then we become fat and lazy until someone comes along and questions the status quo. We need rebels, just as we need heroes. It would be a dull, sad world without them."

"Maybe." Though she was far from convinced. "But we also need rules."

"Oh, yes." Mrs. Greenbaum grinned. "We need rules. How else could we break them?"

* * *

Gage kept his eyes closed as his driver guided the limo across town. Through the night after the explosion and the day that followed, he had thought of a dozen reasons why he should cancel his date with Deborah O'Roarke.

They were all very practical, very logical, very sane reasons. To offset them had been only one impractical, illogical and potentially insane reason.

He needed her.

She was interfering with his work, both day and night. Since the moment he'd seen her, he hadn't been able to think of anyone else. He'd used his vast network of computers to dig out every scrap of available information on her. He knew she'd been born in Atlanta, twenty-five years before. He knew she had lost her parents, tragically and brutally, at the age of eight. Her sister had raised her, and together they had hopscotched across the country. The sister worked in radio and was now station manager at KHIP in Denver where Deborah had gone to college.

Deborah had passed the bar the first time and had applied for a position in the D.A.'s office in Urbana, where she had earned a reputation for being thorough, meticulous and ambitious.

He knew she had had one serious love affair in college, but he didn't know what had ended it. She dated a variety of men, none seriously.

He hated the fact that that one last piece of information had given him tremendous relief.

She was a danger to him. He knew it, understood it and seemed unable to avoid it. Even after their encounter the night before when she had come within a hair's breadth of making him lose control—of his temper and his desire—he wasn't able to shove her out of his mind.

To go on seeing her was to go on deceiving her. And himself.

But when the car pulled to the curb in front of her building, he got out, walked into the lobby and took the elevator up to her floor.

When Deborah heard the knock, she stopped pacing the living room. For the past twenty minutes she'd been asking herself why she had agreed to go out with a man she barely knew. And one with a reputation of being a connoisseur of women but married to his business.

She'd fallen for the charm, she admitted, that smooth, careless charm with the hint of underlying danger. Maybe she'd even been intrigued, and challenged, by his tendency to dominate. She stood for a moment, hand on the knob. It didn't matter, she assured herself. It was only one evening, a simple dinner date. She wasn't naïve and wide-eyed, and expected no more than good food and intelligent conversation.

She wore blue. Somehow he'd known she would. The deep midnight-blue silk of her dinner suit matched her eyes. The skirt was snug and short, celebrating the length of long, smooth legs. The tailored, almost mannish jacket made him wonder if she wore more silk, or simply her skin, beneath it. The lamp she had left on beside the door caught the gleam of the waterfall of blue and white stones she wore at her ears.

The easy flattery he was so used to dispensing lodged in his throat. "You're prompt," he managed.

"Always." She smiled at him. "It's like a vice." She closed the door behind her without inviting him in. It seemed safer that way.

A few moments later, she settled back in the limo and

vowed to enjoy herself. "Do you always travel this way?"

"No. Just when it seems more convenient."

Unable to resist, she slipped off her shoes and let her feet sink into the deep pewter carpet. "I would. No hassling for cabs or scurrying to the subway."

"But you miss a lot of life on, and under, the streets."

She turned to him. In his dark suit and subtly striped tie he looked elegant and successful. There were burnished gold links at the cuffs of his white shirt. "You're not going to tell me you ride the subway."

He only smiled. "When it seems most convenient. You don't believe that money should be used as an insulator against reality?"

"No. No, I don't." But she was surprised he didn't. "Actually, I've never had enough to be tempted to try it."

"You wouldn't be." He contented himself, or tried, by toying with the ends of her hair. "You could have gone into private practice with a dozen top firms at a salary that would have made your paycheck at the D.A.'s office look like pin money. You didn't."

She shrugged it off. "Don't think there aren't moments when I question my own sanity." Thinking it would be safer to move to more impersonal ground, she glanced out the window. "Where are we going?"

"To dinner."

"I'm relieved to hear that since I missed lunch. I meant where."

"Here." He took her hand as the limo stopped. They had driven to the very edge of the city, to the world of old money and prestige. Here the sound of traffic was only a distant echo, and there was the light, delicate scent of roses in bloom.

Deborah stifled a gasp as she stepped onto the curb. She had seen pictures of his home. But it was entirely different to be faced with it. It loomed over the street, spreading for half a block.

It was Gothic in style, having been built by a philanthropist at the turn of the century. She'd read somewhere that Gage had purchased it before he'd been released from the hospital.

Towers and turrets rose up into the sky. High mullioned windows gleamed with the sun that was lowering slowly in the west. Terraces jutted out, then danced around corners. The top story was dominated by a huge curving glass where one could stand and look out over the entire city.

"I see you take the notion that a man's home is his castle literally."

"I like space, and privacy. But I decided to postpone the moat."

With a laugh, she walked up to the carved doors at the entrance.

"Would you like a tour before we eat?"

"Are you kidding?" She hooked her arm through his. "Where do we start?"

He led her through winding corridors, under lofty ceilings, into rooms both enormous and cramped. And he couldn't remember enjoying his home more than now, seeing it through her eyes.

There was a two-level library packed with books—from first editions to dog-eared paperbacks. Parlors with curvy old couches and delicate porcelain. Ming vases, Tang horses, Lalique crystal and Mayan pottery. Walls were done in rich, deep colors, offset by gleaming wood and Impressionist paintings.

The east wing held a tropical greenery, an indoor pool

and a fully equipped gymnasium with a separate whirl-pool and sauna. Through another corridor, up a curving staircase, there were bedrooms furnished with four-posters or heavy carved headboards.

She stopped counting rooms.

More stairs, then a huge office with a black marble desk and a wide sheer window that was growing rosy with sundown. Computers silent and waiting.

A music room, complete with a white grand piano and an old Wurlitzer jukebox. Almost dizzy, she stepped into a mirrored ballroom and stared at her own multiplied reflection. Above, a trio of magnificent chandeliers blazed with sumptuous light.

"It's like something out of a movie," she murmured. "I feel as though I should be wearing a hooped skirt and a powdered wig."

"No." He touched her hair again. "I think it suits you just fine as it is."

With a shake of her head, she stepped further inside, then went with impulse and turned three quick circles. "It's incredible, really. Don't you ever get the urge to just come into this room and dance?"

"Not until now." Surprising himself as much as her, he caught her around the waist and swung her into a waltz.

She should have laughed—have shot him an amused and flirtatious look and have taken the impulsive gesture for what it was. But she couldn't. All she could do was stare up at him, stare into his eyes as he spun her around and around the mirrored room.

Her hand lay on his shoulder, her other caught firmly in his. Their steps matched, though she gave no thought to them. She wondered, foolishly, if he heard the same music in his head that she did.

He heard nothing but the steady give and take of her breathing. Never in his life could he remember being so totally, so exclusively aware of one person. The way her long, dark lashes framed her eyes. The subtle trace of bronze she had smudged on the lids. The pale, moist gloss of rose on her lips.

Where his hand gripped her waist, the silk was warm from her body. And that body seemed to flow with his, anticipating each step, each turn. Her hair fanned out, making him ache to let his hands dive into it. Her scent floated around him, not quite sweet and utterly tempting. He wondered if he would taste it if he pressed his lips to the long, white column of her throat.

She saw the change in his eyes, the deepening, the darkening of them as desire grew. As her steps matched his, so did her need. She felt it build and spread, like a living thing, until her body thrummed with it. She leaned toward him, wondering.

He stopped. For a moment they stood, reflected dozens and dozens of times. A man and a woman caught in a tentative embrace, on the brink of something neither of them understood.

She moved first, a cautious half step in retreat. It was her nature to think carefully before making any decision. His hand tightened on hers. For some reason she thought it was a warning.

"I…my head's spinning."

Very slowly his hand slipped away from her waist and the embrace was broken. "Then I'd better feed you."

"Yes." She nearly managed to smile. "You'd better."

They dined on sautéed shrimp flavored with orange and rosemary. Though he'd shown her the enormous dining room with its heavy mahogany servers and sideboards, they took their meal in a small salon at a table by a curved window. Between sips of champagne, they could watch the sunset over the city. On the table, between them, were two slender white candles and a single red rose.

"It's beautiful here," she commented. "The city. You can see all its possibilities, and none of its problems."

"Sometimes it helps to take a step back." He stared out at the city himself, then turned away as if dismissing it. "Or else those problems can eat you alive."

"But you're still aware of them. I know you donate a lot of money to the homeless and rehabilitation centers, and other charities."

"It's easy to give money away when you have more than you need."

"That sounds cynical."

"Realistic." His smile was cool and easy. "I'm a businessman, Deborah. Donations are tax deductible."

She frowned, studying him. "It would be a great pity, I think, if people were only generous when it benefited them."

"Now you sound like an idealist."

Riled, she tapped a finger against the champagne goblet. "That's the second time in a matter of days you've accused me of that. I don't think I like it."

"It wasn't meant as an insult, just an observation." He glanced up when Frank came in with individual chocolate soufflés. "We won't need anything else tonight."

The big man shrugged. "Okay."

Deborah noted that Frank moved with a dancer's grace, an odd talent in a man who was big and bulky. Thoughtful, she dipped a spoon into the dessert. "Is he your driver or your butler?" she asked.

"Both. And neither." He topped off her wine. "You might say he's an associate from a former life."

Intrigued, she lifted a brow. "Which means?"

"He was a pickpocket I collared a time or two when I was a cop. Then he was my snitch. Now...he drives my car and answers my door, among other things."

She noted that Gage's fingers fit easily around the slender stem of the crystal glass. "It's hard to imagine you working the streets."

He grinned at her. "Yes, I suppose it is." He watched the way the candlelight flickered in her eyes. Last night, he had seen the reflection of fire there, from the burning building and her own smothered desires.

"How long were you a cop?"

"One night too long," he said flatly, then reached for her hand. "Would you like to see the view from the roof?"

"Yes, I would." She pushed back from the table, understanding that the subject of his past was a closed book.

Rather than the stairs, he took her up in a small smoked-glass elevator. "All the comforts," she said as they started their ascent. "I'm surprised the place doesn't come equipped with a dungeon and secret passageways."

"Oh, but it does. Perhaps I'll show you...another time."

Another time, she thought. Did she want there to be another time? It had certainly been a fascinating evening, and with the exception of that moment of tension in the ballroom, a cordial one. Yet despite his polished manners, she sensed something restless and dangerous beneath the tailored suit.

That was what attracted her, she admitted. Just as that was what made her uneasy.

"What are you thinking?"

She decided it was best to be perfectly honest. "I was wondering who you were, and if I wanted to stick around long enough to find out."

The doors to the elevator whispered open, but he stayed where he was. "And do you?"

"I'm not sure." She stepped out and into the topmost turret of the building. With a sound of surprise and pleasure, she moved toward the wide curve of glass. Beyond it, the sun had set and the city was all shadow and light. "It's spectacular." She turned to him, smiling. "Just spectacular."

"It gets better." He pushed a button on the wall. Silently, magically, the curved glass parted. Taking her hand, he led her onto the stone terrace beyond.

Setting her palms on the stone railing, she leaned out into the hot wind that stirred the air. "You can see the trees in City Park, and the river." Impatiently she brushed her blowing hair out of her eyes. "The buildings look so pretty with their lights on." In the distance, she could see the twinkling lights of the Dover Heights suspension bridge. They draped like a necklace of diamonds against the dark.

"At dawn, when it's clear, the buildings are pearly gray and rose. And the sun turns all the glass into fire."

She looked at him and the city he faced. "Is that why you bought the house, for the view?"

"I grew up a few blocks from here. Whenever we walked in the park, my aunt would always point it out to me. She loved this house. She'd been to parties here as a child—she and my mother. They had been friends since childhood. I was the only child, for my parents, and then for my aunt and uncle. When I came back and learned they were gone…well, I couldn't think of much of anything at first. Then I began to think about this house. It seemed right that I take it, live in it.''

She laid a hand over his on the rail. ''There's nothing more difficult, is there, than to lose people you love and need?''

''No.'' When he looked at her, he saw that her eyes were dark and glowing with her own memories and with empathy for his. He brought a hand to her face, skimming back her hair with his fingers, molding her jawline with his palm. Her hand fluttered up to light on his wrist and trembled. Her voice was just as unsteady.

''I should go.''

''Yes, you should.'' But he kept his hand on her face, his eyes on hers as he shifted to trap her body between his and the stone parapet. His free hand slid gently up her throat until her face was framed. ''Have you ever been compelled to take a step that you knew was a mistake? You knew, but you couldn't stop.''

A haze was drifting over her mind, and she shook her head to clear it. ''I—no. No, I don't like to make mistakes.'' But she already knew she was about to make one. His palms were rough and warm against her skin. His eyes were so dark, so intense. For a moment she blinked, assaulted by a powerful sense of déjà vu.

But she'd never been here before, she assured herself as he skimmed his thumbs over the sensitive skin under her jawline.

''Neither do I.''

She moaned and shut her eyes, but he only brushed his lips over her brow. The light whisper of contact shot a spear of reaction through her. In the hot night she shuddered while his mouth moved gently over her temple.

"I want you." His voice was rough and tense as his fingers tightened in her hair. Her eyes were open again, wide and aware. In his she could see edgy desire. "I can barely breathe from wanting you. You're my mistake, Deborah. The one I never thought I would make."

His mouth came down on hers, hard and hungry, with none of the teasing seduction she had expected and told herself she would have resisted. There was nothing of the smooth and sophisticated man she had dined with here. This was the reckless and dangerous man she had caught only glimpses of.

He frightened her. He fascinated her. He seduced her.

With no hesitation, no caution, no thought, she responded, meeting power for power and need for need.

She didn't feel the rough stone against her back, only the hard long length of him as his body pressed to hers. She could taste the zing of wine on his tongue and something darker, the potent flavor of passion barely in check. With a groan of pleasure, she pulled him closer until she could feel his heart thudding against hers. Beat for beat.

She was more than he had dreamed. All silk and scent and long limbs. Her mouth was heated, yielding against his, then demanding. Her hands slid under his jacket, fingers flexing even as her head fell back in a taunting surrender that drove him mad.

A pulse hammered in her throat, enticing him to press his lips there and explore the new texture, the new flavor, before he brought his mouth back to hers. With teeth he nipped, with tongue he soothed, pushing them closer and closer to the edge of reason. He swallowed her gasp as he stroked his hands down her, seeking, cupping, molding.

He felt her shudder, then his own before he forced himself to grip tight to a last thin line of control. Very cautiously, like a man backing away from a sheer drop, he stepped away from her.

Dazed, Deborah brought a hand to her head. Fighting to catch her breath, she stared at him. What kind of power did he have, she wondered, that he could turn her from a sensible woman into a trembling puddle of need?

She turned, learning over the rail and gulping air as though it were water and she dying of thirst. "I don't think I'm ready for you," she managed at length.

"No. I don't think I'm ready for you, either. But there won't be any going back."

She shook her head. Her palms were pressed so hard into the rail that the stone was biting her skin. "I'll have to think about that."

"Once you've turned certain corners, there's no place to go but forward."

Calmer, she turned back to him. It was time, past time, to set the ground rules. For both of them. "Gage, however it might appear after what just happened, I don't have affairs with men I hardly know."

"Good." He, too, was calmer. His decision was made. "When we have ours, I want it to be exclusive."

Her voice chilled. "Obviously I'm not making myself clear. I haven't decided if I want to be involved with you, and I'm a long way from sure if I'd want that involvement to end up in bed."

"You are involved with me." Reaching out, he cupped the back of her neck before she could evade. "And we both want that involvement to end up in bed."

Very deliberately, she reached up and removed his hand. "I realize you're used to women falling obligingly at your feet. I have no intention of joining the horde. And I make up my own mind.''

''Should I kiss you again?''

''No.'' She threw a hand up and planted it solidly against his chest. In an instant she was reminded of how she had stood, just like this, with the man called Nemesis. The comparison left her shaken. ''No. It was a lovely evening, Gage.'' She took a long steadying breath. ''I mean that. I enjoyed the company, the dinner and…and the view. I'd hate to see you spoil it completely by being arrogant and argumentative.''

''It's not being either to accept the inevitable. I don't have to like it to accept it.'' Something flickered in his eyes. ''There is such a thing as destiny, Deborah. I had a long time to consider, and to come to terms with that.'' His brows drew together in a frown as he looked at her. ''God help both of us, but you're part of mine.'' He looked back, then offered a hand. ''I'll take you home.''

Chapter 4

Groaning, her eyes firmly shut, Deborah groped for the shrilling phone on her nightstand. She knocked over a book, a brass candlestick and a notepad before she managed to snag the receiver and drag it under the pillow.

"Hello?"

"O'Roarke?"

She cleared her throat. "Yes."

"Mitchell here. We've got a problem."

"Problem?" She shoved the pillow off her head and squinted at her alarm clock. The only problem she could see was that her boss was calling her at 6:15 a.m. "Has the Slagerman trial been postponed? I'm scheduled for court at nine."

"No. It's Parino."

"Parino?" Scrubbing a hand over her face, she struggled to sit up. "What about him?"

"He's dead."

"Dead." She shook her head to clear her groggy brain. "What do you mean he's dead?"

"As in doornail," Mitchell said tersely. "Guard found him about half an hour ago."

She wasn't groggy now, but was sitting ramrod straight, brain racing. "But—but how?"

"Knifed. Looks like he went up to the bars to talk to someone, and they shoved a stiletto through his heart."

"Oh, God."

"Nobody heard anything. Nobody saw anything," Mitchell said in disgust. "There was a note taped to the bars. It said, 'Dead birds don't sing.'"

"Somebody leaked that he was feeding us information."

"And you can bet that I'm going to find out who. Listen, O'Roarke, we're not going to be able to muzzle the press on this one. I figured you'd want to hear it from me instead of on the news during your morning coffee."

"Yeah." She pressed a hand to her queasy stomach. "Yeah, thanks. What about Santiago?"

"No show yet. We've got feelers out, but if he's gone to ground, it might be a while before we dig him up."

"They'll be after him, too," she said quietly. "Whoever arranged for Parino to be murdered will be after Ray Santiago."

"Then we'll just have to find him first. You're going to have to shake this off," he told her. "I know it's a tough break all around, but the Slagerman case is your priority now. The guy's got himself a real slick lawyer."

"I can handle it."

"Never figured otherwise. Give him hell, kid."

"Yeah. Yeah, I will." Deborah hung up and stared blankly into space until her alarm went off at 6:30.

* * *

"Hey! Hey, beautiful." Jerry Bower charged up the courthouse steps after Deborah. "Boy, that's concentration," he panted when he finally snagged her arm and stopped her. "I've been calling you for half a block."

"Sorry. I'm due in court in fifteen minutes."

He gave her a quick, smiling going-over. She'd pinned her hair back into a simple twist and wore pearl buttons at her ears. Her red linen suit was severely tailored and still managed to show off each subtle curve. The result was competent, professional and completely feminine.

"If I was on the jury, I'd give you a guilty verdict before you finished your opening statement. You look incredible."

"I'm a lawyer," she said tightly. "Not Miss November."

"Hey." He had to race up three more steps to catch her. "Hey, look, I'm sorry. That was a poorly phrased compliment."

She found a slippery hold on her temper. "No, I'm sorry. I'm a little touchy this morning."

"I heard about Parino."

With a grim nod, Deborah continued up the steps to the high carved doors of city courthouse. "News travels fast."

"He was a walking statistic, Deb. You can't let it get to you."

"He deserved his day in court," she said as she crossed the marble floor of the lobby and started toward a bank of elevators. "Even he deserved that. I knew he was afraid, but I didn't take it seriously enough."

"Do you think it would have mattered?"

"I don't know." It was that single question she would have to live with. "I just don't know."

"Look, the mayor's got a tough schedule today. There's this dinner tonight, but I can probably slip out before the brandy and cigar stage. How about a late movie?"

"I'm lousy company, Jerry."

"You know that doesn't matter."

"It matters to me." A ghost of a smile touched her lips. "I'd bite your head off again and hate myself." She stepped into the elevator.

"Counselor." Jerry grinned and gave her a thumbs-up before the doors slid shut.

The press was waiting for her on the fourth floor. Deborah had expected no less. Moving quickly, she waded through them, dispensing curt answers and no comments.

"Do you really expect to get a jury to convict a pimp for knocking around a couple of his girls?"

"I always expect to win when I go into court."

"Are you going to put the prostitutes on the stand?"

"Former prostitutes," she corrected, and let the question go unanswered.

"Is it true Mitchell assigned you to this case because you're a woman?"

"The D.A. doesn't choose his prosecutors by their sex."

"Do you feel responsible for the death of Carl Parino?"

That stopped her on the threshold of the courtroom. She looked around and saw the reporter with curly brown hair, hungry brown eyes and a sarcastic smirk. Chuck Wisner. She'd run foul of him before and would again. In his daily column in the *World*, he preferred the sensational to the factual.

"The D.A.'s office regrets that Carl Parino was murdered and not allowed his day in court."

In a quick, practiced move, he blocked her way. "But do you feel responsible? After all, you're the one who turned the deal."

She choked back the urge to defend herself and met his eyes levelly. "We're all responsible, Mr. Wisner. Excuse me."

He simply shifted, crowding her back from the door. "Any more encounters with Nemesis? What can you tell us about your personal experiences with the city's newest hero?"

She could feel her temper begin to fray, strand by strand. Worse, she knew that was exactly what he was hoping for. "Nothing that could compete with your fabrications. Now if you'll move aside, I'm busy."

"Not too busy to socialize with Gage Guthrie. Are you and he romantically involved? It makes a wild kind of triangle, doesn't it? Nemesis, you, Guthrie."

"Get a life, Chuck," she suggested, then elbowed him aside.

She barely had enough time to settle behind the prosecutor's table and open her briefcase when the jury filed in. She and the defense counsel had taken two days to select them, and she was satisfied with the mix of genders and races and walks of life. Still, she would have to convince those twelve men and women that a couple of prostitutes deserved justice.

Turning slightly, she studied the two women in the first row. They had both followed her instructions and dressed simply, with a minimum of makeup and hair spray. She knew they were on trial today, as much as the man charged with assault and battery. They huddled together, two young, pretty women who might have been mistaken for college students. Deborah sent them a reassuring smile before she shifted again.

James P. Slagerman sat at the defense table. He was thirty-two, dashingly blond and handsome in a dark suit and tie. He looked precisely like what he claimed he was, a young executive. His escort service was perfectly legitimate. He paid his taxes, contributed to charity and belonged to the Jaycees.

It would be Deborah's primary job to convince the jury that he was no different than a street pimp, taking his cut from the sale of a woman's body. Until she did that, she had no hope of convicting him on assault.

As the bailiff announced the judge, the courtroom rose.

Deborah kept her opening statement brief, working the jury, dispensing facts. She didn't attempt to dazzle them. She was already aware that this was the defense counsel's style. Instead, she would underplay, drawing their attention with the contrast of simplicity.

She began her direct examination by calling the doctor who had attended Marjorie Lovitz. With a few brief questions she established the extent of Marjorie's injuries on the night she and Suzanne McRoy had been brought into Emergency. She wanted the jury to hear of the broken jaw, the blackened eyes, the cracked ribs, even before she entered the photographs taken of the women that night into evidence.

She picked her way slowly, carefully through the technicalities, doctors, ambulance attendants, uniformed cops, social workers. She weathered her opponent's parries. By the noon recess, she had laid her groundwork.

She hustled Marjorie and Suzanne into a cab and took them across town for lunch and a last briefing.

"Do I have to go on the stand today, Miss

O'Roarke?'' Marjorie fidgeted in her seat and ate nothing. Though her bruises had faded over the weeks since the beating, her jaw still tended to ache. ''Maybe what the doctors and all said was enough, and Suzanne and I won't have to testify.''

''Marjorie.'' She laid a hand over the girl's and found it ice-cold and trembly. ''They'll listen to the doctors, and they'll look at the pictures. They'll believe you and Suzanne were beaten. But it's you, both of you, who will convince them that Slagerman was the one who did it, that he is not the nice young businessman he pretends to be. Without you, he'll walk away and do it again.''

Suzanne bit her lip. ''Jimmy says he's going to get off anyway. That people will know we're whores, even though you helped us get regular jobs. He says when it's over he's going to find us, and hurt us real bad.''

''When did he say that?''

''He called last night.'' Marjorie's eyes filled with tears. ''He found out where we're living and he called. He said he was going to mess us up.'' She wiped at a tear with the heel of her hand. ''He said he was going to make us wish we'd never started this. I don't want him to hurt me again.''

''He won't. I can't help you unless you help me. Unless you trust me.''

For the next hour, she talked, soothing, bullying, cajoling and promising. At two o'clock, both frightened women were back in court.

''The State calls Marjorie Lovitz,'' Deborah announced, and flicked a cool glance at Slagerman.

Gage slipped into the courtroom just as she called her first witness for the afternoon session. He'd had to cancel two meetings in order to be there. The need to see her had been a great deal stronger than the need to hear quarterly reports. It had been, Gage admitted, stronger than any need he had ever experienced.

For three days he'd kept his distance. Three very long days.

Life was often a chess match, he thought. And you took what time you needed to work out your next move. He chose a seat in the rear of the courtroom and settled back to watch her work.

"How old are you, Marjorie?" Deborah asked.

"Twenty-one."

"Have you always lived in Urbana?"

"No, I grew up in Pennsylvania."

With a few casual questions, she helped Marjorie paint a picture of her background, the poverty, the unhappiness, the parental abuse.

"When did you come to the city?"

"About four years ago."

"When you were seventeen. Why did you come?"

"I wanted to be an actress. That sounds pretty dumb, but I used to be in plays in school. I thought it would be easy."

"Was it?"

"No. No, it was hard. Real hard. Most of the time I didn't even get to audition, you know? And I ran out of money. I got a job waiting tables part-time, but it wasn't enough. They turned off the heat, and the lights."

"Did you ever think of going home?"

"I couldn't. My mother said if I took off then she was done with me. And I guess I thought, I still thought I could do okay, if I just got a break."

"Did you get one?"

"I thought I did. This guy came into the grill where I worked. We got kind of friendly, talking, you know. I told him how I was an actress. He said he'd known it as soon as he'd seen me, and what was I doing working in a dump like that when I was so pretty, and so talented. He told me he knew lots of people, and that if I came to work for him, he'd introduce me. He gave me a business card and everything.''

"Is the man you met that night in the courtroom, Marjorie?''

"Sure, it was Jimmy.'' She looked down quickly at her twisting fingers. "Jimmy Slagerman.''

"Did you go to work for him?''

"Yeah. I went the next day to his offices. He had a whole suite, all these desks and phones and leather chairs. A real nice place, uptown. He called it Elegant Escorts. He said I could make a hundred dollars a night just by going to dinner and parties with these businessmen. He even bought me clothes, pretty clothes and had my hair done and everything.''

"And for this hundred dollars a night, all you had to do was go to dinner or parties?''

"That's what he told me, at first.''

"And did that change?''

"After a while…he took me out to nice restaurants and places. Dress rehearsals, he called them. He bought me flowers and…''

"Did you have sex with him?''

"Objection. Irrelevant.''

"Your Honor, the witness's relationship, her physical relationship with the defendant is very relevant.''

"Overruled. You'll answer the question, Miss Lovitz.''

"Yes. I went to bed with him. He treated me so nice. After, he gave me money—for the bills, he said.''

"And you accepted it?''

"Yes. I guess I knew what was going on. I knew, but

I pretended I didn't. A few days later, he told me he had a customer for me. He said I was to dress up real nice, and go out to dinner with this man from D.C.''

"What instructions were you given by Mr. Slagerman?"

"He said, 'Marjorie, you're going to have to earn that hundred dollars.' I said I knew that, and he told me I was going to have to be real nice to this guy. I said I would.''

"Did Mr. Slagerman define 'nice' for you, Marjorie?"

She hesitated, then looked down at her hands again. "He said I was to do whatever I was told. That if the guy wanted me to go back to his hotel after, I had to go or I wouldn't get my money. It was all acting, he said. I acted like I enjoyed the guy's company, like I was attracted to him, and I acted like I had a great time in bed with him.''

"Did Mr. Slagerman specifically tell you that you would be required to have sex with this customer?"

"He said it was part of the job, the same as smiling at bad jokes. And if I was good at it, he'd introduce me to this director he knew.''

"And you agreed?"

"He made it sound okay. Yes.''

"And were there other occasions when you agreed to exchange sex for money in your capacity as an escort for Mr. Slagerman's firm?"

"Objection.''

"I'll rephrase.'' She flicked a glance at the jury. "Did you continue in Mr. Slagerman's employ?"

"Yes, ma'am.''

"For how long?"

"Three years.''

"And were you satisfied with the arrangement?"

"I don't know."

"You don't know if you were satisfied?"

"I got used to the money," Marjorie said, painfully honest. "And after a while you get so you can forget what you're doing, if you think about something else when it's going on."

"And was Mr. Slagerman happy with you?"

"Sometimes." Fearful, she looked up at the judge. "Sometimes he'd get real mad, at me or one of the other girls."

"There were other girls?"

"About a dozen, sometimes more."

"And what did he do when he got mad?"

"He'd smack you around."

"You mean he'd hit you?"

"He'd just go crazy and—"

"Objection."

"Sustained."

"Did he ever strike you, Marjorie?"

"Yes."

Deborah let the simplicity of the answer hang over the jury. "Will you tell me the events that took place on the night of February 25 of this year?"

As she'd been instructed, Marjorie kept her eyes on Deborah and didn't let them waver back to Slagerman. "I had a job, but I got sick. The flu or something. I had a fever and my stomach was really upset. I couldn't keep anything down. Suzanne came over to take care of me."

"Suzanne?"

"Suzanne McRoy. She worked for Jimmy, too, and we got to be friends. I just couldn't get up and go to work, so Suzanne called Jimmy to tell him." Her hands began to twist in her lap. "I could hear her arguing with him over the phone, telling him I was sick. Suzanne said

he could come over and see for himself if he didn't
believe her."

"And did he come over?"

"Yes." The tears started, big silent drops that cruised
down her cheeks. "He was really mad. He was yelling
at Suzanne, and she was yelling back, telling him I was
really sick, that I had a fever line a hundred and two.
He said—" She licked her lips. "He said we were both
lazy, lying sluts. I heard something crash and she was
crying. I got up, but I was dizzy." She rubbed the heel
of her hands under her eyes, smearing mascara. "He
came into the bedroom. He knocked me down."

"You mean he bumped into you?"

"No, he knocked me down. Backhanded me, you
know?"

"Yes. Go on."

"Then he told me to get my butt up and get dressed.
He said the customer had asked for me, I was going to
do it. He said all I had to do was lie on my back and
close my eyes anyway." She fumbled for a tissue, blew
her nose. "I told him I was sick, that I couldn't do it.
He was yelling and throwing things. Then he said he'd
show me how it felt to be sick. And he started hitting
me."

"Where did he hit you?"

"Everywhere. In the face, in the stomach. Mostly my
face. He just wouldn't stop."

"Did you call for help?"

"I couldn't. I couldn't hardly breathe."

"Did you try to defend yourself?"

"I tried to crawl away, but he kept coming after me,
kept hitting me. I passed out. When I woke up, Suzanne
was there, and her face was all bloody. She called an
ambulance."

Gently Deborah continued to question. When she took her seat at the prosecutor's table, she prayed that Marjorie would hold up under cross-examination.

After almost three hours on the witness stand, Marjorie was pale and shaky. Despite the defense counselor's attempt to destroy her character, she stepped down looking young and vulnerable.

And it was that picture, Deborah thought with satisfaction, that would remain in the jury's mind.

"Excellent job, Counselor."

Deborah turned her head and, with twin pricks of annoyance and pleasure, glanced up at Gage. "What are you doing here?"

"Watching you work. If I ever need a lawyer..."

"I'm a prosecutor, remember?"

He smiled. "Then I'll just have to make sure I don't get caught breaking the law." When she stood, he took her hand. A casual gesture, even a friendly one. She couldn't have said why it seemed so possessive. "Can I offer you a lift? Dinner, dessert? A quiet evening?"

And she'd said he wouldn't tempt her again. Fat chance. "I'm sorry, I have something to do."

Tilting his head, he studied her. "I think you mean it."

"I do have work."

"No, I mean that you're sorry."

His eyes were so deep, so warm, she nearly sighed. "Against my better judgment, I am." She started out of the courtroom into the hall.

"Just the lift then."

She sent him a quick, exasperated look over her shoulder. "Didn't I tell you once how I felt about persistent men?"

"Yes, but you had dinner with me anyway."

She had to laugh. After all the tense hours in court, it was a relief. "Well, since my car's in the shop, I could use a lift."

He stepped into the elevator with her. "It's a tough case you've taken on here. And a reputation maker."

Her eyes cooled. "Really?"

"You're getting national press."

"I don't take cases for clippings." Her voice was as frigid as her eyes.

"If you're going to be in for the long haul, you'll have to develop a thicker skin."

"My skin's just fine, thanks."

"I noticed." Relaxed, he leaned back against the wall. "I think anyone who knows you realizes the press is a by-product, not the purpose. You're making a point here, that no one, no matter who or what they are, should be victimized. I hope you win."

She wondered why it should have unnerved her that he understood precisely what she was reaching for. "I will win."

She stepped out of the elevator into the marble lobby.

"I like your hair that way," he commented, pleased to see he'd thrown her off. "Very cool, very competent. How many pins would I have to pull out to have it fall loose?"

"I don't think that's—"

"Relevant?" he supplied. "It is to me. Everything about you is, since I don't seem to be able to stop thinking about you."

She kept walking quickly. It was typical, she imagined, that he would say such things to a woman in a lobby swarming with people—and make her feel as though they were completely alone. "I'm sure you've managed to keep busy. I noticed a picture of you in this morning's paper—there was a blonde attached to your arm. Candidate Tarrington's dinner party.'' She set her teeth when he kept smiling. ''You switch your allegiances quickly, politically speaking.''

''I have no allegiances, politically speaking. I was interested to hear what Fields's opposition had to say. I was impressed.''

She remembered the lush blonde in the skinny black dress. ''I bet.''

This time he grinned. ''I'm sorry you weren't there.''

''I told you before I don't intend to be part of a horde.'' At the wide glass doors, she stopped, braced. ''Speaking of hordes.'' Head up, she walked into the crowd of reporters waiting on the courthouse steps.

They fired questions. She fired answers. Still, as annoyed as she was with him, she was grateful to see Gage's big black limo with its hulk of a driver waiting at the curb.

''Mr. Guthrie, what's your interest in this case?''

''I enjoy watching justice at work.''

''You enjoy watching gorgeous D.A.s at work.'' Wisner pushed his way through his associates to shove a recorder into Gage's face. ''Come on, Guthrie, what's happening between you and Darling Deb?''

Hearing her low snarl, Gage put a warning hand on Deborah's arm and turned to the reporter. ''I know you, don't I?''

Wisner smirked. ''Sure. We ran into each other plenty in those bad old days when you worked for the city instead of owning it.''

''Yeah. Wisner.'' He summed the man up with one quick, careless look. ''Maybe my memory's faulty, but

I don't recall you being as big a jerk then as you are now." He bundled a chuckling Deborah into the limo.

"Nicely done," she said.

"I'll have to consider buying *The World*, just to have the pleasure of firing him."

"I have to admire the way you think." With a sigh, she slipped out of her shoes and shut her tired eyes. She could get used to traveling this way, she thought. Big cushy seats and Mozart playing softly in the speakers. A pity it wasn't reality. "My feet are killing me. I'm going to have to buy a pedometer to see how many miles I put in during an average day in court."

"Will you come home with me if I promise you a foot massage?"

She opened one eye. He'd be good at it, she thought. At massaging a woman's foot—or anything else that happened to ache. "No." She shut her eye again. "I have to get back to my office. And I'm sure there are plenty of other feet you can rub."

Gage opened the glass long enough to give Frank their destination. "Is that what concerns you? The other...feet in my life?"

She hated the fact that it did. "They're your business."

"I like yours. Your feet, your legs, your face. And everything in between."

She ignored, tried to ignore, the quick frisson of response. "Do you always try to seduce women in the back of limos?"

"Would you prefer someplace else?"

She opened both eyes. Some things, she thought, were better handled face-to-face. "Gage, I've done some thinking about this situation."

His mouth curved charmingly. "Situation?"

"Yes." She didn't chose to call it a relationship. "I'm not going to pretend I'm not attracted to you, or that I'm not flattered you seem to be attracted to me. But—"

"But?" He picked up her hand, rubbed his lips over her knuckles. The skin there smelled as fresh and clear as rainwater.

"Don't." Her breath caught when he turned her hand over to press a slow, warm kiss in the palm. "Don't do that."

"I love it when you're cool and logical, Deborah. It makes me crazy to see how quickly I can make you heat up." He brushed his lips over her wrist and felt the fast thud of her pulse. "You were saying?"

Was she? What woman could be cool and logical when he was looking at her? Touching her. She snatched her hand away, reminding herself that was precisely the problem. "I don't want this—situation to go any further, for several good reasons."

"Mmm-hmm."

She knocked his hand away when he began to toy with the pearl at her ear. "I mean it. I realize you're used to picking and discarding women like poker chips, but I'm not interested. So ante up with someone else."

Yes, she was heating up nicely. "That's a very interesting metaphor. I could say that there are some winnings I prefer to hold on to rather than gamble with."

Firing up, she turned to him. "Let's get this straight. I'm not this week's prize. I have no intention of being Wednesday's brunette following Tuesday's blonde."

"So, we're back to those feet again."

"You might consider it a joke, but I take my life, personally and professionally, very seriously."

"Maybe too seriously."

She stiffened. "That's my business. The bottom line

here is that I'm not interested in becoming one of your conquests. I'm not interested in becoming tangled up with you in any way, shape or form." She glanced over when the limo glided to the curb. "And this is my stop."

He moved quickly, surprising them both, dragging her across the seat so that she lay across his lap. "I'm going to see to it that you're so tangled up you'll never pull free." Hard and sure, his mouth met hers.

She didn't struggle. She didn't hesitate. Every emotion she had felt along the drive had been honed down to one: desire. Irrevocable. Instantaneous. Irresistible. Her fingers dived into his hair as her mouth moved restless and hungry under his.

She wanted, as she had never wanted before. Never dreamed of wanting. The ache of it was so huge it left no room for reason. The rightness of it was so clear it left no room for doubt. There was only the moment— and the taking.

He wasn't patient as he once had been. Instead, his mouth was fevered as it raced over her face, streaked down her throat. With an urgent murmur, she pulled his lips back to hers.

Never before had he known anyone who had matched his needs so exactly. There was a fire burning in her, and he had only to touch to make it leap and spark. He'd known desire before, but not this gnawing, tearing desperation.

He wanted to drag her down on the seat, pull and tug at that slim, tidy suit until she was naked and burning beneath him.

But he also wanted to give her comfort and compassion and love. He would have to wait until she was ready to accept it.

With real regret, he gentled his hands and drew her

away. "You're everything I want," he told her. "And I've learned to take what I want."

Her eyes were wide. As the passion faded from them, it was replaced by a dazed fear that disturbed him. "It's not right," she whispered. "It's not right that you should be able to do this to me."

"No, it's not right for either of us. But it's real."

"I won't be controlled by my emotions."

"We all are."

"Not me." Shaky, she reached down for her shoes. "I've got to go."

He reached across her to unlatch the door. "You will belong to me."

She shook her head. "I have to belong to myself first." Climbing out, she bolted.

Gage watched her retreat before he opened his fisted hand. He counted six hairpins and smiled.

Deborah spent the evening with Suzanne and Marjorie in their tiny apartment. Over the Chinese takeout she'd supplied, she discussed the case with them. It helped, pouring herself into her work helped. It left little time to brood about Gage and her response to him. A response that worried her all the more since she had felt much the same stunning sexual pull toward another man.

Because she wanted to turn to both, she couldn't turn to either. It was a matter of ethics. To Deborah, when a woman began to doubt her ethics, she had to doubt everything.

It helped to remind herself that there were things she could control. Her work, her life-style, her ambitions. Tonight she hoped to do something to control the outcome of the case she was trying.

Each time the phone rang, she answered it herself

while Marjorie and Suzanne sat on the sofa, hands clutched. On the fifth call, she hit pay dirt.

"Marjorie?"

She took a chance. "No."

"Suzanne, you bitch."

Though a grim smile touched her lips, she made her voice shake. "Who is this?"

"You know damn well who it is. It's Jimmy."

"I'm not supposed to talk to you."

"Fine. Just listen. If you think I messed you up before, it's nothing to what I'm going to do to you if you testify tomorrow. You little slut, I picked you up off the street where you were earning twenty a trick and set you up with high rolling johns. I own you, and don't you forget it. Do yourself a favor, Suze, tell that tight-assed D.A. that you've changed your mind, that you and Marjorie lied about everything. Otherwise, I'll hurt you, real bad. Understand?"

"Yes." She hung up and stared at the phone. "Oh, yeah. I understand." Deborah turned to Marjorie and Suzanne. "Keep your door locked tonight and don't go out. He doesn't know it yet, but he just hanged himself."

Pleased with herself, she left them. It had taken a great deal of fast talking to get a tap on Marjorie and Suzanne's line. And it would take more to subpoena Slagerman's phone records. But she would do it. When Slagerman took the stand in a few days, both he and his defense counsel were in for a surprise.

She decided to walk a few blocks before trying to hunt up a cab. The night was steamy. Even the buildings were sweating. Across town there was a cool room, a cool shower, a cool drink waiting. But she didn't want to go home, alone, yet. Alone it would be too easy to think about her life. About Gage.

She had lost control in his arms in the afternoon. That was becoming a habit she didn't care for. It wasn't possible to deny that she was attracted to him. More, pulled toward him in a basic, almost primitive way that was all but impossible to resist.

Yet, she also felt something, a very strong something, for a man who wore a mask.

How could she, who had always prized loyalty, fidelity, above all else, have such deep and dramatic feelings for two different men?

She hoped she could blame her own physicality. To want a man wasn't the same as to need one. She wasn't ready to need one, much less two.

What she needed was control, over her emotions, her life, her career. For too much of her life she had been a victim of circumstance. Her parents' tragic deaths, and the depthless well of fear and grief that had followed it. The demands of her sister's job that had taken them both from city to city to city.

Now she was making her own mark, in her own way, in her own time. For the past eighteen months she had worked hard, with a single-minded determination to earn and deserve the reputation as a strong and honest representative of the justice system. All she had to do was keep moving forward on the same straight path.

As she stepped into the shadows of the World Building, she heard someone whisper her name. She knew that voice, had heard it in her dreams—dreams she'd refused to acknowledge.

He seemed to flow out of the dark, a shadow, a silhouette, then a man. She could see his eyes, the gleam of them behind the mask. The longing came so quickly, so strongly, she nearly moaned aloud.

And when he took her hand to draw her into the shadows, she didn't resist.

"You seem to be making it a habit to walk the streets at night alone."

"I had work." Automatically she pitched her voice low to match his. "Are you following me?"

He didn't answer, but his fingers curled around hers in a way that spoke of possession.

"What do you want?"

"It's dangerous for you." She'd left her hair down, he saw, so that it flowed around her shoulders. "Those who murdered Parino will be watching you." He felt her pulse jump, but not with fear. He recognized the difference between fear and excitement.

"What do you know about Parino?"

"They won't be bothered by the fact you're a woman, not if you're in their way. I don't want to see you hurt."

Unable to help herself, she leaned toward him. "Why?"

As helpless as she, he lifted both of her hands to his lips. He clutched them there, his grip painfully tight. His eyes met hers over them. "You know why."

"It isn't possible." But she didn't, couldn't step away when he brushed a hand over her hair. "I don't know who you are. I don't understand what you do."

"Sometimes neither do I."

She wanted badly to step into his arms, to learn what it was like to be held by him, to have his mouth hot on hers. But there were reasons, she told herself as she held back. Too many reasons. She had to be strong, strong enough not only to resist him, but to use him.

"Tell me what you know. About Parino, about his murder. Let me do my job."

"Leave it alone. That's all I have to tell you."

"You know something. I can see it." With a disgusted breath, she stepped back. She needed the distance, enough of it so that she could hear her brain and remember that she was an officer of the court and he a wrench in the system in which she believed fervently. "It's your duty to tell me."

"I know my duty."

She tossed back her hair. Attracted to him? Hell, no, she was infuriated by him. "Sure, skulking around shadows, dispensing your own personal sense of justice when and where the whim strikes. That's not duty, Captain Bonehead, it's ego." When he didn't respond, she let out a hiss of breath and stepped toward him again. "I could bring you up on charges for withholding information. This is police business, D.A.'s business, not a game."

"No, it isn't a game." His voice remained low, but she thought she caught hints of both amusement and annoyance. "But it has pawns. I wouldn't like to see you used as one."

"I can take care of myself."

"So you continue to say. You're out of your league this time, Counselor. Leave it alone." He stepped back.

"Just hold on." She rushed forward, but he was gone. "Damn it, I wasn't finished arguing with you." Frustrated, she kicked the side of the building, missing his shin by inches. "Leave it alone," she muttered. "Not on your life."

Chapter 5

Dripping, swearing, Deborah rushed toward the door. Knocks at 6:45 a.m. were the same as phone calls at three in the morning. They spelled trouble. When she opened the door and found Gage, she knew her instincts had been on target.

"Get you out of the shower?" he asked her.

She pushed an impatient hand through her wet hair. "Yes. What do you want?"

"Breakfast." Without waiting for an invitation, he strolled inside. "Very nice," he decided.

She'd used the soft cream of ivory with slashes of color—emerald, crimson, sapphire—in the upholstery of the low sofa, in the scatter of rugs on the buffed wood floor. He noted, too, that she had left a damp trail on that same floor.

"Looks like I'm about five minutes early."

Realizing the belt of her robe was loose, she snapped

it tight. "No, you're not, because you shouldn't be here at all. Now—"

But he cut her off with a long, hard kiss. "Mmm, you're still wet."

She was surprised the water wasn't steaming off her. Surprised with the sudden urge that poured through her just to lay her head against his shoulder. "Look, I don't have time for this. I have to be in court—"

"In two hours," he said with a nod. "Plenty of time for breakfast."

"If you think I'm going to fix you breakfast, you're doomed to disappointment."

"I wouldn't dream of it." He skimmed a glance down her short silky robe. The single embrace had made him achingly aware that she wore nothing else. "I like you in blue. You should always wear blue."

"I appreciate the fashion advice, but—" She broke off when another knock sounded.

"I'll get it," he offered.

"I can answer my own door." She stomped over to it, her temper fraying. She was never at her best in the morning, even when she only had herself to deal with. "I'd like to know who hung out the sign that said I was having an open house this morning." Wrenching the door open, she was confronted by a white-jacketed waiter pushing an enormous tray.

"Ah, that would be breakfast. Over by the window, I think," Gage said, gesturing the waiter in. "The lady likes a view."

"Yes, sir, Mr. Guthrie."

Deborah set her hands on her hips. It was difficult to take a stand before seven in the morning, but it had to be done. "Gage, I don't know what you're up to, but it isn't going to work. I've tried to make my position clear, and at the moment, I don't have the time or the inclination…is that coffee?''

"Yes." Smiling, Gage lifted the big silver pot and poured a cup. The scent of it seduced her. "Would you like some?"

Her mouth moved into a pout. "Maybe."

"You should like this blend." Crossing to her, he held the cup under her nose. "It's one of my personal favorites."

She sipped, shut her eyes. "You don't play fair."

"No."

She opened her eyes to study the waiter, who moved briskly about his business. "What else is there?"

"Shirred eggs, grilled ham, croissants, orange juice—fresh, of course."

"Of course." She hoped she wasn't drooling.

"Raspberries and cream."

"Oh." She folded her tongue inside her mouth to keep it from hanging out.

"Would you like to sit?"

She wasn't a weak woman, Deborah assured herself of that. But there were rich and wonderful smells filling her living room. "I guess." Giving up, she took one of the ladder-back chairs the waiter had pulled up to the table.

Gage passed the waiter a bill and gave him instructions to pick up the dishes in an hour. She couldn't bring herself to complain when Gage topped off her cup.

"I suppose I should ask what brought all this on."

"I wanted to see what you looked like in the morning." He poured juice out of a crystal pitcher. "This seemed like the best way. For now." He toasted her with his cup, his eyes lingering on her face, free of makeup and unframed by her slicked-back hair. "You're beautiful."

"And you're charming." She touched the petals of the red rose beside her plate. "But that doesn't change anything." Thoughtful, she tapped a finger on the peach-colored cloth. "Still, I don't see any reason to let all this food go to waste."

"You're a practical woman." He'd counted on it. "It's one of the things I find most attractive about you."

"I don't see what's attractive about being practical." She cut a small slice of ham and slipped it between her lips. His stomach muscles tightened.

"It can be…very attractive."

She did her best to ignore the tingles sprinting through her system and concentrate on a safer kind of hunger. "Tell me, do you always breakfast this extravagantly?"

"When it seems appropriate." He laid a hand over hers. "Your eyes are shadowed. Didn't you sleep well?"

She thought of the long and restless night behind her. "No, I didn't."

"The case?"

She only shrugged. Her insomnia had had nothing to do with the case and everything to do with the man she had met in the shadows. Yet now she was here, just as fascinated with, just as frustrated by the man she sat with in the sunlight.

"Would you like to talk about it?"

She glanced up. In his eyes she saw patience, understanding and something beneath it all she knew would burn to the touch. "No." Cautious, she drew her hand away again.

He found himself enjoying the not-so-subtle pursuit and retreat. "You work too hard."

"I do what I have to do. What about you? I don't even know what you do, not really."

"Buy and sell, attend meetings, read reports."

"I'm sure it's more complicated than that."

"And often more boring."

"That's hard to believe."

Steam and fragrance erupted when he broke open a flaky croissant. "I build things, buy things."

She wouldn't be put off that easily. "Such as?"

He smiled at her. "I own this building."

"Trojan Enterprises owns this building."

"Right. I own Trojan."

"Oh."

Her reaction delighted him. "Most of the Guthrie money came from real estate, and that's still the basis. We've diversified quite a bit over the past ten years. So, one branch handles the shipping, another the mining, another the manufacturing."

"I see." He wasn't an ordinary man, she thought. Then again she didn't seem to be attracted to ordinary men lately. "You're a long way from the twenty-fifth."

"Yeah." A shadow flickered into his eyes. "Looks that way." He lifted a spoonful of berries and cream and offered it.

Deborah let the fruit lie on her tongue a moment. "Do you miss it?"

He knew if he kissed her now she would taste sharp, fresh, alive. "I don't let myself miss it. There's a difference."

"Yes." She understood. It was the same way she didn't let herself miss her family, those who were gone and those who were so many miles away.

"You're very appealing when you're sad, Deborah."

He trailed a finger over the back of her hand. "In fact, irresistible."

"I'm not sad."

"You are irresistible."

"Don't start." She made a production out of pouring more coffee. "Can I ask you a business question?"

"Sure."

"If the owner, or owners, of a particular piece of property didn't want that ownership publicized, could they hide it?"

"Easily. Bury it in paper corporations, in different tax numbers. One corporation owns another, another owns that, and so on. Why?"

But she leaned forward, waving his question aside. "How difficult would it be to track down the actual owners?"

"That would depend on how much trouble they'd gone to, and how much reason they had to keep their names off the books."

"If someone was determined enough, and patient enough, those names could be found?"

"Eventually. If you found the common thread."

"Common thread?"

"A name, a number, a place. Something that would pop up over and over." He would have been concerned by her line of questioning if he hadn't been one step ahead of her. Still, it was best to be cautious. "What are you up to, Deborah?"

"My job."

Very carefully, he set his cup back in its saucer. "Does this have anything to do with Parino?"

Her eyes sharpened. "What do you know about Parino?"

"I still have contacts at the twenty-fifth. Don't you have enough to do with the Slagerman trial?"

"I don't have the luxury of working on one case at a time."

"This is one you shouldn't be working on at all."

"Excuse me?" Her tone had dropped twenty degrees.

"It's dangerous. The men who had Parino murdered are dangerous. You don't have any idea what you're playing with."

"I'm not playing."

"No, and neither are they. They're well protected, and well-informed. They'll know what your next move is before you do." His eyes darkened, seemed to turn inward. "If they see you as an obstacle, they'll remove you, very quickly, very finally."

"How do you know so much about the men who killed Parino?"

He brought himself back. "I was a cop, remember? This isn't something you should be involved in. I want you to turn it over to someone else."

"That's ridiculous."

He gripped her hand before she could spring up. "I don't want you hurt."

"I wish people would stop saying that to me." Pulling her hand away, she rose. "This is my case, and it's going to stay mine."

His eyes darkened, but he remained seated. "Ambition is another attractive trait, Deborah. Until you let it blind you."

She turned back to him slowly, fury shimmering around her. "All right, part of it is ambition. But that's not all of it, not nearly. I believe in what I do, Gage, and in my ability to do it well. It started out with a kid named Rico Mendez. He wasn't a pillar of the community. In fact, he was a petty thief who had already done time, and would have done more. But he was gunned down while standing on a street corner. Because he belonged to the wrong gang, wore the wrong colors.''

She began to pace, her hands gesturing and emphasizing. "Then his killer is killed, because he talked to me. Because I made a deal with him. So when does it stop, when do we stop and say this is not acceptable, I'll take the responsibility and change it?''

He stood then and came toward her. "I'm not questioning your integrity, Deborah.''

"Just my judgment?''

"Yes, and my own.'' His hands slid up, inside the sleeves of her robe. "I care about you.''

"I don't think—''

"No, don't. Don't think.'' He covered her mouth with his, his fingers tightening on her arms as he pulled her against him.

Instant heat, instant need. How was she to fight it? His body was so solid against hers, his lips were so skilled. And she could feel the waves, not just of desire, but of something deeper and truer, pouring out of him and into her. As if he were already inside her.

She was everything. When he held her he didn't question the power she had to both empty his mind and fill it, to sate his hunger even as she incited it. She made him strong; she left him weak. With her, he began, almost, to believe in miracles again.

When he stepped away, his hands were still on her arms. She struggled for balance. How could he do this to her each time, every time, with only a touch?

"I'm not ready for this,'' she managed.

"Neither am I. I don't think it matters.'' He brought

her close again. "I want to see you tonight." He crushed his mouth to hers. "I want to be with you tonight."

"No, I can't." She could hardly breathe. "The trial."

He bit back an oath. "All right. After the trial is over. Neither one of us can keep walking away from this."

"No." He was right. It was time to resolve it. "No, we can't. But I need time. Please don't push me."

"I may have to." He turned for the door, but paused with his hand on the knob. "Deborah, is there someone else?"

She started to deny it, but found she could only be honest with him. "I don't know."

Nodding, he closed the door at his back. With a bitter kind of irony, he realized he was competing with himself.

She worked late that night, poring over papers and law books at the desk in her bedroom. After court she had spent hours cleaning her already clean apartment. It was one of the best ways she knew to relieve tension. Or to ignore it. The other was work, and she had dived into it, knowing sleep was impossible.

As she reached for her mug of coffee, the phone rang.

"Hello."

"O'Roarke? Deborah O'Roarke?"

"Yes, who is this?"

"Santiago."

Instantly alert, she grabbed a pencil. "Mr. Santiago, we've been looking for you."

"Yeah. Right."

"I'd like very much to talk to you. The D.A.'s office is prepared to offer you cooperation and protection."

"Like Parino got?"

She smothered the quick pang of guilt. "You'll be safer with us than on your own."

"Maybe." There was fear in his voice, tight and nervy.

"I'm willing to set up an interview any time you agree to come in."

"No way. I'm not going nowhere. They'd hit me before I got two blocks." He began to talk quickly, words tumbling over each other. "You come to me. Listen, I got more than Parino had. Lots more. I got names, I got papers. You want to hear about it, sister, you come to me."

"All right. I'll have the police—"

"No cops!" His voice turned vicious with terror. "No cops or no deal. You come, and you come alone. That's it."

"We'll do it your way then. When?"

"Now, right now. I'm at the Darcy Hotel, 38 East 167th. Room 27."

"Give me twenty minutes."

"You're sure this is where you want to go, lady?" Though his fare was wearing worn jeans and a T-shirt, the cabbie could see she had too much class for an armpit like the Darcy.

Deborah looked through the hard mean rain that was falling. She could see the dark windows, the scarred surface of the building and the deserted street. "Yes. I don't suppose I could convince you to wait."

"No, ma'am."

"I didn't think so." She pushed a bill through the slot in the thick security glass. "Keep it." Taking a breath, holding it, she plunged into the rain and up the broken steps to the entrance.

In the lobby she stood, dripping. The check-in desk was behind rusty iron bars and was deserted. There was a light, shooting its yellow beam over the sticky linoleum floor. The air smelled of sweat and garbage and something worse. Turning, she started up the stairs.

A baby was crying in long, steady wails. The sound of misery rolled down the graffiti-washed stairwell. Deborah watched something small and quick scuttle past her foot and into a crack. With a shudder, she continued up.

She could hear a man and woman, voices raised in a vicious argument. As she turned into the hallway of the second floor, a door creaked open. She saw a pair of small, frightened eyes before it creaked shut again and a chain rattled into place.

Her feet crunched over broken glass that had once been the ceiling light. Down the dim hall, she heard the bad-tempered squeal of brakes from a television car chase. Lightning flashed outside the windows as the storm broke directly overhead.

At Room 27, she stopped. The raucous television boomed on the other side of the door. Lifting a hand, she knocked hard.

"Mr. Santiago."

When she received no response, she knocked and called again. Cautious, she tried the knob. The door opened easily.

In the gray, flickering light of the television, she saw a cramped room with one dingy window. There were heaps of clothes and garbage. The single dresser had a drawer missing. There was the stench of beer gone hot and food gone bad.

She saw the figure stretched across the bed and swore. Not only would she have the pleasure of conducting an interview in this hellhole, she would have to sober up her witness first.

Annoyed, she switched off the television so that there was only the sound of drumming rain and the shouts of the argument down the hall. She spotted a stained sink bolted to the wall, a chunk of its porcelain missing. It would come in handy, she thought, if she could manage to hold Santiago's head in it.

"Mr. Santiago." She raised her voice as she picked her way across the room, trying to avoid greasy take-out bags and spilled beer. "Ray." Reaching him, she started to shake him by the shoulder, then noted his eyes were open. "I'm Deborah O'Roarke," she began. Then she realized he wasn't looking at her. He wasn't looking at all. Lifting her trembling hand, she saw it was wet with blood.

"Oh, God." She took one stumbling step back, fighting down the hot nausea that churned in her stomach. Another drunken step, then another. She turned and all but ran into a small well-built man with a mustache.

"*Señorita,*" he said quietly.

"The police," she managed. "We have to call the police. He's dead."

"I know." He smiled. She saw the glint of gold in his mouth. And the glint of silver when he lifted the stiletto. "Miss O'Roarke. I've been waiting for you."

He grabbed her by the hair when she lunged toward the door. She cried out in pain, then was silent, deathly still as she felt the prick of the knife at the base of her throat.

"No one listens to screams in a place such as this," he said, and the gentleness in his voice made her shudder as he turned her to face him. "You are very beautiful, *señorita*. What a pity it would be to damage that cheek."

Watching her, he laid the shaft of the knife against it. "You will tell me, *por favor,* what Parino discussed with you before his…accident. All names, all details. And with whom you shared this information."

Struggling to think through her terror, she looked into his eyes. And saw her fate. "You'll kill me anyway."

He smiled again. "Wise and beautiful. But there are ways, and ways. Some are very slow, very painful." He glided the blade lightly down her cheek. "You will tell me what I need to know."

She had no names, nothing to bargain with. She had only her wits. "I wrote them down, I wrote all of it down and locked it away."

"And told?"

"No one." She swallowed. "I told no one."

He studied her for a moment, twirling the stiletto. "I think you lie. Perhaps after I show you what I can do with this, you'll be willing to cooperate. Ah, that cheek. Like satin. What a pity I must tear it."

Even as she braced, there was another flash of lighting and the sound of the window glass crashing.

He was there, all in black, illuminated by a new spear of lightning. This time the thunder shook the room. Before she could so much as breathe, the knife was at her throat and a beefy arm banded her waist.

"Come closer," her captor warned, "and I will slit her throat from ear to ear."

Nemesis stood where he was. He didn't look at her. Didn't dare. But in his mind's eye he could see her, face pale with fear. Eyes glazed with it. Was it her fear, or his own that had made him unable to concentrate, unable to come into the room as a shadow instead of a man? If he was able to do so now, to divorce himself from his fear for her and vanish, would it be a weapon, or would it cause the stiletto to strike home before he could act? He hadn't been quick enough to save her. Now he had to be clever enough.

"If you kill her, you lose your shield."

"A risk we both take. No closer." He slid the blade more truly against her throat until she whimpered.

There was fear now, and fury. "If you hurt her, I will do things to you that even in your own nightmares you have never imagined."

Then he saw the face, the full looping mustache, the gleam of gold. He was back, back on the docks with the smell of fish and garbage, the sound of water lapping. He felt the hot explosion in his chest and nearly staggered.

"I know you, Montega." His voice was low, harsh. "I've been looking for you for a long time."

"So, you have found me." Though his tone was arrogant, Deborah could smell his sweat. It gave her hope. "Put down your weapon."

"I don't have a weapon," Nemesis said, his hands held out from his sides. "I don't need one."

"Then you are a fool." Montega eased his arm from around Deborah's waist and slipped a hand into his pocket. Just as the shot rang out, Nemesis lunged to the side.

It happened so fast. Afterward, Deborah couldn't be sure who had moved first. She saw the bullet smash into the stained wallpaper and plaster of the wall, saw Nemesis fall. With a strength fueled by rage and terror, she slammed her elbow into Montega's stomach.

More concerned with his new quarry than her, he shoved her away. Her head struck the edge of the sink. There was another flash of lightning. Then the dark.

* * *

"Deborah. Deborah, I need you to open your eyes. Please."

She didn't want to. Small vicious explosions were going off behind them. But the voice was so desperate, so pleading. She forced her eyelids to lift. Nemesis swam into focus.

He was holding her, cradling her head, rocking her. For a moment, she could only see his eyes. Beautiful eyes, she thought dizzily. She had fallen in love with them the first time she'd seen them. She had looked through the crowd of people through the dazzle of lights and had seen him, seen them.

With a little groan, she lifted a hand to the knot already forming on her temple. She must be concussed, she thought. The first time she had seen Nemesis she had been in a dark alley. And there had been a knife. Like tonight.

"A knife," she murmured. "He had a knife."

Stunned by relief, he lowered his brow to hers. "It's all right. He didn't get a chance to use it."

"I thought he'd killed you." She lifted a hand to his face, found it warm.

"No."

"Did you kill him?"

His eyes changed. Concern rushed out as fury rushed in. "No." He had seen Deborah crumpled on the floor and had known such blank terror, the kind he thought he'd forgotten how to feel. It had been easy for Montega to get away. But there would be another time. He promised himself that. And he would have his justice. And his revenge.

"He got away?"

"For now."

"You knew him." Over the pounding in her head, she tried to think. "You called him by name."

"Yes, I knew him."

"He had a gun." She squeezed her eyes tight, but the pain continued to roll. "Where did he have a gun?"

"In his pocket. He makes it a habit to ruin his suits."

That was something she would have to consider later. "We have to call the police." She put a hand on his arm for balance and felt the warm stickiness on her fingers. "You're bleeding."

He glanced down to where the bullet had grazed him. "Some."

"How badly?" Ignoring the throbbing in her temple, she pushed away. Before he could answer, she was ripping his sleeve to expose the wound. The long, ugly graze had her stomach doing flip-flops. "We need to stop the bleeding."

She couldn't see his lifted brow, but heard it in his voice. "You could tear your T-shirt into a tourniquet."

"You should be so lucky." She glanced around the room, scrupulously avoiding looking at the form sprawled over the bed. "There's nothing in here that wouldn't give you blood poisoning."

"Try this." He offered her a square of black cloth.

She fumbled with the bandage. "It's my first gunshot wound, but I think this should be cleaned."

"I'll see to it later." He enjoyed having her tend to him. Her fingers were gentle on his skin, her brows drawn together in concentration. She had found a murdered man, had nearly been murdered herself. But she had bounced back and was doing competently what needed to be done.

Practicality. His lips curved slightly. Yes, it could be very attractive. Added to that, he could smell her hair as she bent close, feel the softness of it as it brushed against his cheek. He heard her breathing, slow, steady, under the sound of the quieting rain.

Having done her best, Deborah sat back on her heels. "Well, so much for invulnerability."

He smiled and stopped her heart. "There goes my reputation."

She could only stare, spellbound as they knelt on the floor of the filthy little room. She forgot where she was, who she was. Unable to stop herself, she lowered her gaze to his mouth. What tastes would she find there? What wonders would he show her?

He could barely breathe when she lifted her eyes to his again. In hers he saw passion smoldering, and an acceptance that was terrifying. Her fingers were still on his skin, gently stroking. He could see each quick beat of her heart in the pulse that hammered at her throat.

"I dream of you." He reached out to bring her unresistingly against him. "Even when I'm awake I dream of you. Of touching you." His hands slid up to cup, to caress her breasts. "Of tasting you." Compelled, he buried his mouth at her throat where the flavor and the scent were hot.

She leaned toward him, into him, stunned and shattered by the wildly primitive urges beating in her blood. His lips were like a brand on her skin. And his hands... Oh, Lord, his hands. With a deep, throaty moan, she arched back, eager and willing.

And Gage's face swam in front of her eyes.

"No." She jerked away, shocked and shamed. "No, this isn't right."

He cursed himself. Her. Circumstance. How could he have touched her now, here? "No, it isn't." He rose, stepped away. "You don't belong here."

Because she was on the verge of tears, her voice was sharp. "And you do?"

"More than you," he murmured. "Much more than you."

"I was doing my job. Santiago called me."

"Santiago's dead."

"He wasn't." She pressed her fingers to her eyes and prayed for composure. "He called, asked me to come."

"Montega got here first."

"Yes." Telling herself she was strong, she lowered her hands and looked at him. "But how? How did he know where to find Santiago? How did he know I was coming here tonight? He was waiting for me. He called me by name."

Interested, Nemesis studied her. "Did you tell anyone you were coming here tonight?"

"No."

"I'm beginning to believe you are a fool." He swung away from her. "You come here, to a place like this, alone, to see a man who would as soon put a bullet in your brain as speak to you."

"He wouldn't have hurt me. He was terrified, ready to talk. And I know what I'm doing."

He turned back. "You don't begin to know."

"But you do, of course." She pushed at her tousled hair and had fresh pain shooting through her head. "Oh, why the hell don't you go away? Stay away? I don't need this kind of grief from you. I've got work to do."

"You need to go home, leave this to others."

"Santiago didn't call others," she snapped. "He called me, talked to me. And if I had gotten to him first I would know everything I need to know. I don't…" She trailed off as a thought struck. "My phone. Damn it, they've got a tap on my phone. They knew I was coming here tonight. My office phone, too. That's how they knew I was about to get a court order to deal with the antique shop.'' Her eyes blazed. ''Well, we can fix that in a hurry.''

She sprang up. The room spun. He caught her before she slid to the floor again.

''You're not going to be doing anything in a hurry for a day or two.'' Smoothly he hooked an arm under her knees and lifted her.

She liked the feeling of being carried by him, a bit too much. ''I walked into this room, Zorro, I'll walk out.''

He carried her into the hall. ''Are you always so thick-headed?''

''Yes. I don't need your help.''

''I can see you're doing just dandy on your own.''

''I may have had some trouble before,'' she said as he started down the stairs. ''But now I have a name. Montega. Five-eight, a hundred and sixty. Brown hair, brown eyes, brown mustache. Two gold incisors. It shouldn't be too hard to run a make on him.''

He stopped and his eyes were ice. ''Montega's mine.''

''The law doesn't make room for personal vendettas.''

''You're right. The law doesn't.'' He shifted her slightly as he came to the base of the stairs.

There was something in his tone—disillusionment?— that had her lifting a hand to his cheek. ''Was it very bad?''

''Yes.'' God, how he wished he could turn to her, bury his face in her hair and let her soothe him. ''It was very bad.''

''Let me help you. Tell me what you know and I swear I'll do everything I can do to see that Montega and whoever is behind him pays for what they've done to you.''

She would try. Realizing it moved something in him, even as it frightened him. ''I pay my own debts, my own way.''

''Damn it, talk about thickheaded.'' She squirmed as he carried her into the rain. ''I'm willing to bend my principles and work with you, to form a partnership, and you—''

''I don't want a partner.''

She could feel him stiffen with the words, all but feel the pain rush through him. But she wouldn't soften. Not again. ''Fine, just great. Oh, put me down, you can hardly carry me a hundred blocks.''

''I don't intend to.'' But he could have. He could imagine carrying her through the rain to her apartment, inside, to the bed. Instead, he walked to the end of the block, toward the lights and the traffic. At the curb he stopped. ''Hail a cab.''

''Hail a cab? Like this?''

He wondered why she could make him burn and want to laugh at the same time. He turned his head and watched the heat flare in her eyes as their lips hovered an inch apart. ''You can still lift your arm, can't you?''

''Yes, I can lift my arm.'' She did so, stewing as they stood and waited. After five soaking minutes, a cab cruised up the curb. Miffed as she was, she had to bite back a smile at the way the driver's mouth fell open when he got a load of her companion.

''Jeez, you're him, ain't ya? You're Nemesis. Hey, buddy, want a ride?''

''No, but the lady does.'' Effortlessly he slid Deborah into the back seat. His gloved hand brushed once over her cheek, like a memory. "I'd try an ice pack and some aspirin."

"Thanks. Thanks a lot. Listen, I'm not finished—"

But he stepped back, disappearing into the dark, thin rain.

"That was really him, wasn't it?" The cabbie craned his neck around to Deborah, ignoring the bad-tempered honks around him. "What'd he do, save your life or something?"

"Or something," she muttered.

"Jeez. Wait till I tell the wife." Grinning, he switched off the meter. "This ride's on me."

Chapter 6

Grunting, his body running with sweat, Gage lifted the weights again. He was on his back on the bench press, stripped down to a pair of jogging shorts. His muscles were singing, but he was determined to reach his quota of a hundred presses. Perspiration soaked his sweatband and ran into his eyes as he concentrated on one small spot on the ceiling. There was a satisfaction even in pain.

He remembered, too well, when he'd been so weak he'd barely been able to lift a magazine. There had been a time when his legs had turned to rubber and his breath had been ragged at trying to walk the length of the hospital corridor. He remembered the frustration of it, and more, the helplessness.

He'd resisted therapy at first, preferring to sit alone and brood. Then he'd used it, like a punishment because he'd been alive and Jack had been dead. The pain had been excruciating.

And one day, weak, sick, darkly depressed, he'd stood

weaving in his hospital room, braced against the wall. He'd wished with all of his strength, with all of his will, that he could simply vanish.

And he had.

He'd thought he'd been hallucinating. Going mad. Then, terrified and fascinated, he'd tried it again and again, going so far as to tilt a mirror across the room so that he could watch himself fade back, fade into the pastel wall beside his bed.

He would never forget the morning a nurse came in with his breakfast tray, walked right past him without seeing him, grumbling about patients who didn't stay in bed where they belonged.

And he'd known what he'd brought out of the coma with him. He'd known it had come with him for a purpose.

So therapy had become like a religion, something he'd dedicated every ounce of strength to, every particle of will. He'd pushed himself harder, harder still, until his muscles had toned and firmed. He had thrown himself into lessons in the martial arts, spent hours with weight lifting, the treadmills, the punishing laps in the pool every day.

He had exercised his mind, as well, reading everything, pushing himself to understand the myriad businesses he had inherited, spending hours day after day until he was skilled with complex computer systems.

Now he was stronger, faster, sharper than he had been during his years on the force. But he would never wear a badge again. He would never take another partner.

He would never be helpless.

His breath hissed out, and he continued to lift when Frank strolled in with a tall glass of iced juice.

Setting the glass on the table beside the bench press,

Frank watched in silence for a moment. "Pushing it a bit today," he commented. "Course you pushed it a bit yesterday, too, and the day before." Frank grinned. "What is it about some women that makes guys go out and lift heavy objects?"

"Go to hell, Frank."

"She's a looker, all right," he said, unoffended. "Smart, too, I guess, being a lawyer and all. Must be hard to think about her mind though when she looks at you with those big, blue eyes."

With a last grunt, Gage set the bar in the safety. "Go lift a wallet."

"Now, you know I don't do that anymore." His wide face split with a new grin. "Nemesis might get me." He plucked up a towel from the neatly folded pile beside the bench.

Saying nothing, Gage took it and swiped at the sweat on his face and chest.

"How's the arm?"

"Fine." Gage didn't bother to glance at the neat white bandage Frank had used to replace Deborah's effort.

"Must be getting slow. Never known you to catch one before."

"Do you want to be fired?"

"Again? Nah." He waited, patient, while Gage switched to leg presses. "I'm looking for job security. If you go out and get yourself killed, I'll have to go back to fleecing tourists."

"Then I'll have to stay alive. The tourists have enough trouble in Urbana."

"Wouldn't have happened if I'd been with you."

Gage flashed him a look and continued to push. "I work alone. You know the deal."

"She was there."

"And that was the problem. She doesn't belong on the streets, she belongs in a courtroom."

"You don't want her in a courtroom, you want her in the bedroom."

The weights came down with a crash. "Drop it."

He'd known Gage too long to be intimidated. "Look, you're crazy about her, and it's throwing you off, messing up your concentration. It isn't good for you."

"I'm not good for her." He stood and grabbed the glass of juice. "She has feelings for me, and she has feelings for Nemesis. It's making her unhappy."

"So, tell her she's only got feelings for one guy, and make her happy."

"What the hell am I supposed to do?" He drained the glass and barely prevented himself from heaving it against the wall. "Take her out to dinner, and over cocktails I could say, oh, by the way, Deborah, besides being a businessman and a pillar of the damn community, I have this sideline. An alter ego. The press likes to call him Nemesis. And we're both nuts about you. So, when I take you to bed, do you want it with the mask or without?"

Frank considered a moment. "Something like that."

With a half laugh, Gage set down the glass. "She's a straight arrow, Frank. I know, because I used to be one myself. She sees things in black and white—the law and the crime." Suddenly tired, he looked out over the sparkling water of the pool. "She'd never understand what I do or why I do it. And she'd hate me for lying to her, because every time I'm with her, I'm deceiving her."

"I don't think you're giving her enough credit. You've got reasons for what you do."

"Yeah." Absently he touched the jagged scar on his chest. "I've got reasons."

"You could make her understand. If she really does have feelings for you, she'd have to understand."

"Maybe, just maybe she'd listen, even accept without agreeing. She might even forgive the lies. But what about the rest?" He set his hand down on the bench, waited, watched it disappear into the damp leather. "How do I ask her to share her life with a freak?"

Frank swore once, violently. "You're not a freak. You've got a gift."

"Yeah." Gage lifted his hand, flexed his fingers. "But I'm the one who has to live with it."

At twelve-fifteen sharp, Deborah walked into City Hall. She made her way to the mayor's office, walking under the stern-faced portraits of former mayors, governors, presidents. She moved past marble busts of the country's founding fathers. The current mayor of Urbana liked having his walls lined with tradition, his floor carpeted in red.

She didn't begrudge him. In fact, Deborah appreciated the hushed, reverential feel of tradition. She enjoyed walking past the doors and hearing the quiet hum of keyboards, the click of copiers, the muted phone conversations as people worked for the city.

She paused in the reception area. Tucker Fields's secretary glanced up and, recognizing her, smiled. "Miss O'Roarke. He's expecting you. Just let me buzz him."

Within an efficient twenty seconds, she was escorted into the mayor's office. Fields sat behind his desk, a trim and tidy man with a fringe of snowy hair and the ruddy outdoor complexion of his farmer forebears. Beside him, Jerry looked like a preppy executive.

Fields had earned a reputation during his six years in

office as a man not afraid to get his hands dirty to keep his city clean.

At the moment, his jacket was off, his white shirtsleeves rolled up his sinewy forearms. His tie was askew and he reached up to straighten it as Deborah entered.

"Deborah, always a pleasure to see you."

"Good to see you, Mayor. Hello, Jerry."

"Have a seat, have a seat." Fields gestured her to a chair as he settled back against the cushy leather of his own. "So, how's the Slagerman trial going?"

"Very well. I think he'll take the stand after the noon recess."

"And you're ready for him."

"More than."

"Good, good." He waved in his secretary as she came to the door with a tray. "I thought since I'm making you miss lunch, I could at least offer you some coffee and a Danish."

"Thank you." She took the cup, exchanged idle conversation, though she knew she hadn't been sent for to drink coffee and chat.

"Heard you had some excitement last night."

"Yes." It was no more than she'd expected. "We lost Ray Santiago."

"Yes, I heard. It's unfortunate. And this Nemesis character, he was there, as well?"

"Yes, he was."

"He was also there the night the antique store on Seventh blew up." Steepling his fingers, Fields sat back. "One might begin to think he was involved."

"No, not in the way you mean. If he hadn't been there last night, I wouldn't be sitting here now." Though it annoyed her, she was compelled to defend him. "He's not a criminal—at least not in the standard sense."

The mayor merely lifted a brow. "In whatever sense, I prefer to have the police enforce the law in my city."

"Yes, I agree."

Satisfied, he nodded. "And this man..." He pushed through the papers on his desk. "Montega?"

"Enrico Montega," Deborah supplied. "Also known as Ricardo Sanchez and Enrico Toya. A Colombian national who entered the U.S. about six years ago. He's suspected of the murder of two drug merchants in Colombia. He was based in Miami for a while, and Vice there has a fat file on him. As does Interpol. Allegedly, he is the top enforcer on the East Coast. Four years ago, he murdered a police officer, and seriously wounded another." She paused, thinking of Gage.

"You've been doing your homework," Fields commented.

"I always like a firm foundation when I go after someone."

"Hmm. You know, Deborah, Mitchell considers you his top prosecutor." Fields grinned. "Not that he'd admit it. Mitch doesn't like to hand out compliments."

"I'm aware of that."

"We're all very pleased with your record, and particularly with the way the Slagerman case seems to be going. Both Mitch and I agree that we want you to concentrate more fully on your litigation. So, we've decided to take you off this particular case."

She blinked, stunned. "I beg your pardon?"

"We've decided you should turn your notes, your files over to another D.A."

"You're pulling me?"

He held up a hand. "We're simply beefing up the police investigation. With your caseload, we prefer to have you turn over your files on this to someone else."

She set her cup down with a snap. "Parino was mine."

"Parino is dead."

She shot a glance at Jerry, but he only lifted his hands. She rose, fighting to hold her temper. "This sprang out of that. All of it. This is my case, it has been all along."

"And you've endangered yourself, and the case, twice already."

"I've been doing my job."

"Someone else will be doing it, this part of it, after today." He spread his hands. "Deborah, this isn't a punishment, merely a shifting of responsibilities."

She shook her head and snatched up her briefcase. "Not good enough, not nearly. I'm going to speak with Mitchell myself." Turning, she stormed out. She had to struggle to maintain her dignity and not give in to the urge to slam the door behind her.

Jerry caught up with her at the elevators. "Deb, wait."

"Don't even try it."

"What?"

"To soothe and placate." After jamming the Down button, she whirled on him. "What the hell is this, Jerry?"

"Like the mayor said—"

"Don't hand me that. You knew, you knew what was going on, why I was being called in, and you didn't tell me. Not even a warning so I could prepare myself."

"Deb—" He laid a hand on her shoulder, but she shrugged it off. "Look, not that I don't agree with everything the mayor said—"

"You always do."

"I didn't know. I didn't know, damn it," he repeated

when she only stared at him. "Not until ten o'clock this morning. And whatever I think, I would have told you."

She stopped pounding her fist against the Down button. "Okay, I'm sorry I jumped all over you. But it's not right. Something's not right about all this."

"You nearly got yourself killed," he reminded her. "When Guthrie came in this morning—"

"Gage?" she interrupted. "Gage was here?"

"The ten-o'clock appointment."

"I see." Hands fisted, she whirled back to the elevator. "So he's behind it."

"He was concerned, that's all. He suggested—"

"I get the picture." She cut him off again and stepped into the elevator. "This isn't finished. And you can tell your boss I said so."

She had to bank her temper when she walked into court. Personal feelings, personal problems had no place here. There were two frightened young women and the justice system depending on her.

She sat, taking careful notes as the defense counsel questioned Slagerman. She blanked Gage and his handiwork out of her mind.

When it came time for cross-examination, she was ready. She remained seated a moment, studying Slagerman.

"You consider yourself a businessman, Mr. Slagerman?"

"Yes."

"And your business consists of hiring escorts, both male and female, for clients?"

"That's right. Elegant Escorts provides a service, finding suitable companions for other businessmen and women, often from out of town."

She let him ramble a few moments, describing his

profession. "I see." Rising, she strolled past the jury. "And is it in—let's say the job description—of any of your employees to exchange sex for money with these clients?"

"Absolutely not." Attractive and earnest, he leaned forward. "My staff is well screened and well trained. It's a firm policy that if anyone on staff develops this kind of a relationship with a client, it would result in termination."

"Are you aware that any of your employees have indeed exchanged sex for money?"

"I am now." He aimed a pained look at Suzanne and Marjorie.

"Did you request that Marjorie Lovitz or Suzanne McRoy entertain a client on a sexual level?"

"No."

"But you're aware that they did so?"

If he was surprised by her train of questioning, he didn't bat an eye. "Yes, of course. They admitted to it under oath."

"Yes, they were under oath, Mr. Slagerman. Just as you are. Have you ever struck an employee?"

"Certainly not."

"Yet both Miss Lovitz and Miss McRoy claim, under oath, that you did."

"They're lying." And he smiled at her.

"Mr. Slagerman, didn't you go to Miss Lovitz's apartment on the night of February 25th, angry that she was unable to work, and in your anger, beat her?"

"That's ridiculous."

"You swear that, under oath?"

"Objection. Asked and answered."

"Withdrawn. Mr. Slagerman, have you contacted either Miss Lovitz or Miss McRoy since this trial began?"

"No."

"You have not telephoned either of them?"

"No."

Nodding, she walked back to her table and picked up a stack of papers. "Is the number 555-2520 familiar to you?"

He hesitated. "No."

"That's odd. It's your private line, Mr. Slagerman. Shouldn't you recognize your own private telephone number?"

Though he smiled, she saw the icy hate in his eyes. "I call from it, not to it, so I don't have to remember it."

"I see. And did you, on the night of June 18, use that private line to call the apartment where both Miss Lovitz and Miss McRoy now live?"

"No."

"Objection, Your Honor. This is leading nowhere."

Deborah shifted again, facing the judge and leaving the jury's view of Slagerman unobstructed. "Your Honor. I'll show you where it leads in just a moment."

"Overruled."

"Mr. Slagerman, perhaps you could explain why, according to your phone records, a call was placed from your private line to the number at Miss Lovitz and Miss McRoy's apartment at 10:47 p.m. on June 18?"

"Anybody could have used my phone."

"Your private line?" She lifted a brow. "It's hardly worth having a private line if anyone can use it. The caller identified himself as Jimmy. You are known as Jimmy, aren't you?"

"Me and a lot of other people."

"Did you speak to me on the phone on the night of June 18?"

"I've never spoken with you on the phone."

She smiled coolly and moved closer to the chair. "Have you ever noticed, Mr. Slagerman, how to some men all women's voices sound alike? How, to some men, all women look alike? How to some men, women's bodies are for one purpose?"

"Your Honor." Defense counsel leaped to his feet.

"Withdrawn." Deborah kept her eyes level with Slagerman's. "Can you explain, Mr. Slagerman, how someone using your private line, using your name, called Miss McRoy on the night of June 18? And how when I answered the phone, this person, using your line and your name, mistook my voice for hers, and threatened Miss McRoy?" She waited a beat. "Would you like to know what that person said?"

Sweat was beading on his upper lip. "You can make up whatever you want."

"That's true. Fortunately we had a tap on Miss McRoy's phone. I have the transcript." She turned over a sheet of paper. "Should I refresh your memory?"

She had won. Though there were still closing arguments to take place, she knew she had won. Now, as she stormed through the Justice Building, she had other business to tend to.

She found Mitchell in his office, a phone to his ear. He was a big bull-chested man who had played linebacker in college. Pictures of him in his jersey were scattered on the wall among his degrees. He had short red hair and a sprinkling of freckles that did nothing to soften his leathered looks.

When he spotted Deborah, he waved her in, gestured toward a chair. But she remained standing until he'd completed his call.

"Slagerman?"

"I've got him nailed." She took a step closer to the desk. "You sold me out."

"That's bull."

"What the hell do you call it? I get pulled into the mayor's office and get the brush-off. Damn it, Mitch, this is my case."

"It's the state's case," he corrected, chomping on the end of his unlit cigar. "You're not the only one who can handle it."

"I made Parino, I made the deal." She slapped her palms down on his desk so they were eye to eye. "I'm the one who's been busting my tail over this."

"And you've been overstepping your bounds."

"You're the one who taught me that trying a case takes more than putting on a pin-striped suit and dancing in front of a jury. I know my job, damn it."

"Going to see Santiago alone was an error in judgment."

"Now, that *is* bull. He called me. He asked for me. You tell me what you'd have done if he'd called you."

He scowled at her. "That's entirely different."

"That's entirely the same," she snapped back, certain from the look in his eyes that he knew it. "If I'd screwed things up I'd expect to get bumped, but I haven't. I'm the one who's been sweating and frying my brains over this case. Now when I get a lead, I find out Guthrie chirps up and you and the mayor keel over. Still the old boy's network, is it, Mitch?"

He stabbed the cigar toward her face. "Don't pull that feminist crap on me. I don't care what way you button your shirt."

"I'm telling you, Mitch, if you pull me off this without good cause, I'm gone. I can't work for you if I can't depend on you, so I might as well go out on my own and take on divorce cases for three hundred an hour.''

"I don't like ultimatums."

"Neither do I."

He leaned back, measuring her. "Sit down."

"I don't want—"

"Damn it, O'Roarke, sit."

Tight-lipped and fuming, she did. "So?"

He rolled the cigar between his fingers. "If Santiago had called me, I would have gone, just like you. But," he continued before she could speak, "your handling of this case isn't the only reason I've considered pulling you."

"Considered" took her position back several notches. Calming a bit, she nodded. "Well, then?"

"You've been getting a lot of press on this."

"I hardly see what that has to do with it."

"Did you see this morning's paper?" He snatched it up from his desk and waved it in her face. "Read the headline?" Because she had, and had winced over it already, she simply shrugged. Darling Deb Swept Through City In Arms of Nemesis.

"So, some cab driver wanted his name in the paper, what does that have to do with the case?"

"When my prosecutors start having their names linked with the masked marauder, it has everything to do with everything." He popped the cigar back in his mouth, gnashing it. "I don't like the way you keep running into him."

Neither did she. "Look, if the police can't stop him, I can hardly be responsible for his popping up all over the place. And I'd hate to think you'd take me off a case because some jerk had to fill his column."

Personally Mitch hated the weasely reporter. And he

hadn't cared for the strong-arm tactics the mayor had used. "You've got two weeks."

"That's hardly enough time to—"

"Two weeks, take it or leave it. You bring me something we can take to a jury, or I pass the ball. Got it?"

"Yeah." She rose. "I got it."

She stormed out, past snickering associates. A paper was tacked on the door of her office. Someone had used magic markers and highlighter pens to draw a caricature of Deborah being carried in the arms of a lantern-jawed, muscle-bound masked man. Under it was a caption. The Continuing Adventures Of Darling Deb.

On a snarl, she ripped it down, balling it into her pocket as she stomped out. She had another stop to make.

She kept her finger pressed to the button of Gage's doorbell until Frank pulled the door open.

"Is he in?"

"Yes, ma'am." He stepped back as she pushed past him. He'd seen furious women before. Frank would have preferred to have faced a pack of hungry wolves.

"Where?"

"He's up in his office. I'll be glad to tell him you're here."

"I'll announce myself," she said as she started up the steps.

Frank looked after her, lips pursed. He considered buzzing Gage on the intercom and giving him fair warning. But he only grinned. Surprises were good for you.

Deborah didn't bother to knock, but pushed open the door and strode in. Gage was behind his desk, a phone in one hand, a pen in the other. Computer screens blinked. Across from him sat a trim, middle-aged woman with a steno pad. At Deborah's unannounced entrance she rose and glanced curiously at Gage.

"I'll get back to you," he said into the receiver before lowering it to the cradle. "Hello, Deborah."

She tossed her briefcase onto a chair. "I think you might prefer to have this conversation in private."

He nodded. "You can transcribe those notes tomorrow, Mrs. Brickman. It's late. Why don't you go home?"

"Yes, sir." She gathered her things and made a fast, discreet exit.

Deborah hooked her thumbs in the pockets of her skirt. Like a gunfighter hooking thumbs in a holster. He'd seen her take that pose in court. "It must be nice," she began, "sitting up here in your lofty tower and dispensing orders. I bet it feels just dandy. Not all of us are so fortunate. We don't have enough money to buy castles, or private planes or thousand-dollar suits. We work on the streets. But most of us are pretty good at our jobs, and happy enough." As she spoke, she walked slowly toward him. "But you know what makes us mad, Gage? You know what really ticks us off? That's when someone in one of those lofty towers sticks his rich, influential nose in our business. It makes us so mad that we think real hard about taking a punch at that interfering nose."

"Should we break out the boxing gloves?"

"I prefer my bare hands." As she had in Mitchell's office, she slapped them down on his desk. "Who the hell do you think you are, going to the mayor, pressuring him to take me off this case?"

"I went to the mayor," he said slowly, "and gave him my opinion."

"Your opinion." She blew a breath between her teeth

and snatched up an onyx paperweight from the desk. Though she gave careful consideration to heaving it through the plate glass at his back, she contented herself with passing it from hand to hand. "And I bet he just fell all over himself to accommodate you and your thirty million."

Gage watched her pace and waited until he was sure he could speak rationally. "He agreed with me that you're more suitable to a courtroom than a murder scene."

"Who are you to say what's more suitable for me?" She whirled back, her voice rich with fury. "I say it, not you. All my life I've prepared myself for this job and I'm not having anyone come along and tell me I'm not suitable for any case I take on." She snapped the paperweight back on the desk, a hard crack of stone against stone. "You stay out of my business, and out of my life."

No, he realized, he wasn't going to be able to be rational. "Are you finished?"

"No. Before I leave I want you to know that it didn't work. I'm still on this case, and I'm staying on. So you wasted your time, and mine. And lastly, I think you're arrogant, officious and overbearing."

His hands were fisted beneath the desk. "Is that all?"

"You bet it is." She snatched up her briefcase, turned on her heel and headed for the door.

Gage pushed a button under the desk and had the locks snap into place. "I'm not," he said quietly.

She hadn't known she could be more furious. But as she spun back to him, a red haze formed in front of her eyes. "Unlock that door immediately, or I'll have you up on charges."

"You've had your say, Counselor." He rose. "Now I'll have mine."

"Not interested."

He came around the desk, but only leaned back against it. He didn't trust himself to approach her, not yet. "You've got all the evidence, don't you, Counselor? All your neat little facts. So, I'll save time and plead guilty as charged."

"Then we have nothing more to say."

"Isn't the prosecution interested in motive?"

She tossed back her head, bracing as he crossed to her. Something about the way he moved just then, slowly, soundlessly, set off a flash of memory. But it was gone, overwhelmed by her own temper.

"Motive isn't relevant in this case, results are."

"You're wrong. I went to the mayor, I asked him to use his influence to have you taken off the case. But I'm guilty of more than that—I'm guilty of being in love with you."

Her tensed hands went limp at her side so that the briefcase fell to the floor. Though she opened her mouth to speak, she could say nothing.

"Amazing." His eyes were dark and furious as he took that final step toward her. "A sharp woman like you being surprised by that. You should have seen it every time I looked at you. You should have seen it every time I touched you." He put his hands on her shoulders. "You should have tasted it, every time I kissed you."

Pushing her back against the door, he brushed his mouth over hers, once, twice. Then he devoured her lips.

Her knees were weak. She hadn't thought it was possible, but they were shaking so she had to hold on to him or slide bonelessly to the floor. Even clinging, she was afraid. For she had seen it, had felt it, had tasted it. But that was nothing compared to hearing him say it, or to hearing the echo of her own voice repeating the words inside her mind.

He was lost in her. And the more she opened to him, the deeper he fell. He took his hands over her face, through her hair, down her body, wanting to touch all of her. And to know as he did, that she trembled in response.

When he lifted his head, she saw the love, and she saw the desire. With them was a kind of war she didn't understand.

"There were nights," he said quietly, "hundreds of nights when I lay awake sweating and waiting for morning. I'd wonder if I'd ever find someone I could love, that I could need. No matter how I drew the fantasy, it's nothing compared to what I feel for you."

"Gage." She lifted her hands to his face, wishing with all her heart. Knowing well that heart was already lost to him. But she remembered that she had swayed close to another man only the night before. "I don't know what I'm feeling."

"Yes, you do."

"All right, I do, but I'm afraid to feel it. It's not fair. I'm not being fair, but I have to ask you to let me think this through."

"I'm not sure I can."

"A little while longer, please. Unlock the door, and let me go."

"It is unlocked." He stepped back to open it for her. But he blocked her exit for one last moment. "Deborah. I won't let you go the next time."

She looked up again and saw the truth of his words in his eyes. "I know."

Chapter 7

The jury was out. Deborah spent their deliberating time in her office, using both her telephone and computer to try to track down what Gage had referred to as the common thread. The antique shop, Timeless, had been owned by Imports Incorporated, whose address was a vacant lot downtown. The company had filed no insurance claim on the loss, and the manager of the shop had vanished. The police had yet to locate the man Parino had referred to as Mouse.

More digging turned up the Triad Corporation, based in Philadelphia. A phone call to Triad put Deborah in touch with a recording telling her that the number had been disconnected. As she placed a call to the D.A.'s office in Philadelphia, she inputted all of her known data into the computer.

Two hours later, she had a list of names, social security numbers and the beginnings of a headache.

Before she could make her next call, the receiver rang under her hand. "Deborah O'Roarke."

"Is this the same Deborah O'Roarke who can't keep her name out of the paper?"

"Cilla." At the sound of her sister's voice, the headache faded a bit. "How are you?"

"Worried about you."

"What else is new?" Deborah rolled her shoulders to relieve the stiff muscles, then leaned back in the chair. Coming tinnily through the earpiece was the music Deborah imagined was pulsing in Cilla's office at the radio station. "How's Boyd?"

"That's Captain Fletcher to you."

"Captain?" She sat straight again. "When did that happen?"

"Yesterday." The pride and pleasure came through clearly. "I guess I'll really have to watch myself now, sleeping with a police captain."

"Tell him I'm proud of him."

"I will. We all are. Now—"

"How are the kids?" Deborah had learned to stall and evade long before taking the bar exam.

"It's dangerous to ask a mother how her kids are during summer vacation, no elementary school, no kindergarten, so they outnumber me and the cop three to two." Cilla gave a rich, warm laugh. "All three members of the demon brigade are fine. Allison pitched a shutout in a Little League game last week—then got into a wrestling match with the opposing pitcher."

"Sounds like he was a rotten loser."

"Yeah. And Allison's always been a rotten winner. I practically had to sit on her to make her give over. Let's see…Bryant knocked out a tooth roller-skating then, being a clever little capitalist, sold it to the boy next door for fifty cents. Keenan swallowed it.''

''Swallowed what?''

''The fifty cents. Five dimes. My youngest son eats anything. I'm thinking about putting in a hot line to the Emergency room. Now let's talk about you.''

''I'm fine. How are things at KHIP?''

''About as chaotic as they are around the house. All in all, I'd rather be in Maui.'' Cilla recognized the delaying tactics well and pushed a little harder. ''Deborah, I want to know what you're up to.''

''Work. In fact, I'm about to win a case.'' She glanced at the clock and calculated how long the jury had been out. ''I hope.''

Sometimes, Cilla mused, you just had to be direct. ''Since when have you started dating guys in masks?''

Stalling couldn't last forever, she thought with regret. ''Come on, Cilla, you don't believe everything you read in the paper.''

''Right. Or everything that comes over the wire, even though we ran your latest adventure at the top of every hour yesterday. Even if I didn't go to the trouble to get the Urbana papers, I'd have heard all the noise. You're making national news out there, kid, and I want to know what's going on. That's why I'm asking you.''

It was usually easier to evade if you added a couple of dashes of truth. ''This Nemesis character is a nuisance. The press is glorifying him—and worse. Just this morning at a shop two blocks from the courthouse, I saw a display of Nemesis T-shirts.''

''Isn't merchandising wonderful?'' But Cilla wasn't about to be distracted again. ''Deborah, I've been in radio too long not to be able to read voices—especially my baby sister's. What's between you?''

"Nothing," she insisted, wanting it to be true. "I've simply run into him a couple of times during this investigation I'm doing. The press plays it up."

"I've noticed, Darling Deb."

"Oh, please."

"I do want to know what's going on, but it's more to the point right now why you're involved in something so dangerous. And why I had to read in the paper that some maniac had a knife to my sister's throat."

"It's exaggerated."

"Oh, so no one held a knife to your throat?"

No matter how well she lied, Deborah thought, Cilla would know. "It wasn't as dramatic as it sounds. And I wasn't hurt."

"Knives at your throat," Cilla muttered. "Buildings blowing up in your face. Damn it, Deb, don't you have a police force out there?"

"I was just doing some legwork. Don't start," she said quickly. "Cilla, do you know how frustrating it is to have to keep repeating that you know what you're doing, that you can take care of yourself and do your job?"

Cilla let out a long breath. "Yeah. I can't stop worrying about you, Deborah, just because you're a couple thousand miles away. It's taken me years to finally accept what happened to Mom and Dad. If I lost you, I couldn't handle it."

"You're not going to lose me. Right now, the most dangerous thing I'm facing is my computer."

"Okay. Okay." Arguing with her sister wouldn't change a thing, Cilla knew. And whatever answers Deborah gave her, she would keep right on worrying. "Listen, I also saw a picture of my little sister with some millionaire. I'm going to have to start a scrapbook. Anything you want to tell me?''

The automatic no caught in her throat. ''I don't know. Things are pretty complicated right now and I haven't had time to think it through.''

''Is there something to think through?''

''Yes.'' The headache was coming back. She reached into her drawer for a bottle of aspirin. ''A couple of things,'' she murmured, thinking of Gage and of Nemesis. That was something not even Cilla could help her with. But there were other matters. ''Cilla, since you're married to a police captain, how about using your influence to have him do me a favor?''

''I'll threaten to cook. He'll do anything I want.''

With a laugh, Deborah picked up one of her printouts. ''I'd like him to check out a couple of names for me. George P. Drummond and a Charles R. Meyers, both with Denver addresses.'' She spelled out both names, then added social security numbers. ''Got it?''

''Mmm-hmm,'' Cilla murmured as she scribbled the information.

''And there's a Solar Corporation, also based in Denver. Drummond and Meyers are on the board of directors. If Boyd could run these through the police computer, it would save me several steps through the bureaucracy.''

''I'll threaten him with my pot roast.''

''That should do the trick.''

''Deb, you will be careful, won't you?''

''Absolutely. Give everyone a hug for me. I miss you. All of you.'' Mitchell came to the door and signaled. ''I've got to go, Cilla. The jury's coming back.''

Deep in the recesses of his home, in an echoing cavern of a room, Gage studied a bank of computers. There was some work he couldn't do in his office. Some work he preferred to do in secret. With his hands hooked in the pockets of his jeans, he watched the monitors. Names and numbers flashed by.

He could see on one of the monitors just what Deborah had inputted in her computer across town. She was making progress, he thought. Slow, it was true, but it still worried him. If he could follow the steps she was taking, so could others.

Eyes intent, face sober, he took his fingers flying over one keyboard, then another and still another. He had to find the link. Once he did, he would carefully, systematically locate the name of the man responsible for Jack's death. As long as he found it before Deborah, she was safe.

The computers offered him one way. Or he could take another. Leaving the machines to their work, he turned, pressed a button. On the wall on the far side of the high-ceilinged, curving room a huge map slid into place. Crossing to it, he studied a very large scaled detail of the city of Urbana.

Using yet another keyboard, he had colored lights blinking at various parts of the city. Each represented a major drug exchange, many of which were as yet unknown to the UPD.

They flashed in the East End, and the West, in the exclusive neighborhoods uptown, in the barrios, in the financial district. There seemed to be no pattern. Yet there was always a pattern. He had only to find it.

As he studied the map, his gaze lit and lingered on one building. Deborah's apartment. Was she home yet? he wondered. Was she safe inside? Was she wearing her blue robe and studying files, the television news murmuring in the background?

Was she thinking of him?

Gage rubbed his hands over his face. Frank was right, she was interfering with his concentration. But what could he do about it? Every attempt he made to see that she withdrew from the case had failed. She was too stubborn to listen.

He smiled a bit. He hadn't believed he would ever fall in love. How inconvenient, he thought wryly, that when he did, it was with a dedicated public servant. She wouldn't budge. He knew it. And neither would he. But however much discipline he had over his body and his mind, he seemed to have none over his heart.

It wasn't just her beauty. Though he had always loved beautiful things and had grown up learning to appreciate them for no more than their existence. After he'd come out of the coma, he had found a certain comfort in surrounding himself with beauty. All that color, all that texture after so much flat gray.

It wasn't just her mind. Though he respected intelligence. As a cop and as a businessman, he had learned that a sharp mind was the most powerful and the most dangerous weapon.

There was something, some indefinable something beyond her looks and her mind that had captured him. Because he was just as much her prisoner as he was of his own fate. And he had no idea how to resolve the two.

He was only sure that the first step would be to find the key himself, to find the name and to find the justice. When this was behind him, and her, there might be a chance for a future.

Clearing his mind, he studied the lights then, bending over a computer, went to work.

Balancing a pizza box, a bottle of Lambrusco and a briefcase full of paperwork, Deborah stepped off the elevator. As she wondered how she would manage to dig for her keys, she glanced up at the door of her apartment. Colorful draping letters crossed the door. CONGRATU-LATIONS, DEBORAH.

Mrs. Greenbaum, she thought with a grin. Even as she turned toward her neighbor's apartment, Mrs. Greenbaum's door opened.

"I heard it on the six-o'clock news. You put that little weasel away." Mrs. Greenbaum adjusted the hem of her tie-dyed T-shirt. "How do you feel?"

"Good. I feel good. How about some celebratory pizza?"

"You twisted my arm." Mrs. Greenbaum let her door slam, then crossed the hall in her bare feet. "I guess you noticed the air-conditioning's on the fritz again."

"I got the picture during my steam bath in the elevator."

"This time I think we should mobilize the rest of the tenants." She gave Deborah a shrewd look. "Especially if we had some sharp, fast-talking lawyer lead the way."

"You're already leading the way," Deborah said as she shifted the wine. "But if it's not on within twenty-four hours, I'll contact the landlord and put on the pressure." She fumbled around in her pocket. "Now if I could just get my keys."

"I've got the copy you gave me." Reaching into the pocket of her baggy jeans, Mrs. Greenbaum produced a key ring crowded with keys. "Here we go."

"Thanks." Inside, Deborah set the pizza box on a table. "I'll get some glasses and plates."

Lil lifted the lid and saw with approval that the pizza was loaded with everything. "You know, a pretty young girl like you should be celebrating with some pretty young boy on a Friday night instead of with an old woman."

"What old woman?" Deborah called from the kitchen and made Lil laugh.

"With a slightly above-middle-aged woman then. What about that mouth-watering Gage Guthrie?"

"I can't imagine him eating pizza and drinking cheap wine." She walked back in, carrying the bottle and two glasses, paper plates and napkins tucked under her arm. "He's more the caviar type."

"Something wrong with that?"

"No." She frowned. "No, but I'm in the mood for pizza. And after I gorge myself, I have work."

"Honey, don't you ever let up?"

"I've got a deadline," Deborah said, and found she still resented it. She poured two glasses, handed one to her friend. "To justice," she said. "The most beautiful lady I know."

Just as they sat, gooey slices of pizza split between them, there was a knock on the door. Licking sauce from her fingers, Deborah went to answer. She saw a huge basket of red roses that appeared to have legs.

"Delivery for Deborah O'Roarke. Got someplace I can put this thing, lady?"

"Oh…yes, ah. Here." She stood on tiptoe and got a glimpse of the deliveryman's head under the blossoms. "On the coffee table."

They not only sat on the coffee table, Deborah noted

as she signed the clipboard, they covered it from end to end. "Thanks." She dug into her wallet for a bill.

"Well?" Lil demanded when they were alone again. "Who are they from?"

Though she already knew, Deborah picked up the card.

Nice work, Counselor.
Gage

She couldn't prevent the softening, or the smile that bloomed on her lips. "They're from Gage."

"The man knows how to make a statement." Behind her lenses, Lil's eyes sparkled. There was nothing she liked better than romance—unless it was a good protest rally. "Must be five dozen in there."

"They're beautiful." She slipped the card into her pocket. "I suppose I'll have to call him and thank him."

"At least." Lil bit into the pizza. "Why don't you do it now, while it's on your mind?" And while she could eavesdrop.

Deborah hesitated, the scent of the flowers surrounding her. No, she thought with a shake of her head. If she called him now, while his gesture weakened her, she might do or say something rash. "Later," she decided. "I'll call him later."

"Stalling," Lil said over a mouthful of pizza.

"Yeah." Not ashamed to admit it, Deborah sat again. She ate for a moment in silence, then picked up her wine. "Mrs. Greenbaum," she began, frowning into her glass. "You were married twice."

"So far," Lil answered with a grin.

"You loved both of them?"

"Absolutely. They were good men." Her sharp little

eyes became young and dreamy. "Both times I thought it was going to be forever. I was about your age when I lost my first husband in the war. We only had a few years together. Mr. Greenbaum and I were a bit luckier. I miss both of them."

"Have you ever wondered…I guess it's an odd sort of question, but have you ever wondered what would have happened if you'd met both of them at the same time?"

Lil arched her eyebrows, intrigued with the notion. "That would have been a problem."

"You see what I mean. You loved both of them, but if they had come into your life at the same time, you couldn't have loved both of them."

"There's no telling what tricks the heart will play."

"But you can't love two men the same way at the same time." She leaned forward, her own conflict showing clearly on her face. "And if somehow you did, or thought you did, you couldn't make a commitment to either one, without being unfaithful to the other."

Taking her time, Lil topped off both glasses. "Are you in love with Gage Guthrie?"

"I might be." Deborah glanced back at the basket bursting with roses. "Yes, I think I am."

"And with someone else?"

With her glass cupped in her hand, Deborah pushed away from the table and rose to pace. "Yes. But that's crazy, isn't it?"

Not crazy, Lil thought. Nothing to do with love was ever crazy. And for some, such a situation would be delightful and exciting. Not for Deborah. For Deborah, she understood it would only be painful.

"Are you sure it's love on either side, and not just sex?"

After letting out a long breath, Deborah sat again. "I thought it was just physical. I wanted it to be. But I've thought about it, tried to be honest with myself, and I know it's not. I even get them mixed up in my mind. Not just comparisons, but well, as if I'm trying to make them one man, so it would be simpler." She drank again. "Gage told me he loves me, and I believe him. I don't know what to do."

"Follow your heart," Lil told her. "I know that sounds trite, the truest things often do. Let your mind take a back seat and listen to your heart. It usually makes the right choice."

At eleven, Deborah switched on the late news. She wasn't displeased to see her victory in the Slagerman case as the top story. She watched her own image give a brief statement on the courthouse steps, frowning a bit when Wisner pushed through to ask his usual nonsense about Nemesis.

The news team segued from that into Nemesis's latest exploits—the liquor store robbery he had scotched, the mugger he had captured, the murder he had prevented.

"Busy man," Deborah muttered, and drained the last of the wine. If Mrs. Greenbaum hadn't spent most of the evening with her, Deborah thought, she would have contented herself with one glass of wine rather than half the bottle.

Well, tomorrow was Saturday, she thought with a shrug, as the anchorman reported on the upcoming mayoral debates. She could sleep a little late before she went into the office. Or, if she was lucky, she would uncover something that evening. But she wouldn't get anything done if she continued to sit in front of the television.

She waited long enough to hear the weather report,

which promised continuing heat, raging humidity and chances of thunderstorms. Switching off the set, she went to the bedroom to settle at her desk.

She'd left the window open in the vain hope of catching a breeze. The traffic noise was a steady din from five stories down. The heat rose from the street, intensifying on its upward journey. She could all but see it.

Hot nights. Hot needs.

She walked to the window, hoping for a breath of air to ease the aching even the wine hadn't dulled. But it remained, a deep, slow throb. Was he out there? she wondered, then put a hand to her temple. She wasn't even sure which man she was thinking of. And it would be best, she knew, if she thought of neither.

Turning on her desk lamp, she opened a file, then glanced at the phone.

She'd called Gage an hour before, only to be told by the taciturn Frank that Mr. Guthrie was out for the evening. She could hardly call him again, she thought. It would look as though she were checking up on him. Something she had no right to do—especially since she was the one who had asked for the time and space.

That was what she wanted, she assured herself. What she had to have. And thinking of him wouldn't help her find the answers that were buried somewhere in the papers on her desk.

She began to read through them again, making notations on a legal pad. As she worked, time slipped past and thunder muttered in the distance.

He shouldn't have come. He knew it wasn't right. But as he had walked the streets, his steps had taken him closer and closer to her apartment. Draped in shadows, he looked up and saw the light in her window. In the heat-drenched night he waited, telling himself if the light switched off, he would leave. He would go.

But it remained, a pale yet steady beacon.

He wondered if he could convince himself he wanted only to see her, to speak with her. It was true that he needed to find out how much she knew, how close she was. Facts on her computer didn't take in her intuition or her suspicions. The closer she came to answers, the more jeopardy she was in.

Even more than he wanted to love her, he needed to protect her.

But that wasn't why he crossed the street, why he swung himself onto the fire escape and began to climb. What he did he did because he couldn't stop himself.

Through the open window, he saw her. She was seated at a desk, the slant of light directed onto the papers she read through. A pencil moved quickly in her hand.

He could smell her. The tauntingly sexy scent she wore reached out to him like an invitation. Or a dare.

He could see only her profile, the curve of her cheek and jaw, the shape of her mouth. Her short blue robe was loosely tied, and he could see the long white column of her throat. As he watched, she lifted a hand to rub at the back of her neck. The robe shifted, sliding up her thighs, parting gently as she crossed her legs and bent over her work again.

Deborah read the same paragraph three times before she realized her concentration had been broken. She rubbed her eyes, intending to begin again. And her whole body stiffened. Heat rushed over her skin. Slowly she turned and saw him.

He was standing inside the window, away from the light. Her heart was hammering—not in shock, she realized. In anticipation.

"Taking a break from crime fighting?" she asked, hoping the sharp tone of her voice would cover her trembling. "According to the eleven-o'clock news, you've been busy."

He hadn't bothered to concentrate. This time, at least this time, he'd needed to come to her whole. "So have you."

"And I still am." She pushed at her hair and discovered her hand wasn't quite steady. "How did you get in?" When he glanced toward the window, she nodded. "I'll have to remember to keep that locked."

"It wouldn't have mattered. Not after I saw you."

Every nerve in her body was on edge. Telling herself it would add more authority, she rose. "I'm not going to let this go on."

"You can't stop it." He stepped toward her. "Neither can I." His gaze shifted to the papers on her desk. "You haven't listened."

"No. I don't intend to. I'll wade through all the lies, navigate all the dead ends until I find the truth. Then I'll finish it." Her stance was tense and watchful. Her eyes challenged him. "If you want to help me, then tell me what you know."

"I know I want you." He hooked a hand in the belt of her robe to hold her still. At that moment, she was his only need, his only quest, his only hunger. "Now. Tonight."

"You have to go." She could do nothing to prevent the shudder of response or the flare of desire. Integrity warred with passion. "You have to leave."

"Do you know how I ache for you?" His voice was harsh as he jerked her against him. "There is no law I wouldn't break, no value I wouldn't sacrifice to have you. Do you understand that kind of need?"

"Yes." It was clawing her. "Yes. It's wrong."

"Right or wrong, it's tonight." With one sweep of his hand, he sent the lamp crashing to the floor. As the room was plunged into darkness, he lifted her into his arms.

"We can't." But her fingers dug hard into his shoulder, negating the denial.

"We will."

Even as she shook her head, his mouth came down on hers, fast and fevered, strong and seductive. The power of it slammed into her, leaving her reeling and rocky—and helpless, helpless to resist her own answering need. Her lips softened without yielding, parted without surrendering. As she tumbled deaf and blind into the kiss, her mind heard what her heart had been trying to tell her.

He pressed her into the mattress, his mouth frantic and impatient as it roamed her face, his hands already tearing at the thin robe that covered her. Beneath it she was just as he'd dreamed. Hot and smooth and fragrant. Stripping off his gloves he let himself feel what he had craved.

Like a river she flowed under his hands. He could have drowned in her. Though he burned to see what he was making his, he contented himself with texture, with taste, with scent. In the hot storm-haunted night, he was relentless.

He was still a shadow, but she knew him. And wanted him. With all reason, all rationality aside, she clung to him, mouth seeking mouth as they rolled over the bed. Desperate to feel him against her, to feel the wild beat of his heart match the wild beat of hers, she pulled at his shirt. There were harshly whispered words against her lips, against her throat, her breast, as she frantically undressed him.

Then he was as vulnerable as she, his skin as slick,

his hands as greedy. Thunder rumbled, lightning flickered in the moonless night. The scent of roses and passion hung heavy in the air. She shuddered, mindless with the pleasures he so recklessly showed her.

It was all heat, all ache, all glory. Even as she wept with it, she strained against him, demanding more. Before she could demand, he gave, sending her soaring again. Dark, secret delights. Moans and whispers. Bruising caresses. Insatiable hungers.

When she thought she would surely go mad, he plunged inside her. And it was madness. She gave herself to it, to him, with all her strength, all her eagerness.

"I love you." She wrapped tight around him as the words poured out.

They filled him, even as he filled her. They moved him even as their bodies moved together. He buried his face in her hair. Her nails dug into his back. He felt his own shattering release, then hers as she cried out his name.

He lay in the dark. The roaring in his head gradually subsided until all he heard was the sound of traffic on the street below and Deborah's deep, unsteady breaths. Her arms were no longer tight around him, but had slid off. She was still now, and quiet.

Slowly, unnerved by his own weakness, he shifted from her. She didn't move, didn't speak. In the dark, he touched a hand to her face and found it damp. And he hated that part of him that had caused her grief.

"How long have you known?"

"Not until tonight." Before he could touch her again, she turned away and groped for her robe. "Did you think I wouldn't know when you kissed me? Didn't you realize that no matter how dark it was, no matter how

confused you made me, once this happened I would
know?''

It wasn't just anger in her voice, but pain. He could
have withstood the anger. "No, I didn't think of it."

"Didn't you?" She switched on the bedside lamp and
stared at him. "But you're so clever, Gage, so damn
clever to have made such a mistake."

He looked at her. Her hair was tumbled, her pale skin
still flushed and warm from his hands. There were tears
in her eyes, and behind them a bright anger. "Maybe I
did know. Maybe I just didn't want to let it matter." He
rose and reached for her. "Deborah—"

She slapped him once, then twice. "Damn you, you
lied to me. You made me doubt myself, my values. You
knew, you had to know I was falling in love with you."
With a half laugh she turned away. "With both of you."

"Please listen." When he touched her on the shoulder, she jerked away.

"It wouldn't be wise to touch me just now."

"All right." He curled his hand into a fist. "I fell in
love with you so fast, I couldn't think. All I knew was
that I needed you, and that I wanted you to be safe."

"So, you put on your mask and looked out for me. I
won't thank you for it. For any of it."

The finality in her voice had panic racing through him.
"Deborah, what happened here tonight—"

"Yes, what happened here. You trusted me enough
for this." She gestured to the bed. "But not for the rest.
Not for the truth."

"No, I didn't. I couldn't because I know how you feel
about what I'm doing."

"That's a whole different story, isn't it?" She swiped
away tears. The anger was dying away to misery. "If

you knew you had to lie to me, why didn't you just stay away from me?''

He forced himself not to reach for her again. He had lied and, by lying, hurt her. Now he could only offer the truth and hope it would begin to heal. "You're the only thing in four years I haven't been able to overcome. You're the only thing in four years I've needed as much as I've needed to live. I don't expect you to understand or even accept, but I need you to believe me."

"I don't know what to believe. Gage, since I met you I've been torn in two different directions, believing I was falling in love with two different men. But it's just you. I don't know what to do." On a sigh, she shut her eyes. "I don't know what's right."

"I love you, Deborah. Nothing's righter than that. Give me a chance to show you, time to explain the rest."

"I don't seem to have much choice. Gage, I can't condone—" She opened her eyes and for the first time focused on the long, jagged scars on his chest. Pain slammed into her, all but bringing her to her knees. Dulled with horror, her eyes lifted to his. "They did that to you?" she whispered.

His body stiffened. "I don't want pity, Deborah."

"Be quiet." She moved quickly, going to him, wrapping her arms around him. "Hold me." She shook her head. "No, tighter. I might have lost you all those years ago before I ever had the chance to have you." There were tears in her eyes again as she lifted her head. "I don't know what to do, or what's right. But tonight it's enough that you're here. You'll stay?"

He touched his lips to hers. "As long as you want."

Chapter 8

Deborah always awakened reluctantly. She snuggled into sleep, easily blocking out the honks and gunning engines from the street. A jackhammer was machine-gunning the concrete, but she only yawned and shifted. If she put her mind to it, she could sleep through an atomic bomb.

It wasn't the noise that had her opening her groggy eyes. It was the faint and glorious scent of brewing coffee.

Ten-thirty, she noted, peering at the clock. *Ten-thirty!* Deborah struggled to sit up and discovered she was alone in bed.

Gage, she thought, pressing the heels of her hands to her eyes. Had he ordered breakfast again? Eggs Benedict? Belgian waffles? Strawberries and champagne? God, what she would have given for a simple cup of black coffee and a stale doughnut.

Pushing herself from the bed, she reached down for

her robe, which was lying in a heap on the floor. Beneath it was a swatch of black cloth. She picked it up, then lowered herself to the bed again.

A mask. She balled the material in her hand. So, it hadn't been a dream. It was real, all of it. He had come to her in the night, loved her in the night. Both of her fantasies. The charming businessman, the arrogant stranger in black. They were one man, one lover.

On a low groan, she buried her face in her hands. What was she going to do? How the hell was she going to handle this? As a woman? As a D.A.?

God, she loved him. And by loving him, she betrayed her principles. If she revealed his secret, she betrayed her heart.

And how could she love him without understanding him?

Yet she did, and there was no way she could take back her heart.

They had to talk, she decided. Calmly and sensibly. She could only pray she would find the strength and the right words. It wouldn't be enough to tell him she disapproved. He already knew it. It wouldn't be enough to tell him she was afraid. That would only prompt him to reassure. Somehow, she had to find the words to convince him that the path he had taken was not only dangerous, but wrong.

Deborah braced herself, prepared.

When the phone rang, she muttered an oath. Struggling into her robe, she climbed across the bed to snatch up the receiver.

"...Deborah's sister." Cilla's voice held both amusement and curiosity. "And how are you?"

"Fine, thanks," Gage said. "Deborah's still sleeping. Would you like me to—"

"I'm right here." Sighing, Deborah pushed at her tousled hair. "Hello, Cilla."

"Hi."

"Goodbye, Cilla." Deborah heard Gage set the phone on the hook. There was a moment of humming silence.

"Ah...I guess I called at a bad time."

"No. I was just getting up. Isn't it a bit early in Denver?"

"With three kids, this is the middle of the day. Bryant, take that basketball outside. *Out!* No dribbling in the kitchen. Deb?"

"Yes?"

"Sorry. Anyway, Boyd checked out those names, and I thought you'd like the information right away."

"That's great." She picked up a pen.

"I'll let Boyd fill you in." The phone rattled. "No, I'll take him. Keenan, don't put that in your mouth. Good grief, Boyd, what's all over his face?" There was some giggling, a crash as the receiver hit the kitchen floor and the sound of running feet.

"Deb?"

"Congratulations, Captain Fletcher."

"Thanks. I guess Cilla's been bragging again. How's it going?"

She looked down at the mask she still held in her hand. "I'm not at all sure." Shaking off the mood, she smiled into the phone. "Things sound normal out there."

"Nothing's ever normal out here. Hey, Allison, don't let that dog—" There was another crash and a flurry of barking. "Too late."

Yes, it sounded perfectly normal. "Boyd, I appreciate you moving so fast on this."

"No problem. It sounded important."

"It is."

"Well, it isn't much. George P. Drummond was a plumber, owned his own business—"

"Was?" Deborah interrupted.

"Yeah. He died three years ago. Natural causes. He was eighty-two and had no connection with a Solar Corporation or any other."

She shut her eyes. "And the other?"

"Charles R. Meyers. High school science teacher and football coach. Deceased five years. They were both clean as a whistle."

"And the Solar Corporation?"

"We can't find much so far. The address you gave Cilla was nonexistent."

"I should have guessed. Every time I turn a corner on this, I run into a dead end."

"I know the feeling. I'll do some more digging. Sorry I can't be more helpful."

"But you have been."

"Two dead guys and a phony address? Not much. Deborah, we've been following the papers out here. Can you tell me if this business has anything to do with your masked phantom?"

She balled the black cloth in her hand again. "Off the record, yes."

"I imagine Cilla's already said it, but be careful, okay?"

"I will."

"She wants to talk to you again." There was some muttering, a chuckle. "Something about a man answering your phone." Boyd laughed again, and Deborah could almost see them wrestling over the receiver.

"I just want to know—" Cilla was breathless. "Boyd, cut it out. Go feed the dog or something. I just want to know,'' she repeated into the receiver, ''who owns the terrific, sexy voice.''

''A man.''

''I figured that out. Does he have a name?''

''Yes.''

''Well, do you want me to guess? Phil, Tony, Maximillion?''

''Gage,'' Deborah muttered, giving up.

''The millionaire? Nice going.''

''Cilla—''

''I know, I know. You're a grown woman. A sensible woman with a life of her own. I won't say another word. But is he—''

''Before you take this any further, I should warn you I haven't had coffee yet.''

''Okay. But I want you to call me, and soon. I need details.''

''I'll let you know when I have them. I'll be in touch.''

''You'd better.''

She hung up and sat a moment. It seemed she was back to square one, all around. But first things first, she reminded herself, and followed the scent of coffee into the kitchen.

Gage was at the stove, in jeans and bare feet, his shirt unbuttoned. She wasn't surprised to see him there, but she was surprised at what he was doing.

''You're cooking?'' she said from the doorway.

He turned. The impact of seeing her there in the strong sunlight, her eyes sleepy and cautious, nearly bowled him over. ''Hi. Sorry about the phone, I thought I could get it before it woke you up.''

''It's all right. I was…awake.'' Feeling awkward, she

took a mug from a hook over the sink and poured coffee. "It was my sister."

"Right." He put his hands on her shoulders, running his hands gently down to her elbows and back. When she stiffened, he felt the pain knife into him. "Would you rather I wasn't here?"

"I don't know." She drank without turning around. "I guess we have to talk." But she couldn't bring herself to face it yet. "What are you making?"

"French toast. You didn't have much in the fridge, so I went down to the corner and picked some things up."

So normal, she thought as her stomach clenched. So easy. "How long have you been up?"

"Two or three hours."

When he walked back to the stove, she turned around. "You didn't get much sleep."

His eyes met hers. She was holding back, he thought, on both the hurt and the anger. But they were there. "I don't need much—not anymore." He added two eggs to the milk he already had in a bowl. "I spent the better part of a year doing nothing but sleeping. After I came back I didn't seem to need more than four hours a night."

"I guess that's how you manage to run your businesses, and...the other."

"Yeah." He continued to mix ingredients, then dunked bread into the bowl. "You could say my metabolism changed—among other things." Coated bread sizzled when he placed it in the skillet. "Do you want me to apologize for what happened last night?"

She didn't speak for a moment, then opened a cupboard. "I'll get some plates."

He bit off an oath. "Fine. This only takes a few minutes."

He waited until they were seated by the window. Deborah said nothing while she toyed with her breakfast. Her silence and the miserable look in her eyes were more disturbing to him than a hundred shouted accusations.

"It's your call," he said quietly.

Her eyes lifted to his. "I know."

"I won't apologize for being in love with you. Or for making love with you. Being with you last night was the most important thing that's ever happened to me."

He waited, watching her. "You don't believe that, do you?"

"I'm not sure what I believe. What I can believe." She cupped her hands around her mug, her fingers tense. "You've lied to me, Gage, from the very beginning."

"Yes, I have." He banked down on the need to reach out for her, just to touch her. "Apologies for that really don't matter much. It was deliberate, and if it had been possible, I would have continued to lie to you."

She pushed away from the table to wrap her arms around herself. "Do you know how that makes me feel?"

"I think I do."

Hurting, she shook her head. "You couldn't possibly know. You made me doubt myself on the most basic of levels. I was falling in love with you—with both of you, and I was ashamed. Oh, I can see now that I was a fool not to have realized it sooner. My feelings were exactly the same for what I thought were two different men. I would look at you, and think of him. Look at him, and think of you." She pressed her fingers to her lips. The words were pouring out too quickly.

"That night, in Santiago's room, after I came to and you were holding me. I looked up into your eyes and remembered the first time I had seen you in the ballroom at the Stuart Palace. I thought I was going crazy.''

''It wasn't done to hurt you, only to protect you.''

''From what?'' she demanded. ''From myself, from you? Every time you touched me, I...'' Her breath hitched as she fought for composure. That was her problem, after all. Her emotions. ''I don't know if I can forgive you, Gage, or trust you. Even loving you, I don't know.''

He sat where he was, knowing she would resist if he tried to approach her. ''I can't make up for what was done. I didn't want you, Deborah. I didn't want anyone who could make me vulnerable enough to make a mistake.'' He thought of his gift. His curse. ''I don't even have the right to ask you to take me as I am.''

''With this?'' She pulled the mask from the pocket of her robe. ''No, you don't have the right to ask me to accept this. But that's just what you're doing. You're asking me to love you. And you're asking me to close my eyes to what you're doing. I dedicated my life to the law. Am I supposed to say nothing while you ignore it?''

His eyes darkened. ''I nearly lost my life to the law. My partner died for it. I've never ignored it.''

''Gage, this can't be personal.''

''The hell it can't. It's all personal. Whatever you read in your law books, whatever precedents or procedures you find, it all comes down to people. You know that. You feel that. I've seen you work.''

''Within the law,'' she insisted. ''Gage, you must see what you're doing is wrong, not even to mention dangerous. You have to stop.''

His eyes were very dark, very clear. ''Not even for you.''

''And if I go to Mitchell, to the police commissioner, to Fields?''

''Then I'll do whatever I have to do. But I won't stop.''

''Why?'' She crossed to him, the mask fisted in her hand. ''Damn it, why?''

''Because I don't have a choice.'' He rose, his hands gripping her shoulders hard before he let go and turned away. ''There's nothing I can do to change it. Nothing I would do.''

''I know about Montega.'' When he turned back, she saw the pain. ''I'm sorry, Gage, so sorry for what happened to you. For what happened to your partner. We'll bring Montega in, I swear it. But revenge isn't the answer for you. It can't be.''

''What happened to me four years ago changed my life. That's not trite. That's reality.'' He laid his hand against the wall, stared at it, then pulled it back to stick it into his pocket. ''You read the reports of what happened the night Jack was killed?''

''Yes, I read them.''

''All the facts,'' he murmured. ''But not all the truth. Was it in the report that I loved him? That he had a pretty wife and a little boy who liked to ride a red tricycle?''

''Oh, Gage.'' She couldn't prevent her eyes from filling, or her arms from reaching out. But he shook his head and moved away.

''Was it in the report that we had given nearly two years of our lives to break that case? Two years of dealing with the kind of slime who have big yachts, big houses, fat portfolios all from the money they earn selling drugs to smaller dealers, who pay the rent by putting it out on the streets, and the playgrounds and the projects. Two years working our way in, our way up. Because we were cops and we believed we could make a difference.''

He put his hands on the back of the chair, fingers curling, uncurling. She could only stand and watch in silence as he remembered.

''Jack was going to take a vacation when it was over. Not to go anywhere, just to sit around the house, mow the grass, fix a leaky sink, spend time with Jenny and his kid. That's what he said. I was thinking about going to Aruba for a couple of weeks, but Jack, he didn't have big dreams. Just ordinary ones.''

He looked up, out the window, but he didn't see the sunlight or the traffic crowding the streets. Effortlessly he slid into the past. ''We got out of the car. We had a case full of marked bills, plenty of backup and a solid cover. What could go wrong? We were both ready, really ready. We were going to meet the man in charge. It was hot. You could smell the water, hear it lapping against the docks. I was sweating, not just because of the heat, but because it didn't feel right. But I didn't listen to my instincts. And then Montega…''

Gage could see him, standing in the shadows of the docks, gold glinting in his grin.

Stinking cops.

''He killed Jack before I could even reach for my weapon. And I froze. Just for an instant, just for a heartbeat, but I froze. And he had me.''

She thought of the scars on his chest and could hardly breathe. To have watched his partner murdered. To have had that moment, that instant of time to see his own death coming. The sharp, shuddering pain that ripped through her was all for him.

''Don't. What good does it do to go back and remember? You couldn't have saved Jack. No matter how quick you had been, no matter what you had done, you couldn't have saved him.''

He looked back at her. ''Not then. I died that night.''

The way he said it, so flat, so passionlessly, had her blood going cold. ''You're alive.''

''Death's almost a technical term these days. Technically, I died. And part of me slipped right out of my body.'' Her face grew only paler as he spoke, but she had to know. He had to tell her. ''I watched them working on me, there on the docks. And again in the operating room. I almost—almost floated free. And then...I was trapped.''

''I don't understand.''

''Back in my body, but not *back*.'' He lifted his hands, spread them. He'd never tried to explain it to anyone before, and wasn't certain he could. ''Sometimes I could hear—voices, the classical music the nurse left playing by the bed, crying. Or I'd smell flowers. I couldn't speak, I couldn't see. But more than that I couldn't feel anything.'' He let his hands drop again. ''I didn't want to. Then I came back—and I felt too much.''

It was impossible to imagine, but she felt the pain and the despair in her own heart. ''I won't say I understand what you went through. No one could. But it hurts me to think of it, of what you're still going through.''

He looked at her, watched a tear slide down her cheek. ''When I saw you that night, in the alley, my life changed again. I was just as helpless to stop it as I had been the first time.'' His gaze shifted down to the mask she held tight. ''Now, my life's in your hands.''

''I wish I knew what was right.''

He came to her again, lifting his hands to her face. ''Give me some time. A few more days.''

"You don't know what you're asking me."

"I do," he said, holding her still when she would have turned away. "But I don't have a choice. Deborah, if I don't finish what I've started I might as well have died four years ago."

Her mouth opened to argue, to protest, but she saw the truth of his words in his eyes. "Isn't there another way?"

"Not for me. A few more days," he repeated. "After that, if you feel you have to take what you know to your superiors, I'll accept it. And take the consequences."

She shut her eyes. She knew what he could not. That she would have given him anything. "Mitchell gave me two weeks," she said dully. "I can't promise you any longer."

He knew what it cost her and prayed he would find the time and the place to balance the scales. "I love you."

She opened her eyes, looked into his. "I know," she murmured, then laid her head against his chest. The mask dangled from her fingers. "I know you do."

She felt his arms around her, the solid reality of them. She lifted her head again to meet his lips with hers, to let the kiss linger, warm and promising, even while her conscience waged a silent battle.

What was going to happen to them? Afraid, she tightened her grip and held on. "Why can't it be simple?" she whispered. "Why can't it be ordinary?"

He couldn't count the times he had asked himself the same questions. "I'm sorry."

"No." Shaking her head, she drew away. "I'm sorry. It doesn't do any good to stand here whining about it." With a sniffle, she brushed away tears. "I may not know what's going to happen, but I know what has to be done.

I have to go to work. Maybe I can find a way out of this thing." She lifted a brow. "Why are you smiling?"

"Because you're perfect. Absolutely perfect." As he had the night before, he hooked a hand in the belt of her robe. "Come to bed with me. I'll show you what I mean."

"It's nearly noon," she said as he lowered his head to nibble at her ear. "I have work."

"Are you sure?"

Her eyes drifted closed. Her body swayed toward his. "Ah…yes." She pulled away, holding both palms out. "Yes, really. I don't have much time. Neither of us do."

"All right." He smiled again when her lips moved into a pout at his easy acquiescence. Perhaps, with luck, he could give her something ordinary. "On one condition."

"Which is?"

"I have a charity function tonight. A dinner, a couple of performers, dancing. At the Parkside."

"The Parkside." She thought of the old, exclusive and elegant hotel overlooking City Park. "Are you talking about the summer ball?"

"Yeah, that's it. I'd considered skipping it, but I've changed my mind. Will you go with me?"

She lifted a brow. "You're asking me at noon, if I'll go with you to the biggest, glitziest event in the city— which begins eight hours from now. And you're asking me when I've got to go to work, have absolutely no hope of getting an appointment at a hairdresser, no time to shop for the right dress."

"That about covers it," he said after a moment.

She blew out a breath. "What time are you going to pick me up?"

* * *

At seven, Deborah stepped under a steaming hot shower. She didn't believe it could possibly ease all the aches, and she was over her quota of aspirin for the day. Six hours in front of a computer terminal, a phone receiver at her ear, had brought her minimal results.

Each name she had checked had turned out to belong to someone long dead. Each address was a blind alley, and each corporation she investigated led only to a maze of others.

The common thread, as Gage had termed it, seemed to be frustration.

More than ever she needed to find the truth. It wasn't only a matter of justice now. It was personal. Though she knew that warped her objectivity, it couldn't be helped. Until this was resolved, she couldn't begin to know where her future, and Gage's, lay.

Perhaps nowhere, she thought as she bundled into a towel. They had come together like lightning and thunder. But storms passed. She knew that an enduring relationship required more than passion. Her parents had had passion—and no understanding. It required even more than love. Her parents had loved, but they had been unhappy.

Trust. Without trust, love and passion faded, paled and vanished.

She wanted to trust him. And to believe in him. Yet he didn't trust her. There were things he knew that could bring her closer to the truth in the case they were both so involved in. Instead, he kept them to himself, determined that his way and only his way was the right one.

With a sigh, she began to dry her hair. Wasn't she just as determined that her way, only her way, was the right one?

If they were so opposed on this one fundamental belief, how could love be enough?

But she had agreed to see him that night. Not because she wanted to go to a fancy ball, she thought. If he had asked her for hot dogs and bowling, she would have gone. Because she couldn't stay away. If she was honest, she would admit she didn't want to stay away.

She would give herself tonight, Deborah thought, carefully applying blusher. But like Cinderella, when the ball was over, she would have to face reality.

Moving briskly, she walked into the bedroom. Spread over the bed was the dress she had bought less than an hour before. Fate, she mused, running a hand over its shimmering sequins. He'd said he liked her in blue. When she'd rushed into the dress shop, frantic, it had been there, waiting. A liquid column of rich, royal blue, studded with silvery sequins. And it fit like a glove from its high-banded collar to its ankle-skimming hem.

Deborah had winced at the price tag, then had gritted her teeth. She'd thrown caution and a month's pay to the winds.

Now, looking in the mirror, she couldn't regret it. The rhinestone swirls at her ears were the perfect match. With her hair swept up and back, her shoulders were bare. She shifted. So was most of her back.

She was just slipping on her shoes when Gage knocked.

His smile faded when she opened the door. Her own lips curved at the sudden and intense desire she saw in his eyes. Very slowly she turned a full circle.

"What do you think?"

He discovered, if he did so very slowly, he could breathe. "I'm glad I didn't give you more time to prepare."

"Why?"

"I couldn't have handled it if you were any more beautiful."

She tilted her chin. "Show me."

He was almost afraid to touch her. Very gently he laid his hands on her shoulders, lowered his mouth to hers. But the taste of her punched into his system, making his fingers tighten, his mouth greedy. With a murmur, he shifted, reaching out to shut the door.

"Oh, no." She was breathless, and unsteady enough to have to lean back against the door. But she was also determined. "For what I paid for this dress, I want to take it out in public."

"Always practical." He gave her one last, lingering kiss. "We could be late."

She smiled at him. "We'll leave early."

When they arrived, the ballroom was already crowded with the glamorous, the influential, the wealthy. Over champagne and appetizers, Deborah scanned the tables and the table-hoppers.

She saw the governor glad-handing a well-known actress, a publishing tycoon cheek-bussing an opera star, the mayor exchanging grins and guffaws with a best-selling author.

"Your usual crowd?" Deborah murmured, smiling at Gage.

"A few acquaintances." He touched his glass to hers.

"Mmm. That's Tarrington, isn't it?" She nodded her head toward a young, earnest-looking man. "What do you think his chances are in the debates?"

"He has a lot to say," Gage commented. "Sometimes a bit tactlessly, but he has a point. Still, he'll have a hard time swaying the over-forty vote."

"Gage." Arlo Stuart stopped at their table, patting his hand on Gage's shoulder. "Good to see you."

"Glad you could make it."

"Wouldn't have missed it." A tall, tanned man with a wavy mane of snowy hair and clear green eyes, he gestured with his glass of Scotch. "You've done nice things in here. I haven't been in since you finished the renovations."

"We like it."

It took Deborah only a minute to realize they were talking about the hotel. And that the hotel belonged to Gage. She glanced up at the opulent crystal chandeliers. She should have known.

"I like knowing my competition has class." His gaze flicked to Deborah. "Speaking of class. Your face is very familiar. And I'm too old for you to consider that a line."

"Arlo Stuart, Deborah O'Roarke."

He took Deborah's hand, holding it in a hearty squeeze. "O'Roarke—O'Roarke." His eyes were both friendly and crafty. "You're the hot lawyer, aren't you? The D.A. who knocked that little creep Slagerman down a peg. The newspaper pictures aren't even close."

"Mr. Stuart."

"The mayor has good things to say about you. Very good things. We'll have to have a dance later so you can tell me all you know about our friend, Nemesis."

Her hand jerked in his, but she managed to keep her eyes level. "It would be a short conversation."

"Not according to our favorite journalist. Of course Wisner's an ass." He had yet to release her hand. "Where did you meet our up-and-coming D.A., Gage? I must be frequenting the wrong places."

"At your hotel," he said easily. "The mayor's fund-raiser."

Stuart gave a hearty laugh. "Well, that will teach me to run around drumming up votes for Fields, won't it? Don't forget that dance."

"I won't," she said, grateful to have her hand, sore fingers and all, back in her lap.

When he walked away, Deborah wiggled her fingers. "Is he always so…exuberant?"

"Yes." Gage picked up her hand and kissed it. "Anything broken?"

"I don't think so." Content to have her hand in his, she glanced around the room. Lush palms, a musical fountain, mirrored ceilings. "This is your hotel?"

"Yeah. Do you like it?"

"It's okay." She gave a little shrug when he grinned. "Shouldn't you be socializing?"

"I am." He touched his lips to hers.

"If you keep looking at me like that—"

"Go on. Please."

She let out one long, unsteady breath. "I think I'll take a trip to the powder room."

Halfway across the ballroom, she was waylaid by the mayor. "I'd like a moment, Deborah."

"Of course."

With an arm around her waist, flashing a broad political smile, he steered her expertly through the crowd and through the high ballroom doors.

"I thought we could use a little privacy."

Glancing back, she noted that Jerry was moving their way. At a signal from the mayor, he stopped, sent Deborah an apologetic look and merged back with the crowd.

"It's quite an elaborate event," Deborah began,

schooled enough to know the mayor preferred to launch
a topic himself.

"I was surprised to see you here." He nudged her
away from the doors toward an alcove that held potted
plants and pay phones. "Then again, perhaps I shouldn't
have been, since your and Guthrie's names have been
linked so often lately."

"I'm seeing Gage," she said coolly. "If that's what
you mean. On a personal level." She was already weary
of playing politics. "Is that what you wanted to talk to
me about, Mayor? My social life?"

"Only as it affects your professional one. I was disturbed and disappointed to learn that against my wishes
you're remaining on this investigation."

"Your wishes?" she countered. "Or Mr. Guthrie's?"

"I respected and agreed with his viewpoint." There
was a flash of anger in his eyes he rarely showed outside
of the privacy of his own offices. "Frankly, I'm displeased with your performance on this matter. Your excellent record in the courtroom does not override your
reckless mistakes outside of it."

"Reckless? Believe me, Mayor Fields, I haven't begun to be reckless. I'm following my superior's orders
in pursuing this matter. I began it, and I intend to finish
it. Since we're supposed to be on the same side, I'd think
you'd be pleased with the dedication of the D.A.'s office
in this case, not only with our persistence in tracking
down and prosecuting the men trafficking drugs, but in
finding Montega, a known cop killer, and bringing him
to justice."

"Don't tell me whose side I'm on." Clearly on the
edge of losing control, he wagged a finger in her face.
"I've worked for this city since before you could tie
your own shoes. You don't want to make an enemy of

me, young lady. I run Urbana, and I intend to keep right on running it. Young, overeager prosecutors are a dime a dozen.''

"Are you threatening to have me fired?"

"I'm warning you." With an obvious effort of will, he brought himself under control. "You either work with the system, or you work against it."

"I know that." Her fingers tightened on her evening bag.

"I admire you, Deborah," he said more calmly. "But while you have enthusiasm, you lack experience, and a case like this requires more experienced hands and minds."

She stood her ground. "Mitchell gave me two weeks."

"I'm aware of that. Make sure you play by the book for the time you have left." Though his eyes were still hot, he laid an avuncular hand on her arm. "Enjoy yourself this evening. The menu's excellent."

When he left her, she stood there for a moment, quietly shaking with rage. Grappling for control, she strode toward the ladies' room. Inside, she stormed through two arching ficus trees and into the adjoining room with its rose-colored chairs and mint-green counters. Still seething, she tossed her bag onto the counter and plopped down into a chair in front of one of the oval lighted mirrors.

So the mayor was displeased, she thought. He was disappointed. He was disturbed. She grabbed a lipstick out of her purse and concentrated on painting her lips. What he was, she thought, was spitting mad because she had bucked him.

Did he think there was only one way to do things, only one route to take? What the hell was wrong with taking a few detours, as long as they led to the same destination? Especially if they got you there quicker.

She tossed the lipstick back into her purse and reached for her compact. In the glass, she met her own eyes.

What was she thinking? Only twenty-four hours before, she had been sure there was only one way, only one route. And though she wouldn't have appreciated the mayor's tactics, she would have applauded his sentiments.

And now? She dropped her chin on her hand. And now she just wasn't sure. Wasn't she, even at this moment, veering outside of the system that she believed in? Wasn't she allowing her feelings, her personal feelings for Gage, to interfere with her professional ethics?

Or did it all come down to a matter of right and wrong, with her not knowing which was which? How could she continue, how could she function as a lawyer, if she couldn't see clearly what was right?

Maybe it was time to examine the facts, along with her own conscience, and ask herself if it wouldn't be better for everyone if she did withdraw.

As she sat studying her own face and her own values, the lights went out.

Chapter 9

Deborah clutched her evening bag and set one hand on the counter to orient herself. Big, fancy hotel like this, she thought, and it blows a fuse. Though she tried to see the humor of it as she stood, her heart was pounding. She swore when her hip bumped the chair as she groped through the dark.

Though it was foolish, she was afraid, and felt both trapped and smothered by the dark.

The door creaked open. There was a shaft of light, then blackness.

"Hey, pretty lady."

She froze, holding her breath.

"I got a message for you." The voice was high and piping with a giggle at the end of each sentence. "Don't worry. I'm not going to hurt you. Montega wants you all for himself, and he'd get real mad if I messed you up any first."

Her skin iced over. He couldn't see her, Deborah reminded herself as she fought the paralyzing fear. That evened the odds. "Who are you?"

"Me?" Another giggle. "You've been looking for me, but I'm hard to find. That's why they call me Mouse. I can get in and out of anyplace."

He was moving toward her soundlessly. Deborah could only guess at the direction of his voice. "You must be very clever." After she spoke, she too moved, shifting a careful foot to the left.

"I'm good. I'm the best. Ain't nobody better than old Mouse. Montega wanted me to tell you he's real sorry you didn't get to talk more before. He wants you to know he's keeping an eye on you. All the time. And on your family."

For an instant her blood stopped flowing. Her thoughts of outmaneuvering him, of slipping past him to the door vanished. "My family?"

"He knows people in Denver, too. Real slick people." He was closer now, so close she could smell him. But she didn't move away. "If you cooperate, he'll make sure your sister and the rest stay safe and snug in their beds tonight. Get the picture?"

She reached into her bag, felt the cool metal in her hand. "Yes, I get the picture." Pulling it out, she aimed in the direction of his voice and fired.

Screaming, he crashed into the chairs. Deborah sprinted around him, ramming her shoulder against one wall, then another until she located the door. Mouse was weeping and cursing as she tugged and found the door jammed.

"Oh, God. Oh, God." Panicked, she continued to pull.

"Deborah!" She heard her name shouted. "Get away from the door. Step back from the door."

She took one stumbling step backward and heard the heavy thud. Another, and the door crashed open. She ran into the light and Gage's arms.

"You're all right?" His hands were running over her, checking for hurts.

"Yes. Yes." She buried her face in his shoulder, ignoring the gathering crowd. "He's inside." When he started to push away, Deborah held on tighter. "No, please."

His face grim, Gage nodded to a pair of security guards. "Come and sit down."

"No, I'm okay." Though her breath was still shuddering, she drew away to look at his face. She saw murder there and tightened her hold on him. "Really. He didn't even touch me. He was trying to frighten me, Gage. He didn't hurt me."

His voice was low as he studied her pale face. "Is that supposed to make me want to kill him less?"

With a burly guard on each arm, the weeping Mouse stumbled out, his hands covering his face. Deborah noted he was wearing a waiter's uniform.

Alarmed by the look in Gage's eyes, she pulled his attention back to her. "He's in a lot worse shape than I am. I used this." With an unsteady hand, Deborah held up a can of Mace. "I've been carrying it with me since that night in the alley."

Gage wasn't sure if he should laugh or swear. Instead, he pulled her against him and kissed her. "It looks as though I can't let you out of my sight."

"Deborah." Jerry elbowed through the onlookers. "Are you all right?"

"I am now. The police?"

"I called them myself." Jerry glanced up at Gage. "You should get her out of here."

"I'm fine," Deborah insisted, glad the full-length dress concealed her knocking knees. "I'll have to go down to the police station and make a statement. But I need to make a phone call first."

"I'll call whomever you like." Jerry gave her hand a quick squeeze.

"Thanks, but I need to do this." Behind him, she spotted the mayor. "You could do me a favor and hold Fields off my back for a while."

"Done." He looked at Gage again. "Take care of her."

"I intend to." Keeping Deborah tight at his side, Gage led her away from the crowd. He moved quickly across the lobby and toward a bank of elevators.

"Where are we going?"

"I keep an office here, you can make the call from there." Inside the elevator, he turned her to him again and held tight. "What happened?"

"Well, I didn't get to powder my nose." She turned her face into his collar, breathing deeply. "First, Fields waylaid me and read me the riot act. He's not pleased with my performance." When the elevator doors opened, she loosened her hold so they could walk into the hallway. "When we parted ways, I was seeing red. I sat down in the powder room to repair my makeup and my composure." She was calming, and grateful the shaking had stopped. "Very elegant, by the way."

He shot her a look as he slid a key into a lock. "I'm glad you approve."

"I liked it a lot." She stepped into the parlor of a suite and crossed the thick oatmeal-colored carpet. "Until the lights went out. I was just orienting myself when the door opened, and he came in. The elusive Mouse," she said as her stomach began to churn again. "He had a message for me from Montega."

The name, just the name, had Gage's muscles tensing. "Sit down. I'll get you a brandy."

"The phone?"

"Right there. Go ahead."

Gage was fighting his own demons as he moved to the bar for the decanter and two snifters. She'd been alone, and however resourceful she was, she'd been vulnerable. When he'd heard the screaming… His fingers went white on the decanter. If it had been Montega instead of his messenger boy, she could have been dead. And he would have been too late.

Nothing that had happened to him before, nothing that could happen to him in the future would be more devastating than losing her.

She was sitting now, very straight, very tense, her face too pale, her eyes too dark. In one hand she held the receiver while the other vised around the cord. She was talking fast, to her brother-in-law, Gage realized after a moment.

They had threatened her family. He could see the possibility they would be harmed was more terrifying to her than any attempt on her own life.

"I need you to call me every day," she insisted. "You'll make sure Cilla has guards at the radio station. The children…" She covered her face with her hand. "God, Boyd." She listened a moment, nodding, trying to smile. "Yes, I know, I know. You didn't make captain for nothing. I'll be fine. Yes, and careful. I love you. All of you." She paused again, inhaling deeply. "Yes, I know. Bye."

She replaced the receiver. Saying nothing, Gage pushed the snifter into her hands. She cupped it a moment, staring down at the amber liquid. On another deep breath, she tipped the glass to her lips and drank deeply. She shuddered, drank again.

"Thanks."

"Your brother-in-law's a good cop. He won't let anything happen to them."

"He saved Cilla's life years ago. That's when they fell in love." Abruptly she looked up, her eyes wet and eloquent. "I hate this, Gage. They're my family, all I have left of family. The idea that something I've done, something I'm doing could—" She broke off, pulling herself back from the unthinkable. "When I lost my parents, I didn't think anything would ever be as bad. But this…" With a shake of her head, she looked down at the brandy again. "My mother was a cop."

He knew. He knew it all, but he only covered her hand with his and let her talk.

"She was a good one, or so I was told. I was only eight when it happened. I didn't know her very well, not really. She wasn't cut out to be a mother."

She shrugged it off, but even in that casual, dismissive gesture, he saw the scars.

"And my father," she continued. "He was a lawyer. A public defender. He tried hard to keep it all together, the family—the illusion of family. But he and my mother just couldn't pull it off." She sipped the brandy again, grateful for its numbing smoothness. "Two uniforms came to school that day, picked me up, took me back to the house. I guess I knew. I knew my mother was dead. They told me, as gently as possible, that it was both of them. Both of them. Some creep my father was defending managed to smuggle in a gun. When they were in the conference room, he cut loose."

"I'm sorry, Deborah. I know how hard it is to lose family."

She nodded, setting the empty snifter aside. "I guess that's why I was determined to be a lawyer, a prosecutor. Both of my parents dedicated their lives, and lost them defending the law. I didn't want it to have been for nothing. Do you understand?"

"Yes." He brought her hands to his lips. "For whatever reason you chose to be a lawyer, it was the right decision. You're a good one."

"Thanks."

"Deborah." He hesitated, wanting to phrase his thoughts carefully. "I respect both your integrity and your abilities."

"I feel a *but* coming on."

"I want to ask you again to back off from this. To leave the rest to me. You'll have your chance to do what you do best, and that's prosecute Montega and the rest of them."

She gave herself a moment, wanting, as he had, to make her thoughts clear. "Gage, tonight, after the mayor came down on me, I sat in the powder room. Once I got over being mad, I started to think, to examine my position, and my motives. I began to think maybe the mayor was right, maybe it would be better if I turned this over to someone with more experience and less personal involvement." Then she shook her head. "And I can't, especially now. They threatened my family. If I stepped back, I'd never be able to trust myself again, to believe in myself. I have to finish this." Before he could speak, she put her hands on his shoulders. "I don't agree with you. I don't know if I ever can, but I understand, in my heart, what you're doing and why you have to do it. That's all I'm asking from you."

How could he refuse? "Then I guess we have a stale-mate, for now."

"I have to go down and make my statement." She rose, held out a hand. "Will you come with me?"

They wouldn't let her talk to Mouse. Deborah figured she could work around that eventually. By Monday, she would have the police reports if nothing else. With Mouse under tight security, it was unlikely the same kind of accident could befall him as it had Parino.

For the answers she needed, she would bargain with Mouse, just as she would have bargained with the devil.

She gave her statement, wearily waited while it was typed for her signature. On Saturday night, the station was hopping. Hookers and pimps, dealers and mugging victims, gang members and harried public defenders. It was reality, an aspect of the system she represented and believed in. But it was with relief that she stepped outside.

"Long night," she murmured.

"You handled yourself very well." He laid a hand on her cheek. "You must be exhausted."

"Actually, I'm starving." Her lips curved. "We never did have dinner."

"I'll buy you a hamburger."

With a laugh, she threw her arms around him. Perhaps some things, some very precious things, could be simple. "My hero."

He pressed his lips to the side of her throat. "I'll buy you a dozen hamburgers," he murmured. "Then for God's sake, Deborah, come home with me."

"Yes." She turned her lips to his. "Yes."

He knew how to set the stage. Perfectly. When Deborah walked into the bedroom beside him, there was moonlight drifting through the windows, stardust filtering through the skylight, candle glow warming the shadows. Roses—the scent of them sweetened the air. The sound of a hundred violins romanced it.

She didn't know how he'd managed it all with the single phone call he'd made from the noisy little diner where they had eaten. She didn't care. It was enough to know he would have thought of it.

"It's lovely." She was nervous, she realized, ridiculously so after the passion of the previous night. But her legs were unsteady as she crossed to where a bottle of champagne sat nestled in a crystal bowl of ice. "You thought of everything."

"Only of you." His lips brushed her shoulder before he poured the wine. "I've pictured you here a hundred times. A thousand." He offered her a glass.

"So have I." Her hand trembled as she lifted her glass. Desire, fighting to break free. "The first time you kissed me, up in the tower, whole worlds opened up. It's never been like that for me before."

"I nearly begged you to stay that night, even though you were angry." He slipped off one of her earrings, then let his fingers rub over the sensitive lobe. "I wonder if you would have."

"I don't know. I would have wanted to."

"That's almost enough." He drew off her other earring, set them both on the table. Slowly he slid out one of her hairpins, then another, watching her. Always watching her. "You're shivering."

His hands were so gentle, his eyes so urgent. "I know."

He took the glass from her limp fingers and set it aside. With his eyes on hers, he continued to free her hair. The whisper of his fingertips on the nape of her neck. "You're not afraid of me?"

"Of what you can do to me."

Something flared in his eyes, dark and dangerous. But he lowered his head to gently kiss her temple.

Heavy eyed and sultry, she looked up at him. "Kiss me, Gage."

"I will." His mouth trailed over her face, teasing, never satisfying her. "I am."

Her breath was already coming fast. "You don't have to seduce me."

He ran a finger up and down her bare spine, smiling when she shuddered. "It's my pleasure." And he wanted it to be hers.

The night before, all the passion, all the fierce and angry needs had clawed their way out of him. Tonight he wanted to show her the softer side of love. When she swayed against him, he withstood the swift arrows of desire.

"We made love in the dark," he murmured as his fingers flicked open the trio of buttons at the back of her neck. "Tonight I want to see you."

The dress shimmered down her, a glittery blue pool at her feet. She wore only a lacy woman's fancy that lifted her breasts and skimmed transparent to her hips. Her beauty struck him breathless.

"Every time I look at you, I fall in love again."

"Then don't stop looking." She reached up to undo the formal tie. Her fingers slid down to unfasten the unfamiliar studs. "Don't ever stop." She parted his shirt with her hands, then pressed her mouth to the heated skin beneath. The tip of her tongue left a moist trail before she lifted her head, let it fall back in invitation. Her eyes were a rich blue gleam beneath her lashes. "Kiss me now."

As seduced as she, he branded her lips with his. Twin moans, low and throaty, shuddered through the room. Her hands slid slowly up his chest to his shoulders to push the dinner jacket aside. Her fingers tightened, then went bonelessly lax as he softened the kiss, deepened it, gentled it.

He lifted her into his arms as though she were fragile crystal rather than flesh and blood. With his eyes on hers, he held her there a moment, letting his mouth tease and torment hers. He continued those feather-light kisses as he carried her to the bed.

He sat, holding her cradled in his lap. His mouth continued its quiet devastation of her reason. He could almost see her float. Her eyes drifted shut. Her limbs were fluid. In arousing contrast, her heart pounded under his hand. He wanted her like this. Totally pleasured. Totally his. As he drew more and more of that warm exotic flavor from her mouth, he thought he could stay just so for hours. For days.

She felt each impossible tender touch, the stroke of a fingertip, the brush of his palm, the oh-so-patient quest of his lips. Her body seemed as light as the rose-scented air, yet her arms were too heavy to lift. The music and his murmurs merged in her mind into one seducing song. Beneath it was the violent roar of her own speeding pulse.

She knew she had never been more vulnerable or more willing to go wherever he chose to take her.

And this was love—a need more basic than hunger, than thirst.

One quiet, helpless gasp escaped her when his lips

whispered over the tops of her breasts. Slowly, erotically, his tongue slid under the lace to tease her hardened
nipples. His fingers played over the skin above her stockings, lightly, so lightly, gliding beneath the sheer triangle
of material.

With one touch, he sent her over the first towering
peak. She arched like a bow, and the pleasure arrowed
out of her into him. Then she seemed to melt in his arms.

Breathless, almost delirious, she reached for him.
"Gage, let me…"

"I will." He covered her next stunned cry with his
mouth. And while she was still shuddering, he laid her
on the bed.

Now, he thought. He could take her now, while she
lay hot and damp in surrender. There was moonlight on
her skin, on her hair. The white lace she wore was like
an illusion. When she looked at him from beneath those
heavy lashes, he saw the dark flicker of desire.

He had more to show her.

His knuckles brushed her skin, making her jolt as he
unhooked her stocking. Almost lazily, he slid it down
her leg, following the route with soft, openmouthed
kisses. His tongue glided over the back of her knee,
down her calf until she was writhing in mindless pleasures.

Trapped in gauzy layers of sensation, she reached for
him again, only to have him evade and repeat each devastating delight on her other leg. His mouth journeyed
up, lingering, pausing, until it found her. His name burst
from her lips as she reared up. Nearly weeping, she
grasped him against her.

And at the first touch, the strength seemed to pour
into her.

Furnace hot, her flesh met his. But it wasn't enough.

Urgent, her fingers pulled at his open shirt, tearing seams in her desperation to find more of him. As she ripped the silk away, her teeth nipped into his shoulder. She felt his stomach muscles quiver, heard the quick intake of his breath as she pulled at the waistband of his trousers. Buttons popped off.

"I want you." Her mouth fixed ravenously to his. "Oh, Lord, I want you."

The control he had held so tightly slipped through his tensed fingers. Desire overpowered him. She overpowered him with her desperate hands, her greedy mouth. The breath was clogging in his lungs, burning as he struggled out of his clothes.

Then they were kneeling in the middle of the ravaged bed, bodies trembling, eyes locked. He hooked a hand in the bodice of the lace and rent it ruthlessly down the center. With his fingers digging into her hips, he pulled her against him.

During the rough, reckless ride, she arched back. Her hands slid down his slick shoulders, then found purchase. She sobbed out his name as she tumbled off the razor's edge of sanity. He gripped her hair in his hand and drove her up again. Again. Then he closed his mouth over hers and followed.

Weak, she lay on the bed, one arm tossed across her eyes, the other hanging limply off the mattress. She knew she couldn't move, wasn't sure she could speak, doubted that she was even breathing.

Yet when he pressed a kiss to her shoulder, she shuddered again.

"I meant to be gentle with you."

She managed to open her eyes. His face was close.

She felt his fingers move in her hair. "Then I guess you'll just have to try again until you get it right."

A smile curved his mouth. "I have a feeling that's going to take a long time."

"Good." She traced his smile with a fingertip. "I love you, Gage. That's the only thing that seems to matter tonight."

"It's the only thing that matters." He put a hand over hers. There was a bond in the touch, every bit as deep and as intimate as their lovemaking. "I'll get you some wine."

With a contented sigh, she settled back as he got up. "I never thought it could be like this. I never thought I could be like this."

"Like what?"

She caught a glimpse of herself in the wide mirror across the room—sprawled naked over pillows and rumpled sheets. "So wanton, I guess." She laughed at her choice of words. "In college I had a reputation for being very cool, very studious and very unapproachable."

"School's out." He sat on the bed, handed her a glass then tapped his against it.

"I guess. But even after, when I started in the D.A.'s office, the reputation remained." She wrinkled her nose. "Earnest O'Roarke."

"I like it when you're earnest." He sipped. "I can see you in a law library, poring over thick, dusty books, scribbling notes."

She made a face. "That's not exactly the image I prefer at the moment."

"I like it." He lowered his head to capture her chin gently between his teeth. "You'd be wearing one of those conservatively tailored suits, in those very unconservative colors you like." She frowned a bit, making him chuckle. "Sensible shoes and very discreet jewelry."

"You make me sound like a prude."

"And under it all would be something thin and sexy." He hooked a finger in a torn swatch of lace and lifted it to the light. "A very personal choice for a very proper attorney. Then you'd start quoting precedents and making me crazy."

"Like *Warner v. Kowaski?*"

"Mmm." He switched to her ear. "Just like. And I'd be the only one who knew that it takes six pins to hold your hair back in that very proper twist."

"I know I can be too serious," she murmured. "It's only because what I do is so important to me." She looked down at her wine. "I have to know what I'm doing is right. That the system I represent works." When he drew away to study her, she sighed. "I know part of it's ego and ambition, but another part of it is so basic, Gage, so ingrained. That's why I worry how you and I are going to resolve this."

"We won't resolve it tonight."

"I know, but—"

"Not tonight," he said, laying a finger over her lips. "Tonight it's just you and me. I need that, Deborah. And so do you."

She nodded. "You're right. I'm being too earnest again."

"We can fix that." He grinned and held up his glass to the light. The champagne bubbled.

"By getting drunk?" she said, brow lifted.

"More or less." When his eyes met hers, there was

a smile in them. ''Why don't I show you a…less serious way to drink champagne?'' He tilted his glass and had a trickle of cool wine sliding over her breast.

Chapter 10

Gage lost track of time as he watched her sleep. The candles had gutted out in their own hot, fragrant wax so that their scent drifted, quiet as a memory. She had a hand in his, holding lightly even in sleep.

The shadows lifted, fading in the pearl gray of dawn. He watched the growing light fall over her hair, her face, her shoulders. Just as softly, he followed its path with his lips. But he didn't want to wake her.

There was too much to be done, too much he still refused to make her a part of. He knew that over a matter of weeks, the goals he carried inside him for more than four years had become mixed. It was not enough now to avenge his partner's death. It was not enough now to seek and find payment for the time and the life that had been stolen from him. Even justice, that driving force, was not enough.

He would have to move quickly now, for each day that passed without answers was another day Deborah was in jeopardy. There was nothing more important than keeping her safe.

He slid away from her, moving soundlessly from the bed to dress. There was time to make up, all the hours he had spent with her rather than on the streets or at his work. He glanced back when she shifted and snuggled deeper into the pillow. She would sleep through the morning. And he would work.

He pushed a button beneath the carved wood on the wall farthest from the bed. A panel slid open. Gage stepped into the dark and let it close again at his back.

With the husky morning greeting still on her tongue, Deborah blinked sleepily. Had she been dreaming? she wondered. She would have sworn Gage had stepped into some kind of secret passageway. Baffled, she pushed up on her elbows. In sleep she had reached for him and, finding him gone, had awakened just at the moment when the wall had opened.

Not a dream, she assured herself. For he wasn't beside her, and the sheets where he had lain were already cooling.

More secrets, she thought and felt the sorrow of his distrust envelop her. After the nights they had spent together, the love he had shown her, he still wouldn't give her his trust.

So she would take it, Deborah told herself as she pushed herself out of bed. She would not sit and sulk or wish and whine, but demand. Fumbling in his closet, she located a robe. Soft cotton in steel gray, it hit her mid-calf. Impatient, she bundled the sleeves up out of her way and began to search for the mechanism that opened the panel.

Even knowing the approximate location, it took her ten frustrating minutes to find it and another two to figure out how it worked. Her breath hissed out in satisfaction as the panel slid open. Without hesitation, she stepped into the dark, narrow corridor.

Keeping one hand on the wall for guidance, she started forward. There was no dank, disused smell as she might have expected. The air was clean, the wall smooth and dry. Even when the panel behind her closed her completely into the dark, she wasn't uneasy. There would be no scratching or skittering sounds here. It was obvious Gage used the passage, and whatever it led to, often.

She picked her way along, straining her eyes and ears. Corridors veered off, twisting like snakes from the main passage, but she followed instinct and kept to the same straight path. After a moment, she saw a dim glow up ahead and moved a bit more quickly. A set of stone stairs with pie-shaped treads curved into a tight semicircle as it plunged downward. With one hand tight on the thin iron rail, she wove her way to the bottom, where she was faced with three tunnels leading in different directions.

The lady or the tiger, she thought, then shook her head at her own fancy. "Damn you, Gage. Where did you go?" Her whisper echoed faint and hollow, then died.

Bracing her shoulders, she started through one archway, changed her mind and backtracked to the middle. Again she hesitated. Then she heard it, dim and dreamy down the last tunnel. Music.

She plunged into the dark again, following the sound, moving cautiously down the sloping stone floor. She had no idea how deep she was traveling underground, but the air was cooling rapidly. The music grew in volume as degree by faint degree the tunnel's light increased.

She heard a mechanical hum, and a clatter—like typewriter keys hitting a platen.

When she stepped into the mouth of the tunnel, she could only stand and stare.

It was an enormous room with curving stone walls. Cavernlike with its arching ceiling and echoes, it spread more than fifty feet in every direction. But it wasn't primitive, she thought as she gathered Gage's robe close around her throat. Rather than appearing gloomy, it was brilliantly lit, equipped with a vast computer system, printers and monitors blinking away. Television screens were bolted to one wall. An enormous topographic map of Urbana spread over another. Music, eerily romantic, poured out of speakers she couldn't see. Granite-gray counters held work stations, telephones, stacks of photographs and papers.

There was a control panel, studded with switches and buttons and levers. Gage sat in front of it, his fingers moving. Over the map, lights blinked on. He shifted, working the controls. On a computer screen, the map was reproduced.

He looked like a stranger, his face grimly set and intense. She wondered if his choice of a black sweater and jeans had been deliberate.

She stepped forward, down a trio of stone steps. "Well," she began as he turned quickly, "you didn't include this on my tour."

"Deborah." He stood, automatically turning off the monitor. "I'd hoped you'd sleep longer."

"I'm sure you did." She stuck her tensed hands into the deep pockets of his robe. "Apparently I've interrupted your work. An interesting…getaway," she decided. "Nemesis's style, I'd say. Dramatic, secretive." She moved past a bank of computers toward the map.

"And thorough," she murmured. "Very thorough." She whirled around. "One question. Just the one that seems to matter the most at the moment. Who am I sleeping with?"

"I'm the same man you were with last night."

"Are you? Are you the same man who told me he loved me, who showed me he did in dozens of beautiful ways? Is that the same man who left me in bed to come down here? How long are you going to lie to me?"

"It isn't a matter of lying to you. This is something I have to do. I thought you understood that."

"Then you were wrong. I didn't understand that you would keep this from me. That you would work without me, holding information from me."

He seemed to change before her eyes, growing distant and cool and aloof. "You gave me two weeks."

"Damn you, I gave you more than that. I gave you everything." Her eyes were brilliant with emotion as hurt and anger battled for priority. But she flung up a hand before he could cross to her. "No, don't. You won't use my feelings this time."

"All right." Though his own were straining for release. "It isn't a matter of feelings, but logic. You should appreciate that, Deborah. This is my work. Your presence here is as unnecessary as mine would be in the courtroom with you."

"Logic?" She spat out the word. "It's only logical if it suits your purposes. Do you think I'm a fool? Do you think I can't see what's happening here?" She gestured sharply toward one of the monitors. "And we'll keep it strictly professional. You have all the information I've been painfully digging up. All the names, all the numbers, and more, much more than I've been able to uncover. Yet you haven't told me. And wouldn't have."

The cloak came around him again, impenetrable. "I work alone."

"Yes, I'm aware of that." The bitterness seeped into her voice as she walked toward him. "No partners. Except in bed. I'm good enough to be your partner there."

"One has nothing to do with the other."

"Everything," she all but shouted. "One has everything to do with the other. If you can't trust me, in every way, respect me, in every way and be honest with me, in every way, then there's nothing between us."

"Damn it, Deborah, you don't know everything." He gripped her arms. "You don't understand everything."

"No, I don't. Because you won't let me."

"Can't let you," he corrected, holding her still when she would have pulled away. "There's a difference between lying to you and holding back information. This isn't black-and-white."

"Yes, it is."

"These are vicious men. Without conscience, without morals. They've already tried to kill you, and you'd hardly broken the surface. I won't risk you. If you want black-and-white, there it is." He shook her, punctuating each word. "I will not risk you."

"You can't prevent me from doing my job, or what I feel is right."

"By God, if I have to lock you upstairs until I'm done with this to keep you safe, I will."

"And then what? Will the same thing happen the next time, and the next?"

"I'll do whatever it takes to protect you. That won't change."

"Maybe you've got a nice little plastic bubble you could stick me in." She put her hands on his forearms, willing him to understand. "If you love me, then you have to love the whole person I am. I demand that, just as I demand to know and love the whole person you are.'' She saw something flicker in his eyes and pushed her point. ''I can't become something different for you, someone who sits and waits to be taken care of.''

''I'm not asking you to.''

''Aren't you? If you can't accept me now, you never will. Gage, I want a life with you. Not just a few nights in bed, but a life. Children, a home, a history. But if you can't share with me what you know, and who you are, there can't be a future for us.'' She broke away from him. ''And if that's the case, it would be better for both of us if I left now.''

''Don't.'' He reached out for her before she could turn away. However deep his own need for survival ran, it was nothing compared to the possibility of life without her. ''I need your word.'' His fingers tightened on hers. ''That you won't take any chances, and that you'll move in here with me at least until it's over. Whatever we find here has to stay here. You can't risk taking it to the D.A. Not yet.''

''Gage, I'm obligated to—''

''No.'' He cut her off. ''Whatever we do, whatever we find stays here until we're ready to move. I can't give you more than that, Deborah. I'm only asking for a compromise.''

And it was costing him. She could see that. ''All right. I won't take anything to Mitchell until we're both sure. But I want it all, Gage. Everything.'' Her voice calmed, her hands gentled. ''Don't you see I know you're holding something back from me, something basic that has nothing to do with secret rooms or data? I know, and it hurts me.''

He turned away. If he was to give her everything, he

had no choice but to begin with himself. The silence stretched between them before he broke it. "There are things you don't know about me, Deborah. Things you may not like or be able to accept."

The tone of his voice had her mouth growing dry and her pulse beating irregularly. "Do you have such little faith in me?"

He was putting all his faith in her, he thought. "I've had no right to let things go as far as they have between us without letting you know what I am." He reached out to touch her cheek, hoping it wouldn't be the last time. "I didn't want to frighten you."

"You're frightening me now. Whatever you have to tell me, just tell me. We'll work it out."

Without speaking, he walked away from her, toward the stone wall. He turned and, with his eyes on her, vanished.

Deborah's mouth opened, but the only sound she could make was a strangled gasp. With her eyes riveted to where Gage should be—had to be, her confused brain insisted—she stumbled back. Her unsteady hand gripped the arm of a chair as she let her numbed body slide into it.

Even while her mind rejected what her eyes had seen, he returned—materializing ten feet from where he had disappeared. For an instant she could see through him, as if he were no more than the ghost of the man who stood in front of her.

Deborah started to rise, decided against it, then cleared her throat. "It's an odd time for magic tricks."

"It isn't a trick." Her eyes were still huge with shock as he walked toward her, wondering if she would stiffen or jerk away. "At least not the way you mean."

"All these gadgets you've got down here," she said,

clinging desperately to the lifeline of logic in a sea of confusion. "Whatever you're using, it produces quite an optical illusion." She swallowed. "I imagine the Pentagon would be very interested."

"It's not an illusion." He touched her arm, and though she didn't pull away as he'd feared she would, her skin was cold and clammy. "You're afraid of me now."

"That's absurd." But her voice was shaking. She forced herself to stand. "It was just a trick, an effective one, but—"

She broke off when he placed his hand, palm down on the counter beside them. It vanished to the wrist. Dark and dazed, her eyes lifted to his.

"Oh, God. It's not possible." Terrified, she pulled his arm and was almost faint with relief when she saw his hand, whole and warm.

"It's possible." He brought the hand gently to her face. "It's real."

She lifted her trembling fingers to his. "Give me a minute." Moving carefully, she turned and walked a few steps away. Rejection sliced through him, a dull, angry blade.

"I'm sorry." With great effort he controlled his voice, kept it even. "I didn't know of a better way, an easier way, to show you. If I had tried to explain, you wouldn't have believed me."

"No, no, I wouldn't have." She had seen it. Yet her mind still wanted to argue that she could not have seen it. A game, a trick, nothing more. Though there was a comfort in the denial, she remembered how time and again, Nemesis had seemed to vanish before her eyes.

She turned back and saw that he was watching her, his body tensed and ready. No game. When she accepted the truth her trembling only increased. Briskly, she rubbed her hands up and down her arms, hoping to warm and steady the muscles.

"How do you do this?"

"I'm not completely sure." He opened his hands, stared at them, then fisted them to push them impotently into his pockets. "Something happened to me when I was in the coma. Something changed me. A few weeks after I came back I discovered it, almost by accident. I had to learn to accept it, to use it, because I know it was given to me for a reason."

"And so—Nemesis."

"Yes, and so Nemesis." He seemed to steady himself. Deborah saw that his eyes were level and curiously blank when he looked at her. "I have no choice in this, Deborah. But you do."

"I don't think I understand." She lifted a hand to her head and gave a quick, shaky laugh. "I know I don't understand."

"I wasn't honest with you, about what I am. The man you fell in love with was normal."

Baffled, she let her hand fall to her side again. "I'm not following you. I fell in love with you."

"Damn it, I'm not normal." His eyes were suddenly furious. "I'll never be. I'll carry this thing with me until I die. I can't tell you how I know, I just do."

"Gage—" But when she reached out to him, he backed away.

"I don't want your pity."

"You don't have it," she snapped back. "Why should you? You're not ill. You're whole and you're healthy. If anything, I'm angry because you held *this* back from me, too. And I know why." She dragged both hands through her hair as she paced away from him. "You thought I'd walk, didn't you? You thought I was too weak, too stupid, or too fragile to handle it. You didn't trust me to love you." Her fury built so quickly, she was all but blind with it. "You didn't trust me to love you," she repeated. "Well, the hell with you. I do, and I always will."

She turned, sprinting for the stairs. He caught her at the base of them, turning her back to him and pulling her close while she cursed at him and struggled.

"Call me anything you like." He grabbed her shoulders and shook once. "Slap me again if you want. But don't leave."

"You expected me to, didn't you?" she demanded. She tossed her head back as she strained away from him. "You expected me to turn around and walk away."

"Yes."

She started to shout at him. Then she saw what was in his eyes, what he held back with such rigid control. It was fear. Accusations melted away. "You were wrong," she said quietly. With her eyes still on his, she lifted her hands to his face, rose on her toes and kissed him.

A shudder. From him, from her. Twin waves of relief. He drew her closer, crushing, consuming. As huge as his fear had been, a need sprang up to replace it. It was not pity he tasted on her lips, but passion.

Small, seductive sounds hummed in her throat as she struggled out of the robe. It was more than an offering of herself. It was a demand that he take her as she was, that he allow himself to be taken. With an oath that ended in a groan, he moved his hands over her. He was caught in the madness, a purifying madness.

Impatient, she tugged at his shirt. "Make love with

me.'' Her head fell back and her eyes were as challenging as her voice. ''Make love with me now.''

She pulled at his clothes even as they lowered to the floor.

Frenzied and frantic. Heated and hungry. They came together. Power leaped like wind-fed flames. It was always so between them, she thought as her body shuddered, shuddered, shuddered. Yet now there was more. Here was a unity. Here was compassion, trust, vulnerability to mix with hungers. She had never wanted him more.

Her hands clenched in his dark hair as she rose above him. She needed to see his face, his eyes. ''I love you.'' The breath tore in her throat. ''Let me show you how I love you.''

Agile, quick, greedy, she moved over him, taking her mouth down his throat, over his chest, down to where his taut stomach muscles quivered under her moist, seeking lips. The blood pounded in his head, his heart, his loins.

She was a miracle, the second he'd been given in a lifetime. When he reached for her, he reached for love and for salvation.

They rolled, a tangle of limbs and needs, unmindful of the hard, unyielding floor, the clatter and hum of machines blindly working. Breath came fast, heartbeats galloped. Each taste, each touch seemed more potent, more pungent than ever before.

His fingers dug into her hips when he lifted her. She sheathed him, surrounded him. The pleasure speared them both. Their hands slid toward each other's, palm against palm, then fingers locked tight.

They held on, eyes open, bodies joined, until they took the final leap together.

Boneless, she slid down to him. Her mouth brushed his once, then again, before she lay her head on his shoulder. Never had she felt more beautiful, more desirable, more complete, than in feeling his heart thunder wildly beneath hers.

Her lips curved as she turned and pressed them to his throat. "That was my way of saying you're stuck with me."

"I like the way you get your point across." Gently he ran a hand up and down her spine. She was his. He'd been a fool to ever doubt it, or her. "Does this mean I'm forgiven?"

"Not necessarily." Bracing her hands on his shoulders, she pushed herself up. "I don't understand who you are. Maybe I never will. But understand this. I want all, or I want nothing. I saw what evasions, denials, refusals did to my parents' marriage. I won't live with that."

He put a hand on hers, very lightly. "Is that a proposal?"

She didn't hesitate. "Yes."

"Do you want an answer now?"

Her eyes narrowed. "Yes. And don't think you can get out of it by disappearing. I'll just wait until you come back."

He laughed, amazed that she could joke about something he'd been so sure would repel her. "Then I guess you'll have to make an honest man out of me."

"I intend to." She kissed him briefly, then shifted away to bundle into the robe. "No long engagement."

"Okay."

"As soon as we put a cap on this thing and Cilla and Boyd can arrange to bring the kids out, we get married."

"Agreed." Humor danced in his eyes. "Anything else?"

"I want children right away."

He hitched on his jeans. "Any particular number?"

"One at a time."

"Sounds reasonable."

"And—"

"Shut up a minute." He took her hands. "Deborah, I want to be married to you, to spend the rest of my life knowing when I reach out, I'll find you there. And I want a family, our family." He pressed his lips to the fingers that curled over his. "I want forever with you." He watched her blink back tears and kissed her gently. "Right now I want something else."

"What?"

"Breakfast."

With a strangled laugh, she threw her arms around him. "Me, too."

They ate in the kitchen, laughing and cozy, as if they always shared the first meal of the day together. The sun was bright, the coffee strong. Deborah had dozens of questions to ask him, but she held them back. For this one hour, she wanted them to be two ordinary people in love.

Ordinary, she thought. Strange, but she felt they were and could be ordinary, even with the very extraordinary aspects of their lives. All they needed were moments like this, where they could sit in the sunshine and talk of inconsequential things.

When Frank walked in, he paused at the kitchen doorway and gave Deborah a polite nod. "Is there anything you need this morning, Mr. Guthrie?"

"She knows, Frank." Gage laid a hand over Deborah's. "She knows everything."

A grin split Frank's wide, sober face. "Well, it's about time." All pretense of formality dropped as he lumbered across the room to pluck up a piece of toast. He took a seat at the semicircular breakfast nook, bit into the toast and gestured with the half that was left. "I told him you wouldn't head for the hills when you found out about his little vanishing act. You're too tough for that."

"Thank you. I think." Deborah chuckled and the rest of the toast disappeared in one healthy bite.

"I know people," Frank said, taking the tray of bacon Gage passed him. "In my profession—my former profession—you had to be able to make somebody quick. And I was good, real good, right, Gage?"

"That's right, Frank."

"I could spot a patsy two blocks away." He wagged a piece of bacon at Deborah. "You ain't no patsy."

And she'd thought of him as the strong, silent type, Deborah mused. She was fascinated by the way he made up for lost time, rattling quickly as he steam-shoveled food away. "You've been with Gage a long time."

"Eight years—not counting the couple of times he sent me up."

"Kind of like Kato to his Green Hornet."

He grinned again, then let out a series of guffaws. "Hey, I like her, Gage. She's okay. I told you she was okay."

"Yes, you did. Deborah's going to be staying, Frank. How would you like to be best man?"

"No kidding?" Deborah didn't think Frank's grin could stretch any wider. Then she saw the gleam of tears in his eyes. At that moment, her heart was lost to him.

"No kidding." She shifted, took his big face in her

hands and kissed him firmly on the mouth. "There, you're first to kiss the bride-to-be."

"How about that." Deborah had to bite back a chuckle as a beet-red blush stained Frank's face. "How about that."

"I'd like Deborah to move in a few things today," Gage put in.

She glanced down at the robe. Besides the borrowed garment, she had an evening dress, a pair of stockings and an evening bag. "I could use a few things." But she was thinking of the big room downstairs, the computers, the information Gage had at his fingertips.

Gage had little trouble following the direction of her thoughts. "Do you have someone who could put what you need together? Frank could go by your apartment and pick them up."

"Yes." She thought of Mrs. Greenbaum. "I'll just make a call."

Within a half an hour, she was back in Gage's secret room, wearing a pair of his jeans hitched up with the belt of his robe and a crisply pressed linen shirt skimming her thighs. Hands on her hips, she studied the map as Gage explained.

"These are drop points, major drug deals. I've been able to run makes on a handful of the messengers."

"Why haven't you fed this information to the police?"

He glanced at her briefly. On this point they might never agree. "It wouldn't help them get any closer to the top men. Right now, I'm working on the pattern." He moved to one of the computers and, after a moment, signaled to her. "None of the drops are less than twenty blocks apart." He motioned to the reproduction on the monitor. "The time span between them is fairly steady."

He punched a few buttons. A list of dates rolled onto the screen. "Two weeks, sometimes three."

Frowning in concentration, she studied the screen. "Can I have a printout of this?"

"Why?"

"I'd like to run it through my computer at the office. See if I can find any correlation."

"It isn't safe." Before she could argue, he took her hand and led her to another work station. He tapped a code in the keyboard and brought up a file. Deborah's mouth opened in surprise as she saw her own work reproduced on the screen.

"You've tapped into my system," she murmured. "In more ways than one."

"The point is, if I can, so can someone else. Anything you need, you can find here."

"Apparently." She sat, far from sure how she felt about Gage or anyone else peeking over her shoulder as she worked. "Am I on the right track?"

Saying nothing, he tapped in a new code. "You've been going after the corporations, and the directors. A logical place to start. Whoever set up the organization knows business. Four years ago, we didn't have the information or the technology to get this close, so we had to go in and physically infiltrate." Names flipped by, some she recognized, some she didn't. They were all tagged Deceased. "It didn't work because there was a leak. Someone who knew about the undercover operation passed the information to the other side. Montega was waiting for us, and he knew we were cops." Though Deborah felt a chill, he said it calmly. "He also had to know exactly how we were set up that night, to the man. Otherwise he could never have slipped through the backup."

"Another cop?"

"It's a possibility. We had ten handpicked men on the team that night. I've checked out every one of them, their bank accounts, their records, their life-style. So far, I haven't found a thing."

"Who else knew?"

"My captain, the commissioner, the mayor." He made a restless movement with his shoulders. "Maybe more. We were only cops. They didn't tell us everything."

"When you find the pattern, what then?"

"I wait, I watch, and I follow. The man with the money leads me to the man in charge. And he's the one I want."

She suppressed a shudder, promising herself she would somehow convince him to let the police take over when they had enough information. "While you're looking for that, I'd like to concentrate on finding names— that common thread."

"All right." He ran a hand over her hair until it rested on her shoulder. "This machine is similar to the one you use in the office. It has a few more—"

"How do you know?" she interrupted.

"How do I know what?"

"What machine I use in the office?"

He had to smile. "Deborah…" Lightly, lingering, he bent down to kiss her. "There's nothing about you I don't know."

Uncomfortable, she shifted away, then rose. "Will I find my name programmed on one of these machines?"

He watched her, knowing he would have to tread lightly. "Yes. I told myself it was routine, but the truth was I was in love with you and greedy for every detail. I know when you were born, to the minute, and where.

I know you broke your wrist falling off a bike when you were five, that you moved in with your sister and her husband after the death of your parents. And when your sister divorced, you moved with her. Richmond, Chicago, Dallas. Finally Denver where you zipped through college in three years, *cum laude,* drove yourself through law school to graduate in the top five percent of your class, and passed your bar on the first attempt. With enough finesse to bring you offers from four of the top law firms in the country. But you chose to come here, and work in the D.A.'s office.''

She rubbed her palms over the thighs of her jeans. ''It's odd to hear an encapsulated version of my life story.''

''There were things I couldn't learn from the computer.'' The important things, he thought. The vital things. ''The way your hair smells, the way your eyes go to indigo when you're angry or aroused. The way you make me feel when you touch me. I won't deny I invaded your privacy, but I won't apologize for it.''

''No, you wouldn't,'' she said after a moment. She let out a little breath. ''And I suppose I can't be overly offended, since I ran a make on you, too.''

He smiled. ''I know.''

She laughed, shaking her head. ''Okay. Let's get to work.''

They had hardly settled when one of the three phones on the long counter rang. Deborah barely glanced over as Gage lifted a receiver.

''Guthrie.''

''Gage, it's Frank. I'm at Deborah's apartment. You'd better get over here.''

Chapter 11

Her heart beating erratically, Deborah sprinted out of the elevator and down the hall one step in front of Gage. Frank's phone call had had them shooting across town in Gage's Aston Martin in record time.

The door was open. Deborah's breath stopped as she stood on the threshold and saw the destruction of her apartment. Curtains slashed, mementos crushed, tables and chairs viciously broken and tossed in pieces on the floor. The first groan escaped before she spotted Lil Greenbaum propped on the remains of the torn and tattered sofa, her face deathly white.

"Oh, God." Kicking debris aside, she rushed over to drop to her knees. "Mrs. Greenbaum." She took the cold, frail hand in hers.

Lil's thin lids fluttered up, and her myopic eyes struggled to focus without the benefit of her glasses. "Deborah." Though her voice was weak, she managed a faint smile. "They never would have done it if they hadn't caught me by surprise."

"They hurt you." She looked up as Frank came out of the bedroom carrying a pillow. "Did you call an ambulance?"

"She wouldn't let me." Gently he slipped the pillow under Lil's head.

"Don't need one. Hate hospitals. Just a bump on the head," Lil said, and squeezed Deborah's hand. "I've had one before."

"Do you want me to worry myself sick?" As she spoke, Deborah slipped her fingers down to monitor Lil's pulse.

"Your apartment's in worse shape than I am."

"It's easy to replace my things. How would I replace you?" She kissed Lil's gnarled knuckles. "Please. For me."

Defeated, Lil let out a sigh. "Okay, I'll let them poke at me. But I won't stay in the hospital."

"Good enough." She turned, but Gage was already lifting the phone.

"It's dead."

"Mrs. Greenbaum's apartment is right across the hall."

Gage nodded to Frank.

"The keys—" Deborah began.

"Frank doesn't need keys." He crossed over to crouch beside Deborah. "Mrs. Greenbaum, can you tell us what happened?"

She studied him, narrowing and widening her eyes until she brought him into shaky focus. "I know you, don't I? You picked Deborah up last night, all spiffed up in a tux. You sure can kiss.''

He grinned at her, but his hand slipped to her wrist just as Deborah's had. "Thanks."

"You're the one with pots of money, right?"

She may have had a bump on the head, Gage thought, but her mind seemed to work quickly enough. "Right."

"She liked the roses. Mooned over them."

"Mrs. Greenbaum." Deborah sat back on her heels. "You don't have to play matchmaker—we've taken care of it ourselves. Tell us what happened to you."

"I'm glad to hear it. Young people today waste too much time."

"Mrs. Greenbaum."

"All right, all right. I had the list of things you'd called for. I was in the bedroom, going through the closet. Neat as a pin, by the way," she said to Gage. "The girl's very tidy."

"I'm relieved to hear it."

"I was just taking out the navy pin-striped suit when I heard a sound behind me." She grimaced, more embarrassed now than shaken. "I'd have heard it before, but I turned on the radio when I came in. That'll teach me to listen to the Top 40 countdown. I started to turn, and, boom. Somebody put my lights out."

Deborah lowered her head to Lil's hand. Emotions screamed through her, tangled and tearing. Fury, terror, guilt. She was an old woman, Deborah thought as she struggled for control. What kind of person strikes a seventy-year-old woman?

"I'm sorry," she said as levelly as she could. "I'm so sorry."

"It's not your fault."

"Yes, it is." She lifted her head. "This was all for my benefit. All of it. I knew they were after me, and I asked you to come in here. I didn't think. I just didn't think."

"Now, this is nonsense. I'm the one who got bashed, and I can tell you I'm damn mad about it. If I hadn't been caught off guard, I'd have put some of my karate training into use." Lil's mouth firmed. "I'd like to have another go at it. Wasn't too many years ago I could deck Mr. Greenbaum, and I'm still in shape." She glanced up as the paramedics came through the door. "Oh, Lord," she said in disgust. "Now I'm in for it."

With Gage's arm around her shoulders, Deborah stood back while Lil ordered the paramedics around, complaining about every poke and prod. She was still chattering when they lifted her onto a stretcher and carried her out.

"She's quite a woman," Gage commented.

"She's the best." When tears threatened, she bit her lip. "I don't know what I'd do if…"

"She's going to be fine. Her pulse was strong, her mind was clear." He gave her a quick squeeze then turned to Frank. "What's the story?"

"The door wasn't locked when I got here." The big man jerked his thumb toward the opening. "They did a messy job forcing it. I walked into this." He gestured around the chaos of the living room. "I thought I should check out the rest of the place before I called you, and found the lady in the bedroom. She was just coming to. Tried to take a swing at me." He smiled at Deborah. "She's one tough old lady. I calmed her down, then I called you.'' His mouth tightened. There had been a time he hadn't been above pinching a purse from a nice little old lady, but he'd never laid a finger on one. ''I figure I missed them by ten or fifteen minutes.'' His big fists bunched. ''Otherwise they wouldn't have walked out of here.''

Gage nodded. ''I have a couple of things I'd like you to do.'' He turned back to Deborah, gently cradling her face in his hands. ''I'll have him call the police,'' he said, knowing how her mind worked. ''Meanwhile, why don't you see if you can salvage anything you might need until tomorrow?''

''All right.'' She agreed because she needed a moment alone. In the bedroom, she pressed her hands to her mouth. There had been such viciousness here, such fury, yet there was a cold kind of organization to the destruction that made it all the more frightening.

Her clothes were torn and shredded, the little antique bottles and jars she'd collected over the years broken and smashed over the heaps of silk and cotton. Her bed had been destroyed, her desk littered with ugly words someone had carved deeply in the wood with a knife. Everything she owned had been pulled out or torn down.

Kneeling, she picked up a ragged scrap of paper. It had once been a photograph, one of the many of her family she had treasured.

Gage came in quietly. After a moment, he knelt beside her and laid a hand on her shoulder. ''Deborah, let me take you out of here.''

''There's nothing left.'' She pressed her lips together, determined to keep her voice from shaking. ''I know they're only things, but there's nothing left.'' Slowly she curled her fingers around the remains of the photograph. "My parents—" She shook her head, then turned her face into his shoulder.

His own anger was a bright steady flame in his chest. He held her, letting her grieve while he promised himself he would find the men who had hurt her. And all the while he couldn't get past the sick terror that lodged in his throat.

She might have been there. She might have been alone in this room when they'd come in. Instead of trinkets and mementos, he could have found her broken on the floor.

"They'll pay," he promised her. "I swear it."

"Yes, they will." When she lifted her head, he saw that her grief had passed into fury. It was just as deep, just as sharp. "Whatever I have to do, I'm going to bring them down." After pushing back her hair, she stood up. "If they thought they could scare me away by doing this, they're going to be disappointed." She kicked at the remains of her favorite red suit. "Let's go to work."

They spent hours in the cavern beneath his house, checking data, inputting more. Deborah's head was throbbing in time with the machines, but she continued to push. Gage busied himself across the room, but they rarely spoke. They didn't need to. Perhaps for the first time, their purposes meshed and their differences in viewpoints no longer seemed to matter.

They were both anxious to make up the time lost while talking to the police—and evading the enterprising Wisner, who had shown up at the apartment in their wake. She'd be a Monday-morning headline again, Deborah thought impatiently. The press would only bring more pressure from City Hall. She was ready for it.

She no longer swore when she slammed into a dead end, but meticulously backtracked with a patience she hadn't been aware of possessing. When the phone rang, she didn't even hear it. Gage had to call her name twice before she broke out of her concentrated trance.

"Yes, what?"

"It's for you." He held up the receiver. "Jerry Bower."

With a frown for the interruption, she walked over to take the call. "Jerry."

"Good God, Deborah, are you all right?"

"Yes, I'm fine. How did you know where I was?"

She could hear him take two long breaths. "I've been trying to reach you for hours, to make sure you were okay after last night. I finally decided just to go by your place and see for myself. I ran into a pack of cops and that little weasel Wisner. Your place—"

"I know. I wasn't there."

"Thank God. What the hell's going on, Deb? We're supposed to have a handle on these things down at City Hall, but I feel like I'm boxing in the dark. The mayor's going to blow when he hears this. What am I supposed to tell him?"

"Tell him to concentrate on the debates next week." She rubbed her temple. "I already know his stand on this, and he knows mine. You're only going to drive yourself crazy trying to arbitrate."

"Look, I work for him, but you're a friend. There might be something I can do."

"I don't know." She frowned at the blinking lights

on the map. "Someone's sending me a message, loud and clear, but I haven't worked out how to send one back. You can tell the mayor this. If I manage to work this out before the election, he's going to win by a landslide."

There was a slight hesitation. "I guess you're right," Jerry said thoughtfully. "That might be the best way to keep him from breathing down your neck. Just be careful, okay?"

"I will."

She hung up, then tilted her head from one side to the other to work out kinks.

Gage glanced over. "I wouldn't mind taking out a full page ad in the *World* to announce our engagement."

Confused, she blinked. Then laughed. "Jerry? Don't be stupid. We're just pals."

"Mmm-hmm."

She smiled, then walked over to hook her arms around his waist. "Not one big, sloppy kiss between us. Which is exactly what I could use right now."

"I guess I've got at least one in me." He lowered his head.

When his lips met hers, she felt the tension seep out of her, layer by layer, degree by degree. With a murmur, she slid her hands up his back, gently kneading the muscles, soothing them as his lips soothed her.

Quiet, content, relaxed. She could bring him to that, just as she could make him shudder and ache. With a soft sound of pleasure, he changed the angle of the kiss and deepened it for both of them.

"Sorry to break this up." Frank came through the tunnel, bearing a large tray. "But since you're working so hard..." He grinned hugely. "I figured you should eat to keep up your strength."

"Thanks." Deborah drew away from Gage and took a sniff. "Oh, Lord, what is it?"

"My special burn-through-the-ribs chili." He winked at her. "Believe me, it'll keep you awake."

"It smells incredible."

"Dig in. You got a couple of beers, a thermos of coffee and some cheese nachos."

Deborah rolled a chair over. "Frank, you are a man among men." He blushed again, delighting her. She took her first bite, scorched her mouth, her throat and her stomach lining. "And this," she said with real pleasure, "is a bowl of chili."

He shuffled his feet. "Glad you like it. I put Mrs. Greenbaum in the gold room," he told Gage. "I thought she'd get a kick out of the bed curtains and stuff. She's having some chicken soup and watching *King Kong* on the VCR."

"Thanks, Frank." Gage scooped up his own spoon of chili.

"Just give me a ring if you need anything else."

Deborah listened to the echo of Frank's footsteps in the tunnel. "You had her brought here?" she said quietly.

"She didn't like the hospital." He shrugged. "Frank talked to the doctor. She only had a mild concussion, which was a miracle in someone her age. Her heart's strong as an elephant. All she needs is some quiet and pampering for a few days."

"So you had her brought here."

"She shouldn't be alone."

She leaned over and kissed his cheek. "I love you very much."

When they had finished and were back to work, Deborah couldn't stop her mind from wandering in his direction. He was such a complicated man. Arrogant as the devil when it suited him, rude when it pleased him, and as smooth and charming as an Irish poet when the mood struck him. He ran a multimillion-dollar business. And he walked the streets at night to ward off muggers, thieves, rapists. He was the lover every woman dreamed about. Romantic, erotic, yet solid and dependable as granite. Yet he carried something intangible inside him that allowed him to vanish like smoke into the wall, slip without a shadow through the night.

She shook her head. She was far from ready, far from able to dwell on that aspect of him.

How could he, a man she knew to be flesh and blood, become insubstantial at will? Yet she had seen it with her own eyes. She pressed her fingers against those eyes for a moment and sighed. Things weren't always what they seemed.

Straightening her shoulders, she doubled her concentration. If numbers began to blur, she downed more coffee. Already she had a half dozen more names, names she was sure she would find attached to death certificates.

It seemed hopeless. But until this avenue was exhausted, she had no other. Mumbling to herself, she punched up screen after screen. Abruptly she stopped. Cautious, eyes sharpened, she backtracked—one screen, two. She held back a smile, afraid to believe she'd finally broken through. After another five minutes of careful work, she called Gage.

"I think I've found something."

So had he, but he chose to keep his information to himself. "What?"

"This number." When he bent over her shoulder, she ran a finger below it on the screen. "It's all mixed with the corporation number, the tax number, and all the other identification numbers of this company." When he lifted a hand to rub at the base of her neck, she leaned back into the massage gratefully. "A supposedly bankrupt corporation, by the way. Out of business for eighteen months. Now look at this." She punch up a new screen. "Different company, different location, different names and numbers. Except…this one." She tapped a finger on the screen. "It's in a different place here, but the number's the same. And here." She showed him again, screen after screen. "It's the corporation number on one, the company branch on another, tax ID here, a file code there."

"Social security number," Gage muttered.

"What?"

"Nine digits. I'd say it's a social security number. An important one." He turned to walk quickly to the control board.

"What are you doing?"

"Finding out who it belongs to."

She blew out a breath, a bit annoyed that he hadn't seemed more enthusiastic about her find. Her eyes were all but falling out of her head, and she didn't even get a pat on the back. "How?"

"It seems worth going to the main source." The screen above him began to blink.

"Which is?"

"The IRS."

"The—" She was out of her chair like a shot. "You're telling me you can tap into the IRS computers?"

"That's right." His concentration was focused on the panel. "Almost got it."

"That's illegal. A federal offense."

"Mmm-hmm. Want to recommend a good lawyer?"

Torn, she gripped her hands together. "It's not a joke."

"No." But his lips curved as he followed the information on the screen. "All right. We're in." He shot her a look. The internal war she was waging showed clearly on her face. "You could go upstairs until I've finished."

"That hardly matters. I know what you're doing. That makes me a part of it." She closed her eyes and saw Lil Greenbaum lying pale and hurt on her broken couch. "Go ahead," she said, and put a hand on his arm. "We're in this together."

He tapped in the numbers she had found, pushed a series of buttons and waited. A name flashed up on the screen.

"Oh, God." Deborah's fingers dug into Gage's shoulder.

He seemed to be made of stone at that moment, unmoving, almost unbreathing, his muscles hard as rock.

"Tucker Fields," he murmured. "Son of a bitch."

Then he moved so quickly, Deborah nearly stumbled.

With a strength born of desperation, she grabbed him. "Don't. You can't." She saw his eyes burn, as she had seen them behind the mask. They were full of fury and deadly purpose. "I know what you want," she said quickly, clinging. "You want to go find him right now. You want to tear him apart. But you can't. That isn't the way."

"I'm going to kill him." His voice was cold and flat. "Understand that. Nothing's going to stop me."

The breath was searing and clogging in her lungs. If he left now, she would lose him. "And accomplish what? It won't bring Jack back. It won't change what happened to you. It won't even finish what you both started that night on the docks. If you kill Fields, someone will replace him, and it'll go on. We need to break the back of the organization, Gage, to bring it all out to the public so that people will see. If Fields is responsible—"

"If?"

She took a careful, steadying breath and kept her grip on him tight. "We don't have enough, not yet. I can build a case if you give me time, and bring them down. Bring them all down."

"My God, Deborah, do you really think you'll get him in court? A man with that much power? He'll slip through your fingers like sand. The minute you start an investigation, he'll know, and he'll cover himself."

"Then you'll do the investigating here, and I'll throw dust in his eyes from my office." She spoke quickly, desperate to convince him and, she was sure, to save them both. "I'll make him think I'm on the wrong track. Gage, we have to be sure. You must see that. If you go after him now, like this, everything you've worked for, everything we've started to build together, will be destroyed.''

"He tried to have you killed." Gage put his hands to her face, and though his touch was light, she could feel the tension in each finger. "Don't you understand that nothing, not even Jack's murder, signed his death warrant more indelibly?"

She brought her hands to his wrists. "I'm here, with you. That's what's important. We have more work to do, to prove that Fields is involved, to find out how far down the line the corruption runs. You'll have justice, Gage. I promise."

Slowly he relaxed. She was right—at least in some ways she was right. Killing Fields with his bare hands would have been satisfying, but it wouldn't complete the job he had begun. So he could wait for that. There was another stone to uncover, and he had less than a week to wait until he did so.

"All right." He watched the color seep slowly back into her face. "I didn't mean to frighten you."

"Well, I hope you never mean to, because you scared me to death." She turned her head, pressing her lips to his palm, then managed a shaky smile. "Since we've already broken a federal law, why don't we go a step forward and look at the mayor's tax records for the last few years?"

Minutes later, she was seated beside Gage at the console.

"Five hundred and sixty-two thousand," she murmured, when she read Fields's declared income for the previous tax year. "A bit more than the annual salary for Urbana's mayor."

"It's hard to believe he's stupid enough to put that much on record." Gage flipped back another year. "I imagine he's got several times that much in Swiss accounts."

"I never liked him, personally," Deborah put in. "But I always respected him." She rose to pace. "When I think about the kind of position he's been in, a direct line to the police, to the D.A.'s office, to businesses, utilities. Nothing goes on in Urbana he doesn't know about. And he can put his people everywhere. How many city officials are on his private payroll, how many cops, how many judges?"

"He thinks he's got it covered." Gage pushed away from the console. "What about Bower?"

"Jerry?" Deborah sighed and rubbed her stiff neck. "Loyal to the bone, and with political aspirations of his own. He might overlook a few under-the-table machinations, but nothing so big as this. Fields was clever enough to pick someone young and eager, with a good background and unblemished reputation." She shook her head. "I feel badly that I can't pass this along to him."

"Mitchell?"

"No, I'd bet my life on Mitch. He's been around a long time. He's never been Fields's biggest fan but he respects the office. He's by the book because he believes in the book. He even pays his parking tickets. What are you doing?"

"It doesn't hurt to check."

To Deborah's consternation, he pulled up Jerry's then

Mitchell's tax returns. Finding nothing out of the ordinary, he moved toward another console.

"We can start pulling up bank accounts. We need a list of people who work at City Hall, the department, the D.A.'s office." He glanced up at her. "You've got a headache."

She realized she was rubbing at her temple. "Just a little one."

Instead of turning on the machine, he shut the others down. "You've been working too hard."

"I'm fine. We've got a lot to do."

"We've already done a lot." And he was cursing himself for pushing her so hard for so long. "A couple of hours off won't change anything." He slipped an arm around her waist. "How about a hot bath and a nap?"

"Mmm." She leaned her head against his shoulder as they started down the tunnel. "That sounds incredible."

"And a back rub."

"Yes. Oh, yes."

"And why don't I give you that foot rub that's long overdue."

She smiled. Had she ever really been worried about something as foolish as other women? "Why don't you?"

Deborah was already half-asleep by the time they came through the panel into Gage's bedroom. She stopped in mid-yawn and stared at the boxes covering the bed.

"What's all this?"

"At the moment all you have is my shirt on your back. And though I like it—" he flicked a finger down the buttons "—a lot, I thought you might want some replacements."

"Replacements?" She pushed at her tumbled hair. "How?"

"I gave Frank a list. He can be very enterprising."

"Frank? But it's Sunday. Half the stores are closed." She pressed a hand to her stomach. "Oh, God, he didn't steal them, did he?"

"I don't think so." Then he laughed and caught her in his arms. "How am I going to live with such a scrupulously honest woman? No, they're paid for, I promise. It's as easy as making a few calls. You'll notice the boxes are from Athena's."

She nodded. It was one of the biggest and slickest department stores in the city. And the light dawned. "You own it."

"Guilty." He kissed her. "Anything you don't like can go back. But I think I know your style and your size."

"You didn't have to do this."

From the tone of her voice, he understood she wished he hadn't done it. Patient, he tucked her tumbled hair behind her ear. "This wasn't an attempt to usurp your independence, Counselor."

"No." And she was sounding very ungrateful. "But—"

"Be practical. How would it look for you to show up at the office tomorrow in my pants?" He tugged the belt loose and had the jeans sliding to her feet.

"Outrageous," she agreed, and smiled when he lifted her up and set her down beside the heap of denim.

"And my shirt." He began to undo the buttons.

"Ridiculous. You're right, you were being very practical." She took his hands to still them before he could distract her. "And I appreciate it. But it doesn't feel right, you buying my clothes."

"You can pay me back. Over the next sixty or seventy years." He cupped her chin when she started to speak again. "Deborah, I've got more money than any one man needs. You're willing to share my problems, then it should follow that you'll share my fortunes."

"I don't want you to think that the money matters to me, that it makes any difference in the way I feel about you."

He studied her thoughtfully. "You know, I didn't realize you could come up with anything quite that stupid."

She lifted her chin, but when he smiled at her she could only sigh. "It is stupid. I love you even though you do own hotels, and apartment buildings, and department stores. And if I don't open one of these boxes, I'm going to go crazy."

"Why don't you keep your sanity then, and I'll go run the bath?"

When he walked into the adjoining room, she grabbed one at random, shook it, then pulled off the lid. Under the tissue paper she found a long, sheer sleeping gown in pale blue silk.

"Well." She held it up, noting the back was cut below the waist. "Frank certainly has an eye for lingerie. I wonder what the boys in the office will say if I wear this in tomorrow."

Unable to resist, she stripped off the shirt and let the cool thin silk slide over her head and shoulders. A perfect fit, she mused, running her hands over her hips. Delighted, she turned to the mirror just as Gage came back into the room.

He couldn't speak any more than he could take his eyes from her. The long, sleek shimmer of silk whispered against her skin as she turned to him. Her eyes were dark as midnight and glistening with a woman's secret pleasure.

Her lips curved slowly. Was there a woman alive who didn't dream about having the man she loved stare at her with such avid hunger? Deliberately she tilted her head and lifted one hand to run her fingertips lazily down the center of the gown—and just as lazily up again—watching his eyes follow the movement.

"What do you think?"

His gaze trailed up until it met hers again. "I think Frank deserves a very large raise."

As she laughed, he came toward her.

Chapter 12

Over the next three days and the next three evenings, they worked together. Piece by steady piece they built a case against Tucker Fields. At her office Deborah pursued avenues she knew would lead nowhere, carefully laying a false trail.

As she worked, she continued to fight the rugged tug-of-war inside her. Ethics versus instinct.

Each night, Gage would slip out of bed, clothe himself in black and roam the streets. They didn't speak of it. If he knew how often Deborah lay awake, anxious and torn until he returned just before dawn, he offered no excuses or apologies. There were none he could give her.

The press continued to herald Nemesis's exploits. Those secret nocturnal activities were never mentioned and stood between them like a thick, silent wall that couldn't be breached on either side.

She understood, but couldn't agree.

He understood, but couldn't acquiesce.

Even as they worked toward a single goal, their individual beliefs forced them at cross-purposes.

She sat in her office, the evening paper beside a stack of law books.

Nemesis Bags East End Ripper

She hadn't read the copy, couldn't bring herself to read it. She already knew about the man who had killed four people in the past ten days, with his favored weapon, a hunting knife. The headline was enough to tell her why she had found traces of blood in the bathroom sink.

When was it going to end? she asked herself. When was he going to stop? A psychotic with a knife had nothing to do with Fields and the drug cartel. How much longer could they go on pretending that their relationship, their future, could be normal?

He wasn't pretending, Deborah admitted with a sigh. She was.

"O'Roarke." Mitchell slapped a file on her desk. "The city doesn't pay you this princely salary to daydream."

She looked at the file that had just landed on a pile of others. "I don't suppose it would do any good to remind you that my caseload has already broken the world's record."

"So's the city's crime rate." Because she looked exhausted, he walked over to her coffee machine to pour her a cup of the bitter bottom-of-the-pot brew. "Maybe if Nemesis would take some time off, we wouldn't be so overworked.''

Her frown turned into a grimace as she sipped the coffee. ''That sounded almost like a compliment.''

''Just stating facts. I don't have to approve of his methods to like the results.''

Surprised, she looked up into Mitchell's round, sturdy face. ''Do you mean that?''

''This Ripper character carved up four innocent people and was starting on a fifth when Nemesis got there. It's hard to complain when anybody, even a misguided masked wonder, drops a creep like that in our laps and saves the life of an eighteen-year-old girl.''

''Yes.'' Deborah murmured. ''Yes, it is.''

''Not that I'm going out and buying a T-shirt and joining his fan club.'' Mitchell pulled out a cigar and ran it through his stubby fingers. ''So, making any progress on your favorite case?''

She shrugged evasively. ''I've got another week.''

''You're hardheaded, O'Roarke. I like that.''

Her brows rose. ''Now, that was definitely a compliment.''

''Don't let it swell your pinstripes. The mayor's still unhappy with you—and the polls are happy with him. If he knocks Tarrington out in the debates tomorrow, you could have a hard road until the next election.''

''The mayor doesn't worry me.''

''Suit yourself. Wisner's still pumping your name into copy.'' He held up a hand before she could snarl. ''I'm holding Fields off, but if you could keep a lower profile—''

"Yeah, it was really stupid of me to have my apartment trashed."

"Okay, okay." He had the grace to flush. "We're all sorry about that, but if you could try to keep out of trouble for a while, it would make it easy on everyone."

"I'll chain myself to my desk," she said between her teeth. "And the minute I get the chance, I'm going to kick Wisner right in his press card."

Mitchell grinned. "Get in line. Hey, ah, let me know if you need a few extra bucks before the insurance takes over."

"Thanks, but I'm fine." She looked at the files. "Besides, with all this, who needs an apartment?"

When he left her alone, Deborah opened the new case file. And dropped her head in her hands. Was it a twisted kind of irony or fate that she'd been assigned to prosecute the East End Ripper? Her chief witness, she thought, her lover, was the one man she couldn't even discuss it with.

At seven Gage waited for her at a quiet corner table in a French restaurant skirting City Park. He knew it was almost over and that when it was, he would have to explain to Deborah why he hadn't trusted her with all the details.

She would be hurt and angry. Rightfully so. But he preferred her hurt and angry, and alive. He was well aware how difficult the past few days—and nights—had been for her. If there had been a choice, he would have given up everything, including his conscience, to keep her happy.

But he had no choice, hadn't had a choice since the moment he'd come out of the coma.

He could do nothing but tell her and show her how completely he loved her. And to hope that between the very strong and opposing forces that drove each of them, there could be a compromise.

He saw her come in, slim and lovely in a sapphire-colored suit trimmed and lined with chartreuse. Flashy colors and sensible shoes. Was there lace or silk or satin beneath? He had an urge to sweep her up then and there, take her away and discover the answer for himself.

"I'm sorry I'm late," she began, but before the mâitre d' could seat her, Gage had risen to pull her to him. His kiss was not discreet, not brief. Before he released her, nearby diners were looking on with curiosity and envy.

The breath she hadn't been aware of holding rushed out between her parted lips. Her eyes were heavy, her body vibrating.

"I—I'm awfully glad I wasn't on time."

"You worked late." There were shadows under her eyes. He hated seeing them. Knowing he'd caused them.

"Yes." Still breathless, she took her seat. "I had another case dumped on my desk just before five."

"Anything interesting?"

Her gaze came to his and held. "The East End Ripper."

He watched her unwaveringly. "I see."

"Do you, Gage? I wonder if you do." She drew her hand from his and laid it in her lap. "I felt I should disqualify myself, but what reason could I give?"

"There is no reason, Deborah. I stopped him, but it's

your job to see that he pays for the crimes. One does not have to interfere with the other.''

"I wish I could be sure.'' She took up her napkin, pleating it between her fingers. "Part of me sees you as a vigilante, another part a hero.''

"And the truth lies somewhere in between.'' He reached for her hand again. "Whatever I am, I love you.''

"I know.'' Her fingers tightened on his. "I know, but, Gage—'' She broke off when the waiter brought over the champagne Gage had ordered while waiting for her.

"The drink of the gods,'' the waiter said in a rich French accent. "For a celebration, *n'est-ce pas?* A beautiful woman. A beautiful wine.'' At Gage's nod of approval, he popped the cork with a flourish that had the bubbling froth lapping at the lip of the bottle before teasingly retreating. *"Monsieur* will taste?'' He poured a small amount into Gage's glass.

"Excellent,'' Gage murmured, but his eyes were on Deborah.

"Mais, oui.'' The waiter's gaze slid approvingly over Deborah before he filled her glass, then Gage's. *"Monsieur* has the most exquisite taste.'' When the waiter bowed away, Deborah chuckled and touched her glass to Gage's.

"You're not going to tell me you own this place, too?''

"No. Would you like to?''

Though she shook her head, she had to laugh. "Are we celebrating?''

"Yes. To tonight. And to tomorrow.'' He took a small velvet box from his pocket and offered it to her. When she only stared at it, his fingers tensed. Panic rushed through him, but he kept his voice light. "You asked me to marry you, but I felt this privilege was mine."

She opened the box. In the candlelight, the center sapphire glittered a deep and dark blue. Surrounding that bold square was a symphony of ice-white diamonds. They flashed triumphantly in the setting of pale gold.

"It's exquisite."

He'd chosen the stones himself. But he had hoped to see pleasure in her eyes, not fear. Nor had he thought to feel fear himself.

"Are you having doubts?"

She looked up at him and let her heart speak. "Not about the way I feel about you. I never will. I'm afraid, Gage. I've tried to pretend I'm not, but I'm afraid. Not only of what you do, but that it might take you away from me."

He wouldn't make her promises that could be impossible to keep. "I was brought out of that coma the way I was brought out for a reason. I can't give you logic and facts on this one, Deborah. Only feelings and instinct. If I turned my back on what I'm meant to do, I'd die again."

Her automatic protest clogged in her throat. "You believe that?"

"I know that."

How could she look at him and not see it, too? How many times had she looked in his eyes and seen—something? Different, special, frightening. She knew he was flesh and blood, yet he was more. It wouldn't be possible to change that. And for the first time, she realized she didn't want to.

"I fell in love with you twice. With both sides of you." She looked down at the ring, took it out of its box where it flashed like lightning in her hand. "Until then, I was sure of my direction, of what I wanted, needed, and was working for. I was certain, so certain that when I fell in love it would be with a very calm, very ordinary man." She held the ring out to him. "I was wrong. You didn't come back just to fight for your justice, Gage. You came back for me." Then she smiled and held her hand out to him. "Thank God."

He slipped the ring on her finger. "I want to take you home." Even as he brought her hand to his lips, the waiter bounced back to their table.

"I knew it. Henri is never wrong." Deborah chuckled as he made a business out of topping off their glasses. "You have chosen my table. So, you have chosen well. You must leave the menu to me. You must! I will make a night such as you will never forget. It is my pleasure. Ah, *monsieur,* you are the most fortunate of men." He grabbed Deborah's hand and kissed it noisily.

Deborah was still laughing as he hurried away, but when she looked at Gage, she saw his attention was elsewhere. "What is it?"

"Fields." Gage lifted his glass, but his eyes followed the mayor's progress across the room. "He just came in with Arlo Stuart and a couple of other big guns with your friend Bower bringing up the rear."

Tensed, Deborah turned her head. They were heading for a table for eight. She recognized a prominent actress and the president of a major auto manufacturer. "Power meeting," she muttered.

"He's got the theater, industry, finance and the art

worlds all represented neatly at one table. Before the evening's over, someone will come along and take a few 'candid' shots.''

"It won't matter." She covered Gage's hand with hers. "In another week, it won't matter."

In less than that, he thought, but nodded. "Stuart's coming over."

"Well, now." Stuart clamped a hand on Gage's shoulder. "This is a nice coincidence. You look stunning as always, Miss O'Roarke."

"Thank you."

"Great restaurant this. Nobody does snails better." He beamed at both of them. "Hate to waste them talking business and politics. Now, you've got the right idea here. Champagne, candlelight." His sharp gaze fell on Deborah's ring hand. "Well, that's a pretty little thing." He grinned at Gage. "Got an announcement to make?"

"You caught us in the act, Arlo."

"Glad to hear it. You take your honeymoon in any of my hotels." He winked at Deborah. "On the house." Still grinning, he signaled to the mayor. It wouldn't hurt Fields's image, he thought, to be in on the first congratulations to one of the city's top businessmen and the most recognizable D.A.

"Gage, Deborah." Though Fields's smile was broad, his nod of greeting was stiff. "Nice to see you. If you haven't ordered, perhaps you'd like to join us."

"Not tonight." Stuart answered before Gage could. "We've got ourself a newly engaged couple here, Tuck. They don't want to waste the evening talking campaign strategy."

Fields glanced down at Deborah's ring, the smile still in place. But he wasn't pleased. "Congratulations."

"I like to think we brought them together." Always exuberant, Stuart tossed an arm around Fields's shoulder. "After all, they met at my hotel during your fundraiser."

"I guess that makes us one big, happy family." Fields looked at Gage. He needed Guthrie's support. "You're marrying a fine woman, a tough lawyer. She's given me a few headaches, but I admire her integrity."

Gage's voice was cool, but perfectly polite. "So do I."

Stuart gave another booming laugh. "I've admired more than her integrity." He winked at Deborah again. "No offense. Now we'll get back to politics and leave you two alone."

"Bastard," Deborah mumbled when they were out of earshot. She snatched up her wine. "He was sucking up to you."

"No." Gage tapped his glass to hers. "To both of us." Over her shoulder, he saw the minute Jerry Bower heard the news. The man jolted, glanced up and over. Gage could almost hear him sigh as he stared at Deborah's back.

"I can't wait until we nail him."

There was such venom in her voice that Gage covered her hand with his and squeezed. "Just hold on. It won't take much longer."

She was so lovely. Gage lingered in bed, just looking at her. He knew she was sleeping deeply, sated by love, exhausted from passion. He wanted to know that she would dream content until morning.

He hated knowing there were times she woke in the middle of the night to find him gone. But tonight, when he could all but feel the danger tripping through his blood, he needed to be sure she would sleep, safe.

Silently he rose to dress. He could hear her breathing, slow and steady, and it soothed him. In the sprinkle of moonlight, he saw his reflection in the mirror. No, not a reflection, he thought. A shadow.

After flexing his hands in the snug black gloves, he opened a drawer. Inside was a .38, a regulation police issue revolver whose grip was as familiar to him as a brother's handshake. Yet he had not carried it since the night on the docks four years before.

He had never needed to.

But tonight, he felt that need. He no longer questioned instinct, but tucked the gun into a holster and belted it on so that the weapon fit at the small of his back.

He opened the panel, then paused. He wanted to see her again, sleeping. He could taste the danger now— bitter on his tongue, in his throat. His only respite from it was knowing she wouldn't be affected. He would come back. He promised himself, and her. Fate could not deal such a killing blow twice in one lifetime.

He slipped away in the dark.

More than an hour later, the phone rang, pulling Deborah from sleep. Out of habit, she groped for it, murmuring to Gage as she rattled the receiver from the hook.

"Hello."

"*Señorita.*"

The sound of Montega's voice had her icy and awake. "What do you want?"

"We have him. The trap was so easily sprung."

"What?" Panicked, she reached out for Gage. But even before her hands slid over empty sheets, she knew. Terror made her voice shake. "What do you mean?"

"He's alive. We want to keep him alive, for now. If you wish the same you'll come, quickly and alone. We'll trade him for all your papers, all your files. Everything you have."

She pressed a hand to her mouth, trying to stall until she could think. "You'll kill us both."

"Possibly. But I will surely kill him if you don't come. There is a warehouse on East River Drive. Three twenty-five East River Drive. It will take you thirty minutes. Any longer and I remove his right hand."

A rancid sickness heaved her stomach. "I'll come. Don't hurt him. Please, let me talk to him first—"

But the phone went dead.

Deborah sprang out of bed. Dragging on a robe, she rushed out to Frank's room. When one glance told her it was empty, she bounded down the hall to find Mrs. Greenbaum sitting up in bed with an old movie and a can of peanuts.

"Frank. Where is he?"

"He went out to the all-night video store, and for pizza. We decided to have a Marx Brothers festival. What's wrong?"

But Deborah only covered her face with her hands and rocked. She had to think.

"He'll be back in twenty minutes."

"That's too late." She dropped her hands. She

couldn't waste another moment. "You tell him I got a call, I had to go. Tell him it involves Gage."

"You're in trouble, tell me."

"Just tell him, please. The moment he comes in. I've gone to 325 East River Drive."

"You can't." Lil was climbing out of bed. "You can't go there at this time of night by yourself."

"I have to. Tell Frank I had to." She gripped Lil's hands. "It's life or death."

"We'll call the police—"

"No. No, just Frank. Tell him everything I said, and tell him what time I left. Promise me."

"Of course, but—"

But Deborah was already racing out.

It took several precious minutes to throw on clothes and to push stacks of printouts in her briefcase. Her hands were slick with sweat when she reached her car. In her mind, like a chant, she said Gage's name over and over as she streaked down the streets. Sickness stayed lodged in her throat as she watched the clock on the dash tick away the minutes.

Like a ghost, Nemesis watched the exchange of drugs for money. Thousands of bills for thousands of pounds of pain. The buyer slit one sample bag open, scooped out a touch of white powder and tapped it into a vial to test the purity. The seller flipped through stacks of bills.

When both were satisfied, the deal was made. There were few words exchanged. It was not a friendly business.

He watched the buyer take his miserable product and walk away. Even though Nemesis understood he would find the man again, and quickly, there was regret. If he had not been stalking larger game, it would have given him great pleasure to have thrown both merchants and their product into the river.

Footsteps echoed. The acoustics were good in the high, spreading cinderblock building. Boxes and crates were piled beside walls and on long metal shelves. Tools and two-by-fours crowded workbenches. A large forklift was parked by the aluminum garage doors, there to lift the stacks of lumber stored within. Though the scent of sawdust remained, the enormous saws were silent.

He saw, with blood-boiling fury, Montega walk into the room.

"Our first prize tonight." He strode to the suitcase of cash, waving the underlings aside. "But we have richer coming." He closed the suitcase, locked it. "When he comes, show him here."

As he stood, as insubstantial as the air he breathed, Nemesis fisted his hands. It was now, he thought. It was tonight. A part of him that thirsted only for revenge burned to take the gun he carried and fire it. Cold-blooded.

But his blood was too hot for such a quick and anonymous solution. His lips curved humorlessly. There were better ways. More judicious ways.

Even as he opened his mouth to speak, he heard voices, the sound of shoes rushing over the concrete floor. His heart froze to a ball of ice in his chest.

He had left her sleeping.

While his blood ran cold, the sweat of terror pearled on his brow. The danger he had tasted. Not for himself. Dear God, not for himself, but for her. He watched Deborah rush into the room, followed by two armed guards. For an instant, he slipped, wavering between Nemesis's world of shadows and hers.

"Where? Where is he?" She faced Montega like a tigress, head back, eyes blazing. "If you've hurt him, I'll see you dead. I swear it."

With an inclination of his head, Montega tapped his hands together in applause. "Magnificent. A woman in love."

There was no room for fear of him, not when all her fear was for Gage. "I want to see him."

"You are prompt, *señorita,* but have you come with what I asked for?"

She heaved the briefcase at him. "Take it to hell with you."

Montega passed the briefcase to a guard and, with a jerk of his head, had the man take it into an adjoining room.

"Patience," Montega said, holding up a hand. "Would you like to sit?"

"No. You have what you want, now give me what I came for."

The door opened again. Eyes wide, she stared. "Jerry?" Over surprise came the first wave of relief. Not Gage, she thought. They had never had Gage. It had been Jerry. Moving quickly, she went over to take his hands. "I'm sorry, I'm so sorry this happened. I had no idea."

"I know." He squeezed her hands. "I knew you'd come. I was counting on it."

"I wish I thought it was going to help either of us."

"It already has." He put an arm around her shoulder

as he faced Montega. "The deal went smoothly, I take it."

"As expected, Mr. Bower."

"Excellent." Jerry gave Deborah's shoulder a friendly pat. "We have to talk."

She knew the color had drained from her face. She had felt it. "You—you're not a hostage here at all, are you?"

He allowed her to step away, even holding up a hand to signal the guards back. There was nowhere for her to go, and he was feeling generous. "No, and unfortunately, neither are you. I regret that."

"I don't believe it." Shaken, she lifted both hands to her temples. "I knew, I knew how blindly you stood behind Fields, but this— in the name of God, Jerry, you can't possibly let yourself be a part of this. You know what he's doing? The drugs, the murders? This isn't politics, it's madness."

"It's all politics, Deb." He smiled. "Mine. You don't honestly believe that a spineless puppet like Fields is behind this organization?" This time he laughed and signaled for a chair. "But you did. You did, because I laid a nice, neat trail of bread crumbs for you and anyone else who decided to look." Putting a hand on her shoulder, he pushed her into the chair.

"You?" She stared at him, head reeling. "You're telling me you're in charge? That Fields—"

"Is no more than a pawn. For more than six years I've stood two paces behind him, picking up all the flack—and pushing all the buttons. Fields couldn't run a dime store much less a city. Or the state…" He took a seat himself. "As I will in five years."

She wasn't afraid. Fear couldn't penetrate the numbness. This was a man she had known for nearly two years, one she had considered a friend and who she had judged as honest, if a bit weak. "How?"

"Money, power, brains." He ticked the three points off on his fingers. "I had the brains. Fields supplied the power. Believe me, he's been more than willing to leave the details, administrative and otherwise, to me. He makes a hell of a speech, knows whose butt to kick and whose to kiss. The rest of it, I do, and have since I was put in his office six years ago."

"By whom?"

"You are sharp." Still smiling, he gave her an admiring nod. "Arlo Stuart—he's the money. The problem has been that his businesses—the legitimate ones—dug a bit deeper into his profits than he cared for. Being a businessman, he saw another way to make that profit margin sing."

"The drugs."

"Right again." Casually he crossed his legs and gave an almost disinterested glance at his watch. There was time yet to indulge her, he thought. Since this was the last time. "He's been the head man on the East Coast for over twelve years. And it pays. I worked my way up in the organization. He likes initiative. I had the knowledge—law, political science—and he had Fields."

Questions, she ordered herself. She had to think of questions and keep him answering. Until…would Gage come? she wondered. Was there a way for Frank to contact him?

"So the three of you worked together," she said.

"Not Fields—I'd hate to give him credit in your mind,

because I do respect your mind. He's nothing but a handy pawn and he hasn't a clue about our enterprise. Or if he does, he's wise enough to overlook it." He moved his shoulders. It didn't matter either way. "When the time is right, we'll expose the tax information and so forth that you've already discovered. No one will be more surprised than Fields. Since I'll be the one who righteously and regretfully exposes him, it should be very simple to step into his place. Then beyond."

"It won't work. I'm not the only one who knows."

"Guthrie." Jerry linked his fingers over his knee. "Oh, I intend to see to Guthrie. I ordered Montega to remove him four years ago, and the job was incomplete."

"You?" she whispered. "You ordered?"

"Arlo leaves that kind of detail to me." He leaned forward so only she could hear him. "I like details—such as what your new fiancé does in his spare time." His lips curved when her color drained. "You led me to him this time, Deborah."

"I don't know what you're talking about."

"I'm a good judge of people. I have to be. And you are a very predictable person. You, a woman of integrity, intelligence and fierce loyalties, involved with two men? It didn't seem likely. Tonight, I became sure of what I've suspected for several weeks. There's only one man, one man who would have recognized Montega, one man who would have won your heart, one man with enough reason to fanatically pursue me." He patted her hand when she remained silent. "That's our little secret. I enjoy secrets."

His eyes chilled again as he rose. "And though I regret it, sincerely, only one of us can walk out of here tonight with that secret. I've asked Montega to be quick. For old times' sake.''

Though her body was shaking, she made herself stand. ''I've learned to believe in destiny, Jerry. You won't win. He'll see to that. You'll kill me, and he'll come after you like a Fury. You think you know him, but you don't. You don't have him, and you never will.''

''If it gives you comfort.'' He stepped away from her. ''We don't have him—at the moment.''

''You're wrong.''

Every head in the room turned at the voice. There was nothing but blank walls and piles of lumber. Deborah's knees went so weak she almost folded to the ground.

Then everything seemed to happen at once.

A guard standing beside the wall jerked back, his eyes bright with surprise. While his body struggled and strained, the rifle he was holding began to spray bullets. Men shouted, diving for cover. The guard screamed, stumbled away from the wall. His own men cut him down.

Dashing behind a line of shelves, Deborah searched frantically for a weapon. Laying her hands on a crowbar, she stepped back, ready to defend herself. Before her astonished eyes, a weapon was grappled away from a goggle-eyed guard. Mad with fear, he raced away, screaming.

''Stay back.'' The voice floated out toward her.

''Thank God, I thought that—''

''Just stay back. I'll deal with you later.''

She stood, gripping the crowbar. Nemesis was back, she thought, and gritted her teeth. And as arrogant as

ever. Sliding a box aside, she peeked through the opening to the melee beyond. There were five men left—the
guards, Montega and Jerry. They were firing wildly, as
terrified as they were confused. When one of the bullets
plowed into the wall a scant foot from her head, she
crouched lower.

Someone screamed. The sound made her squeeze her
eyes shut. A hand grabbed her hair, dragging her up.

"What is he?" Jerry hissed in her ear. Though his
hand was shaking, it maintained a firm grip. "What the
hell is he?"

"He's a hero," she said, looking defiantly into his
wild eyes. "Something you'll never understand."

"He'll be a dead one before this is over. You're coming with me." He jerked her in front of him. "If you
try anything, I'll shoot you in the back and take my
chances."

Deborah took a deep breath and slammed the crowbar
into his stomach. When he keeled over, retching, she
raced out, weaving and dodging around workbenches
and shelving. He recovered quickly, half running, half
crawling until his hand reached out and slipped over her
ankle. Cursing, she kicked him off, knowing any minute
she could feel a bullet slam into her back. She scrambled
up a graduated hack of lumber, thinking if she could
climb to safety, he couldn't use her as a shield.

She could hear him clambering behind her, gaining
ground as he got back his wind. Desperate, she imagined
herself like a lizard, quick and sure, clinging to the
wood. She couldn't fall. All she knew was that she
couldn't fall. Splinters dug into her fingers, unfelt.

With all her strength, she heaved the crowbar at him.

It struck him on the shoulder, making him curse and falter. Knowing better than to look back, she set her teeth and jumped from the stack of lumber to a narrow metal ladder. Sweaty, her hands slipped, but she clung, climbing up to the next level. Her breath was coming fast as she raced across the steel landing crowded with rolls of insulation and building material.

But there was no place to go. As she reached the far side, she saw that she was trapped. He had nearly reached the top. She couldn't go down, had no hope of making the five-foot leap to the overhang of metal shelving that held more supplies.

He was breathing hard, and there was blood on his mouth. And a gun in his hand. Deborah took an unsteady step back, looking down twenty-five feet to where Nemesis battled three to one. She couldn't call to him, she realized. To distract him even for an instant could mean his death.

Instead, she turned and faced her one-time friend. "You won't use me to get him."

With the back of his hand he wiped blood and spittle from his lip. "One way or another."

"No." She stepped back again and bumped into a hoist chain. It was thick and hooked and heavy, used, she realized quickly, to lift the huge stacks of material to the next level for storage. "No," she said again and, using all her strength, swung the chain at his face.

She heard the sound of bones breaking. And then his scream, one horrible scream before she covered her own face.

He had whittled things down to Montega when Nemesis looked up and saw her, white as a ghost and swaying

on the brink of a narrow metal ledge. He didn't spare a
glance for the man who had fallen screaming to the concrete below. As he sprinted toward her, he heard a bullet
whistle past his head.

"No!" she shouted at him, pushing aside the faint-
ness. "He's behind you." She saw with relief, and Montega with disbelief, that he veered left and disappeared.

Cautious, wanting to draw Montega's attention from
Deborah, Nemesis moved along the wall. He would call
tauntingly, then move right or left before Montega could
aim his trembling gun and fire.

"I will kill you!" Shaking with fear, Montega fired
again and again into the walls. "I've seen you bleed. I
will kill you."

It wasn't until he was certain Deborah was down and
safely huddled in the shadows that he reappeared, six
feet from Montega. "You've already killed me once."
Nemesis held his gun steady at Montega's heart. He had
only to pull the trigger, he thought. And it would be
over. Four years of hell would be over.

But he saw Deborah, her face white and sheened with
sweat. Slowly his finger relaxed on the trigger.

"I came back for you, Montega. You'll have a long
time to wonder why. Drop your weapon."

Speechless, he did so, sending it clattering onto the
concrete. Pale but steady, Deborah stepped forward to
pick it up.

"Who are you?" Montega demanded. "What are
you?" A scream of warning burst from Deborah's lips
as Montega slipped a hand into his pocket.

Two more gunshots ripped the air. Even as they echoed, Montega sprawled lifelessly on the floor. Staring at

him, Nemesis stepped closer. "I'm your destiny," he whispered, then turned and caught Deborah in his arms.

"They said they had you. They were going to kill you."

"You should have trusted me." He turned her away, determined to shield her from the death surrounding them.

"But you were here," she said, then stopped. "Why were you here? How did you know?"

"The pattern. Sit down, Deborah. You're shaking."

"I have a feeling it's going to be from anger in a minute. You knew they would be here tonight."

"Yes, I knew. Sit. Let me get you some water."

"Stop it, just stop it." She snatched at his shirtfront with both hands. "You knew, and you didn't tell me. You knew about Stuart, about Jerry."

"Not about Jerry." And he would always regret it. "Until he walked in here tonight and I heard what he told you, I was focused on Fields."

"Then why were you here?"

"I broke the pattern a few days ago. Every drop had been made in a building Stuart owned. And each drop was at least two weeks apart in a different section of the city. I spent a couple of nights casing a few other spots, but honed in here. And I didn't tell you," he continued when her eyes scraped at him, "because I wanted to avoid exactly what happened here tonight. Damn it, when I'm worried about you I can't concentrate. I can't do my job."

Her body was braced as she held out her hand. "Do you see this ring? You gave this to me only hours ago. I'm wearing it because I love you, and because I'm teaching myself how to accept you, your feelings and your needs. If you can't do the same for me, you'll have to take it back.''

Behind his mask his eyes were dark and flat. ''It's not a matter of doing the same—''

''It's exactly that. I killed a man tonight.'' Her voice shook, but she pushed him away when he would have held her again. ''I killed a man I knew. I came here tonight ready, willing to exchange not only my ethics but my life for yours. Don't you ever protect me, pamper me, or think for me again.''

''Are you through?''

''No.'' But she did lean against the chair. ''I know you won't stop what you do. That you can't. I'll worry about you, but I won't stand in your way. You won't stand in mine, either.''

He nodded. ''Is that all?''

''For now.''

''You're right.''

She opened her mouth, shut it, then blew out a long breath. ''Would you say that again?''

''You're right. I kept things from you and instead of protecting you, I put you in more danger. For that, I'm sorry. And besides admitting that, I think you should know I wasn't going to kill him.'' He looked down at Montega, but cupped Deborah's chin in his hand before she could follow his direction. ''I wanted to. For an instant, I tasted it. But if he had surrendered, I would have turned him over to the police.''

She saw the truth of it in his eyes. ''Why?''

''Because I looked at you and I knew I could trust

you to see there was justice.'' He held out a hand. "Deborah, I need a partner.''

She was smiling even as her eyes overflowed. "So do I.'' Instead of taking his hand, she launched herself into his arms. "Nothing's going to stop us,'' she murmured. In the distance, she heard the first sirens. "I think Frank's bringing the cavalry.'' She kissed him. "I'll explain later. At home. You'd better go.'' With a sigh, she stepped back. "It's going to take a good lawyer to explain all of this.''

At the sound of rushing feet, he moved back, then into the wall behind her. "I'll be here.''

She smiled, spreading her palm on the wall, knowing he was doing the same on the shadowy other side. "I'm counting on it.''

* * * * *

*If you've enjoyed NIGHT TALES,
please look out for Boyd's daughter's story
in Silhouette Sensation® right now—
NIGHT SHIELD —and the other two
linked books coming to you in one
volume—NIGHT MOVES—in
February 2002!*

No.1 New York Times *best-selling author*

NORA ROBERTS

*and Silhouette® Books present
the brand-new sequel to NIGHT TALES,*

NIGHT SHIELD

*Available from Silhouette Sensation®
this month!*

Here's a preview…

Night Shield
by
Nora Roberts

Last call was enough to make Ally all but weep with gratitude. She'd been on her feet since eight that morning, having worked at the precinct all day before going undercover at the club that night. Her fondest wish was to go home, fall into bed and sleep for the precious five hours she had before starting it all over again.

Ally stepped out of the lounge and bumped solidly into Jonah.

"Where'd you park?" he asked her.

"I didn't. I walked." Ran, she remembered, but it came to the same thing.

"I'll drive you home."

"I can walk. It's not far."

"It's two in the morning. A block is too far."

"For heaven's sake, Blackhawk, I'm a cop."

"So, naturally, bullets bounce off you."

Before she could argue, he caught her chin in his hand. The gesture, the firm grip of his fingers shocked her to silence. "You're not a cop at the moment," he murmured. "You're a female employee and the daughter of a friend. I'll drive you home."

"Fine. Dandy. My feet hurt anyway."

She started to shove his hand away, but he beat her to it and shifted his grip to her arm.

"Night, boss," Beth called out, grinning at them as they passed the bar. "Get that girl off her feet."

"That's my plan. Later, Will. 'Night, Frannie."

Suspicion was buzzing in Ally's brain as Will lifted his brandy snifter and Frannie watched her with quiet serious eyes.

"What was that?" Ally demanded when they stepped out in the cool air. "What exactly was that?"

"That was me saying good-night to friends and employees. I'm parked across the street."

"Excuse me, my feet have gone numb, not my brain. You gave those people the very distinct impression that we have a thing here."

"That's right. I didn't consider it either until Beth made some remark earlier. It simplifies things."

She stopped beside a sleek black Jaguar. "Just how do you figure that having people think there's a personal thing between us simplifies anything?"

"And you call yourself a detective." He unlocked the passenger door, opened it. "You're a beautiful blonde with legs up to your ears. I hire you, out of the blue, when you have basically no experience. The first assumption from people who know me is

I'm attracted to you. The second would be you're attracted to me. Add all those together and you end up with romance. Or at least sex. Are you going to get in?"

"You haven't explained how those deductions equal simple."

"If people think we're involved they won't think twice if I give you a little leeway, if you come up to my office. They'll be friendlier."

Ally said nothing while she let it run through her head. Then she nodded. "All right. There's an advantage to it."

Going with impulse he shifted, boxed her in between his body and the car door. There was a light breeze, just enough to stir her scent. There was a three-quarter moon, bright enough to sprinkle silver into her eyes. The moment, he decided, seemed to call for it.

"Could be more than one advantage to it."

The thrill that sprinted straight up her spine irritated her. "Oh, you're going to want to step back, Blackhawk."

"Beth's at the window of the bar, and she's got a romantic heart despite everything's that's happened to her. She's hoping for a moment here. A long, slow kiss, the kind that slides over melting sighs and heats the blood."

His hands came to her hips as he spoke, rode up to just under her breasts. Her mouth went dry and the ache in her belly was a wide stretch of longing.

"You're going to have to disappoint her."

Jonah skimmed his gaze down to her mouth.

"She's not the only one." But he released her, stepped back. "Don't worry, Detective. I never hit on cops, or daughters of friends."

"Then I guess I've got a double shield against your wild and irresistible charms."

"Good thing for both of us, because I sure as hell like the look of you. You getting in?"

"Yeah, I'm getting in." She got into the car and waited until the door shut before letting out the long, painful breath she'd been holding.

Wherever that spurt of lust inside her had come from, it would just have to go away again. Cool off and focus on the job, she ordered herself, but her heart was bumping madly against her rib cage...

* * *

Don't forget Night Shield
is on the shelves now!

From the No.1 New York Times
best selling author

NORA ROBERTS

NIGHT SHIELD

Don't miss this exciting, BRAND NEW Night
Tales book in Sensation™ October Series!

Available from 21st September

1001/18/SH21